The Rarest Diamonds

By: Manes Marcellon

THE RAREST DIAMONDS

—105—
PUBLISHING
EST. 2020

Table of Contents

Acknowledgements

I am grateful for several people who had a hand or some influence throughout my writing of this book. To begin, I'd like to express my sincere appreciation to my youngest sister, Linda Marcellon, who on many occasions took time out of her precious day to either listen to, or in most cases read the manuscript. Others I'd like to show my deepest gratitude towards include Kenny Kwon, Robertson Fluerima, Gabrielle Campbell, and Satesh Singh for reading parts of the manuscript and providing some thorough feedback; to my beloved younger sister, Dr. Roselande Marcellon and my web designer, Dillon Cash, who shared some reputable resources which aided me through the process of writing this book, my cousin, rapper Tony T. Placil, House of Sounds records producer, Remy Joseph, and the lovely Poetess and social activist, Krystal "Gypsy" Orellano, who spurred me into action prior to when the book was just seeds of ideas I envisioned, Prof. Angel Clyman, Prof. Tammy Knipp, Prof. Brandon Petite, Prof. Stephan Molinari along with my fellow art contemparies, Kasan Da Julah and Kelly "Y2K" Tanelus, for their part in being a great source of encouragement and motivation. Lastly, I'd like to give thanks to Jason Raynor and his team for all the effort and contribution that went into completing the book.

Chapter 1: Torence

Outside on this gloomy, dismal afternoon sits a twelve-year-old youngster named Torence, who has chosen to isolate himself away from the rest of his peers on the playground. You see, unlike his peers, Torence seems to have no trace of his biological parents. After twelve years of existence, all that remains are memories of his mother and the name of his deceased father. Within five months of his stay at the Bridges, the group home, rumors among his peers are circulating about his story as an orphan. The rumors have only further nurtured his distaste toward his current residence. Now sitting outside, alone on a green bench, he takes a look at the gray clouds. With his eyes fixed on the clouds, out of nowhere he begins to hear what sounds like a violin. Widening his eyes and licking his lips, the sound slowly picks up. As it does, along comes the rhythmic beating of sticks, drums, and bass. Followed by a roar of thunder and some drops of light rain to mute the instrumental in his mind. As he watches his peers head back inside for shelter, a tortured soul inside him asks, *who am I?* A question he asked himself too many times. Yet, a thousand times is still not quite enough. *Who am I,* he asks himself once more. Then, another voice from within speaks up saying: *You are Torence...You're a diamond...You are a diamond.* Something a social worker, Ms. Constant, would often say to him back in his days at the orphanage. In fact, she'd say that to all of the kids at Open Arms. Recalling how she'd say that line with distinct confidence, made Torence think about how pleasing a diamond looked to the eyes. However, Ms. Constant's words weren't enough to convince Torence. That's because he's been rejected by several families. After spending six years at the orphanage, Torence concluded that he must've been that diamond that nobody or no family wanted. The one that someone would pick up and put back on the dirt just moments after being found. But why? How come no one would take him in after six years of living in the orphanage?

Well, for Torence, it all began on the year his mother gave him up to the Blesses. At the time, he was only four years old when his distant cousins decided to take him in. For the first few months, Teresa, his mother, stayed in contact with him, but that didn't last long because the family was constantly on the move when they relocated to several different cities. By the time he was turning six, the Bless family eventually moved him to Open Arms, the orphanage he ended up living in for practically six years.

His first year living at Open Arms seemed to be going relatively well, despite the fact that it was a children's home. He was fed, sheltered, and overall, seemed unaware of what was going on. However, it didn't take him too long to realize what was happening once he stopped hearing from the Bless family. With more and more orphans moving in the orphanage, there soon became far too many kids for him to count. Open arms became a bucket full of leftovers. It was at that point when Torence stopped wondering and started asking the staff who would take him in. That specific question remained unanswered until he met the Innocents several months after he turned eight years old. The Innocents happened to be a family of four, consisting of a mother, father, son, and a daughter on the way. With Torence there, they'd become a party of five.

Mr. and Mrs. Innocent started as a young couple struggling to make ends meet for their son, whom they had in their late teens. They strived, but their efforts eventually paid off, enabling them to raise their child. With Torence in the picture, their son was no longer going to be an only child. Which meant he now had a playmate. In addition, the staff at Open Arms figured the Innocents would play perfect role models knowing that they overcame their struggles. More importantly, they provided the stability that Torence needed. So, Ms. Constant and the rest of the staff assumed that this was a match made in Heaven. Unfortunately, time said otherwise. With half a year gone by, Torence was returned to the orphanage.

Almost nine years old, Torence was beginning to dread the idea of spending the rest of his life at the orphanage, especially since he had already lived there for three years. The Innocents had a number of reasons that led to Torence's return to Open Arms. His fights with their son were perhaps by far the biggest reason. A specialist from the Open Arms staff diagnosed him with Emotional Behavioral Disorder (EBD).

Despite being back in the orphanage, Torence did not miss the Innocents, nor did he ever want to remember them. In fact, having lived with them only made him wonder about his real parents and what his real family would've probably been like. Thinking about them, he'd often take a look at magazines, and sometimes even cut out the images of people he thought might actually be his relatives. And when he didn't have any magazines, he'd take time to sketch out pictures.

In his fifth year living at the orphanage, he noticed how much smaller the number of kids were in comparison to when he first moved there. As a matter of fact, he didn't recognize any of the kids that were there now, because they were recently enrolled in the program. His questions soon turned to frustrations he'd express to the Open Arms staff. At some point, he began to isolate himself from everyone, including the staff. You see, according to Torence's view, the staff neglected to give him the reason that could possibly answer all of his questions, and potentially put an end to his frustration. Evidently, there was some reason behind why families were hesitant to take him in. Yet, no one was coming forward. So, he felt the need to shun them out. His relationship with the staff remained stagnant for some time. Then came news about a family that wanted to take him in as a foster child potentially. This family, from what the staff knew, was said to be very stable. This was essential for Torence. Like the Innocents, this family was a small party of four: A loving mother and father along with two daughters. With an age gap between the two daughters, Torence would fit right in as their middleman. This family was known as the Towns. With just a few more meetings with the staff, Torence was going to move out of the orphanage in a matter of weeks. The news made waves around the orphanage and hopes of living with the Towns made Torence open up. Unfortunately, Torence didn't move in with the Towns. For no particular reason, the Towns and the staff just discontinued the meetings. And once more, Torence remained at Open Arms.

Seven to eight weeks after, the staff got in touch with an alternative family known as the Bridges. Unlike the two previous families, the Bridges happened to be a rather big family. In fact, they housed a number of orphans. Moreover, this family lived pretty far from Open Arms. That was something Torence gradually noticed on his way to the Bridges group home. This time, he didn't take a minute or two to think about what life in this new home was going to be like. Figuring that they were probably going to end up returning him to the orphanage, he disconnected any emotion he'd tie to this new family.

My Thoughts

Who am I? Well, if anyone would like to know, I'm Torence…Torence Murder. At least that's the name my mother gave me when we were together. Before, I lived with her cousins (the Blesses). Besides her naming me, her look is all I remember. I mean she was tall…pretty…and loved to wear her hair tied back. But it's funny; I didn't think I look like her. Hmmm, come to think of it, I thought I looked more like my dad. Yet, I hadn't even ever met him before. But if I looked like anyone in this world, it'd be him…David Boston. That's what I'd always hear from the Blesses. They said I had his look written all over my face. Is it a good thing or a bad thing? Hmm, not really sure what to make of that. Even though my dad was dead, they talked about him like he was right in their living room. He died before I ever showed up, and I was never sure why or how…But I knew it had something to do with why we lived in so many places. Damn, it was like they were running from a ghost…Or even worse: a bunch of monsters. I remember the time we packed our bags and left right in the middle of the night. That had to be one of the coldest nights living with the Blesses. We rushed out, leaving my jacket behind. The one my mother gave me when I used to live with her. Whatever or whoever it was that made them play musical chairs, spooked them pretty bad. So bad that they moved me to Open Arms. And that's how I ended up living there for so long. Staying there, I saw many other kids like me who didn't have parents. But at least, some of them lived there with brothers and sisters. They were probably the ones I hated the most about living there at Open Arms. At least they had another person they could call family. I had no one.

Staying there all those years was where I learned about math and reading. All the other kids hated learning, but I ain't mind it so much. Especially when it came to reading and writing. That helped me take my mind off my parents and…who I was. Ms. Constant, a smart lady who was just as pretty as my mother, used to always remind me that I was a diamond in the rough: something special that hasn't been found. Hearing her say that was always nice to hear. And she knew I liked hearing her say that, so she said it to me more than the other kids. But all of the other kids there ain't think so. And even though I'd never say it to Ms. Constant's face, I ain't think so either. Shit, all of these kids at the orphanage found new homes and families to stay with! Yet, I still hadn't! And I knew it had something to do with my dad, but no one (not even Ms. Constant) was telling me why! Maybe they didn't know…Maybe…That's what my voice would say when it'd sit still inside my mind. But then, the voice in me would say something else, and speak even louder saying: THEY DO KNOW! AND THEY JUST DON'T WANNA TELL ME! Sometimes, the voice in me just spoke loudly that everyone heard me. At some point after I turned ten, I started thinking that my dad wasn't dead. Maybe he's out somewhere trying to find me. Maybe he thinks I'm with my mother's cousins, but he can't reach me because they keep moving to other places. In that year, I was really into looking at the magazines Ms. Constant use to bring in. I liked cutting pictures of people who I thought might have been in my father's family. But there was one picture in one of the magazines that I couldn't cut out. That one was special to me because it had a picture of a man who looked like me. He was tall, had nice black clothes on, and just seemed respected. He also wore a shiny necklace with a music note on it, but I couldn't figure out why. The Blesses told me that my dad, used to have big hair and a mustache. Hmm, this guy in the front cover didn't have any of that. He just looked respected, like he was somebody. I figured that this probably what my dad looked like…Yeah, this is who he was…A man with respect…Hmm…but behind him was another guy with pale skin and long brown hair. His hair looked like silk tied up into ropes. Oh, and they stretched down to his back. He was just as tall and held up two fingers with his left hand. I didn't take time to wonder about him, but he looked like he belonged in the picture. In the front cover, it read Dopa...Dopa...Ugh, I can't pronounce it, but it was spelled d-o-p-a-m-i-n-e. I held on to that picture up until I moved here at the Bridges. I drew so many pictures about that man in the front cover. So much that Ms. Constant kept some of them before I moved away.

Now I'm staying with the Bridges. They're the third family I've lived with and the fourth I've known in total. Out of any family I've lived with, this one is the biggest of them all. The home I'm staying in is really big and next to it is a small art center. They even got a little playground around the corner. But...the Bridges don't seem anything like a real family at all. Six other kids lived here, and most of the grown-ups worked with us. It was just like Open arms all over again. Only this time a bit smaller. Ugh, I don't like me here anymore than the other kids do. One of the grownups here told me that things would turn around. A lot of them did, but this has been going on for five months, and I still don't like it here. No...I can't stand it here.

On my way here, I thought maybe there'd be something different about this place. I mean it was so far and the buildings I saw on my way here were so huge. Oh, and the wind here just never stops blowing. Could that be the reason why the people here call it the Windy City? I admit it; I guess part of me was excited. Really excited till I came here with the Bridges...The grownups here are a bit meaner than the ones I knew at Open Arms. I heard some of them told me they'd send me back to Open Arms if I continued to give them more problems. But its not my fault that I stick out like a sore thumb to the other kids! They don't like me, so I don't like them, and they knew it. That's why I wanna sit here right now on this green bench, away from the playground, away from them. Trying to make friends with them is only getting me in more fights. I'd rather stay here and get wet by the rain than pretend like this is my family. Sometimes, I get so sad that I think I'm a turn into a raindrop. But other times, I feel like I'm a strike like some ole lightning bolt. Everyone doesn't want me here, but that's okay because, after today, they won't have to worry about that anymore. You see tonight, when the grownups take us out to our next outing, this will be the last time they'll ever deal with me. Tonight's the night where I'm going to take care of myself. I will run so far away from the Bridges and never come back if I could. Even though I may not still be strong enough to live on my own, but hey, I'm a lot stronger now than I once was before. Besides, no family outside the Bridges wants me anyway. Shoot, the Bridges were probably gonna send me back to Open Arms anyway. So, they don't even want me. I guess I might as well look after myself. And while I'm doing that, I will find my mother. I have questions she needs to answer. She better have some good answers! As for my pa…dead or alive, I'm a find out what really happened since no one else here can seem to tell me. Hmm, I think I'm calling today, "day one." The day I chose to take myself in.

Chapter 2: Day One

After several months of living with the Bridges, Torence concluded that the wait was over. In the feeling that the moment was now. It was time for him not to expect acceptance from the Bridges nor any family. Now it was time for him to take care of himself. It was time to leave the Bridges. Although he still had quite a way to grow before he could take care of himself, he didn't want to entertain the idea of being sent back to Open Arms. So, on day one he took off on the next outing with the Bridges. He took off, drifting out and away into the realm of the unknown, which was the Windy City, Chicago.

Several distances away, there lived another rebellious soul in the city of Chicago, who, like Torence, didn't necessarily know much about his parents either. In fact, he was staying with a legal guardian, and like Torence, things always just seem to start off at the wrong end. His name was Lantino Soulberg, and he happened to be the offspring of an interracial couple (Black and Latino). Unlike Torence, he was older by just a couple of years. Besides that, everything else in terms of their physique and circumstances was identical.

Again, Lantino always seemed to be on the wrong side of things. At home, he couldn't seem to get along with Loriana, his legal guardian. Nor could he get by without arguing with Loraine, his half-sister. In school, things weren't any better. Lantino was labeled an at-risk student, because his grades were spiraling downhill. This factor landed him a seat in the dropout prevention program. Moreover, he seemed to be making friends with the wrong crowd.

On one particular day, Lantino, for some unknown reason, got in a physical altercation with the school's resource officer, which led him to getting a twenty-two-day suspension. On that same day, Loriana, his legal guardian, was called in for an informal parent conference with the school's principal. For Lantino, it was a long day at school, but the meeting made it feel longer. It was a gloomy, dismal afternoon on the way home from school, and Lantino could feel some light rain about to touch down. Fortunately, he and Loriana managed to beat the rain. However, he still hadn't received a full blast of Loriana's tongue-lash. As if the day couldn't get any worse… "So, Tino," said the frustrated Loriana.

"Yeah…So," responding Lantino as he reciprocates his frustration towards her.

"So…"

"So, what?"

"Tell me what happened!"

"Ugh!"

"Hey, I asked you a question!"

"Stuhh!"

"And I want an answer! Oh, and don't you suck your teeth or roll your eyes at me when I'm talking, Lantino!"

"Man, please…"

"Oh… 'Man, please,' huh…Is that how you talk to your mother? Huh!?"

"Stuh, first of all, you ain't my momma! And second of all, she wouldn't leave me hanging the same way you just did today at the principal's office!"

"Lantino, I did not leave you hanging!"

"Yes, you did! Security and Mr. Lawson were just straight up bashing me, and you sat back and did nothing!"

"That is not true, Lantino!"

"Oh yeah, then what was that at the principal's office?! My real mother would've stuck up for me! She wouldn't just sit still and take their side!"

"Tino, you tell me?! What am I to say to your principal?! After I come to find my kid gets kicked out of school for twenty days! Twenty days for fighting!"

"You mean to say twenty-two days?"

"Iyee! Twenty-two! Twenty-two days Lantino!"

"Why does it matter? You took their side anyway."

"Well, Tino, I'm giving you a chance to tell me your side! So, what happened?"

"Why do you wanna hear my side now?"

"So, you're not gonna tell me what happened?"

"You should've let me do that when we were with Mr. Lawson. Shit, it's no wonder my mother ain't like you. I see why she told me what she told me."

"You know what?! Callate! That's enough! I've had it with all this talk about Ms. Lopez, your mother, that woman…I don't want to hear any more about that woman!"

"Stuh…"

"Just tell me one thing, Tino. Why? Why did you punch him?"

"Ugh! I told you already, he touched me first!"

"But Lantino, he's a cop!"

"No, he's not! He's security!"

"Did you have to hit him, though?"

"Well, what about him? Did he tell you how he grabbed my right arm? He started it first!"

"So, he is an adult! You're not supposed to put your hands on him at all!"

"I thought you wanted to hear my side?!"

"Wait, hear your side?" asked Loraine, who just happened to walk right through the front door unexpectedly. "Wait, so Tino, you mean to tell me that was you in that big fight with security earlier today?" She asked with a bewildered look on her face. Staring down at the floor, Lantino sucks his teeth and shakes his head saying, "Stuh…".

"Aye, yie, yie and you wanna know what else?" asked Loriana to Loraine. "He's also suspended for twenty-five days!" she says.

"Gosh, it is twenty-two" Lantino said.

"Twenty-two! Damn, so Tino that really was you in that big fight with security," said Loraine to Lantino.

"Good, well now that you know all about the story of my day, I guess you probably wanna hear my side now," says Lantino to Loraine.

"Hunny please, you could tell that to the next person because as far as I know, you ain't got no side to tell," replied Loraine to Lantino.

"You know what, I think I need to be somewhere else." Lantino walks toward the front door.

"Where you heading to Lantino?" asked Loriana.

"Away from here, that's for sure," he replied. "I don't think I can handle both of you in my face right now."

"So, you're gonna walk out on us like your dad?" Loraine taunted Lantino.

"Say what?" Lantino responded.

"Stuh, just go ahead, walk out on us," Loraine shouted angrily.

"First of all, he didn't walk out on us. Second, last time I checked, he's your dad too," he says to Loraine.

"Hmp, whatever." Loraine responded turning her face away from him.

"Stuh, see y'all when I get back," he said shutting the door behind him.

Stepping outside, Lantino noticed how soaked everything looked, and began to wonder how Loraine managed to stay dry the whole time while it was raining earlier. Doing himself a favor, Lantino decided not to put neither Loraine nor his legal guardian on his mind. *Tuh, now that I'm out the door, they can be all up in each other's ear for all I care,* he thought as he made his way down the street. Things were beginning to dry up outside, allowing Lantino to buy some time into thinking about what he could do for the rest of the evening while he wandered around the neighborhood. It had been no more than ten minutes from when Lantino stepped out. Yet, delving into his own bubble as an effort to put the earlier part of the day behind him, Lantino seemed to have walked a lot further than where he was prior. For the moment, he looked like someone on pace walking a marathon. However, that's when he heard a whisper come from one of the alleys he passed by.

Coming to a halt, Lantino took a moment to make out what was being said. That's when he heard the voice from the alley. "Yo Tino, hold up," said the voice as its volume grew louder. As he waited, he could hear footsteps coming from the direction of the alleyway. Creeping out from the alleyway was not one, but two boys. Two in which Lantino recognized from school. They were both high school sophomores, making them older than he was by just a year. They were also slightly taller than Lantino. At school, everyone knew them as Vern and J-Roc. When they had a substitute, they'd skip class to hang out in other classes and this is how Lantino met them. Vern usually showed up to school always wearing the same cap. And normally, his cap would be tilted sideways. He had light brown eyes and light-skin complexion. He could often be seen in the main areas of the school campus drawing unwanted attention to other kids, especially during lunchtime. J-Roc, on the other hand, tends to show up to school with a flashing red bandana wrapped either around his neck or head. It was against the school's dress code policy for him to wear it, so, therefore, he'd often try to conceal it. The school was rather lenient on the dress code, but due to recent gang-related fights among cliques, the school developed a zero-tolerance for gang attire. One of them specifically was the red bandana. Also wearing big clothes, particularly for boys around Lantino's age group was a trend, so the school's principal gave it a pass. Most people suspected that J-Roc was a member of the hardcore gang, the Vice Lords. When gang-related activity got around, his name somehow was usually always sitting in the middle of it all. It was almost as though he was some kind of smooth orchestrator. All these made him gain popularity around the school. It was only a matter of time before his name spread around the streets. Respecting him, Lantino figured he could potentially be someone who could stand by J-Roc's side. However, doing that fell out of Lantino's favor very fast. And surely, Lantino had his own reasons.

"Tuh, haha...See Vern," said J-Roc, "I told you it was Lil' Tino."

"Sup Roc," said Lantino to J-Roc.

"What's up Lil' Tino," J-Roc replied. "Crazy because we were just talking about you haha..."

"Haha, I kept wondering if we were talking about the same person," said Vern to J-Roc. "But now I know for sure haha..."

"Who are you?" asked Lantino to Vern with his guard up.

"Haha c'mon Lil' Tino, I know you remember Vern," J-Roc replied.

"Hmmm, I think so."

"Oh...that's right, Vern wasn't with us at the last work out we handed you" J-Roc laughed. "Hmmm you only met 'em a few times at school."

"You know what, that's probably why," Vern said.

"Hey well that's alright Vern, Lil' Tino's gonna get to know more about you real soon, ain't that right?" said J-Roc to Lantino.

"Actually, I think I'm a chill today," Lantino responded.

"Well, in that case, why don't you just come chill with us," J-Roc suggested to Lantino.

"Hmmm I don't know," replied a hesitant Lantino.

"Look Lil' Tino," said J-Roc interrupting Lantino, "I know you ain't like that last workout, but to be real with you, none of us did...But it's all part of the steps to getting in, like I told you before, remember."

"Yeah, I hear ya trying to get in," Vern added.

"Yeah, Lil' Tino, I told him a thing or two about you wanting in," J-Roc said.

"Hmmm...Am I really gonna be in this time?!" responded Lantino to J-Roc.

"I guarantee it haha," answered J-Roc.

"Hmmm...So when's it all going down?" Lantino asked.

"Don't worry about it," J-Roc cut in. "I can set all that up tonight in a couple of hours."

"The same spot?" Lantino asked.

"Yeah, same spot, the junkyard," J-Roc replied.

"Man damn, it's gonna be the same shit," Lantino lamented. "That's it; I'm out!"

"Wait, so you're bailing?" asked Vern in a rather forceful manner.

"Man, what does it look like I'm doing? Get outta my face!" responding Lantino to Vern.

"Alright, alright, alright fine..." said J-Roc pulling Lantino back. "Here's another option."

"What now, man?" Lantino asked facing J-Roc.

"You know about Stone Park, right? Okay, well tonight we're gonna rumble with a few of them boys from Folk Nation. It's gonna be me, Vern, and a couple more of us that's gonna come through." J-Roc said.

"Yeah, I know about Stone Park. Rumble with who, though?" Lantino asked.

"Tell 'em Vern," said J-Roc.

"The KCs..." Vern said with a grin on his face.

"The Cobras…Th…The King Cobras?" Lantino asked mockingly.

"That's right, and tonight you get to come along," replied J-Roc.

"Yeah, but I heard about them," said Lantino. "Aren't they a soft crew? Wouldn't y'all wanna thump with a real clique?"

"Fool, haven't you been listening to anything my man here been saying?" Vern cuts in.

"What you mean?" asked Lantino

"What I'm saying is that by letting you come, that's like earning you a spot in the clique," said Vern to Lantino.

"Yeah, Lil' Tino...He's right," said J-Roc to Lantino. "After tonight, you basically sealed your spot."

"And this time, it's you that's gonna be working them out," said Vern.

"Yeah, that's how it's always gonna be beyond that point Lil' Tino," said J-Roc.

"Yep, you'll have respect, and the best part about it is we'll always have your back," said Vern.

"Always?" Lantino asked facing both Vern and J-Roc.

"Always," answered J-Roc.

"Like blood," added Vern, "So what do ya say? You're in?" he asked Lantino.

"When y'all trying to do this?" Lantino asked.

"Soon…So there's no time to think," answered J-Roc.

"And it's not like us to spill to outsiders," said Vern, "So think about it? If we're letting you in on this, then it's gotta be official."

"Alright, alright, I'm in," Lantino responded.

"Ha ha ha my dawg, I knew you wouldn't let us down," said Vern.

"Ha ha ha ha yeah he'd better not," laughed J-Roc. "Anyway, now that we got you on deck Lil' Tino, come with us so we could show you how it's all gonna go down."

"Hmmm…Where we headed?" asked a slightly suspicious Lantino.

"To Stone Park like we said before," answered Vern. "But first, we gotta go scoop up the others."

"Yeah, so follow us Lil' Tino," said J-Roc.

Lantino followed them, until they reached their destination. After walking way down from where they started, Lantino found the three of them standing in an area that seemed rather secluded. They stood on what once appeared to be a parking garage. However, there weren't any cars parked outside, which indicated the area was abandoned. And looking around, Lantino could see there were scraps of objects lying everywhere. Thus, reminding him of the junkyard, it gave him an eerie feeling that something wasn't right. With suspicions growing, Lantino tilted his head and said "This ain't no Stone Park." Taking a moment to stare at one another, both Vern and J-Roc shrug their shoulders with a look of bewilderedness on each of their faces. Drawing his attention back on Lantino, J-Roc lifts his left eyebrow and said, "Okay, and what's that supposed to mean," while slightly spreading his arms out. With his head still tilted sideways, a suspicious Lantino responded with a question: "Why are we here and not Stone Park?"

"We're on our way Lil' Tino," replied a slightly irritated Vern.

"Then why are we out here and not there?" Lantino asked.

"Because we're gonna head there as soon as the others get here, Lil' Tino," answered J-Roc.

"So, they're meeting us out here?" asked Lantino.

"Yeah, just like we told you Lil' Tino! Now relax. We're gonna go to Stone Park," said a vexed Vern.

"Yeah, just like he said Lil' Tino…just relax and be easy," laughed J-Roc. "They're gonna be here any minute," he assured Lantino.

"Hmmm, alright," Lantino responded.

"Ding, for someone who wants in, he sure asks a lot of questions J," said Vern to J-Roc. Staring back at Lantino with a crooked smile, J-Roc laughed.

"Like some interrogator…what are you five-O?" asked Vern to Lantino.

"Naw, naw he cool," laughed J-Roc.

"Tuh, whatever," muttered Lantino.

"Hey, but yo Lil' Tino," said J-Roc, "he right though. If you want in, you're gonna have to do something about all that twenty-one questions shit, ya dig? Hmmm, speaking of which…I gotta question for you."

"Hmmm, what?".

"Where were you all day at school".

"Hey, that's right!" said Vern as he interrupted J-Roc. "Yeah, we ain't seen you around all day. What happened?" he asked Lantino.

"Seems like you been hiding Lil' Tino…ever since that last workout," said J-Roc.

"Naw, naw…" replied Lantino.

"Okay…Guess we'll take your word for it Lil' Tino," said J-Roc.

"Man, bump all that!" said Vern. "He's chilling with us now, ain't it? The real question is if you heard about it."

"Wait, huh? Heard about what?" asked Lantino.

"The fight Lil' Tino!" answered J-Roc.

"The fight? Wait, the fight with who?" Lantino asked.

"Wow, you missed it Lil' Tino!" answered J-Roc, "Some kid got into it with security earlier today!"

"Yeah, news about that got around real quick!" said Vern. "I mean real quick."

"Damn, and now the whole school knows about it?" Lantino tried to sound surprised.

"Yeah," J-Roc answered, "Everyone was talking about it today at lunch."

"Tuh, whoever he is, we definitely gotta introduce him to the crew," Vern said.

"Yeah, we do," agreeing J-Roc. "Speaking of the crew, I'm a tag up a few more of our turfs. You got the spray on deck?" he asked Vern.

"Yep, and it's still full," answered Vern to J-Roc.

"Cool then, all is well," J-Roc responded. "C'mon, lets clear it."

"So now where we're heading?" asked Lantino.

"You know what, Lil' Tino I want you to stand here and be our look-out," J-Roc said.

"But Roc, how do you expect me to do that if y'all ain't even around?" Lantino complained.

"Chill out Lil' Tino, we'll be right here in the garage just marking territory," replied J-Roc. "And while we're doing that, this where you come in to signal us if anybody else besides us comes through."

"Oooooh..." Lantino responded.

"Ya got me?" asked J-Roc.

"Yeah, yeah, I gotchu Roc," answered Lantino.

"Cool…So, if anyone else comes through this turf, I want you to just say the words, code blue," said J-Roc.

"Code blue…" Lantino repeated.

"Yeah, just like that," responded J-Roc. "Yeah, that there means enemy alert; Vern and I will know right away."

"What should I say when the others get here, though?" asked Lantino as Vern and J-Roc were heading out.

"Just tell 'em to wait," answered J-Roc "We won't stay long."

"Hmmm…" responded Lantino while nodding his head.

"Alright," said J-Roc.

"Hmmm…Alright," responded Lantino as he watched them set out to go vandalize the area. After having started the earlier part of the day in an altercation with the school resource officer, Lantino now found himself in a fairly unique position. *Hmmm, I don't think they'd believe me if I told them that it was me who fought security,* he thought as he stood there on his p's and q's. Trying not to dwell on the earlier part of the day at school, Lantino focused and kept his eyes peeled on his surroundings. However, darkness was nearly all he could see as the night slowly began to settle in. Now relying heavily on his auditory senses, Lantino could hear what sounded like something wrestling against leaves and rocks just outside the old parking garage. Staring back towards the direction in which the sound was coming from, Lantino slowly began to notice movements. Unable to make out exactly what or who it was, he kept his eyes fixed on that same direction for some minutes. As he continued to stare, he figured out what appeared to be some tall shadowy figures. Four of them, to be exact. *Hmmm, that's funny Roc did say there'd be others coming, but what's up with the hoodies,* Lantino thought as he took note of their attire. Wearing hoodie jackets wasn't part of the VL dress code. Rather than approaching them, Lantino waved a few hand signals at them. However, all four shadowy figures showed no response, which sent back an odd vibe, leaving Lantino with more anxiety. In fact, Lantino received an awfully sinister vibe from them the moment he set eyes on them. And when they began to spread out and walk up towards him, Lantino then began taking steps back. At that point, Lantino stuttered out the words "Code blue, code blue," just like Vern and J-Roc instructed him to do. Unfortunately, he received no response. Though to him, it didn't matter whether he got a response or not because he had already decided to take off even before shouting out "code blue."

It was without question that they weren't the other vice Lords J-Roc had told him about. Neither were they the King Cobras. Whoever they were, one thing Lantino undoubtedly knew was that they were out to get him. And he knew that if he couldn't outrun them, then this would possibly mean the end of his life. By now, Lantino was out of the old parking garage area, and very far from the trail he had taken to come there. He was far and away from the garage, but not from his pursuers. He could hear their footsteps gaining on him as he kept scrambling away on foot for his dear life. Doing so, he ended up finding himself in a labyrinth of alleyways, continuously running around in circles. Lost in the midst of chaos, Lantino stopped, turned his head left and right before deciding which path to run to next. That's when he crashes right into someone, knocking him right off his feet and on to the floor. Taking a moment to sit up with a wide eye, Lantino figured his enemies caught him. *This is it; I'm dead meat*, he thought as he blinked for a quick second. But taking a second look, he comes to find that the person he bumped into, isn't one of the four guys on his tail. In fact, it's just a boy about his age and size, who, like Lantino ironically, seems to be on the run. With some air coming back to his lungs, Lantino instantaneously asks, "Where'd you come –" but then his question gets interrupted by the sound of muffled voices and footsteps. Consumed with fear, Lantino looks around as he gets ready to dash. But tapping him on the right shoulder, the same boy he crashed into tells him, "Here! This way! Follow me!" Lantino does reluctantly. Following him, they ran to a corner that brings them to a dead end. At that point, there's no turning back because two of the pursuers were behind them. Evidently, there with nowhere else to run, Lantino bulges his knuckles as he gets ready for the inevitable. That's when the boy jumped up a few feet into the air pulling down a fire escape ladder. Within seconds, the boys were up the ladder and on a balcony which the ladder's attached to. Pulling the fire escape ladder back up, the boys then crouched in the balcony, hoping that all four pursuers didn't hear or notice them.

Chapter 3: Life in the Greens

Trying not to make a sound while hiding on the balcony, the boys heard the footsteps coming from below. It was the four hooded shadowy figures Lantino ran from earlier at the old parking garage. As sweat continued to pour down Lantino's cheeks, he could hear them taking their time trying to scorch the dead end. Listening to them attentively, he could hear their voices. Though, he couldn't quite make out what they were saying.

It took a while, but eventually, Lantino took a peek to check after some time. "Hey, I think they're gone; we should head back now," he whispered to the boy who was with him. "No, wait," the boy replied, "I know another way."

"Another way? Another way where? Out of here?" asked Lantino.

"Yeah, c'mon follow me."

"Wait, where you're climbing up to?"

"I told you I know another way."

"Hmmm…but what about going back down where we came from?"

"You think they're really gone?"

"Hmmm…Okay, show me this other way."

So rather than climbing back down and risking the possibility of doing more running or getting caught, the boys continued climbing their way up the building. They climbed up every fire escape ladder until they reached the building's rooftop. Once they made it to the rooftop, the boy who led the way took a moment to sigh in relief, basically stating that they both survived the horror they encountered below in the alleyways. Realizing that the building's rooftop was the other way the boy was talking about, Lantino slowly looked around while spreading his arms out, calmly asking him, "So, this…this is it? This is this other way you were telling me about?"

"Yeah," responding the boy, "we're good here for now."

"So, tell me, how do you know they won't come up this way through the building?" asked Lantino.

"Because they won't…No one knows about up here except for the people that stay in this building. Besides, no one ever comes up here."

"No one?"

"No one."

"But wait, how'd you know that, though?"

"Because I snuck out my group home a couple of times to come out here, and no one ever said anything to me. I had my eye on this building."

"Hmmm…Okay, I guess we could chill here then."

"Yeah, man, we're good. Nobody's gonna come give us any trouble here."

"Stuh, that's good. Hmp, so you said you had your eye on this building?"

"Yeah, that's how I know about out here."

"Hmmm…why?"

"What do you mean?"

"I mean like…why here? What for?"

"I just needed a spot I could find before I ran away from my group home. So after I did that, I knew this place would be the right one. Matter of fact, when I came here earlier today, no one was up here again."

"Hold up, so you have been here for how many hours now?"

"I don't know…For a while now. But when my stomach started to hurt, I went down to see if I could find some food somewhere. And then, out of nowhere, these creepy dudes in dark hoodies showed up and started chasing me all over these corners."

"Ahhh so that's how I bumped into you."

"Or maybe that's how I bumped into you."

"Shit, better you than them…"

"Wait, were they after you?"

"Yeah…they were…but somehow, they must've thought you were me when they came through the alleys…"

"Were…were they gonna kill you? I mean us? If they caught us?"

"Yeah…I think so…"

"Who were those guys?"

"I don't know…I have never seen Folks like them around here before…"

"Never?"

"Naw, never…Not ever…But whoever they were, they roll with the Folks."

"The Folks?"

"Yeah, members of Folk Nation."

"Huh? What is that?"

"Tuh, things you don't know about. People you probably don't wanna ever know about."

"Hmmm…Why were they after you?"

"Because I rock the five-point star."

"The what point star?"

"The People Nation."

"Huh?"

"You know the VLs…five high six die."

"Uh…"

"You're not from here, are you?"

"Hmmm…No, I'm not. Honestly…I'm not sure where I'm from."

"Tuh, well, it ain't here; that's for sure."

"Yeah, I know."

"Hey, well, don't feel bad. Ain't much special for someone to wanna be from out here anyway."

"What makes you say that?"

"Life's hard here in the Chi. Especially in the Greens, where I stay."

"The Chi?"

"It's short for Chicago, the name of this big city."

"Oooooh…"

"Yeah…Anyway, you'll see what I'm talking about if you stay out here long enough. Wait, so how long you been around here since you're not from here?"

"I just moved here about five months ago."

"Oh, okay."

"Yeah, I stayed with the Bridges."

"Who are they?"

"A bunch of people I lived with at a group home who tried to pretend to be a family."

"A group home...What's a group home?"

"Just a stupid place. A stupid place I was forced to stay at. That's until I finally ran away. And now I'm here on this rooftop."

"What made you run away?"

"It was either that, or I'd get sent back to Open Arms."

"Sent back where?"

"Open Arms! The orphanage! A place for kids with no family or place to go!"

"Wow, you really don't like out there."

"No...I hate it. It's just a stupid place."

"And up this rooftop is better?"

"Anywhere is better than there!"

"Hmp...Okay."

"Look, you don't have to stay up here. If you wanna go, then you can go."

"Oh, okay..."

"Just take the stairwell downstairs. I think that way's a quieter route for you to run home."

"Yo...thanks..."

"Yeah..."

"But hey, what about you?"

"I'll be alright up here."

"But won't you need a place to stay? I mean a real place anyway..."

"Hmmm, who do you live with?"

"I live with two people right now. The place isn't very big, but it's only the three of us, which means there's room for you."

"Hmmm...I don't do too well living with new people, though..."

"Hmmm that's alright, just stay for a couple of nights, and if you still think it's a stupid place later on, then you can just leave. No one's gonna force you to stay. That I can guarantee!"

"You sure?"

"Of course, after helping me out tonight, it's the least I could do."

"Hmmm…well, thanks, uh…"

"Lantino…My name's Lantino. And you?"

"I'm Torence."

After their unexpected meeting, they went back to Lantino's place, where Torence gladly stayed. After having survived their encounter with Folk Nation, an affinity between the two immediately began to develop. Despite not having many answers to his questions about Torence, Lantino could feel that having him around was going to make life with the Tourezes more interesting. Moreover, it was going to make life out in the Greens somewhat more bearable, now that Lantino had a real friend. For Torence, staying with Lantino was conflicting with everything he had conjured up in his thoughts prior to the events of day one. For once, he was actually accepted by someone, which he felt was complicated. Though, at the same time, he was just as glad to be in the picture. However, there was only one uncertainty that stood in the way. How long was Torence going to stay? It is now a week since he came over. Torence had stayed at the residence a bit longer than expected. It was apparent that Torence didn't mind staying with the Tourezes, but it was only a matter of time before Loriana would say something. Serving a suspension from school had proved convenient for Lantino because he'd normally be home while Ms. Tourez and Loraine were out during the day. So, on that note, he and Torence could hang out. And on days his legal guardian and half-sister were home, he'd just have Torence come over in the later part of the day. However, like Torence, Lantino knew the questions were coming. The eventual questions about his new friend.

On an early Friday in the Fall, Torence and Lantino got up to start the day as they usually do. This time, they got up earlier than usual. According to Lantino, it was time to spend their day slightly different. Lantino led the trail outside, where the two now stood just yards away in front of Lantino's building. Fortunately, it didn't rain outside. But on the flip side, the rain left an uncomfortable chill in the air. While Torence borrowed a red sweater, Lantino figured his baggy clothes should suffice in keeping him warm. Wrapping a red striped bandana around his head, Lantino asked Torence if he's probably wondering what they're doing outside so early. "Hmmm, yeah kind of." Torence replied.

"Well, I figured since you're not from around here, why not show you around," said Lantino.

"You mean like a tour?" asked Torence.

"Hmmm yeah…You know, like a tour…to welcome you to the Greens…Your new home."

"My new home?"

"Yeah…This way."

"Hey, but wait, what are we going to see?"

"Tuh, the places I'm taking you out to are only a small part."

"A small part?"

"Yeah, think of it as a small piece of a pie."

"Whoa…"

"Yeah, this city is big, which means I probably won't get to show you the whole thing in one day."

"Wait, so what are we gonna see first?"

"Hmmm, you'll see once we get there."

"Hmp, okay…"

"Ready for this tour?"

"Hmmm, just one thing. What's up with the handkerchief?"

"Handkerchief? Ahhh, you mean what I got around my head now?"

"Yeah…"

"You're asking because it makes me look different with it on?"

"Yeaaah."

"Hmp, that's what everyone says, haha."

"Everyone?"

"People at school…Anyway, if you're gonna live here in this part of town, you're gonna have to get you one of these."

"Hmmm…why?"

"This part of town can get really rough out here unless you're wearing what I've got on."

"A handkerchief?"

"Yeah, but not just any handkerchief. It's a flag."

"All I just see is red stripes, though."

"That's the thing; the red gives you protection."

"Protection?"

"Yeah…Protection…You remember those four people that chased us a few nights ago?"

"Oh yeah, them!"

"Okay, well, they wouldn't be able to do that to us here…"

"Hmmm, can I get one?"

"This is the only one I've got, but I can probably get you one. For now, just stay next to me when you're out of the house. I'll watch your back."

"Okay…How come people aren't safe if they're not wearing red?"

"Hmmm, because this is how life out here is in the Greens. That's why I think I need to show you around if you plan on staying out here for long."

"Hmp okay…I guess I'm ready to take a tour now."

"Oh, you ready now?"

"Yeah…"

"Okay, c'mon this way."

Just as Lantino drew a gesture that indicated it was time to move on, the sudden sound of a shout echoed through the streets. Both Torence and Lantino paused and turned towards one another. The shout is heard a couple of more times, putting silence to practically all of their thoughts and next moves. Now clearly hearing his name being called out loud, Lantino tilts his head up and finds that its Loraine calling him from the high-rise building. Just the very sight of her begins to create an irritable sensation on Lantino. Staring back at him, Loraine could immediately feel his mood as she watched the change in his facial expression. "Yeah nigga, that's right, I'm talking to you," she says to him.

"Man, what do you want?" he asked her.

"Um, excuse me, but don't you 'what do you want' at me. You need to remember Tino; this is my house, my momma gotchu staying in so, you need to come at me correct."

"Stuh, whatever…What you need?"

"What I need…No, I don't need ANYTHING from you. More like, what mami needs from you."

"Man, I'm on my way out right now, and you're holding me up. So, spit it out."

"Mami said she needs to see you."

"Okay…"

"Like right now."

"Right now? For what?"

"I don't know. Maybe that's why you need to come up here and find out."

"Stuh, I'm doing something right now. My friend and I gotta head somewhere."

"I don't give a care to what you or your lil' friend gotta do. You come up here right now and talk it out to mami."

"Stuh…damn…"

"Hurry up; she's waiting for you!"

"Shit, I'm on my way! Can't you see I'm walking."

"Tuh, you need to get a step on it already!"

With a bit of reluctance, Lantino made his way back inside the building to meet with Loriana, his legal guardian. Not too far behind him, his new friend Torence followed his trail. Watching Torence from the kitchen window, Loraine took the opportunity to introduce herself bringing Torence to an immediate halt. "Um, hold on lil' boy!" said Loraine to Torence, "but did anybody ask to see you upstairs?!"

"Uh…No," replying Torence as he slowly shook his head.

"I didn't think so," said Loraine. "Which probably means you have to wait."

Torence stood silently still as he's stopped on his track by the pissy Loraine. Looking back at her from where he's standing, their eyes connected, and as this is happening, a sensation begins to come upon him. It's like he's going through a state of hypnosis. The annoying look on Torence face made Loraine so uncomfortable that she asked, "do you have an eye problem?" He was so lost in his thought that he didn't hear her at first. Then Loraine asked again, "boy, do you have an eye problem. Do you need glasses or something?" He answered by shaking his head; the embarrassed Torence looked away. Loraine poked her head back inside and closed the window shut.

Walking through the front door, Lantino slowly made his way through the living room before stopping near the sofa. Standing there, his eyes began to travel around the room. While doing that, he noticed everything appeared to be the same way he left it prior to him stepping out with Torence. Present in the kitchen was Loraine staring him down condescendingly. "Mami, Tino's here," she said out loud while heading back to her room. Watching her as she headed back to her room, Lantino could then began to feel an atmospheric change in the living room. Hearing sounds coming from the restroom, Lantino automatically inferred that Ms. Tourez was going to be joining him soon in the living room. *Stuh, what the heck does she want,* he thought as he waited with a lot of suspense. "Tino," Loriana said out loud while making her way out the restroom. "You know why you're here, right?" she asked him. Nodding his head, he looks on vacantly at her as she slowly comes near the other end of the sofa. Standing directly across from him, she was wearing a bathrobe with her hair wrapped in a shower cap. "Hmmm… yeah, Loraine told me you wanted to speak with me," said Lantino.

"Si, that's right…I need to have a talk with you about that boy."

"The boy…You mean, my friend?"

"Si, Tino, that boy…your friend who's been staying here for the past week…"

"Oh…Uh…Yeah…What about him?"

"What about him'…Who is he, Lantino? Where are his parents? Shouldn't he be going back home by now?"

"Tuh…He'll be going soon…"

"Just going…"

"I mean yeah…He'll be going back home soon…"

"Lantino!"

"What?"

"That didn't answer my questions."

"Hmmm, I don't know, we just met a few days ago…"

"Ugh! What's his name, Lantino?"

"His name's…Stuh, you know what, what difference does it make?"

"Ooooh…"

"You never liked any of my friends. So, what's with all the questions?"

"None of them stayed over this long. None of them stayed over at all…"

"Oh…yeah…But that's just cause they ain't like it here."

"Hmp, good for them, and even better for me. Anyways, where are you up to now?"

"Nothing, I just told my friend I'd show him around town today."

"Hmmm…Comprende and am I holding you up?"

"Well, yeah…he's downstairs now waiting on me."

"Hmmm…Have fun with your new friend today."

"Okay…talk to me about him later."

"No, no, no…Don't worry yourself with that."

"Oh word…"

"Si, because he can find another place to sleep over."

"Ahhh…alright, alright, alright…"

"Tell me his name, Lantino!"

"Stuh…Okay…He told me his name's Torence…"

"And…"

"And a few days ago, when we met, he told me that there were problems in his family…"

"He has problems with his family…Is he in some kind of trouble, Lantino?!"

"No…Well…I mean; I don't know…Maybe…All I just know is that he don't wanna stay with them. At least, not right now."

"And so, that's why you brought him here?"

"He's just sleeping over for a few days. That's all…"

"He didn't say anything to you about his family?"

"Hmmm…A last name…the Bridges, and that's about it…"

"Is he in some kind of trouble?!"

"No…I don't know…"

"You better not be hiding anything from me, Lantino. You better not!"

"I told you everything I know…What else you want me to say?"

"Hmmm…"

"I mean, if you wanna know anything else, I guess you should talk to him."

"Fine then…I'll let you know…"

"Know what?"

"When I'm ready to talk to him."

"Hmp…"

"What?"

"Good luck with that?"

"Porque?"

"He seems really top secret with that, but…don't tell 'em I told you that."

"Why hasn't he told you something?"

"No clue…But maybe he'll tell you."

Chapter 4: Trying to Hang

It had been only a few hours into their tour around Lantino's local community, and Torence had already concluded that life in the Greens was an endless struggle. In his walk with Lantino, Torence passed a lot of homes that didn't look like people resided in them. What stuck out to him more was one area that was blocked off by crime scene investigators. It appeared to be some kind of homicide that took place. Whatever happened, he paused and glued his eyes to the scene. "Welcome to the Greens," said Lantino.

"Is this what life out here is like? I mean, is this what I gotta get used to?" asked Torence.

"These days, yeah…" answered Lantino.

"Damn…"

"But I hear it wasn't always like this though. I mean, that's what Ms. Tourez once told me."

"What was it like?"

"She said out here was a lot quieter than this. At least, back in her days when she was growing up."

"Hmp…I can't imagine."

"Yeah, me too. You wanna go somewhere else?"

"Yeah, let's go."

"Let's check out Stone Park."

Torence stood right beside Lantino while making the walk with him, though the park wasn't far. The actual name of the park they were both heading to is called La Villita, though many of the local residents knew it better as Stone park. The name Stone Park was derived from a gang that used to roam the area many years ago. As a group, they were small in number, but they were known for their stone-cold reputation. Thus, giving them their name, the Stone Lords.

Eventually, a majority of them were either run off by rival gangs or mostly caught and placed in boot camps. However, the following decades spawned a new breed of Lords who resurged from the toughest boot camps. Dropping the 'stone' from their name, they called themselves the Vice Lords. Like their predecessors, they were just as hardcore and twice as successful in pushing nearly all but a few of their rivals away from the park. Now Stone Park itself is considered a high valued territory because the zone it sits on, is gang infested. With that said, cops are slow or, in most cases, unwilling to respond to that particular area. So, whoever has hold of Stone Park can run their operations smoothly without police interference. In other words, that gang is considered by far the most dominant. And according to Lantino's knowledge, his clique, the Vice Lords, appear to have the upper hand for the moment.

Finally making their way to the park, the boys decided to rest their legs on the bleachers sitting out near a playground. From there, Torence took a moment to let his eyes do some wandering for a change. Doing that, Torence took mental notes of some of the symbols that were spray-painted mostly throughout the park. Some of them were the same ones he saw while he was en route to Stone Park. Something else he noted was that a majority of the smaller symbols were sprayed with black colors while the bigger ones were done in red. The red ones were symbols like wine glasses, canes, top hats, two cubes, occasionally a pyramid, a bunny, and usually a five-point star with VL letters. The red ones seem to be all over the park, based on what he was able to infer. "So, we're here…" said Lantino.

"This is it?" asked Torence.

"Yep, Stone Park…"

"Hmp…"

"What?"

"Hmmm…don't seem like much to me."

"What? You were expecting to see a mansion or something?"

"Hmmm, I don't know, I just thought there'd be more, I guess."

"Well, hey I know it ain't much, but this out here is where everyone be at."

"Everyone? Who's everyone? So far, it's only us out here."

"Keyword, so far."

"Who are they?"

"They're the Vice Lords."

"So, is that what VL stands for?"

"Yeah, and practically, this whole place is marked by them. That's why you keep seeing the same red signs tagged everywhere we go."

"Ooooh…"

"Yeah, oh…and you remember what I told you earlier about the Greens being a little crazy out here?"

"Yeah, I remember…"

"Well, good then, so now you know why I brought you out here."

"Protection?"

"Bingo. Your backs covered all the time on these grounds."

"Ding, then I better make sure I don't forget the way to the park."

"Stuh, yeah…C'mon, let's have a look around real quick."

"Hey, wait, is that some of them over there? The Vice Lords?"

"Some of them over where?"

"Right over there where I'm pointing at."

Turning away from Torence, Lantino looks over towards the direction Torence is pointing and comes to find a gazebo sitting way across from where they are at the bleachers. In that gazebo were three people, who appeared to be boys around their age group. From the looks of it, it seems as though the three of them came by to hang out. "So, you see what I'm talking about?" asked Torence while pointing at their direction. "Yeah, I see them," replied Lantino. "Here, put your arm down before they notice us," he said to Torence.

"Hmmm, hey look, I think one of them is getting up," said Torence.

"Yeah, he is," replied Lantino, "and it's all due to them spotting us."

"Hmmm, oh yo what's he doing now?"

"He's signaling for us to come over to the gazebo."

"Hmmm…Should we go to them?"

"Yeah, let's go see what they want."

"You sure?"

"Yeah…I think it's safe. They're VLs."

"Hmmm, okay…"

"Hey, but just one thing, if you see someone don't point at them. No matter what."

"Uh…Okay. How come, though?"

"Just don't, I will explain later."

"Okay…"

"Oh, and one more tip, when we get there, don't speak unless spoken to."

"What? Why?"

"Look, Torence, if you're gonna live here, then you're gonna have to try and hang. And the only way to do that is by following me."

"Okay…I gotchu."

"Alright, cool…C'mon, let's go see what they want."

Heading towards the gazebo, Lantino led the way while Torence followed his trail. There were three Vice Lords waiting for them there. Torence felt a bit apprehensive about meeting them. Despite what Lantino mentioned about protection, Torence wasn't necessarily sure what was going to come out of this situation. The question marks surrounding the gazebo were drawing a lot of suspense. Suspense that made Torence feel all the more reluctant to come with Lantino. However, noting Lantino's willingness to head there without hesitation, calmed Torence's nerves in some way. When they arrived near the gazebo, the Vice Lord who signaled them to come over approached them first. He stood slightly taller than both Torence and Lantino and wore a cap sideways; it was Vern.

"Hey Roc, I told you it's him. The look-out we thought got snatched up by the GDs the other week," he said out loud to one of the other Vice Lords who was standing inside of the gazebo. Hearing that, the same one that stood inside the gazebo look like he was trying to keep his jaw from hitting the floor as he stared attentively at Lantino. Like the one who signaled them over, the one standing in the gazebo was slightly taller than Torence and Lantino. He had on a black snap back which he reversed and wore a red flashing bandana around his neck. "Oooooh shit, well, I'll be damned…" he said, looking directly at Lantino. "Lil' Tino, is it actually you?"

"Vern, J-Roc…It's nice to see y'all," Lantino said to both of the Vice Lords. Torence was shocked that his friend Lantino actually knew the two Vice Lords. By now, everyone had entered the gazebo, and Torence, at this point was just trying to remain invisible while quietly listening to the dialogue. "Yeah…Nice to see you too Tino," said J-Roc. "How'd you slip pass the GDs?" he asked.

"Yeah, we thought you were history," said Vern. "I mean, we asked around, but no one had seen you."

"Yeah, no one…Not even in school," said J-Roc.

"Well, I'm glad I was missed," replied Lantino. "Anyway, if it makes y'all feel better, I'm alive and well," he said to J-Roc and Vern.

"Yeah…but how, though?" asked J-Roc.

"I found help," replied Lantino, slightly swinging his head towards Torence's direction. Moving the spotlight on Torence, the pair stared him down from head to toe and back. Not seeing much to look at in Torence, Vern then asked, "Who's this?" to Lantino.

"Stuh, does it matter?" replied Lantino.

"Okay, so you're straight," said J-Roc, "but what I really need to know is where you been at this whole time, you haven't even been at school?" he asked.

"Yeah, cause you been like a ghost…" Vern added.

"I'm suspended from school," replied Lantino.

"Suspended," said both Vern and J-Roc in unison.

"Yeah, for like three weeks or so," answered Lantino.

"You suspended?" asked J-Roc.

"For what?" asked Vern.

"Man, for fighting with security!" said the third Vice Lord who was seated quietly inside the gazebo. All eyes were placed on him the moment he spoke. Somehow his voice seemed to carry weight. Anticipating his next words was like waiting for a green light. Something about his demeanor made him very intimidating. How he talked gave Torence the impression that he was a lot older than he looked. He may have been seated, but he was clearly taller than they all were. Not to mention, he was physically bigger. He wore a thick long-sleeved, red and black buttoned-up flannel shirt with tan baggy khaki pants. His head was shaved bald and wrapped around it was a flashing red bandana, like J-Roc's. "Can't y'all dumbasses see it was him who whooped security's ass?" he said out loud to both J-Roc and Vern. With a convoluted look on each of their faces, they both turned to look at one another. "Wait, you mean that was you Lil' Tino," asked a surprised Vern. Answering him, Lantino nods his head a couple of times. "You, security, fight, whoop, what..." said J-Roc, who's stumbling on his words.

"You're being almighty is all that needs to make sense around me," said the seated Vice Lord to Lantino. "Now my meeting you was the day I was dying for from the moment word got out to me about your fight. I figure we could use another soldier like you for the third chapter," he said to Lantino.

"How'd you know about the fight?" asked a curious Lantino to the seated Vice Lord.

"Tuh, it's all over the school," replied the seated Vice Lord. "It's all everyone's been talking about. Besides, one of my peeps from the school pointed you out a few days ago when he spotted you out here at the park; I have been coming to this park since then. So tell me...You're really him? The kid...the Tino that thumped with security?" he asked Lantino.

"Yeah...I'm Tino..."

"Hmp...Well, Tino, I'm Tyberius. But around here, I'm better known as just Tye. For the People Nation, I run the third chapter. My enemies like to call me TB. Wanna know why?"

"Hmmm...Why?"

"The fuck I know...to hell, anyway those Folk Nation niggas you and your partner managed to outrun a week ago were GDs. Now banging with them is a story that goes way back. Anyway, word around the street has it that the KCs are rolling with them after we took them out of the game. So, we're gonna have to hang tight because the GDs have a bad rep for jumping niggas. If you hang with me Tino, I'll double your protection, your doe, and make you twice as sharp as those edges on the five-point star. What do ya say? We almighty?"

"Yeah...Almighty."

"All is well then. Be back out here after dark. Vern, Roc, round up the troops for a hood meeting tonight."

Chapter 5: On Thin Ice

As usual, Torence's tours around the city with Lantino began with the both of them getting up rather early to step out and take a walk. This time the two toured areas of the north and eastside region. There Torence's eyes ventured around the neighborhood's settings and landmarks, taking note of their every flavor and eye-catching style. They got around to make stops by places like Hyde and Lincoln Park, to name a few. Then ended up at a pizza shop somewhere on the west side where Lantino called the tour a wrap. Heading home after a so-called fun-filled day of sightseeing, Torence opened up a new dialogue asking, "So what now?" to Lantino. "We're heading back to the crib," replied Lantino.

"Hmmm yeah, I know that. But what I mean is...where to after today?"

"Oh, you mean that...Oh naw, that's it. That's the end of the tour."

"Wait, this is it?"

"Yeah, today was the last day. Why do you think we're heading home earlier than usual?"

"Hmp...Okay..."

"So, now that you know your way around the city, what do you think?"

"Uhhh...Well...I don't know if I could say I know my way around."

"Hahaha...I know. I'm just messing with you."

"Stuh oh, okay..."

"I know it's a big city, and you're gonna need more time, but you'll figure out your way around."

"Hmp, I hope so, haha."

"You will..."

"Hmmm, well, I think I like it out here."

"Good...So, you think you'll stay with us for a little longer?"

"Stay?"

"Yeah, I mean, it's going on almost a month now since you showed up."

"Hmmm...well, what about that lady?"

"Wait, what lady?"

"You know...that lady you stay with. The one you always say that's not your mom."

"Oh, you mean Ms. Tourez?"

"Yeah, her..."

"Man, I told you, don't worry about her. I got that covered."

"Ugh...I don't know, Lantino."

"You worried you're gonna end up back at the group home again."

"Stuh...Yeah..."

"Look, you ain't going back."

"I'm never going back!"

"I know...Look, Torence, Ms. Tourez likes you."

"How do you know that?"

"Because if she didn't, then don't you think she would've said something to me by now?"

"Hmmm...Well, has she?"

"No..."

"That's the thing."

"Wait...What you mean?"

"Stuh..."

"Wait, she said something to you?"

"Stuh, yeah..."

"Oh snaps, when was this? I mean what did she say?"

"Hmmm some nights ago, when you went out for the hood meeting, she cooked up a hot plate and –"

"And..."

"And she asked me who am I?"

"Wait, huh?"

"Well...It wasn't really what she said, but it was kinda what she said, if you know what I mean."

"Okay...and what'd you say?"

"Tuh...Well..."

"Yeah..."

"I told her..."

"Hmmm...Told her what?"

"I told her about my name...about the group home...The Bridges."

"You told her?"

"Yeah...I told her about the Bridges. But only what I wanted her to know. The rest I can't talk about."

"That's cool. She said anything else?"

"Yeah...She did. She brought up something about...home study."

"Home study...What the heck is that?"

"I don't know...Everything else she said after that didn't make much sense. I mean, she said that and a whole bunch of things like 'apple-lication'"

" Apple-lication? Wait, you mean application? Is that what you're trying to say?"

"Yeah, yeah that word..."

"Well, what do you think?"

"I don't know, I felt like talking to her for the first time should've and could've been much scarier but..."

"But, it wasn't?"

"Nah, it wasn't."

"Hmp, well, since she ain't kick you out yet, then I'd take that as a good sign."

"Yeah, maybe..."

"Hey, look, I know the ice we're standing on ain't thick, but at least we're still standing."

"Yeah...You're right. Hmmm...Lantino, you may not think so, but you have good peoples in your life."

"Hmp, it's good to know someone thinks so."

"I could be wrong, though...But if I'm right...then Ms. Tourez is different."

"Different?"

"Yeah..."

"Hmmm, like in what way?"

"I don't know...I just feel like she's different from all the other grownups I've met, I guess."

"Hmp, if you say so. What about my sister?"

"Uh...She's alright, I guess."

"Alright? Don't you wanna say something worse?"

"No, I'll just...leave it alone."

"It's okay, shit, it won't hurt me a bit."

"Well, she's a little rough."

"That sounds more like it, haha."

"Especially around me."

"I know she gets crazy, but hey, like I said before, you'll get used to her."

"But you think she'll ever get used to me?"

"I don't know...but she's gonna have to. I mean, you're not going anywhere anytime soon, so..."

"But...What if things get worse?"

"You think it could?"

"Yeah, maybe...On some days when you're not around, she'll say things to me like –"

"Like what?"

"Like 'why are you here or what are you doing here.'"

"Wait, she said that to you?"

"Yeah...She clearly doesn't want me around."

"Well, don't even sweat that, Torence."

"Thanks, Lantino."

"No prob. Look, I know you ain't been with us that long but just know this, until you go, the door will always be open for you."

"Even if Ms. Tourez says otherwise?"

"Even if...But she won't."

"Alright."

"Now let's quit stalling like we're scared to go home."

"Haha yeah, let's go...Oh, hey…"

"What's up?"

"You never told me what happened that night at the hood meeting."

"Hmmm ain't much happen that night. Tye just introduced me to a whole bunch of people he knew."

"The VLs?"

"Yeah...There were about eight people who showed up first, but more came through later."

"What'd y'all end up doing the whole time?"

"I ended up learning some VL talk and things I could say with my hands."

"For real?"

"Yeah, it's all like a secret language. Tye's planning to check me on them the next time we meet."

"Hey, you think you can show me some of what they taught you?"

"Hmmm, okay...When we get home, I'll show you some of the handshakes."

"Must be nice to be a VL."

With both of them now just a few blocks away from home, the tour around the city was surely over. Thanks to Lantino, Torence now gained a better awareness of his surrounding areas. Although there was still much more for him to know, Lantino figured he'd be fine in a matter of time. Lantino, on the other hand had moved from being a pre-gang potential to an official member of the Vice Lords gang. In exchange for their protection, he was going to be their eyes and ears during their activities. In that view, Lantino seems to like the role and name he earned for himself under the likes of Tyberius, which was a shame because his suspension was almost up.

When the boys arrived home, they carried on with conversations about Tye and everything else that was going on. In doing that, Lantino showed Torence how to do one of the few handshakes he learned from the Vice Lords. For Torence, trying the handshake the first couple of times seemed overwhelmingly complicated. However, with repetition and some time, he eventually began picking it up. By then, Loraine had walked through the living room door and seemed to be in a noticeably unhappy mood. Stepping inside, she had deliberately slammed the door behind her, which instantaneously took the boys out of their conversation. With their heads both turned towards her direction, they sat on the living room sofa, looking on a bit stunned. "Well, damn Loraine," said Lantino, "the hell was that for?!" Standing without a response, Loraine just looks on in silence. Then begins to glare not at Lantino, but Torence. Slowly glancing back and forth between Torence and Loraine, Lantino starts questioning what she was doing. But again, he doesn't get a response out of the hostile Loraine. Instead, Loraine belligerently started asking Torence why's he still in their house in a very high tone. "Didn't I tell you to take your sorry ass back to wherever you came from!" she continued.

"Hey, don't talk like that to Torence!" said Lantino standing up for Torence.

"Oh, shut up, Lantino!" shouted Loraine. Fixing her eyes back on Torence, who's still seated on the living room sofa, she continued talking, "Boy, when will you get it? No one wants you here! Don't you have a place to go to? Why you trying to freeload off our meals and shit!?" She pauses for a moment, but in response, Torence quietly looks on without a word. "I guess I ain't make myself clear the last time I told you not to come here," said Loraine to Torence in a bellicose expression. Torence slowly stood up on his two feet. "Ah naw, naw, naw, sit back down, Torence," said Lantino, "you didn't do anything wrong coming here."

"It's about time for him to go, Lantino!" said Loraine.

"Says who? You? Last time I check, you're not Ms. Tourez!"

"Tell him to get out, Lantino!"

"Or else what?!"

"I said, tell him to get out!"

"Make me!"

"You know what, boy just get the fuck out!" said Loraine to Torence.

"Don't listen to her, Torence," Lantino said to Torence pushing him back to the sofa.

"Oh, shut the fuck up, Lantino!" said Loraine to Lantino.

"No, it's you who need to shut up and take all this noise somewhere else!" replied Lantino. Stepping between Lantino and Loraine, Torence tries to calm things down. "Boy, don't you put your crusty fingers on me," said the belligerent Loraine to Torence. "Better be glad he's keeping me away from you," Lantino said to Loraine.

"Forget him! And you too! Fuck both of –" shouting Loraine.

"LORAINE! THAT'S ENOUGH!" said Loriana, who stepped out of her bedroom to take command of the situation.

"Mami," said Loraine, "Can you tell this boy –"

"THAT'S ENOUGH!" Loriana said in a strong voice to Loraine.

"But mami!" said a persistent Loraine, "he needs_ _ _"

"I WILL DEAL WITH IT!" said Loriana interrupting Loraine. "FOR NOW, THAT'S ENOUGH! I HEARD ENOUGH FROM YOU WHILE I WAS IN MY ROOM! No se lo que te pasa. Pero todos estos gritos y' peleas no son como tu. Que esta pasando?"

"What's going on with me?!" asked a frustrated Loraine. "What I can't figure out is porque Lantino se escapa con las cosas por aque? Por que le estas dando a su amigo to do este trato especial como si se lo hubiera ganado? Si me preguntas, eso no esta bien. I get my schoolwork done, pass my classes, and hardly get in trouble. Yet somehow Tino and his new friend get to have all this fun. That's not right Mami!"

"Ahhh si...A horremos otro tiempo para esta discusion. For now, that's enough."

"Ugh! Mami, it's not right!"

"Si, si, but let's save it for another time."

"You know that's not right, mami!"

"LORAINE! WHAT DID I SAY!"

Taking her eyes off her mother, she took one more look around the living room, and when her eyes fell on Torence, she bent them and sucked her teeth, uttering out "Ugh!" She angrily walked into her room, slamming the door shut behind her. While Torence looked at the ground, feeling rather embarrassed about the outcome of tonight's event, Lantino just shook his head. Loriana, in the meantime, stood quietly in the living room as if she was waiting for Loraine to come back out. The look on her face had concerns written all over it. And rightfully so, after dealing with everything that just took place. She stood still processing everything for a couple of more minutes before finally heading back to her room. Fortunately, this was how things concluded for the night at the Tourez's residence. Unfortunately, the following days brought new episodes of Loraine's hostility towards anyone she'd practically come in contact with. Once Loriana reached her limit with Loraine, she sent her to a boot camp.

Chapter 6: Concrete

In Chicago, there were several local boot camps, but Concrete happened to be one of the more reputable ones for at-risk youths like Loraine. The length in which the teen attended the discipline-based program depended on the parent or, at times, the severity of the issue concerning the teen. Although Concrete was well known, some parents and people within their staff argued about its disciplinary program proving to be ineffective. In fact, many people argued that a therapy program that could identify their teen's underlying issues while promoting reform needed to be developed. Whatever the case, Loriana felt the urge to send her daughter to Concrete in hopes that other voices besides her own could snap Loraine back into a good place.

It had only been a week since Loraine moved into Concrete, and she already wanted to leave. In fact, she made no secret about it when her mother came by to see her. Unfortunately, Loraine clearly wasn't going to be leaving any time soon, according to the conversation she had with her mother. Thus, this only doubled Loraine's anger. Noting down the unfavorable results, Loriana left the visitor's lounge feeling discouraged. Loraine got escorted back to her dorm room. While on her way back, she accidentally bumped shoulders with another girl who just so happened to be getting moved to a different room. "Watch where you're fucking going bitch!" shouted Loraine as she made the mistake of calling the girl out of her name. Hearing that, the girl without any thought instantaneously charged at Loraine with the intent of doing physical harm. Fortunately, the same security officers escorting the girls to their rooms were able to keep them apart. "I'm a bitch, huh? Well, guess what? This time around, you messed with the wrong bitch!" she said to Loraine while glaring back at her. By then, a third officer reported to the scene to help restrain the girl. A bit spooked Loraine could only look on in silence before continuing her way back to her dorm. The girl was about her size but clearly taller. She kept her hair short, and most of all, she had a very intense look in her stare. Her name's Isis, but nearly everyone, including the staff, knew her better as Ice. "You messed with the wrong bitch," she said once more.

Part 2: The Sisterhood

Since her encounter with Ice, Loraine, on several occasions, had received letters from an anonymous person. At times, they'd mysteriously show up just outside her dorm room. Other times, she'd find them in various settings around the boot camp. Enclosed in the letter would usually be a short message signed off with the initials SH with a six-point star next to it. If it weren't letters, then it'd be graffiti that just unexpectedly appeared out of nowhere. Letter or graffiti, they each had the same message: 'you messed with the wrong one.'

Though it had been a couple of weeks since the encounter, Loraine strongly believed that Ice was the anonymous person behind those messages. Moreover, Loraine, at this point, saw the messages as threats. She had this gut feeling that she eventually was going to be running into Ice again. She felt like she was constantly being watched and felt an urge to keep looking over her shoulders, specifically when she was out of her dorm room.

On one particular day, she was at the cafeteria when she noticed two girls leaned up against the wall. Both of them were slim and practically the same height as Loraine. One of them had natural flat ironed hair that reached out to her neck while the other one styled her hair in lengthy tiny locks that stretched down to her back. Like Loraine, they were in gray jumpsuits. Besides that, nothing else seemed particularly unusual about them other than the fact that they appeared unfriendly. For some reason, they kept their eyes on Loraine the whole time while she was in the lunch line. However, Loraine didn't bother making any eye contact with them. After running into an odd character like Ice, Loraine figured she made enough enemies.

The food being served was corn dog, brown beans, a slice of flatbread, and green peas on the side. It wasn't much, but it would do, Loraine figured as she placed the food on her tray. Looking for a table, Loraine noticed the same girls who were staring her down were still leaning up against the wall. She found it odd how they never joined the other girls in line to pick up their lunch. *Hmmm...could it be them who's been sending me all those letters this whole time*, Loraine thought. Avoiding eye contact with those girls by the wall, Loraine tried to play like she was grabbing a cup of water from the fountain machines. That's when she bumped into another girl who was actually grabbing a cup of water. With some quick reflex, Loraine was able to hang on to everything on her tray. The same couldn't be said for the other girl. She hung on to her food, but her cup of water spilled all over the floor. Unlike the first time, Loraine apologized and helped her wipe the floor. Shortly after, they both found an empty table to sit and have their lunch. The girl appeared to be Hispanic decent, petite in size, and slightly shorter than Loraine. She was pale-skinned and had long wavy jet-black hair. She also had a lot of piercings on her left ear, but hardly any earrings. Noticing a rather picky eater in the girl, Loraine opened up the dialogue saying, "I'll take your corn dog if you don't want it."

"Hmmm...I think I might finish it," said the girl.

"Hmp, okay, well, in case you change your mind, I'm here."

"Hmmm okay...Hey, you know you didn't have to help me wipe the floor."

"Yes, I did. I spilled your drink."

"Well...thanks uh..."

"Loraine. I'm Loraine."

"Oh...Okay well, I'm Kelisto, but just call me K."

"Sorry, I usually watch where I'm going, but I was just a lil' sidetracked by some watchdogs."

"Watchdogs...wait, are you talking about those hoes way over there by the wall?"

"Ugh, yes them...Wow, you notice them too?"

"Yeah, I think everyone in here does...Don't know what's that about."

"Are they still over there?"

"By the wall? Yes."

"And are they still looking this way?"

"Hmmm...yeah."

"Ugh, okay...Try not to make eye contact with them."

"You know them?"

"No, I've never seen them before. But since the moment I stepped foot in the cafeteria, they've been eyeing me."

"Tuh, they been eyeing everyone here. It's not just you."

"Maybe so…Anyway, forget them. Let's talk about something else."

"Ha, right."

"So, when'd you get here?"

"Hmmm like a couple of days ago. My brother dropped me off."

"Lucky you. I've been here for almost three weeks now, but it already feels like three months."

"Damn yo…That's rough."

"Ugh…I just wanna go home."

"Me too, girl. But I just got here."

"Tuh, anyway, welcome aboard."

"Hah, I guess…"

"So, why'd you end up here?"

"Because of the LKs…"

"Huh? LKs…What's that?"

"The Kings…You know, the Latin Kings?"

"Hmmm…Maybe…"

"Well, whatever. Anyway, it had something to do with them."

"Okay…Like what happened?"

"Ugh, it's embarrassing. Don't ask."

"K, I think every girl in here's ashamed to be here."

"Hmp, you know what…I think I need to use the restroom."

"Now?"

"Yeah, can you watch my food while I'm in there?"

"Does that mean I could have your corn dog?"

"Yeah, take it. I'll be right back."

"Chica, your food will be right here when you get back."

"Ha ha well, Raine if it goes missing, then I guess we'll both know what happened, won't we?"

"Raine, huh?"

"Ha ha, you like?"

"Chica, hurry on back."

Kelisto made a trip to the restroom while Loraine enjoyed her second corn dog. Finishing up her meal, Loraine felt a sense of ease knowing that she may have potentially made a new friend here at Concrete. Unfortunately, finding some comfort in that was short-lived. Out of nowhere, the two girls who were leaning up against the wall had decided to join Loraine at the table. They didn't place any trays on the table, nor did they take any food out of Keliesto's tray. In fact, one of them pushed Keliesto's tray to the side. So, clearly, they wanted something else, and whatever it was, had something to do with Loraine. By now, Loraine had realized that Keliesto still hadn't returned, but at this point, she couldn't worry about that. As her eyes connected with theirs, Loraine could feel her heart fluttering out of intimidation. However, she hid her true feelings with an impassive facial expression. "Nice poker face," said the girl with the flat ironed hair. "You been here for a while, but you're still kinda new. So, I thought it'd be right if we introduced ourselves to you."

"Hmmm…Okay, who are y'all?" Loraine asked the girl with the flat ironed hair.

"I'm Dawn," she replied. "The sistah next to me is my sidekick, Ray. And we're the Sisterhood."

"Hmmm…what do you want?" asked Loraine to Dawn.

"Hmp, I'm glad you asked…A few weeks ago, you met one of our sisters, Ice," replied Dawn.

"Who?" again asking Loraine.

"Ice…"

"I don't know who that is…"

"Oh no? Well, she seems to know you. After all, you did call her out her name…Or did you forget?"

"Ahh…I called her –"

"A bitch…Yeah, and she's sitting just four tables down that way." With her left eyebrow and head, Dawn tilts to her left. Looking at that direction, Loraine saw the table. Four girls were sitting on it and among them was Ice, who happened to be staring right back at Loraine with the same glare. ('I'm a bitch huh? Well, guess what? You messed with the wrong bitch!') "Yeah, I know her," said Loraine with a quiver in her voice.

"Yeah, I figured you did," replied Dawn, "but I just wanted to make sure we were talking about the same person."

"Okay, so I messed –"

"Yes, you did, and you crossed the line, big time! Usually, the Sisterhood would settle this right away, but… I figure since you are new, I'll be fair and give you a chance to fix this."

"How?"

"If you ride with the sisters. But…here's something you gotta do for us. You see that lil' Spanish girl that was just here at your table?"

"Uh, yeah…"

"Well, we were gonna rough her up, but now we'll leave that to you."

"Wait, I don't get it…What did she do?"

"She crossed the line with one of us long before she came to Concrete. Anyway, you're lil' friend is good. None of us touched her while she was in the restroom."

"Wait but –"

"Look! The Sisters think I'm wasting time, but I'm giving you a chance. Handle it, or you'll see what happens next."

"Damn…"

"Yeah damn…Oh and by the way, you have six days to handle this."

Part 3: Milleena

Days had gone by since Loraine's meeting with the Sisterhood at the cafeteria. With the fourth day coming to an end, Loraine was now down to just two more days. Fortunately, she hadn't heard a word from the Sisterhood, let alone a message written in a letter nor graffiti. However, everything that transpired on the day she met Dawn and the Sisterhood was still at the back of her mind. With that said, it was but only a matter of time before she'd inevitably hear from them again. It was either her or Keliesto…*which one was it going to be*, she thought repeatedly.

Thinking about this was beginning to make her head hurt. She had come to a point where all she wanted to do was lie down in bed all day to ease her mind. She figured she was definitely going to take advantage of that now, since she was heading back to her dorm room. Though, when she entered her room, she got a surprise. She noticed two beds in the room. Moreover, all of her things were moved and placed on the new bed, which now sat on the right side of the room. On the left side of the room, was another bed and items that didn't belong to her. Now completely bewildered, Loraine stood silently, trying to register what was going on. And then, another girl entered the room, walking right past her. Like Loraine, she was slim and stood about her height. She was caramel complexioned and had curly shoulder-length hair. Another distinct feature about her was that she had double lid eyes, which suggested that she was biracial. As she casually made her way through the door to settle in Loraine's old bed, Loraine looked at her sideways, asking her, "Who are you?".

"Oh, I'm Milleena," replied Milleena, "but if it helps you remember, you could call me Lee. Anyway, I'm your new roomie."

"Wait, no one told me I was getting a new roommate."

"Yeah, I could tell just by the look on your face. Anyway, I got here around lunchtime. So, now you gotta roomie. Don't like it? Oh, well, get used to it."

"Tuh, so you're just gonna come in here and take my bed like this was your room this entire time?"

"Sorry, girl. I'm just one of those people who can't function on the right side of the room."

"What?"

"I know it's complicated, but trust me, it's just better if I take this side of the room. Your things are still intact, though. You can check; I ain't mess with anything."

"Ugh...whatever..."

"Well, hey, look I'm actually cool...I mean, once you get to know me."

"Hmp, is that right?"

"Yeah...as long as you stay outta my shit, you and I will be as straight as a fine line."

55

"Ha ha ha…"

"Oh, you laugh…girl, I'm serious haha…I'm telling ya, if you can't follow that then you'll end up like my last roommate."

"Hmmm…Did something happen between y'all?"

"Well, to put it in a nice a way, we couldn't be roomies anymore. It had something to do with a boy at our school."

"Uh…Okay…"

"Anyway, I found this letter earlier when I moved my things in."

"A letter?"

"Yeah, I thought it was for me till I opened it up and read some bullshit talking about 'Handle this or you'll see what happens next.'"

Oh damn…it's them, the Sisterhood. "Can I see the letter?"

"Yeah, here ya go…You know anything about this?"

"Hmmm…Maybe it's for someone else."

"Hmp, maybe so…I bet that this came from the Sisterhood, and you know how I know?"

"How?"

"I saw a six-point star on the bottom of the letter. Seems to me like they're looking for someone new to beat up on. Probably some new girl I heard some of the girls talking about before lunch today."

'She crossed the line with one of us long before she came to Concrete. "Wait, what new girl you're talking about?"

"I don't know. Some chica I heard them saying who moved in a few days ago. I hear she stays in one of the baddest blocks around the neighborhood."

Oh snaps…its gotta be Keliesto. "Hmmm…"

"Well, one thing's for sure: you're not her. Even though I never saw your face around here before, you said you been here for a while."

"What about the star on the letter? What's it supposed to mean?"

"You've been here for how long?"

"About a month now."

"And you still ain't heard of the Sisterhood?"

"Well, you seem to know so much."

"Tuh, yeah, and I think I should probably school you real quick about them. Anyway, those bitches are down with Folk Nation because most of them have brothers or boyfriends that are aligned with the Six from different sets. So, that makes all of them sisters of the struggle. You follow me?"

"Yeah...So, what's Folk Nation?"

"Don't worry about that. You just make sure you stay as far away from them as you can because they got a rep for jumping people. You fight one; you might as well get ready to fight more."

"How many people with the sisters?"

"I can't tell you how many, but what I will say is that I can't stand them, and they know not to fuck with me."

Slowly nodding her head, Loraine took a moment just to sigh, saying thanks for the tip. Then, she leaned back against her bed. With her head facing the ceiling, all she could hear was Dawn's voice in the letter playing back repeatedly in her mind: *Handle it, or you'll see what happens next.* It was an utterly long night for Loraine, but the next day eventually came. And when it did, Loraine felt the weight on her shoulders increase as time was winding down. She still hadn't made up her mind about the offer Dawn presented, and she could feel the presence of the Sisterhood just literally somewhere around every corner. Unfortunately, the clock rolled over to lunchtime, and it was time for Loraine to head to the cafeteria. At this point, things just seemed completely unpredictable for her, and it made her feel apprehensive. Stepping inside, she didn't see Dawn, Ice, nor the Sisterhood. In fact, she saw Keliesto sitting alone at a table having lunch. Feeling a bit of relief, Loraine joined the line to grab her tray. Shortly after picking up her lunch, she made her way to sit with her friend Keliesto. But she got cut off by Sherray and another member of the Sisterhood. "C'mon, come sit with us," said Sherray. "Dawn's dying to see you," she said with an unpleasant look on her face. While Loraine picked up her food in the lunch line, Dawn and the Sisterhood made their way in from another entrance. Dawn sat at a table opposite to Keliesto. Seated next to her was Ice and joining them was Sherray and Loraine. "Tuh, we missed you," said Dawn as Loraine approached the table. "Hmp, but it's funny how you don't seem so happy to see us," she said.

"Hmmm...I guess it's the beef," replied Loraine. "Never quite had the stomach for it," she adds.

"Hmp, not feeling today's meal, I see," said Dawn. "I don't know, I think the food smells really good, wouldn't y'all agree, girls?" Both Ice and Sherray simultaneously nod their heads. "Funny, how you're in favor of the food, yet you ain't even got a tray in front of you," said Loraine.

"I see someone doesn't have a watchful eye over their fresh mouth."

"Yeah, so I've been told."

"Tuh...So, you thought about our deal?"

Loraine pauses for a moment, silencing the dialogue between her and Dawn. Suddenly, Dawn's words from the letter began flashing back and forth in her mind. As she could hear them, she also feels an immense amount of stress pressing down on her shoulders from the pressure of uttering a response. Losing her patience, Ice snaps Loraine back to the setting, belligerently saying, "Hey, she asked you a question," while slamming her hand against the table. Making eye contact with Dawn, Loraine responds saying, "Yes."

"Okay, good," replied Dawn, "So when and how you're trying to do this because your time's running out," she says.

"Tuh, that's the thing..." said Loraine in a calm tone of voice. "I ain't."

"Wait, huh?" asked a convoluted Dawn, "you ain't what? I don't follow..."

"I ain't doing it," replied Loraine.

"Hah...Is that so?"

"Yeah..."

"You know, you're really pushing your luck...I'm a give you till tomorrow to change your –"

"No, I dont think I'm making myself clear...I ain't doing this. Period."

"Okay...But you'll see what happens next, foe. I guarantee..."

"Do what you gotta do."

Getting up, Loraine makes her way back towards the other side of the cafeteria. However, just as she's doing that, Ice and one other member rushes to cut her off one more time saying, "Aren't you forgetting your food?"

"It ain't me who likes today's lunch. So, keep it," responding Loraine. Walking past them, Loraine continues on her way but again was cut off by Ice. "We're not done here," says a confrontational Ice, who's now standing in Loraine's personal space. Without turning back, Loraine immediately figures that the other three Sisterhood members surround her. Keeping her poise, she spots a couple of security officers with the corner of her eyes. Concluding that they're most likely going to intervene, she took the opportunity to swing a haymaker to Ice's midsection. She landed several more, but because she was outnumbered, the Sisterhood ultimately ended up landing more. Fortunately, the Sisterhood didn't land as much as they wanted, thanks to the intervention of the security officers.

Chapter 7: Back in the Greens

In the month of February, the coldness of old man winter was really beginning to take its toll on Chicagoans all over the Windy City. Winds had picked up; snow was coming down pretty hard and mounting up to about three feet off the ground. The temperature had dropped, and the word from the meteorologist reported that people were probably going to see subzero degree temperature. Old man winter had everything looking white and frosted. However, Loriana didn't freeze like a popsicle stick during the time she was outside making her way back to her building. That entire evening, she had Loraine on her mind. An hour had passed by the time she got back home from her visit to Concrete facility. Since the time she had sent Loraine away to Concrete, she'd often think about her. But now Loraine was on her mind more than ever after having that conversation with her. She couldn't help the fact that she felt a bit guilty for having sent her daughter there. Thinking about what Loraine said to her, brought feelings of frustration. Frustration, in the sense that she's been raising Loraine for so long and nothing seems to be coming out of the hard work so far. There were all sorts of emotions Loriana was feeling: anger, sympathy, sorrow, depression, hopelessness, restlessness, love, and so forth. Before stepping through the front door, she began to delve deeper about what her relationship with Loraine might be like after she gets back. *Would Loraine ever forgive me*, she thought as she made her way through the living room. *Will she understand why I sent her to Concrete? Will she always hate –*

"Hey Ms Tourez," said Torence, seated quietly in the background.

"Oh hey, sweetie," said a startled Loriana turning over to greet Torence. "I didn't even know you were sitting there that whole time. How long you been home?"

"For most of the day. Did you get to see Loraine?"

"Mmhm."

"Umm, what did she say?"

"She said that she wants to come home."

"Will she?"

"No…At least not anytime soon."

"You must feel really sad."

"No baby, I'm okay," she said, swallowing a gulp of saliva down her throat.

"But your eyes don't say so."

She sighs and then wipes her eyes, trying to dry the tears while thinking of what to say next. "I told her about you guys," she said, "and how you two are getting along like night and day."

"Did she say anything about us?"

"Yeah, she had something to say about everyone."

"Hmmm, bad things?"

"Si papi. Si"

"Did she tell you anything else while you were there?"

"Other than how much she hates that place and that she wants to come home, no."

"Will she come home?"

"Yes, but not anytime soon."

"She cried after you told her that, didn't she?"

"I cried too, and I didn't stop till I got here."

"Really?"

"Yes …You may not think so, but part of me is in that boot camp suffering with her."

"But Ms. Tourez, how?"

"Because Loraine is my firstborn daughter. When I see her, I see another part of me."

"Another part of you?"

"Yes, another part of me who has a chance to live a better life. To win at the areas I messed up at."

"I don't understand. What areas?"

"Areas like school, a good job…that's what I mean by areas."

"When's the next time you plan on visiting her?"

"Sweetie, that I can't say, but what I can say is that I miss her too."

"I know."

Loriana sits still for a few minutes. Her left hand is covered her lips, and her eyes were staring at the floor, though her mind was fixated on something else. The small living room was filled with silence. Sitting down, Torence could practically hear the wind blowing in and out of his nostrils. Wondering what's on Loriana's mind, he broke the silence by asking her a question. "What are you thinking about?"

"I'm thinking way too hard about way too many things," she sighs.

"Like what?"

"Honey, I don't even know where to begin."

"You're gonna be okay?"

"Yes baby, I'm a be just fine. Say, did your brother come back from school?"

"Yeah, he did a while earlier but then he left."

"Any idea where he's up to?"

"Naw, he ain't say. He told me to just come with him like he always does, but this time I chose to sit out. Couldn't put up with that cold out there."

"Hmp, papi I don't blame you. Don't see how Lantino manages to get around in that kind of weather. I wonder where he could be in all this cold weather?"

"Don't know, but when he gets back, could you tell 'em that I'll be on the top floor?"

"Si papi, I'll let 'em know."

"Okay."

Walking out from the living room through the front doorway and now climbing up the stairway, Torence was making his way to the top floor. While Loriana, in the meantime figured she'd fix up a hot plate now that she, for the most part, wasn't feeling as bad as she did earlier. She didn't bother asking herself where Lantino could've been because she knew that he'd come crashing through the front door sometime soon. Besides, her mind was too occupied with what she was trying to make in the kitchen.

After school let out, Lantino had spent most of his afternoon at the park. He heard earlier that something was going on at the park and decided he'd meet with the clique. He and a few others ventured out into other parts around town whenever word came to them that something else was about to take place. By the time he called it a wrap, the temperature outside had dropped, and the breeze started to pick up. Like Loriana predicted, Lantino came crashing through the front door. "Ding it's cold outside," he said.

"I know I was out there earlier," Loriana replied.

"The wind is blow... blow... blowing hard too."

"Don't worry, I believe you. Here I fixed some warm soup if you want any."

"Oh, good...To ...To ...To... Torence got any?"

"No, but if you like, you can take his plate with you to the top floor."

"The top floor..."

"Yeah, that's where he's at now."

"Okay, I'll bring his plate up."

Of course, everything outside got dark, and all the streetlights were lit up. But for Lantino, that didn't matter because surely, he knew not to step outside. Standing by the balcony on the 12th floor was the closest he'd come to stepping outside. Walking down the hall, Lantino saw Torence standing out on the balcony. Looking at him, he noticed some paper along with a pencil in his hand. Coming closer, he also noticed how the breeze didn't seem to bother Torence at all. When he finally made it near the balcony, he sat Torence's plate down to the side and stood just two feet away from his left side.

"Nice view ain't it," he said to Torence.

"Yeah, it is," Torence agreed.

"Standing here, you could see everything."

"Even though everything looks a bit smaller."

"Yeah, but it's a nice view."

"Yeah, it is."

"This all you did since you got here?"

"Yeah. This all I did."

"How long you been up he...here?" Lantino shivered.

"A long while."

"D-ding"

"You feel cold?"

"Yeah, let's go." They move inside and lean on the door side as they look out through the balcony. "So, where'd you go after you left?" Torence asked.

"Somewhere and nowhere," answered Lantino.

"Anything I missed?"

"Naw, you were actually lucky you ain't come."

"Anything happened since your first day back in school?"

"Naw, the heat there has calmed down since. It's so boring now that my girl Ice is gone."

"Ice...Who's that?"

"Oh, you don't know her. She was some girl who stayed by the East and went to my school. I used to see her a lot in I.S –"

"I.S?"

"Internal Suspension...And we'd chill a lot, but after she got kicked out, that all changed."

"Why'd she get kicked out?"

"I think it might have had been her living too far off. I ain't sure. That's just what I think. There was some other girl I knew from the clique, though."

"And who was that?"

"Milleena."

"Milleena...I ain't know there were girls in the clique."

"Yeah, you've seen her before."

"I have?"

"Yeah, she's that one girl who looks so light, that you couldn't tell if she was black."

"Hmmm..."

"C'mon you know who I'm talking about. She's light skinned with long dark black hair. She got small eyes like a Chinese person."

"You say she's black?"

"Yeah. Milleena..."

"Hmmm, let me see. Ding, I can't remember."

"Well, don't think so hard then. Anyways that's why I went out. I was trying to see if I'd catch her at the park somewhere because I haven't seen her since I came back."

"Think she might have gotten kicked out too like the other girl?"

"Maybe, but that wouldn't make any sense."

"How come?"

"Cause Milleena stays right down the street."

"Um, maybe she just disappeared."

"Well, tomorrow I'll check the park if I don't see her again at school. Say, you wanna come?"

"Naw, I can't. Ms Tourez said that she was gonna have me come with her to the post office."

"The post office... How come?"

"She wants to show me how to mail something away."

"Ding, she sure been showing you a lot."

"I know. Hey, you know she saw Loraine."

"When? Today?"

"Yeah, at the boot camp."

"So is Loraine coming back home?"

"Naw...At least not anytime soon."

"Ding it's been a while. I think she'd let Loraine come back by now."

"Yeah, me too."

"Did Loraine say anything at all?"

"Yeah...I heard from Ms Tourez that Loraine had a lot to say about everything, but coming home was what she probably said the most."

"Ding."

"Yeah, I know. Wanna know something else Ms Tourez told me when we talked?"

"What?"

"She said that part of her is in there with Loraine and that she misses her too. I didn't understand, but for some reason, I believed her."

"You think she's telling the truth?"

"Yeah."

"Yeah...I think so too."

Agreeing with one another, both of them turn their faces towards each other and began nodding their heads in unison. Next,

Torence pulls out his piece of paper and holds it against the wall. While doing that, he moves his pencil across the paper. As he's doing this, Lantino steps a bit closer towards the light to take a look at what's on the paper. On it, Lantino noticed some project buildings sitting in the middle of what appears to be a cityscape. Above the cityscape, he notices stars and a crescent moon. Everything else is either well shaded or being shaded by Torence's pencil. "Damn Torence, you drew this?", asked Lantino standing over Torence's shoulder.

"Oh, you mean this…Yeah," answered Torence as he continued to put the finishing touches to his picture.

"Ding, ain't know you could draw like that," said Lantino with an astonished look on his face. "So, is this what you were doing the whole time?" he asked.

"Yeah," answering Torence. "Just wish it wasn't so dark out here now."

"Is that the city?"

"Yep, all this we're looking at right here."

"Now that's BADASS."

"Huh?"

"Oh naw, that means good."

"It does?"

"Yeah…If someone ever says 'that's hot, cool, fresh, or nice,' then that means good. Now you won't hear too many people say 'badass,' but if they ever do then it's the same thing, and right now, your shit is all that!"

"Ding, it is?"

"Yeah…Say what is this for?"

"Oh, I'm making this for Loraine."

Chapter 8: The Reformatory

One early morning Loraine woke up earlier than usual due to all the racket she was hearing outside her dorm room. Outside in the hallway, she could hear what sounded like a loud, jarring sound people make in a riot. As she got up, she turned over to her left to ask Milleena what's going on but didn't see her lying in bed. Instead, she saw two boot camp officers standing and looking at her. One male, one female. One taller and slightly bigger than the other. With matching uniforms, you could have said that they were identical twins. And from the looks of their faces, it was clear that they weren't in the best mood. "For the third and last time, little lady, hurry up and put those damn clothes on!" One of them shouted. Loraine was still a bit dazed and confused, but having heard that, she didn't waste any time jumping into her gray clothes. Neither did she ask any questions making her way to the cafeteria, which is where the officers walked her to. Making her entrance in the cafeteria, Loraine noticed that the tables were all spread out this time. This left a lot of room for everything sitting in the middle of the cafeteria. In the middle, there sat a podium, a microphone, and a few empty chairs. About four empty seats, to be exact. All lined up just right of the podium. Behind the podium stood Kendrick Nobles, someone Loraine remembers seeing before. It had been a long while since she last recalled seeing him. For that time fell on the first night, her mother dropped her off at the boot camp. Kendrick happened to be one of the commanding officers at Concrete, and one of the bigger, if not the biggest, names she heard about since her time there at the facility. Next to him were five other people. Four of them being women on his right and on his left, stood another male boot camp soldier. "Voooom," sounded the microphone as Kendrick gripped hold of it. Seem like he had something long and important to say, Loraine figured. Surely, he must have had because this was the highest number of girls Loraine had ever seen in the cafeteria. She could tell that all of Concrete's boot camp inmates were here. "Now quietly, go find a seat with the rest," a female officer said to Loraine.

Now seated comfortably on the left section, Loraine was now aiming her attention towards the middle of the cafeteria. Listening, she could hear Kendrick's breathing on the microphone through the speakers as he got ready to deliver his speech.

"Morning, ladies," he began. "Good morning, morning to all. So glad we could have you all here to witness and be a part of the change that's about to take place, starting this morning at the facility. Some of you and most of you, I presume, already or should probably have an idea of who I am, but for the rest of you who haven't the slightest clue about me…I am Sgt. Nobles. Sgt. Kendrick Nobles, your commanding…excuse me, the commanding officer and Director of operations here at Concrete correctional facilities. But of course, who I am to you probably means nothing to none of you, and not that it matters to me anyway, because that isn't the reason why we're all here, to begin with. So, moving right along. Surely, you all right now are probably asking yourselves, 'what's going on?' Well, what's going on is a reformatory that's about to be opened. And in this reformatory which you all will eventually be moving to, is a program I, my staff, and a youth specialist from New York have developed. Why ladies? Why the reformatory? Why develop a program for you? Well, ladies, my team, since your stay here at Concrete, have examined your behavior, your progress, your record before and after Concrete, your everything. And over time, well, based on our observations, haven't found your results very pleasing. The results being: overcrowding, disturbing behavior, and numerous conflicts between inmates, we felt were mainly due to the terrible living conditions here at Concrete. And that's where the reformatory came in, which is why we're grateful for you and all the drills and hard labor you ladies put in to fix these spacious rooms. And with the reformatory, that's where our program comes in to finish the rest of the project. This program, the Martin program, is specifically designed to make you ready and better before your return to society. With that said, let me now pass this over to our youth specialist who'll be going over the program with you and be working with us as our program unit manager. Everyone this is Dr. Marianne Martin."

Kendrick hands the mic over to Dr. Martin and moves a little towards the right, as she stands before the podium. She takes a quick moment to thank Kendrick as she glances to her right. Next, turns her face over to everyone in the cafeteria to greet them: "Again, good morning ladies," she said in hopes of resurrecting the dead audience, but they showed no sign of life. So, she went on with her speech pretty much continuing where Kendrick left off. Loraine, in the meantime, was sitting silently just like all the other girls in the cafeteria. When suddenly her attention was taken away by a tap, she felt her right shoulder. She looked over her right shoulder and then paused for a moment. "Hey, sis," she whispered to Kelisto.

"Hey, chica," said Kelisto in a low tone of voice.

"Where you been at ma?" asked Loraine with a bright smile on her face.

"It's a long story," replying Kelisto.

"I bet it is," said Loraine. "Ding, I was beginning to think you weren't here anymore."

"I'm a tell you what happened when this is over."

"Do you know what this program thing's about?"

"It's about a class we're all gonna take to help send us back home."

"Wait...Send us back home?"

"Yep."

"Send us back home?"

"Yep, but only one thing, though..."

"And what's that?"

"You gotta pass this class?"

"Pass?"

"Mmhm."

"What is this class anyway?"

"I don't know. I heard they're just there to help us."

"They're? You mean there's more than one?"

"Maybe...I couldn't tell you."

"Did you hear who was going to teach us?"

"Yeah...You see that black lady standing up there right now?"

"Umm, I see two of them standing."

"I'm talking about the one holding the microphone."

"You mean Dr. Martin?"

"Yep. She and some of the people next to her."

"I wonder when this is going to be over."

"I think it will almost be over when she's done. The others don't look like they have much to say."

"Hmp, I hope so."

"Yeah, I hope so too. Hey, did you see the new dorms?"

"New dorms…"

"Yeah, the new one's outside."

"Oh, you're talking about the portables?"

"Is that what they call 'em here?"

"Yeah, that's what they are K."

"Well, you know some of us are going to be moving in them."

"Why?"

"They say they're trying to make more room since there's too many of us bad bitches."

"Well, I know that. What I'm asking is, how come only some of us get to go?"

"I hear it's for girls they think ain't gonna be too much trouble. You know, like low key."

"Hmmm…"

"What?"

"So that's why they had us clean all them portables this whole time."

"Wait, they made ya do that?"

"Yeah…Ain't you do it too?"

"No, by the time I got here, the new dorms were all clean."

"It ain't all that funny."

"My bad chica, but that's crazy because I thought they were always that way."

"Ha ha, very funny. Say K, where'd you hear about all this anyway?"

"About the classes and the new dorms?"

"Yeah, how'd you know about this?"

"The nurses at the clinic told me."

"Nurses at a clinic…What clinic??"

"The clinic…Raine, are you telling me that you never knew about the clinic? Damn yo, and how long you been here?"

"I don't know. Anyways what were you doing at the clinic?"

"Remember that time in the cafeteria?"

"You're talking about back when we first met?"

"Yeah."

"Okay, what about that day?"

"Well, you remember those hoes that came by the wall, right?"

Oh shit, the Sisterhood. "Yeah, I remember."

"Well, one of them got me jumped."

Oh my god…You were the girl my roommate was talking about that one time. "Is that why I didn't see you after that day?"

"Yep. That's why…Becau –"

"Shhhhh," said a boot camp officer. "More listening and less talking, or else I'll have one of you moved."

"We'll talk more, Raine," whispering Kelisto.

"Gotcha K," replying Loraine.

"Did you girls just hear what I said?" asked the boot camp officer.

"Yes, mister," answering Kelisto and Loraine at unison.

"Okay then show me from this point on," said the boot camp officer; with no problem, the girls complied.

Within twenty minutes, June, Columbia, and Tempest also talked with the audience. June, whose real name is Olive Morrison, is a white woman in her mid-twenties. She was brought up in a home of domestic violence and later became a survivor of a fatal act of domestic violence. She's about 5'6", pretty, petite, blond and blue-eyed. She has a closed-in upper left eye received from one of her previous abusive relationships. Her nickname was given to her after recovering from a deep coma she underwent for three weeks. The time of her recovery fell in June. She comes from a long line of women who has been abused and having survived what looked like an irreversible coma; she looks to break the family cycle.

Columbia is a Latina whose originally from the South American nation. Her family moved to the States when she was entering her preteens. Now in her mid to late twenties, Columbia has grown into a very beautiful woman. However, throughout her life, she has been a victim of numerous rapes. She's tan-skinned, dark-haired with jet black eyes, slim, and has silky pink lips, also standing about 5'6" or 5'7 ½". Her real name is Digna Cardozo. Growing up, she went by the nickname "Columbia" obviously because she's Columbian. Unfortunately, for Columbia, she's been coping with depression and some emotional problems.

Tempest, whose real name is Nefertina Munnings, happens to be the tallest and oldest. She was the black woman Loraine was referring to when Kelisto tried to point out Dr. Martin. Tempest was a former member of the Black Widows gang in New York. Throughout her life, Tempest has been through it all: homeless, poverty, gang conflicts, incarceration, and even near-death experiences. The last time she cheated death, she said that it came to her face to face like a perfect storm. On account of living through the storm nearly her entire life, she chose to go by the name "Tempest." During her incarceration at a corrections facility in New York, she met Dr. Martin, who she teamed up with to encourage reform for troubled teens. Since then, the dynamic duo has worked with some of the nation's most notorious gangs.

Closing the speech off was Officer Sezz, who stood on Kendrick's left. He is Concrete's acting Commanding Officer, and most of the girls were pretty familiar with who he was. So, therefore, life came back to the dead audience. When it was all over, the girls were lined up to receive an individual badge, which the staff knew as the smart card. This was a card that came in a necklace for each inmate to wear for the new reformatory that was about to open. Waiting in line, Kelisto and Loraine managed to kill time by continuing where their conversation left off. "So, how long you stayed at the clinic?" asked Loraine.

"Yo, I was in there for about a week. Could have come back after my third day, but I kept pretending that there was still something wrong with my finger," Kelisto replied.

"What's up with your middle finger?"

"I think that bitch might have broken it because I can't make it straight."

"Damn."

"I know."

"Hey, you know they tried to get me too?"

"When?"

"Like almost three days ago right here at the cafeteria."

"Eww, if only my brother were here!"

"Your brother…"

"Yeah, my big brother. If he were here, none of those hoes would have messed with us."

Seem so innocent…The heck with it, I'm a ask her this. "K, what are you in here for?"

"Huh?"

"Look, I know you say you're part of the Kings and all, but…but you don't look like you've ever done anything wrong before. The fact that you are here means you did something bad, and looking at you, I just can't… I just can't —"

"You just can't what?"

"I just can't picture you doing something bad. What'd you do?"

"Raine, I have done some bad things in my life."

"Right, but what'd you do to end up sitting here?"

"Something…"

"Okay, like what?"

"I stole a car."

"Where? From Argentina?"

"Raine listen, listen…"

"I'm sorry, K, but I ain't buying that."

"Alright, fine yo…I'll tell you."

"What did you do?"

"It wasn't me…It was him who was pushing that nice ride."

"Who?"

"Chil…One of my brother's homies. He pulled over and asked us if we wanted a ride. His homeboy, Wee, was in the front passenger seat, so we all jumped in the back."

"Okay, so then what?"

"Next, he took us everywhere around the neighborhood, just showing off. After a while, the police showed up and had him pull over. Ain't think nothing of it, but when the man had Chil turn off the radio, I knew we were in trouble."

"But for what, though?"

"That bad boy Chil was pushing was stolen; and that's not all…Wee also had dimes stashed in the back."

"Okay, so why'd you get put in here again?"

"For being there."

"For that?"

"Chica, I'm a have my brother come for you too."

"Your brother ain't so tough."

"Yeah huh! My brother can take out five people."

"Five people?"

"That's right chica; you heard correct. Five people, and that's why my brother's not to be fucked with because he's something serious."

"You two get along?"

"What? You mean my brother and I?"

"Yeah, do you get along with him?"

"Umm, yeah chica…I mean he's my brother…Hmp, he's really more like a father to me."

"A father…Your brother seems like a father to you?"

"Yeah."

"But how so, he's only what…eighteen?"

"Yeah, but he takes care of us, he buys me clothes, he gives me money to go shopping, he even makes sure I get to school, and when I was much younger, he bathed and spanked me."

"Okay well, isn't your father supposed to do that? Where is he this whole time?"

"He's dead."

"Dead?"

"Yeah, I heard that he died in a terrible car accident when I was about two or three years old. At least that's what mami and everybody else says. But Esteban told me that he was shot and killed by Latin Disciples."

"How does your brother know for sure?"

"He knows because he heard this from Monalisa."

"Who?"

"Our aunt, who came to stay with us for a while after papi died."

"So, your aunt was staying with you guys?"

"Yeah, because my mother was a house mom when papi was alive. So, after he died, she ain't have a job to feed us. My brother was too young, and mami ain't know how to speak English anyway. That's why my aunt moved in with us at the time because she had money coming from somewhere."

"She made money doing what?"

"I don't know, but it wasn't work, that's for sure."

"She made a lot of money?"

"Oh yeah...Enough to support us for a while."

"For a while...Wait, what happened after?"

"That's the thing; she was always in and out of the house. She had problems of her own too."

"Like what kind of problems?"

"A lot...She ain't bring too many of her drama home because she ain't want the family to know what was going on. But I'm sure mami and everybody else had an idea what it was about. I might not have been old enough, but I wasn't too young to know that her problems might have had something to do with all that money she was bringing home."

"Was she getting money from the gang?"

"Probably...Or her problems could have been coming from somewhere else. Maybe something illegal because I remember the night the cops came knocking on our door asking for her."

"Hmp, wow, that's crazy..."

"Now, one problem she had that everyone did know about involved a legal matter."

"And what was that all about?"

"It was a matter of her trying to win her son back from the custody of his stepmom. This case from what I could remember went on for a while."

"Well, your aunt won, right?"

"Naw yo...The judge sided with his stepmom."

"With the stepmom...But how? Why?"

"Yo that's the same thing I'm still trying to figure out."

"So, what about Monalisa? She at least got to see 'em again, didn't she?"

"Naw yo, all ties to him were cut off after his stepmom won full custody. Even we haven't heard from him. It's been five years now."

"How old were you when you last saw him?"

"About seven years old. All I remember of my cousin was him and I always running when Esteban chased us around the yard."

"How old was he when you last saw him?"

"He was nine."

"How about your aunt? What happened to her after the case was over?"

"Well, the police eventually caught up with her. So, she got arrested and went to jail, last thing I heard. No one but Esteban would tell me something whenever I asked about her coming back. But even he didn't give me a straight answer. I was always stuck wondering why my aunt hadn't come back home after such a long while. And then the truth hit me when I turned eleven."

"Okay, so what happened?

"Her ass got deported."

Chapter 9: The Reformatory

Part Two:

Both Kelisto and Loraine picked up their smart cards and then afterward found a table to continue their conversation. After the cafeteria got too crowded and noisy, they went outside where it was still busy but not as bad. Outside sat a few benches, the officers moved to make room for the announcement that took place earlier. As Loraine and Kelisto rested their legs on one of the benches sitting outside, Loraine, for the first time, admitted to herself that she was actually having a good time. Sitting down next to Kelisto, she stared at her card while holding up both of theirs. "What's the use of having one of these," she asked jokingly to Kelisto.

"Hmp, I don't know…To wear 'em I guess," answering Kelisto.

"They call this the smart card, and yet I don't even feel smart wearing one of these."

"Same here, Raine. Same here"

"Tell me…"

"Okay, what?"

"After your aunt got sent back, how'd you all maintain?"

"Well, after my aunt got deported, the responsibility seemed like it fell on the hands of my brother. With there still being some money left from Monalisa, mami found time to get herself a green card and a work permit. And through the right people, mami managed to find work being a housekeeper. But it wasn't enough to support us. So, it was all up to Esteban to grow up fast and become the man of the house. By then, my brother was fourteen and still ain't know how to speak English too well. School ain't mean much to my brother because he was trying to get money now. Plus, he wasn't born here, which meant that he couldn't find a job. So, he turned to the Kings. Since then, it's been my brother and the LKs that's been looking out for us."

"Did you and your brother ever have any problems?"

"Yeah, sometimes, but he still sees me as his little angel."

Wish I could say the same about my brother. "The Kings ain't ever give y'all any trouble?"

"Naw yo…they always took care of our troubles. Esteban and I know 'em all like family, almost the whole neighborhood does. If there is trouble, then usually it's someone else bringing it to us. Not the other way around. Although…" Kelisto paused for a minute to gather her thoughts about a particular issue. "…the last time I was in town, there was some word going around," she continued.

"Word…," said Loraine. "Word about what?"

"Word about some lady getting raped," answer Kelisto while nodding her head. "I heard it had something to do with Esteban and the gang."

"What do you think?"

"I don't know what to think. Everybody I know has something to say about it, but when my brother's around, they all just act as if nothing ever happened."

"Ump ump."

"Yep, you should see them. When he's around, not a word about that issue is mentioned."

"Hmmm…K, you said your cousin was nine when you last saw 'em, right?"

"Right."

"And it's been about four years now."

"Five."

"Oh, about five years now…"

"Correctomundo. Why wassup?"

"That means he'd be fourteen today. Wow, he'd been the same age as my brother."

"Oh, you have a brother?"

"Yeah, he's back home."

"Is he older than you?"

"Yeah, but only by a couple of months."

"A couple of months…Wait, how so?"

"We don't share the same mom."

"Oh, so that makes you his half-sister."

"Hmp…I guess if that's what you wanna call it."

"So, tell me, is he cute?

"What? Who? My brother? Um, I guess."

"Well, what's he like?"

"He's bad, that's for sure. In our school, he got suspended for fighting the security guard."

"Like yo, for how long was he suspended?"

"Um, like about three weeks."

"Damn, do you know what they fought over?"

"Nope. By the time I got the word, his ass was already sitting in the principal's office. I found out that he had been there for a while, and the reason mami hadn't come get 'em yet was that he ain't know her work number. So that's how the message passed on to me."

"Is he mixed like you?"

"Yeah, he is."

"Mmmm...I bet he's cute."

"Hmp, probably to other girls."

"What does he look like?"

"Looks like his daddy. Except for his skin shade. He took his mom's light-skinned complexion, and her bitchy attitude too. Oh yeah, and he's taller than you and I."

"When I get out of this shit hole, moving to your school is the first thing I'm a do!"

"Girl, you almost had me going for a minute. Say, I notice out here's starting to get quiet. Is it time to go inside?"

"Hmmm, yeah, we should probably be heading back."

"Okay, I'll walk with you...So K, when's the next time I'll see you?"

"I don't know chica...I guess I'll see ya when I see ya."

"Hmp...Well, I guess so too then."

"So, we'll talk more."

"Yep. Later K."

"Choa..."

Chapter 10: The Martin Program

Loraine was sitting silently just like all the rest of the girls in the cafeteria. Looking around, she could tell that nearly all of Concrete's boot camp inmates were present in the cafeteria. Though she hadn't seen Milleena, she was pretty certain that her roommate was sitting somewhere within the midst of the audience. After all, that was the only thing that could explain why she didn't see her in the dorm room when she woke up today. Staring at the right side of the cafeteria, which was way across from where she was sitting, Loraine spotted out a familiar face. It was Ice, and she was making that glare Loraine had come to know her very well for. Seeing Ice here made Loraine know that the Sisterhood were listening to what was going on as well. Though Loraine didn't make eye contact with Ice very long, she could still feel Ice's eyes taking note of her every move. Knowing this made her very uncomfortable; she felt like she needed to cringe. Thoughts about her very first encounter with Ice kept playing back and forth in her head:

I'm a bitch huh? Well, guess what? You messed with the wrong bitch!

A bit apprehensive about her next episode with the Sisterhood, Loraine tries to take her mind off her worries by directing all of her attention to Dr. Martin and this so-called program she was talking about. However, her attention was taken away after Kelisto tapped her right shoulder.

Leaving the cafeteria, Loraine decided to make a stop in one of the bathrooms. Coming in, she saw only one mirror. Heading back out, she noticed a big six-point star drawn in lipstick on that same mirror. Looking not at the sign but at the images the mirror reflected, Loraine noticed a figure standing four feet away from her. It was Dawn, one of the same girls she got in a scuffle with three days ago in the cafeteria. Loraine immediately turned around to bulge her fists. Now facing Dawn, Loraine also noticed Sherray on the left, another one Dawn's associates from the Sisterhood. Sherray, who stood between Loraine and the exit, too, was about four feet away. "Bang!" went one of the doors in the bathroom, as Ice kicked it open. "Wassup!" she roared as she strides towards Loraine.

"Yeah wassup, now bitch!" said Sherray.

"Yeah, since ya can't side with a hoe, then we'll beat ya down like a foe!" said Dawn as she palmed her fist and swung it at Loraine.

Yep, the Sisterhood were back, and this time, they were looking to finish what started three days ago back in the cafeteria. What began as an offer the Sisterhood tried to force on Loraine had now escalated into what you could call a series of fights. In the first sequence, Loraine had to be separated from Ice after standing her ground. Like the first sequence, Loraine stood her ground by swinging punches, but this time, she was outnumbered. Everything was happening too fast for her to tell exactly where the punches were coming from. She felt like the wind got knocked out of her each time she took a blow from one of the girls. Surprisingly, she was still on her feet, but for how long could she stay on them. She was beginning to feel like she had a fever of 102 degrees.

Without question, Loraine's ass was getting jumped, and with no authoritative figure around to stop the Sisterhood; it seemed like the pounding was going to continue without an end. When suddenly, one of the doors in the bathroom slammed open, and this time louder than the first time. Out of nowhere, Milleena showed up and struck Ice twice in the head, knocking her out cold to the ground. Next, she shoved Dawn out of the way and landed a haymaker to Sherray's midsection, sending her straight to her knees. With Ice now on the floor and Sherray gasping for air, Loraine spears Dawn, taking her off her feet. Struggling to get back on her feet, Dawn wrestles with Loraine, but it's no use as she receives not one, not two, but three shots to the nose. "Hah and like a foe I'm a beat ya down to the core!" said Loraine. Another door burst open, but this time, it was Sherray rushing through the exit. Right behind her was Dawn, who managed to shove Loraine out of the way while her back was turned. She made it out but not before getting her head slammed against the mirror by Milleena. Following Dawn was Ice, who got kicked in the ribs as she crawled her way out. "VL here!!" shouting Milleena as she raised a hand signal high to the air.

"How…how…how'd you know they'd be in here?" grunting Loraine.

"That's the thing, I didn't," answering Milleena with a tense look on her face.

"Wait what?"

"Forget that! C'mon let's go!" said Milleena interrupting Loraine. "You think you could run?" she asked dramatically. Loraine looks at Milleena and nods her head even though she wasn't sure she could. "Alright, then c'mon before them boot camp ass holes show up!" again saying Milleena as she drags Loraine's left arm and zooms through the bathroom exit door. It took a while, but the girls made the eventual trip back to their dorm room. Removing her gray jumpsuit, Milleena noticed blood sprinkled on her right sleeve. This made her pause for a moment because she knew it wasn't her blood. Throwing her clothes on the floor, she then recalled the time she smashed Dawn's head on the glass mirror. Figuring that out, Milleena sat comfortably in her bed, wondering where she left her smart card. Loraine was soaked with sweat and still grunting about some of the aches and pains she was feeling. During her run from the bathroom, through the hallway to her dorm room, Loraine saw stars and neon colors. It wasn't until she reached her bed, that she finally stopped seeing stars. "Girl, what I tell you about Dawn and the Sisterhood," asked Milleena.

"They were trying to get to me long before you warned me about 'em," grunted Loraine. "Doesn't matter now."

"Hmp, you're right about that," Milleena agreed. "Say, did you get something called the smartcard?"

"Yeah, I did. Why… didn't you?"

"I did, but I don't seem to know where I placed mine."

"Hey, what made you do that back there?"

"You mean back in the bathroom?"

"Yeah, why'd you jump in?"

"I already told you…I can't stand the Sisterhood. Period."

"But they wanted me that time…"

"So, I should have not come?"

"No. What I wanna say is that I'm grateful for that thing you did back there."

"Hmp...Don't think nothing of it."

"Listen, I got your back next time they try coming for you."

At that moment, Milleena stopped what she was doing and went quiet for a few seconds. With her smartcard no longer on her mind, she continued the conversation, bringing the subject back to the real reason behind why she chose to get involved: "I remember how they did that other girl in the cafeteria," she said. "They all ganged up on her...All ten of 'em. Even after one of them stepped on her middle finger and broke it..." *Oh shit, she's talking about Kelisto,* Loraine figured. "...They just kept going, and that's why when they were ganging up on you, I just let my rage out on them hoes. That one girl you saw me hit in the stomach after I knocked Dawn out my way, was the one who stepped on that other girl's finger at the cafeteria..." *Okay, now that makes sense why she ain't hit Dawn right away,* Loraine thought as she continued to listen to Milleena. "...I was so mad at how that hoe stepped on that girl's finger! Child, you have no idea! I even bet you that she set this whole shit up."

Well, one of them got me jumped. So, it was her Kelisto was talking about, Loraine figured as Kelisto's words played in her mind.

"Raine, had you seen it, you'd probably say the same thing," said Milleena. "That hoe had it in for the lil' jit from the get-go."

"Well, I know if you ain't got her, then you sure gotta good shot off Ice," said Loraine.

"Yeah, that's the first thing I wanted to do, the minute I busted that door open."

"Now, I know that you can't stand her."

"I certainly can't."

"So, was he your brother or something?"

"Huh?"

"The boy..."

"Who? What boy? What are you talking about?"

"You told me that it was some boy that started all this between you and you're old roommate, Ice."

"Oh, you're talking about who we were fighting over?"

"Yeah, was he your brother?"

"Naw…My boyfriend."

"Oh, so that's her brother, and she ain't want you seeing –"

"No, no, no, no, no sis. Let me tell you the story. She had a thing going on with him back when she was in our school. But that all changed after she got booted out. He started chilling with me, that's all…She tried locking him down by claiming they were still together. But I wasn't having that. She wasn't gonna claim him. Especially not him. Not my Tino."

"Tino?"

"Yeah, my Tino. You see, when she was in our school; she stayed trying to push other girls off 'em. He was always on lock when she was with him. And that's the main reason her ass got kicked out because she stayed thinking someone else was always hugging and touching up on 'em. Now the reason she hates me so much is that I was actually the one hugging and touching up on 'em, but that wasn't till her ugly ass got kicked out. So, when she tried to push me out the picture, I pushed her right into another school."

"Are you talking about Lantino?"

"Yeah, my Tino."

Hmp…He ain't never bring any of em home. "That's funny ain't never even knew he had girlfriends."

"Yeah, he's my…hey wait up; how you know about Tino?"

"Lee chill, he's my brother…"

"What?"

Chapter 11: The Final Sessions

One out of the three remaining sessions for the month was currently in progress. This time under the administration of June, the session focused on domestic violence, verbal abuse, and emotional manipulation. Subjects June knew all too well about. In the room, there was a sense of liberty and reform, to a certain degree, that could be felt. Some of the girls were looking at what could be their last days in the program. Overall, positivity was definitely present inside the room. Outside the room was a hallway, at the end of the hall was a small conference room in which Dr. Martin was holding individual face to face meetings. Near the end of the hallway were two chairs and sitting in one of them was Loraine who was doing some reflective thinking.

Hmmm, she thought, *let's see...Sherray pulled out a knife on K, Officer Sezz holds her back. She gets booted out. Then two girls out here are fighting over my BROTHER...Stah, this place is crazy. Hmp, I wonder what's next.*

Sitting on the chair, Loraine bent over to rest her elbows on her knees. Then tilts her head slightly to her left facing the small conference room at the end of the hallway. Looking towards the end of the hallway, she asks herself: *exactly what's going on inside that room? Oh snaps, here comes someone...*

Suddenly, someone steps out of the conference room, and no, it's not Dr. Martin. Instead, that person stepping out happened to be Dawn Boston. *Snaps,* says Loraine, *she's coming this way...what could she possibly want?*

Walking towards Loraine, their eyes immediately met. Though the duration of their conversation wasn't expected to be too long, every look they exchanged between one another was worth more than a thousand words. "Hmp, I still wonder how you ended up sitting in here," said Dawn.

"Oh, believe me, if I could be somewhere else, I would," replying Loraine. "I don't wanna be here anymore than you and your crew do."

"How long you've been waiting here?"

"I don't know…long enough, I guess."

"Stuh…"

"What? What's funny?"

"Your ass could've been got out of here, and you don't even know it."

"If that's what you be telling the sisters then honey, you need to stop lying to them. If you ask me, that ain't sister-like."

"For your information Raine, that ain't a lie."

"Oh, so you expect me to believe that?"

"If it were David, he'd have disappeared outta here."

"Who?"

"David Boston."

"David…Boston? Who's that?"

"My uncle."

"Hmmm, so your uncle could get out of something like this?"

"Please, this ain't nothing compared to what he's got himself out of before."

"Don't sound like no ordinary man."

"Hmp, he was far from ordinary."

"Well, hey listen if you're trying to get out of here your own way, then you could count me out. No point in trying to pull that off if the program is bound to let us out soon."

"Okay, Raine, I heard ya loud and clear. You're out. Anyways it's your turn to see Dr. Martin. She's waiting inside that room I just walked out of."

"Uh okay…"

With Dawn on her way back to the portables, Loraine was now making her way to the conference room because she was the only person left for Dr. Martin to see. After holding a small conversation with Dawn, there was still a lot of thoughts running through Loraine's mind. *Ding, Milleena wasn't kidding that time when she told me that Dawn's crazy self escaped from the camp before,* she thought. *What I don't understand is why she would come back if she had gotten away before? Uh, ummm…okay, whatever. One thing I can say she's got right for sure is that a girl like me doesn't belong in here. CAN'T WAIT TO GET OUT THIS SHIT*

HOLE! It's weird...Her staring at me ain't phase me at all, but what did stick out to me was how deep her stares were. Makes me think of that boy Lantino always has over. He's really the only other person that does that. Damn, why is his name popping up in my head? Dorn could've –.

"Hi there, Loraine. Nice of you to drop by," said a welcoming Dr. Martin.

"Glad I could stop by," replied Loraine.

"Aww, now do you really mean that?"

"Um, yeah."

"Good, now come in and have a seat. For a minute there, I was beginning to think that Dawn went back to her portable without having you know that I needed to see you."

"Oh okay."

"Alright, so you ready to get this started?"

"Uh yeah...what is it that we're doing?"

"I was just about to get to that...basically what we're doing is reflecting on our experience here at the program and highlighting areas in which we've made progress. Particularly areas that gives us value and meaning in our lives. How it works is, I will ask you a few questions in which you'll have to answer."

"Uh, do I have to give right answers?"

"No. There's no right or wrong answer."

"Alright, but what if I don't know what to say to one of your questions?"

"I guarantee; you'll know exactly what to say once I ask you."

"Hmp, okay if you say so."

"Alright, so again, you ready?"

"Yep."

"Okay, good. So...Loraine...Since your stay here at Concrete, what's your experience been like?"

"Ugh, I hate it here!"

"Okay...Could you elaborate for me?"

"Hate being told what to do or how to do. I hate the food they serve here. Can't stand being told when I gotta go to sleep. And every day someone's always trying to beat up on me."

"How's your life here in Concrete different from the one you know out there?"

"Aw man…It's a big difference: I miss being able to go to bed on my own time or doing anything whenever I wanted to. I miss the tacos my mom used to make for us."

"Mmmm sounds like she makes good food."

"Yeah mami fed us pretty good. But Dr. Martin, what I probably don't like the most about out here is all the bull I been going through."

"Like, what do you mean?"

"Like what I mean is all the battles I had to get out of. I mean, before I came here, I was fighting a lot, and that's what landed me a seat here. But at least, I could say that the girls and I had a reason. Over here, girls find any reason to start with you! Shit! I thought my life was BULL until I got here!"

"So basically, you've come to realize that your life outside Concrete was a lot better?"

"Yes…Way better! I don't know how some of the girls could do it."

"Do what exactly?"

"Keep showing up at this hell hole."

"With some of them, it's all about proving some kind of point not just to themselves, but to others as well. With others, the reasons for coming back are different and beyond our understanding."

"Come back to this…Come back to eat food that tastes worse than shit! Come back to girls who'll fight you for looking at them a certain way! Come back to hear stories about other girls getting ganged up on, and having their fingers broken and shit! Or how about you get in a fight with one or two of and come to find out that the same ones are back for a second round! Tough or not, I wouldn't come back here! No way!!"

"Hmmm…you know Loraine, you're one of the few to actually admit what you had taken for granted."

"Really? I am?"

"Yes. But what's different about you is the way you expressed how much you took it for granted. It was very brief."

"Brief?"

"Yeah…It's like you had nothing to hide."

"What about the others?"

"Mmmm…let's just say that they were in the bush, which is okay. If there's something you don't feel comfortable about sharing because it's personal to you, then it's understandable. Just know that everything you do share with me will stay confidential, alright."

"Um, alright."

"Okay, so now tell me your thoughts about the program."

"I know…that Dawn said that this whole thing was about money, but I…think…that you do care. And I appreciate you, Tempest, June, and Columbia for making me think about what gives me meaning in my life."

"I'm glad to see that you're keeping that in mind because it's very important."

"I know."

"So…Loraine…tell me…what progress have you felt that you made so far since entering the program?"

"Well, back home, I thought I had it bad. I mean, even after I came to boot camp, I still thought I had it hard. Until I started coming to the program."

"Oh yeah?"

"Yeah, I mean till I came to the program was when I realized that I didn't have it anywhere near as bad as most of these girls do: I mean, I heard it all. From girls getting raped fourteen times, girls who ran away to different places, people having to take meds for their anger problems."

"So, I take it that, that was your breaking point."

"Yeah…It was because half of the things I know now were things that I… I…didn't know before."

"So now you know more."

"Yeah…Now I do."

"Well, Loraine there's something else I'm a need you to know…"

"Okay, and what's that?"

"Well, I had a word with Kendrick regarding you a few days ago. As a matter of fact, it was just a day ago."

"Uh …what was it about?"

"Hmmm…just know that discussing matters about you turned out to be one of the best conversations that he and I ever had."

"Okay, what makes you say that?"

"Well, for one, he actually smiled a majority of the times your name came up."

"Alright, so he smiled. So what?"

"What that means is that he enjoyed discussing matters regarding you."

"Hmp…Okay."

"By the way, I also had a word with your mother recently ago as well."

"Stuh, did you see my brother too?" *Lady's starting to get on my last nerve, talking to everybody about me, shit.*

"No, your mother and I spoke on the phone. And my talk with her was kept very short and simple."

"Really?"

"Uh huh. Really and you know I must say Loraine, your mother is a very pleasant woman. You ought to feel very fortunate to have her. In two minutes of conversing with her, I was already able to tell what kind of person she is."

"Oh…"

"Well, aren't you going to ask me what we talked about?"

"What did you two talk about?"

"She asked me about you?"

"She did?"

"Yep."

"And what'd you say?"

"I told Ms. Tourez that after next week, she won't have to come pay a visit to Concrete ever again."

"Wait, what? You told her that?"

"Yes, Loraine."

"Wait, but Dr. Martin…WHY?"

"Because Loraine, I'm recommending that you go home."

Part Two: The Final Sessions

After ending her individual meeting with Dr. Martin, Loraine was back in the hallway making her way to the portables as Dawn did before her. Down the hallway Loraine could see students stepping out the room, which meant the session June administered had probably come to an end. Among the students, Loraine noticed three of them: Victoria, Roxanne, and Shakira. She hadn't seen them in a while. One more of June's students had crossed Loraine's mind, but she just couldn't seem to remember her name. Loraine's mind now became too clouded by everything that was shared in her conversation with Dr. Martin. She was feeling ecstatic about the good news back in the conference room. It was the thought of laying down in her own bedroom and doing what she wanted to do, how she wanted to do, and when she wanted to do something. This made her feel all the more delighted in wanting to see her last day at the boot camp. She passed the room in which the session was taking place and was now looking at the letter with a sketch she had received prior to the reformatory opening. She told herself that she couldn't wait to greet and thank her half-brother, Lantino, whom she completely assumed made it.

She stood near the visitor's area after realizing that she gazed at it for too long. So, she folded it up and put it away. But then that's when she noticed a familiar face. "Kelisto," she said as she was waving her friend down. "Hey chica," Kelisto replied walking to her to embrace her immediately. "Wow girl, I ain't think I was gunna get to see you."

"Ding, has it really been that long since you last saw me," Loraine asked.

"Probably not, but it sure feels like it, though."

"Yeah, it does. I think it was after Sherray got kicked out."

"Yeah, it had to be around that time when I last saw you."

"So, she ever showed up in any of your classes then?"

"Naw yo. She just coasted and went ghost from that point on."

"Yeah well, I guess that means that they never let her back in."

"Oh…Oh, well."

"Oh well…So I ain't see you in any of Ms. Columbia's classes nor Tempest's. I even saw V and Kira."

"I got placed with Ms. Morrison's circle."

"Who?"

"Ms. Morrison. You know…the white lady."

"Oh…you mean June."

"Yeah her. She was my favorite."

"Really? Why's that?"

"She was different in the way she did things."

"She was?"

"Yeah…"

"Hmmm…but how?"

"Well, she ain't try and put you on the spotlight like Dr. Martin did. She ain't sit there and try and step in your face either like Tempest."

"Oh ding…well, that's good, but what did she do then?"

"She told us about the shit she had gone through."

"Oh, kind of like Ms. Columbia then, right?"

"Naw naw yo. Not like Ms. Columbia."

"But that is like Ms. Columbia if she's telling y'all about shit she gone through."

"Yeah, but she ain't try and make us feel sorry for her though."

"Hmmmm…yeah I can't front. Ms. Columbia did do that, but that's because her life was real rough, K."

"I know Raine, but what I liked more about Ms. Morrison was the part when she told us that no one was ever going to feel sorry for us. All we could just do was do the best we could for a better life…a better tomorrow."

"She told y'all that?"

"Yeah yo. Those were her exact words to us. I don't know about Dr. Martin and the rest, but I believe that she really does care about us. She's just not in it for the money like Dawn said."

"I didn't think I was gunna show her any respect at first. That's why I was hoping I wasn't going to get stuck with her."

"Yeah, that's what Victoria told me too. So Raine, you weren't the only one."

"Hmp, guess not…"

"But, hey Raine you wanna know what really touched me the most about June?"

"Yeah, what?"

"What got me was when she told us about the nice car and home she has now since leaving the hard times behind in the dust."

"She's got a nice house?"

"Yeah, and a car. And the chica told us that this is what we could have in our lives too, but it starts with not feeling sorry for ourselves, and not waiting for other people to feel bad and bail us out of shit."

"Yeah, that's true. She's right."

"Out of all of them, she's the one I'm going to miss the most."

"I may miss Dr. Martin, but that's really it for me. I just like knowing that I wasn't alone in dealing with problems. That to me is what turned –"

"OKAY KELISTO! Your brother's here to pick you up," said one of the security officers in the visitor's area. The interruption instantly took Loraine off her train of thought as she stuttered to complete her last statement and get a clear question out for Kelisto. "Wait…Did she just say that your brother's here to come get you?".

"Yeah chica," answered Kelisto, "today's my last day here."

"So is that why you're hanging out here all dressed up," asked a bewildered Loraine.

"Yeah, my brother's taking me back home," again answered Kelisto. "That's why I'm so glad I got to see you one more time before I left."

"KELISTO! Your brother's here, and you're holding 'em up!" Shouted the security officer.

"Oh well, I guess this is it after today, huh?" Loraine asked taking one good final look at her friend. She had on a black cap tilted to the side. Her hair was jet black, and it stretched past her shoulders. She wore a black jacket that may have belonged to her older brother. Being that it wasn't zipped up, the golden yellow tank top showed underneath. She wore a white baggy jeans folded in the bottom where the golden yellow color could be seen. She had on a shiny black leather belt holding her baggy jeans up, and they matched with her metallic black shoes, which looked like it had just got burnished. Nodding her head, Loraine smiled and said "Girlfriend, you are beautiful. Stay up, okay…"

"Okay, you too," replied Kelisto. "I'm a tell my brother that it was you who watched my back while I was in here. So, in case you ever do show up in my hood he's gotchu…Naw better yet, the whole block will look out for you."

They both smiled and embraced one more time before the security guards came and escorted Kelisto to the front lobby. "If things get too tough there, remember me, so you know that you ain't alone in this," said Loraine as she squeezed harder.

"Chica, I'll never FORGET you," replied Kelisto.

Dr. Martin walked into the room to find them hugging. It took a while, but Kelisto finally started to let loose her grip on Loraine. However, the same couldn't be said for Loraine, who even kept her eyes closed. That's when Dr. Martin spoke, though she felt a bit reluctant. "Okay, Loraine, she has to go now," she said. But Loraine wasn't complying accordingly. So Rubbing Loraine on her arms, Dr. Martin made a second attempt. "Loraine, it's time for her to go now." After a few more attempts, Loraine at last loosened her grip and opened her eyes. Then she turned over to Dr. Martin, who hugged her as the security guards escorted Kelisto to the front.

A week had gone by a little faster than usual, now it was Loraine's turn to go home. No one was as happy as Loraine when the time to go came. Once she walked through the front entrance, she never looked back. As for the others, Dr. Martin noted some updates. After Loraine left, it wasn't too long before Dawn was recommended to join the staff. This idea was passed to Sgt. Nobles so Dawn and other inmates with her kind of intelligence could use their gifts towards something positive. Once this offer was made, she knew she couldn't deny the fact that Dr. Martin was really here to help her reform. She was very intrigued by the idea but, at the same time, knew that her choice to lead this new path would mark the end of the Sisterhood gang. Her associate, Ice, was moved to another program near her area. Word has it that Ice is getting by just fine. For Sherray, Dawn's other associate, she started showing progress when she learned about her older sister's recovery. She never really asked about Kelisto's whereabouts. Though the staff never lightened their watch on her, a set date for her return in Dr. Martin's program was made. Victoria was the potential associate of the Sisterhood gang. Not much was really said about her during her time in the program. She, like Kelisto and Loraine, soon left the program. However, she showed signs of someone who's going to return to boot camp. Both Shakira and Roxanne became very close to Columbia, Storm, and the rest of the Dr. Martin's team. Both left around the same time and have since kept in touch with Columbia. Milleena was recommended to stay for a couple of months simply for the fact that she had left the boot camp then returned on a number of occasions. Looking through her file made the staff become very particular about her, and why she kept showing up. When Loraine learned that Milleena was still at Concrete, she frequently visited her. Her friendship with Loraine grew. By the time she was released, welcoming her into Loraine's family was no problem. After all, she and Lantino already had some history.

Chapter 12: Nights to Remember

Part 1: The Spot

Suddenly the year began to move fast. The city of Chicago was now looking at its days in Fall, early October to be exact, and the cool breeze was starting to come in. On these days, Milleena was getting in trouble less and making fewer visits to boot camp. With her staying out of boot camp and spending more time by Loraine's place, she now seemed like the fifth member of the Tourez family. It had only been a few weeks, yet she and Loraine were getting by like sisters. Her stuff was always lying in Loraine's room if they weren't sitting in Lantino's space. She shared her clothes and belongings with Loraine. And overall, everyone at Loraine's place liked having her over because there was usually always something new going on with her.

It was now mid-day, and Milleena was at the park making her way to the spot her and Lantino use to hang out before she was sent back to the boot camp. Lantino had already made it there a couple of hours after school let out. Loraine, who Milleena told she'd catch up with earlier when they were home, was also there as well. Torence, Tyberius, and everybody else were going to join them later. "Hey ma," said Lantino greeting Milleena as she made her way to the bench.

"Sup hon-ney," she replied as she found a seat next to him.

"Not much…" said Lantino.

"Hey Raine," said Milleena greeting Loraine.

"Hey sis," replied Loraine with a wave.

"My sis here was telling me y'all ran into Ice at the boot camp," said Lantino. "Heard y'all even got into it."

"Hmp, that's why we should've never run into her," said Milleena.

"Told 'em the same thing," adding Loraine.

"Ding, ain't seen her since that time she got kicked out of our school," said Lantino as he started to trace back. "Damn, I wonder how long it's been."

"Tino, good thing you didn't see her!" exaggerating Milleena. "Trust me; you wouldn't wanna see her now. Ugh…she is just butt ugly! Ain't that right, Raine?"

"Yeah Lantino," cried Loraine, "ain't know how you were able to deal with her and those hard stares."

"Hard stares?" asked Lantino. "What ya talking about?"

"She's talking about the look Ice's ugly ass would make before she gets ready to fight someone," said Milleena.

"Yeah, that girl would just sit there for about twenty minutes straight and look you dead in the eyes without blinking," said Loraine. "Plus, I heard she took medication," she laughed.

"Uh, I don't know what y'all talking about," responded Lantino.

"Yeah, I remember when she said it in Dr. Martin's class," said Milleena.

"Okay, and that was yo chick at one time, Lantino," Loraine laughed.

"Like I said before, I don't know what y'all talking about," said a denying Lantino. "I mean, she wasn't on meds when I was with her."

"Boy, what'd you see in her? Huh?" asked Milleena.

"Yeah…Huh?" said Loraine.

"Man, whatever…Anyways, moving along," said Lantino, whose blood was beginning to boil on account of feeling a bit irritated. "So y'all were in the same boot camp?" he asked.

"Yep," answered Loraine. "Matter of fact, we were roomies."

"For real?" asked Lantino.

"Furreel," answered Loraine.

"I know. Crazy huh?" said Milleena.

"Yeah, it is," replying Lantino. "I remember Ms. Tourez telling me that things happen for a reason. After hearing this, I'm beginning to think that shit is true."

"Lantino, you don't believe in anything," said Loraine.

"Huh? Wait a minute, that's not true," replied Lantino.

"Yeah ha."

"Naw aw."

"Uhhh yeaaah…"

"What you mean? I just got done saying that I believe everything happens for a reason."

"Yeah, and then tomorrow, he'll turn around to tell you he doesn't believe in that shit."

"Hmmm…yeah, for as long as I've known you, Tino, you will do that sometimes," said Milleena.

"See Tino, even our lady friend here says the same thing," said Loraine to Lantino, who by now is just shaking his head. *What's the big deal*, he thought as he sat there on the bench with them choosing to say no more. That's when Torence suddenly dropped in.

"Aww great," said Loraine in a sarcastic manner.

"What's wrong with you?" asked Lantino.

"Your weird friend is coming over," answered Loraine. "Who told 'em that he could come all the way out here?" she asked.

"He knew about the spot," answering Lantino.

"Raine, I don't see anything wrong with him coming," said Milleena.

"I bet it was you, Lantino," said Loraine. "Boy, what do you want?" she asked Torence rudely. "Who told you that you could come?"

Torence stood still for a moment before he attempted to find a seat on the bench. It looked as if he was trying to think of an answer to Loraine's last question. "You could come sit here," said Milleena. "You don't gotta stand there." Listening to Milleena, Torence felt a bit encouraged and decided he'll sit across Milleena.

"Sta! And who said you could sit next to me," said Loraine to Torence, who immediately turned her direction.

"Raine, you need to quit," laughed Milleena. "Here we could switch seats," she suggested.

"Naw, he doesn't need to do that," said Loraine. "What he needs to do is just leave. Go home you." Everyone then waits quietly to hear a response from Torence, but he instead continues to sit there among their presence without making a sound. It's as though he's not even there. Feeling a bit offended for Torence, Lantino calmly let out some air out of his chest. "Loraine, I think you need to listen to Lee and quit with the disrespect. Either that or I'm a pound that ass back to boot camp."

"Hmm…" responded Loraine while rolling her eyes.

"Anyways…Moving along," said Milleena, who's seated next to Loraine.

"Yes, yes," agreed Lantino, "moving along…"

"Ump, ump," sighed Milleena shaking her head at Lantino.

"So Torence," said Lantino, "now that you're here, could you tell these people that I actually do believe in something in life."

Nodding his head, Torence said, "yes, pretty much," confirming that Lantino does believe in some things. "Aw darn it," sighing Milleena, "and I thought we were moving along."

"But we are," replied Lantino. "I just had to backtrack on that topic for lil' bit, that's all."

"Yeah, and cause you did that now, we gotta stop you right there and rewind this whole subject," said Loraine.

"Yeah, you see what you done started Tino?" asked Milleena.

"Yeah, something you can't finish," said Loraine.

"Okay, you know what, Torence name a few things you know I believe in," said Lantino standing on his two feet.

"Hmmm," wondering Torence.

"Okay, just name something," again said Lantino.

"Hmmm, well, I think you were telling the truth that night you told me that you believed Ms. Tourez," replied Torence.

"Y'all hear that?" Asked Lantino to Loraine and Milleena.

"So, what…" said Loraine.

"Yeah, so what…" Milleena said.

"What?" replied Lantino. "So? Is that really what I'm hearing? You know what Torence, I don't think they were listening. Go ahead and tell 'em one more time."

"Uh okay," said Torence. "I think you were telling –"

"You know what HUSH!" said Loraine rudely interrupting him. "I wanna hear something from you Lantino, off rip."

"Yeah Tino," said Milleena, who was now standing on her feet.

"Uh okay," replying Lantino. "Um, um, uh…what about the tales?" he asked like a final guess.

"The tales," Milleena repeated.

"Yeah, the tales," again saying Lantino. "You know some of that talk that spread around the hood?"

"Oh, the tales," again repeated Milleena.

"Yeah, I believe in some of the tales," said Lantino, "like the Latin Queen."

"The Latin Queen…" once again repeating Milleena.

"Wait, wasn't it called 'The Age of a Latin Queen'?" asked Loraine.

"Oh yeah, I think that's what its called," answered Lantino.

"Oh yeah, I know that story," said Milleena.

"Hmp, everyone knows about that story," said Loraine.

"Yeah, the story goes that she was like a diamond in the dirt that ain't been found," said Lantino.

"Yeah, like a beautiful flower that grew out of the hardest concrete," said Milleena.

"But rose into something," said Lantino.

"And ruled more streets than the mayor," said Milleena.

"Shit, I even heard they named a street after her," said Lantino.

"You talking about Lopez lane?" asked Loraine.

"Yeah, that's the street," answering Lantino.

"Lopez lane…" said Milleena sounding mesmerized.

"Hmmm, didn't she get deported at the end," asked Lantino.

"Yeah, from what I heard," answering Loraine, "but that was after they took her son."

"Wait…Naw, that's not what I was told," said Milleena.

"Well, that's how the story goes," said Loraine.

"What'd you hear?" asked Lantino.

"I heard that after she lost her kid, she got shot," answered Milleena, "then her ass got deported."

"Hmmm, I like the other ending to the story better," said Lantino.

"Either way, it's still a tragic," said a soft-spoken Torence.

"True," Lantino agreed.

"What other tales in the hood y'all heard about?" said Loraine.

"Y'all ever heard about the 'Legend of King David'?" asked Lantino.

"Who?" Loraine asked.

"King David," said Lantino. "Y'all ever heard about him?".

"King David," repeating Milleena, "hmmm, I heard of King Arthur," she laughed.

"Yeah, me too," laughing Loraine.

"So y'all ain't never heard about it then?"

"Ain't that some old' story in the Bible?" Loraine asked jokingly.

"Naw, this story came out of the Folk Nation," answered Lantino.

"Hmp, well it sure sounds like it came out of the Bible," said Milleena in a sarcastic manner.

"Yeah, I know right. 'Legend of King David,'" Loraine laughed.

"You know a lot of people believe this story really happened," said Lantino, "especially the ones from the Southside."

"You know what Lee," said Loraine, "what's funny to me is that some girl at the boot camp mentioned that name to me."

"For real, who? Did I know her?" asking Milleena.

"Yeah, you remember Dawn, right?" said Loraine.

"From the Sisterhood, yeah," replied Milleena.

"Well, she said something about this David guy too," said Loraine.

"What did she say?" asked Lantino.

"She was talking about him being her uncle, and some stuff about his knowing how to disappear," Loraine stated.

"Disappear," laughed Milleena. "Okay, now I done heard it all."

"Hmmm, ain't know he had a niece. Ain't even think he had any kids," said Lantino.

"I'm just telling you what she said to me," said Loraine.

"Going ghost on someone was something I did hear about 'em though," said Lantino. "So, she might have been talking about the same David I heard about."

"Okay, next please!" said Milleena.

"What is the Sisterhood?" asked Lantino.

"Just a gang of bitches you don't wanna know," answered Loraine.

"You know ya gurl Ice was down with 'em," said Milleena informing Lantino.

"What, but Ice told me that she was a sister from the B.O.S," said Lantino. "So, if what y'all just told me is true, then that means that the Sisterhood runs with the Folk Nation."

"Can we talk about something else now?" asked an aggravated Milleena.

"Hey, hold up, you know David use to rock the six-point star too," said Lantino, completely dismissing Milleena's question. "Maybe there are ties between that girl y'all met at the boot camp and David."

"Come on, you really believe in that shit?" asked Milleena.

"Hey, I'm just saying," replied Lantino.

"Alright now, can we talk about something else?" again asked Milleena.

"Yeah, alright," answering Lantino.

"Thank you," sighed Milleena, "about time."

"Soooo, can anybody think of another tale?" asked Loraine.

"Hmmm…What about 'A Lawndale Nightmare'?" asked Lantino.

"What's that one about?" asked Loraine.

"Ain't that one about this drug buster who stopped a drug lord?" asked Milleena.

"But then realized that that was the same drug lord who saved his life back when they were small-time drug dealers," said Lantino.

"Yeah, that's the one, right?" asked Milleena.

"Naw," answered Lantino, "but I know the one you're talking about, though."

"Alright, so what's this one about?" Loraine asked.

"Lawndale Nightmare is about this boy from the Southside who rolled with this gang till one day he came across this kid about his age that was beaten to death," Lantino said. "The real nightmare in the story starts when he comes to find out that the kid is him…"

"Damn, now that's crazy," said Loraine.

"Yeah, I know, right!" Milleena agreed.

"Yeah, but tell you what," said Lantino, "that's just another tale from the hood."

"Uh okay…meaning…," said Loraine.

"Meaning that, that was nothing compared to the tales I heard about from the Crips," said Lantino.

Soon three more people showed up to join Lantino and company at his little hangout spot. Lantino's friend from the clique, Tyberius, came through another entrance at the park. "Oh, now I know you ain't gonna tell 'em about one of the tales from the Crips," said Tyberius as he approached the bench. Behind him were two of Milleena's younger twin siblings, who he picked up, Tuwan and Kabrina. They each said "hi" and greeted everyone on the table. Looking for one more person, Lantino began to wonder. "Where's Julisa?" he asked Tyberius.

"I thought she was here earlier at the park," said Tyberius. "Guess she never left the house."

"You know if she's still coming?" asked Lantino.

"Naw," answered Tyberius. "Guess we'll just have to see. Hmmm, why you all worried about her?"

"Shouldn't you?" asked Lantino redirecting Tyberius's question back to him. "I mean, I would be if she were my cousin."

"Alright, back to this talk about the tales from the Crips," said Loraine.

"Okay," said Lantino, "I'ma tell y'all about –"

"Naw, Tino, let's not even go into the tales from the Crips!" said Tyberius. "Skip that!"

"Skip that? Wait, why don't you want him talking about it?" asking Loraine to Tyberius.

"Why," said Tyberius, "Look I'ma tell you why. What he's about to tell you ain't some old tale that the Cripplers made up. It's a FACT. Shit really went down over there!"

"Shit went down over where?" asked a curious Loraine. "You know what, I haven't heard this story yet, and neither have some people on this table."

"Naw Loraine," said Tyberius, "the less you know about this story, the better off you'll be."

"Lantino, I wanna know what happened," said a demanding Loraine.

"Naw Tino," said Tyberius.

"Lee, could you tell me since my brother doesn't want to," said Loraine.

"Tino knows the story better than I do, Raine," replied Milleena.

"Damn well, will somebody on this table tell me what happened?" asked Loraine.

"Lee, Tino," said Tyberius, "even you Rence, don't tellah shit!"

"So that's it Lantino, you're just gonna listen to him," asked Loraine. "So, whatever he tells you to do, you're just gunna do, huh? At the house wasn't it you who said that 'you're the man around here.' Huh, huh –"

"The saying goes…" Lantino interrupts her, "…that they use to hold meetings there," he said.

"Who's they?" Loraine asked. "And Who –"

"They!" again interrupting Lantino. "They...the Satanic Disciples," he said.

"Who are they?" asked Loraine.

"Shut up, and let me tell the story, then maybe you'll know everything," said Lantino.

"I told you not to tell her, but go head on then, Tino," said Tyberius.

"Now that old building," explaining Lantino, "for years used to be a crazy house. Till one day, it got shut down. Reasons why…Not too sure. All I was told was that there was something that people were doing that they should not have done. Something…wicked, I'm guessing. Anyways before the SDs showed up over there for some time became the spot to have rumbles. For that time out there was where kats got stabbed, tased,

104

murked, sprayed, and more. You name it; it happened to dudes who stepped foot out near that old building. Time passed, and things eventually calmed down. The area still wasn't occupied by anyone. So that's when the SDs showed up and claimed it as their turf to practice gang warfare. Soon it became their little outpost to hold all their hood meetings. Hearing this, my thought was that they must been a cult or some kind of secret society. If you go in the old building today, everything is abandoned. Not nann one of them is there. To close it off, people say that over there today is like a cemetery for Gs who died there. Some say that spirits are lurking around there. I've even heard some told me that they could hear things out there. Others think it's just cursed."

"Cuz it is," cried out Tyberius.

"So do y'all know where the old building is?" asked Loraine.

"You don't actually wanna go, do you?" asked Tyberius.

"Actually, I do," answered Loraine.

"You ain't just hear me say that it's cursed!" cried out Tyberius.

"It's just an old tale," said Loraine. "It ain't happen for real."

"See, this is why I ain't wanna have her listen to this," said Tyberius.

"Lee, you don't actually believe in this stuff, do you?" asked Loraine.

"Naw, but if you wanna go, you could go," answered Milleena.

"What! Don't tell me you scared?" asked Loraine.

"Oh naw, I'm uh, uh, uh gonna chill here with Lantino," answered Milleena.

"So, no one else is coming, huh?" asked Loraine. Surely no one responded to her. Standing all alone, Loraine looked around the table then made eye contact with Tuwan and immediately questioned him. "Hey, have you and Bree ever been there before?" she asked. He shook his head slowly after looking at his twin sister. "Good then," replied Loraine, "cause y'all coming with me over there."

"You know what," said Tyberius, "that's it! I'm out of here!" At that moment, he gets up and leaves, taking the same way he came in without a goodbye. No one really cared to say it either, as they watched him make his exit. Now the crew was just down to six people.

"Hmmm now I remember," said Lantino, who just traced back an old memory. "Loraine, the old building sits at Ridgeway."

"Oh good," said Loraine, "take me there."

"Who said anything about me going back there," replied Lantino.

"Lee?" asked Loraine.

"Please, I don't even know the way," replying Milleena. "You'd have to go to Price."

"Yeah, he knows the route better than anybody I know," said Lantino.

"Think he might still be posting up by the train station," asked Milleena.

"Of course," answered Lantino. "You know the station is like his second home. He'll never leave."

"I'm out y'all," said Loraine, who automatically gets up.

"Where you going?" asked Lantino.

"I told you, I'm heading to that old building you just told me about," answering Loraine.

"Naw ah," said Milleena in disbelief. "You are going right at this time of the day?" she asked.

"Yeah," answered Loraine, "what y'all thought I was playing? I told you that story ain't spook me."

"Hey well, good luck with that," said Lantino.

Loraine yells at Milleena's twin siblings, reminding them that they're to keep her company. Choosing not to get her upset, they quietly follow her to exit the park. With Loraine gone now, a silence suddenly began to fill the surrounding area. The lights outside were turning on as darkness fell. The wind continued blowing from that point on. Looking out into space, a randomly selected question just happened to come into Lantino's mind. "So Torence, you doing anything when you get home?" he asked.

"Naw," answered Torence, "I'ma probably just help Ms. Tourez get some work done around the house."

"Oh word," said Lantino.

"Yeah, I should probably head back now," said Torence. "You coming?" he asked Lantino.

"Nann," answered Lantino, "I think I'll just chill out here for lil' bit."

"Alright then," said Torence.

"Yeah," said Lantino. "Well, Lee, I guess it's just you and me."

"Yep," agreed Milleena.

Chapter 13: Nights to Remember

Part 2: Ridgeway

Drawn by a tale well told by her half-brother, Loraine decided to take a tour to one of the smaller areas known to the Windy City, Ridgeway. Away from home, Loraine had never gone any further than Stone Park. And now at Ridgeway meant that she was coming back home late, which was going to affect the satisfactory progress the Martin program was keeping track of. With her was Milleena's twin siblings, Tuwan and Kabrina, who Loraine had practically stapled on to her. For all three of them, the visit to Ridgeway was their first time. And guiding them was Price, an associate of Tyberius' set. "You know I use to live here," he said to Loraine as he continued leading the way.

"Hmp, really," said Loraine.

"Yeah," answered Price, "my old house is just right up the road on 27th avenue."

"Well, I can see why anyone would move from here," said Loraine.

"Hmmm, what makes you say that?"

"For starters, everything is so…black and white around here. It feels like we're walking right back in time. Like things ain't change out here or something."

"Like an old fashion feeling, huh?"

"Yeah, like a 1930-ish type of feeling."

"Yeah, I know, that's what everyone from the Greens says when they come here."

"Out there is way better than up here."

"Hmp, welcome to Ridgeway ma."

"Yeah, whatever…Hey, we almost there yet?"

"You mean Trentonhaven?"

"The what?"

"The Behavior House. You know that old building you said you were tryna get to."

"Oh yeah…that."

Yep, it's coming."

"Good, cause I'm just about done walking."

"That place is probably the only thing to see out here in this little village."

"What you say its name was?"

"The Trentonhaven House."

"The…Trent and what now?"

"The Trentonhaven Behavior House."

"Hmmm…Trentonhaven…"

"Yeah, now you got it."

"Hmp, weird name for a place."

"Yeah, I hear the name came from some guy named Trenton."

"Who's he supposed to be?"

"Heard he was the man who put this house together. Either that or he was one of the top doctors back in the days."

"Dr. Trenton…"

"Yep, that's his name, and after the house got put here, it was supposed to be a 'haven' for crazy people to live here. That's why it's called Trentonhaven."

"Oooooh…Trent-haven. Trentonhaven…It makes sense."

"Yeah, it's crazy, huh?"

"Yeah, it is…So why he closed the place down?"

"Uh, it wasn't him…the house was shut down by people he had to answer to."

"Okay, so the people shut the place down, but why?"

"Mmmhm…heard the crazy people were getting mistreated."

"Did you say 'crazy people'?"

"Yeah, like two times already."

"So, there were actual crazy people staying there?"

"Yeah…I told you it was supposed to be a haven for crazy people."

"How many of them stayed there?"

"T'oin know, I ain't work there. I wasn't even around when they did stay here."

"Oh…uh okay…"

"What I do know for sure, is the fights that happened out there. That's legit."

"Oh yeah, my brother told me about it. Over there's where all the rumbles happen, right?"

"Yeah, the Behavior House for a while was the spot."

"So, it was like a movie theater coming over there to watch people fight?"

"Hell, no!"

"Huh…"

"No one wanted to see people get killed! I know I wouldn't!"

"Oh, so gangsters got killed there?"

"Tased, sprayed, shanked, worked…you name it, it happened!"

"Ding, my brother told me the same thing."

"Yeah, and that's why there's hardly any gangs or cliques left today."

"What do you mean?"

"What I mean is they all died out."

"Who?"

"The Dukes, the Legion, the Clovers, the Colony, the Shepherds, the Imperials, nearly all of them."

"They were all over here at Ridgeway?"

"Yep, the Krazy bunch, the Mad lads, Deuce, and the Clicks. GONE…"

"Ding…"

"Some of them moved out of Ridgeway and hopped with other gangs like the Aces, Action pack, or the King Cobras. I know you've heard of the KCs before."

"The Cobras…Uh naw…"

"Well, back at the Greens, we beat them out of our territory. Even though they linked up with the GDs, something tells me that they ain't never recovered."

"So, if they're still here, you say it's because they allied with other sets?"

"That or they either moved out. I know the inner-city players did that, and so did the Drake Boys. The only real gangs still around are the Refugees near the riverside, and the Cherokees over by the Reservations."

"Sooo I don't get it…"

"Get what?"

"Why'd they go fighting there?"

"It was all about territory, and who could claim it."

"For real?"

"Yeah, at least in the beginning. But then soon, they all seem like they forgot, and it became the hot spot to throw rumbles."

"Stuh! Now no one claims it as a turf today. What a damn shame."

"Hmp, you telling me..."

"So, after things calmed down is that when the Satanics showed up to claim it."

"Yeah…So they say."

"Huh? I thought that's what happened…"

"Naw, the tale of what really went down was held back from the kats that passed it on."

"Hmmm…"

"I did look into it, and as it turns out the Sons of Satan knocked the others out the way to claim the house as their turf too."

"Sons of Satan?"

"You and your brother know 'em as the Satanic Disciples. Around here, they call 'em the Sons of Satan."

"Really?"

"Yeah…At one point, they almost had Ridgeway locked down."

"How'd they do that?"

"Well, you see, they weren't just one set."

"They weren't?"

"Naw, they were a set of cliques who made a pact."

"Oh, kind of like an alliance."

"A what?"

"An alliance."

"What's that?"

"Kind of like what you're talking about. When two people or a bunch of people team up for a reason."

"Hmmm…smart girl throwing some big words at me, huh."

"Yeah, something like that."

"Anyways they made a pact –"

"Wait, wait, who made a pact?"

"A whole bunch of sets, the Renegades, the Raiders, the Vikings, the Rejects, the Insane Hoods, 2-Sixes even the Four Corners gang jumped in."

"…And then what?"

"Then they all became part of the Insane Unknowns Faction."

"The alliance…"

"Yeah, exact-a-fucking mundo!"

"So, then what happened after that?"

"Well, they took over the spot. Once that became official, those bastards started setting niggas on traps and taking 'em back to their turf to jump 'em."

"Damn, that's evil."

"Hah, who you telling?"

"So, one by one, Ridgeway Gs were going missing?"

"Yeah, and that's just how it was. The first victims were the 8-Ball posse. Then it became the 11th Street posse. Next, 42nd Avenue Boyz, and the Alley Kats, and then next after next and you know the rest."

"Okay, so how'd all this end?"

"That's where we came in. The very first of us here in Ridgeway use to stay by a lil' ass park where all the trailers were at. So, because we were always hanging out there, people called us the Parkers. But since the Park's name was Baron, we also called ourselves the Barons. So, when word came to the park about what was going on, we finally got some help from the VLs of the Westside. After the oldest of us promised to side with the VLs forever, everyone from the outside called us the Lords of Ridgeway. That's how we adopted our name 'the Ridgeway Lords.' I had probably turned eight years old or nine when I was finally jumped in."

"That's funny, how come I've never heard of y'all?"

"No one knows about the Ridgeway Lords like that."

"What about this tale about the old place? Where or who that all come from?"

"Ma, those were tales from the Crip Walkers that use to be out here."

"I thought they were called the Cripplers?"

"Same thing…"

"Why were they called the Cripplers or Crip Walkers anyway?"

"Well, after a few of them got away from the beating by the Esses, people who saw 'em said that they walked with a limp. Now the limp was said to represent a soldier who was still standing after battle. I heard it was supposed to rep their originator back somewhere at California."

"California…what the hell?"

"I don't know…the Cripplers are another story within their own selves."

"You got that right."

"Anyways, it was them who found out and spread the word out about the traps and setups. After that, they all bounced."

"Bounced? Where'd they go?"

"I don't know. Away from here. Away from the Sons of Satan that's for sure."

"Can't blame 'em."

"Right, so anyways their words got around, and over time they were worded to other people it passed to. That's why they call these stories the 'Tales from the Crips'."

"Okay, I gotchu…So Price, right?"

"That's me."

"You're gunna take us to that place?"

"Oh, why ma, we already here."

"Say what? I don't see any old building around here."

"No…not right here, but right over there, pass those trees by the dead-end sign."

"Uh, pa, I don't see anything."

Slightly annoyed, Price turned his attention to the twins to check if they knew exactly where he was pointing at. "Hey, you two, y'all see what I'm talking about, right?" he asked them. In unison, they both nodded their heads as their response. Then Tuwan tapped Loraine on her shoulder, and like Price, he pointed his finger directly pass the dead-end sign Price was referring to. From where she was standing, she could tell that it stood about two stories tall, and its surrounding area covered about the same amount of space as a basketball court. The paint on the building was faded, and because it was so dark outside, it was hard to decide what color the building was. The glass windows were filled with dust, and the screens in the front porch were practically ripped up as if someone was trying to get out, the ground was nothing but old dirt, and vines could be seen growing on the building. The building gave each of them this feeling that it nor the area in which it sits on hadn't been occupied for a good amount of time. The look on Tuwan and Kabrina's face gave Price the impression that they wanted to run as fast as track stars. Though they didn't say anything, the look alone on both their faces gave him that idea. Loraine, on the other hand ignored the eerie reaction to the appearance of the property and proceeded to enter. Looking back at Price, Loraine asked him why he didn't escort them to the front since they were already there. In response, he said to her, "Ma, this is as close as I'm gunna step to that house. I ain't stepping any closer to the devil's playground."

'The devil's playground'...damn, that's the same thing my brother said, Loraine thought as Lantino's words played back in her mind. "So you're gunna wait here till we get back, right?" she asked Price.

"No," answered Price while shaking his head.

"Huh? Why?"

"What I do for anyone comes with a price. Why else do you think they call me the 'Price.'"

Oh please, you're way in over your head. "Oh common, just this once. Pleeeseee –"

"Look that because you're Tino's sister don't mean I'm a cut you a break."

"Well, my brother told me to tell you that he'd work something out, but you had to get back with him on that."

"Work what out?"

"Beats me! That's what he said. I figured you know whatever it was he was talking about being that y'all friends."

"Was he talking about money?"

"Boy, I don't know. Whatever it is, it's between y'all."

"Wait a minute, how come you ain't tell me this before by the train station?"

"Well, you ain't never ask!"

"Hmmm...alright fine, you cool."

"So, you're gunna wait for us?"

"Yeah, I'm a be right here."

Sucker "Okay, then good."

"Hey, but just one thing, though…"

"What?"

"If you ain't back by twenty minutes, then I'm out."

"Twenty minutes?!"

"Twenty or none at all! There's no way I'm a be a duck out here especially near Satan's camp!"

"Ugh! Alright, fine, we'll be back!"

"In twenty minutes?"

"In twenty minutes!"

"Okay then…good. Oh! Tino sister!"

"What, man?"

"Just one more thing, I almost forgot to tell you."

"And…what's that?"

"I don't need to know anything that happens to y'all back there. The less I know, the better."

"Before I came here, I was told that this was an old building."

"It is an old building."

"Looks more like a two-story house."

"Yeah, well, it's that too."

"What's the worst that could happen?"

"The worst…"

"Okay…C'mon y'all let's go."

"Remember, the less I know, the better…"

"Alright, Price. C'mon y'all hurry up!"

After hearing so much about the building and the events that occurred in its past, Loraine now could actually use the opportunity necessary to confirm whether if the tale surrounding its reputation was indeed true. So eager to prove her brother wrong, Loraine wasted no time walking through the property's frontcourt. Loraine and the twins noticed pieces of metals and scraps lying around the floor. Those same scraps and metal pieces appeared to be what might have been car parts. They also stepped through a lot of rocks on their way to the front porch. By the time they arrived at the front porch Loraine immediately let her ego get the best of her. "See, I told ya nothing happened down here," she boasted. "It's just an old house my brother tried to scare us with. Talking about some old tale –"

Suddenly Loraine was interrupted by the sound made from the doorknob as it turned. They couldn't really tell if the doorknob turned or not, but they were certain the door made a sound as if the knob was turned, and it opened. Everyone stared at the door with a wide eye. Loraine coerced the twins to stay quiet though she wasn't able to convince them otherwise about what they all had just witnessed. "Look, it was just the wind," she said to them as she tried to deny what really happened. Using her fingertips, she then pushed the door wide open with a light touch. Right there and then, she boldly proceeded to say "Oh yeah, we're going in." Tuwan slowly followed her inside, and then his sister, Kabrina, behind him. He made an effort to talk Loraine out of doing this, but unfortunately, he couldn't seem to get a word out as she kept interrupting him. "Look just shut up Tuwan, I don't wanna hear it!" she'd say.

"But uh –"

"Ap!"

"Buh –"

"AHH!"

"Buhh –"

"AHH!"

"HUSH, boy! I told you we're doing this!"

Again, the house from the exterior had paint that appeared faded. Due to the darkness outside, there was no telling what kind of color the paint was looking from a distance. When they arrived up close, the color of the paint looked to be tarnished. The glass windows in the house were filled with dust. The screens on them were ripped apart and were in urgent need of being replaced. The interior of the house needed an entire makeover as the three discovered. Inside was nothing left but a mess. Paint was all over the place. Ripped carpets, broken glass, pipes, and all sorts of objects were sitting all over the place. Looking up, they were able to see whatever was holding the roof up in the ceiling. "Damn, the least they could've done was clean up the whole place," Loraine said. Out of nowhere that's when they heard a loud banging sound. It sounded like a bunch of pipes someone had fallen on. "What was that?" whispered Tuwan.

"What was what?" asked Loraine continuing her denial.

"Tuwan, I heard it too," said Kabrina. "It was loud."

"Y'all both need to shut up," said Loraine, "that wasn't –"

The loud banging noise could be heard again.

"You heard it?" again quietly asking a startled Tuwan.

"Yeah," answered Kabrina, "and this time, it was louder."

"There it goes again," said Tuwan.

"Sounds like a bunch of bars and pipes," said Kabrina.

"Someone probably fell on…"

"Or something…"

"Now, it keeps playing back…"

"Yeah, and it's getting louder…"

"And louder by the second…"

"I know…where could it be coming from?"

All three of them, for a while, stood there by the lobby, all paused in one spot, trying to look around. But none of them could make out where exactly the sound was coming from. As the noise grew louder, Loraine drew more silence. It was becoming more apparent to the twins that she was scared. However, the acknowledgment of the truth still couldn't seem to outweigh her pig-headedness. "C'mon y'all," she said, "let's ch-ch-check upstairs." Loraine began making her climb upstairs, as did Kabrina. Tuwan, on the other hand, wasn't moving. "C'mon boy!" said Loraine, "we still gotta whole ten minutes left!"

"Raine, we ain't supposed to be here," replied Tuwan.

"Boy, ain't nothing gunna happen to us! Now let's go!"

"Yeah, we should probably leave before things get worse."

"Oh, so what, you're scared now?"

"Raine I'm just saying it's –"

"Naw Wan, you sound like a pussy!"

"It would be better if we –"

"Hey y'all listen!" said Kabrina silencing Loraine's dispute with Tuwan.

"The noise stopped," she said. Once Loraine and Tuwan realized that, they stopped talking. Again, they all stood still and looked at each other. Finally, Loraine made eye contact with Kabrina, signaling to follow her upstairs. This Kabrina did without hesitation. Though the same couldn't be said for Tuwan, who continued to stand motionless at the same spot. Looking at Tuwan, Loraine began to shake her head saying, "Ump, ump, ump, ump." He stared back at her but didn't make any replies.

"When we head back to the Greens, do you really want me to tell everyone what such a wussy you were? Huh?" she asked him. This time he shook his head. "Alright, then com'on!" she said rudely. So, he followed them upstairs.

Heading up to the second floor, they found a work of graffiti done alongside the wall while climbing the stairs. In fact, they were even done on the stairs. "Hey, y'all stop and take a look at this," said Kabrina, who was paying a close attention to the work done on the wall.

"What is it now?" asked Loraine.

"Take another look at the spray paints," suggested Kabrina. "What are these signs supposed to mean?" she asked.

"Why it's all devilish shit!" said Tuwan with a startled tone of voice. "Devilish shit! Nothing but devilish shit!" he said repeatedly.

"Ding, what in the world did these people use to do here?" asked Loraine.

"That's it, Kabrina, we bouncing out of this joint," said Tuwan with a more demanding demeanor.

"Wait, but we can't leave Raine here by herself," said Kabrina.

"Yeah, we can if she doesn't wanna come," said Tuwan.

"I'm the girl, and yet I got bigger balls than you!" said Loraine. "How does that make you feel?"

"Tino could come to get you since you wanna stay here so bad," replied Tuwan.

"Shhhhhh," said Kabrina, "there's some noise coming from downstairs," she whispered.

"Shit, there is, and it sounds like it's coming from outside," acknowledged Tuwan.

"Do you hear it, Raine?" asked Kabrina.

"Yeah, that's probably just Price checking up on us," answered Loraine.

"But it can't be," disagreed Tuwan, "those footsteps sound too much like hooves on a goat or a horse."

"Shit, it slammed the front door shut!" said a frightened Loraine.

"Oh shit, who do you think it is?" asked Tuwan.

"Or what do you think it is?" asked Kabrina.

After the twins asked questions, they then turned to Loraine for some sort of answer, but all they saw was the look of complete fear in her eyes. Like that, their hope, trust, and confidence in her slipped to the abysmal of disappointment. To top it off, Loraine, without a word, zoomed into one of the empty rooms on the second floor. When Tuwan and Kabrina behind her made it inside, she instantly shut the door, and leaned her back against it to keep someone or something from barging in. It felt like someone had recently moved out of the empty room; all three of them were sitting in. It was spacious and appeared like six to ten people could fit in there. Yet, the three of them, for some unknown reason, felt condensed like they were in a tight space. Besides that, there was really nothing else in the room but a light bulb that was suspended in the middle of the ceiling and a few damages done on the wall. Staring at the walls, Kabrina began to wonder if the damages were done by punches people threw at it. These walls in the room don't look very hollow, she thought. "Hey y'all, how thick do you think these walls are?" she asked.

"Hmmm, I don't know," answered Tuwan, "but I sure as hell know I can't bust 'em with my hand."

"Yeah, well, that's the funny thing," said Kabrina, "'cause doesn't it look like someone did that with their hands?"

"Yeah," answered Tuwan, "it does but how could that be?"

"It could have been something else," said Loraine. "You never know."

"Don't think I want to know," said Tuwan.

"Uh neither do I," agreed Kabrina.

"Ugh! Why are there so many bugs in here, and what's that smell?" asking a frustrated Tuwan.

"Oh, stop your whining," said Loraine.

"It so stuffy in here," complained Tuwan, "y'all is it just me or what?"

"No, it is stuffy in here," replied Kabrina.

"Raine, is it time yet?" asked Tuwan.

"Yeah," Loraine answered.

"What?" cried Tuwan.

"Almost!" said Loraine, "We still have time. Just not enough to check out the back."

"Wait, you mean to tell me that you still want to stick around?" asked Tuwan. "Ding, to think Tino said that you're the smart one…"

"Wan, you didn't hear me say anything about sticking around, now did you?!" replying Loraine.

"Naw bu –,".

"Y'all LISTEN, LISTEN!" Kabrina interrupted. There's something else going on downstairs," she said.

Shortly after she said that the noise downstairs suddenly became more and more audible. All three of them in the empty room could hear noises. Noises that sounded like a group of people fighting. Stuff being thrown across the house could be heard. From men falling, running, to beating each other down to a pulp was also heard loud and clear. It sounded like a rumble. Tuwan, Kabrina, and even Loraine acknowledged that they heard what sounded like panting, grunting, and voices. However, none of them was able to make out the words they heard as they listened to the voices. "Help me hold the door," said Loraine to the twins in fear that something was about to burst through the door. It took about six minutes for the noise downstairs to finally die down. Though to the three of them, it felt more like fifteen minutes had gone by.

Unfortunately for the three of them, the horror didn't end there. It seemed to only worsen as it continued, this time inside the empty room they were in. The suspended light bulb in the middle of the ceiling began swinging erratically as all three of them immediately noticed. Some images of that weren't there before mysteriously began to appear in the room's walls. Moreover, the temperature of the room increased dramatically. It was to a point where they could each see steam come through their nostrils as they exhaled. At that moment, they all came to learn that they weren't alone in the room, for there clearly was a presence among them. And this presence was taunting their every move, their every thought, emotion, step, and everything else about their existence.

"You think that boy is still waiting for us back there?" asked Kabrina.

"Uh, you mean Price?" asked Loraine.

"Yeah him," replied Kabrina.

"Um I don't know," replied Loraine, "maybe…"

"He was the smart one," said Tuwan.

"Yeah," Kabrina agreed, "we should've listened to him and everybody else."

SPLANG! Sounded the light bulb as it crashed to the floor from the ceiling and became nothing more than many broken pieces of glass.

"To hell with him," said Tuwan, "I'm a find my own way back to the Greens my own damn self!" Within seconds he was out the room. Loraine drew a crazy look on her face because she could not believe that he was actually going back downstairs to exit the old building, especially after everything they had heard down there. She felt movement by the door coming from her right side, which was where Kabrina was standing. When she turned her head towards there, Kabrina was out of sight. *Damn, they're both crazy,* Loraine thought. *Aren't they worried that whatever's down there might get 'em?* She said to herself.

Suddenly, red smeared handprints of all sizes began to appear on the walls of the room before her very own eyes. Her heart skipped a beat instantaneously. "Hey y'all wait for me," Loraine shouted on top of her lungs. Making her exit, Loraine looked like someone who'd qualify for a foot race.

Chapter 14: Nights to Remember

Part 3: Tor'raine

"So Torence, you doing anything when you get home?" asked Lantino.

"Naw," answered Torence, "I'm a probably just help Ms. Tourez get some work done around the house."

"Oh word," said Lantino.

"Yeah, I should probably head back now," said Torence, "you coming?"

"Nann," answered Lantino, "I think I'll just chill out here for 'lil bit.

"Alright then," said Torence.

"Yeah," said Lantino. "Well, Lee, I guess it's just you and me."

"Yep," agreed Milleena.

"Hmmm, being alone out here with you kind of reminds me of old times."

"You still remember those days, huh?"

"Yeah, even after such a long time."

"The only difference about right now is…"

"What? It ain't white-out?"

"Yeah…this time, everything ain't buried under the snow."

"I still like that tag you put up."

"You talking about the one that put me away in boot camp for a while?"

"Yeah, that one! The way you did the bunny was so nice and crisp!"

"Mr. Nobles and the security guard were so mad."

"Yeah, they were. From what I heard, those buildings you tagged were supposed to be for the school's new programs."

"Oh, so maybe that's what put me away for so long."

"You should feel lucky they ain't do you like they did Ice."

"Hmmm, I do feel lucky…"

"How long they keep you in there?"

"Longer than I could remember, longer than any of the times I'd ever gone."

"If my memory serves me correct, I say it was by last November when I ain't see you here no more."

"Yeah, well, it was too long. So Tino, what'd you do the whole time while I was gone?"

"Well, I wasn't coming to the park as much, and if I did, I wouldn't make a stop out to our spot being that you weren't there."

"Awww, you sound bored."

"Hmp, that's cause I was. I mean, my brother wasn't coming out because it got too cold. And all that ever went down at the park was hood meetings I ain't feel like showing up to."

"So, then you went to other places?"

"Yeah, because you already know I can't stand being at home. So, I did just that till finally, I found someone new to hang out with."

"Someone...New..."

"Uh yeah..."

"Someone new, huh?"

"Aw, c'mon Lee...I had to find something to do while you were gone!"

"Mmmmhmmm..."

"Like I told you already, I was bored, and I ain't like being at the house. Plus, my brother wasn't coming."

"Brother...You ain't never tell me you had a brother."

"Lee, you've seen my adopted brother before."

"Adopted brother?"

"Yeah...Torence who was just sitting here tonight."

"Oh, you mean him...I ain't know he was adopted."

"Yeah, he's our adopted brother."

"How come you ain't never tell me that?"

"Well, uh, that time when you and I were together, he wasn't staying with us."

"Uh hmmm...It's kind of weird how he just popped out of nowhere and became your family."

"Okay, so it is, but he's in our family."

"What happened to his real family?"

"It's a long story."

"Alright, so make it a short story."

"Hmmm, it's too complicated."

"K, then don't make it complicated."

"I can't…"

"Hmmm…You told me he was your friend, Tino."

"And he is. So what?"

"But now I'm hearing that he's your adopted brother."

"Because he is my adopted brother."

"Well, how come Loraine doesn't say so?"

"Um, uh…I don't know."

"Hmmm…He ain't your adopted brother for real."

"Yeah, he is! What do you mean?"

"She says that he's just a boy whose freeloading off our meals and shit."

"My sister doesn't know what she's talking about. Half the things that come out her mouth ain't serious."

"I don't know, Tino. From my point of view, she sounded like she knew what she was saying."

"That's cause you listen to her, but if you look for yourself, you can see that Torence ain't no freeloader."

"Hmmm…well, he did say that he was gonna help Ms. Tourez around the house tonight."

"See! My point exactly!"

"And most of the time I'm there he's always trying to do something for Ms. Tourez."

"Ching! Ching! Two points!"

"You know what…You might be right."

"That's because I am. At home, this is all he'll ever do. While you and Loraine were away, I swear this was all this boy ever use to do. After that, he's either chilling or sketching some pictures up at the balcony on the top floor."

"Hmmm…I don't get it. If he never bugs anyone or anything, then why's your sister always being so mean to him?"

"Beats me."

"That's awkward."

"I ain't never tell you that Loraine be on that SHIT!"

"Wait, she be on it?"

"Naw, but you would think so after seeing her do some of the things she does. Like tonight…"

"Oh yeah, I'm with you on that one. I can't believe she'd wanna go to Ridgeway."

"Yep, and she's my sister."

"Haha Tino, you're funny."

"For real, though."

"Hey Tino…"

"What's up?"

"Hmmmmm, you think maybe she might like him?"

"Who? Loraine?"

"Yeah…You think Loraine might be treating your friend like that because she likes him?"

"Hmmmm, nope."

"Not even one bit?"

"You think a girl would be treating someone this way if she liked him? I mean c'mon, wouldn't that make the guy run from her?"

"Yeah, it would but –"

"But –"

"Hmmm…But still…Have you ever seen how she looks at 'em when she says things to 'em?"

"Hmmm…what do you mean?"

"She acts all strong around 'em and even puts on a show…"

"You're losing me."

"But it's just a cover-up…"

"Wait, huh?"

"I'm talking about Loraine, and when she talks all mean to your friend."

"Uh okay…yeah…"

"You don't ever notice how she looks at 'em with the googly eyes…"

"Uh Lee, what googly eyes?"

"Um okay, like tonight…"

"Okay…Tonight…"

"She put 'em on the spotlight and did what she normally do again."

"Okay. Yeah…"

"Okay, so did you notice her eyes before he even reached the bench?"

"Uh Lee, you're losing me again."

"She did it again."

"Did what again?"

"The googly eyes!"

"Okay, now you completely lost me."

"Ugh! What I'm trying to say is that I think Raine talks mean to him because she's trying to hide how she really feels about 'em!"

"Wait huh?"

"I'm telling you that's what it is, Tino! I can see it!"

"What? I think you're off."

"You know what, Tino, never mind."

"Huh?"

"It's a girl thing; you wouldn't understand."

"What you mean…"

"You have to be a girl to see these things."

"What you mean? I stay with two girls at my place! How you gonna tell me?"

"I can't. It's complicated."

"Oh, so now you're mocking me, huh?"

"Naw honey, I'm just saying."

"Look, I know Loraine longer than you have, and she usually means what she says."

"Oh wait, wasn't it just you who told me that half the things that come out her mouth ain't serious?"

"Lorai-uh…"

"Yeah, can't talk now huh?!"

"Man Lee, please...Look, what I meant –"

"Uh huh! What you meant to say! Yeah, go on…"

"What I meant to say was that my sister, when it comes to boys, is usually the strong type. I mean, she's always been so strong around boys. At least the ones she's seen me brought over."

"I can tell that your sister's always been that type."

"Yeah, well to see her get soft for a boy just don't sound like her."

"Well, I notice she takes her time to dress up these days."

"Hmmm, why do you think that is?"

"Well, long time ago, I once thought it was for boys. Now I think it's just for a boy."

"So, what you're saying is that you think she does that for Torence?"

"I think she likes him, but she doesn't wanna admit it."

"A few months from now, I bet you won't be saying that."

"Hmmm, then I guess we'll see in a few months…"

"Hey, you know what, though?"

"What?"

"Loraine has acted differently since coming back from boot camp."

"Well duh Tino, she has to play like a good girl because the Martin program is keeping an eye on her."

"Naw, I ain't talking about that. What I'm talking about is how she treats Ms. Tourez and me. Especially ME."

"How has she been treating y'all?"

"Compared to how she was before she went to boot camp, she's been…nice."

"Uh what you don't like her being nice."

"It ain't that. It's just that I feel like she's trying too hard to be that way or something. I mean she doesn't say anything slick to me as much anymore. She'll ask me if I want something from the store."

"Oh…I thought she was always like that with y'all."

"Naw, before that, she used to always cuss and fight. She ain't tell you?"

"Oh yeah, she did say that in the reform school she and I went to. That's what she was in boot camp for."

"Well, I'm glad all that fist fighting shit stopped. I was tired of beating her up."

"Boy, stop…"

"But naw, she'll always smile and then say something about the way I made the buildings and stuff like that."

"Oh! That's right; she really liked that picture!"

"What picture?"

"The picture you drew for her."

"Uh I don't know what you're talking about."

"You know the picture you sent to the boot camp?"

"When?"

"I ain't send no picture to some boot camp. I ain't even sure where this boot camp was."

"But she told me it was you who did it."

"Naw, not me."

"So, if it wasn't you, then who?"

"What was in the picture?"

"It was so pretty! It had buildings, a crescent moon with stars, and the shading was nice too!"

"Sta! That wasn't my picture."

"Then, whose?"

"It was Torence."

"Wait, that was him!"

"Yeah, he made that. Damn, he actually sent it to her!"

"So, you're telling me that he drew that?"

"Yeah…I was right there when he drew it."

"And this whole time she's been picking on him. Ump, ump."

"Does she still got it?"

"Boy, what? Loraine loves that picture! Shoot, I love that picture, just looking at it!"

"Hah, you think that's nice! Girl, trust me, you ain't seen some of his real stuff!"

"Say what?"

"If you saw some of the shit I seen, you'd be like damn now that's BADASS!"

"For real?"

"Wait, what can he do? What kind of shit he's drawn?"

"Ma, you should've seen the stuff he made for Ms. Tourez while Loraine was in boot camp!"

"Haaaaa, for real?! What was it?"

"It's a…naw, you know what…I'm a let you see for yourself when we get back."

"Nooooo, just tell me!"

"Chill, I'm a show you when we get back to the house."

"Ugh! Ding, Tino!"

"I'll tell you about his other stuff."

"Ewwww, tell me!"

"Check out this picture he drew for me."

"Hey, that kind of looks like the tag I posted up at school."

"That's cause it is. Well, almost."

"Ding, he's good!"

"Yeah, I know right."

"How long did that take 'em?"

"Hmp, I'oin know…All I do know is that I just told him about your tag at school and next thing you know he handed me this that same day."

"Oh, so wait, he never had seen my tag at our school before?"

"Naw…Never…"

"Damn!"

"Yeah, I know, right! That's the same thing I said!"

"So, what is this picture for?"

"Oh, this?"

"Yeah…"

"That's for my tat."

"Your…tat?"

"Yeah, for my tattoo. I told 'em that I needed a design, and he knew I liked your tag, so he went ahead and did that for me."

"So, you're getting a tattoo?"

"Yeah, and this the sketch I want done on me."

"Nice. So, when are you getting it done on you?"

"Soon as I get some money."

"That's what your friend ought to be doing right now."

"Uh Lee…He already is."

"Naw, for real?"

"Yeah."

"How so?"

"Okay. In some of the last meetings we went to, did you notice that quite a few of 'em showed up with new tattoos?"

"Yeah, yeah I did notice that. So, he makes tattoos too?"

"He doesn't make 'em. He designs pictures for 'em. Then he gets paid when he's done."

"Wow, he's connected around the streets then."

"Yep…with the money he made, we were able to get something for Ms. Tourez on her birthday."

"Could he draw anything?"

"Yeah…Anything…Off rip. I mean, you should see 'em while he's at work."

"What's that like?"

"Shit, I can't explain it. It's like he's in a trance or something. You gotta see 'em for yourself."

"In a trance?"

"Yeah, matter of fact, I'll take you with me to the balcony on the top floor tonight if you wanna see 'em."

"Um okay…think he's there now?"

"There's no doubt in my mind that Torence is up there right now, chilling up at that balcony."

"Well, alright, then take me to the top floor."

"Alright c'mon follow me."

"Yes sir."

"Hey, just one thing, though…"

"What?"

"It's almost funny to me that Loraine thought I could draw."

"Hmp, why?"

"Because Lee, I can't even draw a straight line."

"Ump, ump. Shame."

"Hey, but I bet you Torence could beat you at tagging!"

"What? You know what, take me to 'em!"

Chapter 15: Nights to Remember

Part 4: Tor'raine

As weeks flew by like days, months felt like weeks, and within a matter of time, Chitowners were now living through the days of an entirely new year. On these days, everyone seemed to be living by their own agendas. Milleena was spending more and more of her time in the afterschool programs, which was a plus for the Martin staff. However, that meant less time with Lantino, who momentarily seemed completely fixated on Julisa, Tyberius' cousin. Loraine was back in school, and her grades were pretty much back to where they were long before her trip to the boot camp. Since her return, her popularity had grown to a great extent. Her popularity was centered around Lantino's fight with the school's security guard, and the fact that she was his half-sister. She was well-known among the older crowd, which mainly consisted of Lantino's peers or people who had some affiliation with Tyberius' clique. Boys had become particularly fond of her looks. On top of it all, she seemed to possess the type of personality to match her appearance. Her focus was more towards those who were older as far as her interest in boys was concerned. When she wasn't at home, she'd usually manage to find something to do besides hanging out all day after school. This, by the way, kept her mother out of her case.

As for Torence, marveling in creativity had suddenly become the new thing for him. Spray painting was practically all he did on days Lantino wasn't with him. He'd often venture out into other settings now that he was becoming more comfortable. However, at the same time, he didn't try to get too complacent when he was alone. Given the fact that Lantino as well Tyberius supplied him with some knowledge regarding their rival gang, he considered the possibility of them lurking around. Other than that, his name got around fast because he had skills in tattoo designing. So, a majority of the times, he'd be somewhere else providing service for his clients. And then again sometimes his clients would go out their way to see him. Hanging out at his spot, the balcony on the top floor, was something he started to do less frequently. In fact, he'd show up there on various times, and at nights he isn't there than he is out somewhere near by just spray painting.

On one very windy February evening, Loraine and Milleena were taking a walk together back home from the same party. They decided to go through the subway to avoid the strong wind outside. In addition, it was also everyone's little alternative to beat the bad weather on the way back home. "Ugh! So glad we ain't gotta deal with that wind for now," said Milleena throwing away some old transit cards.

"Yeah, I know right," agreed Loraine, "the wind out there today just won't stop blowing."

"Yeah, it sure won't, but that's alright, though, because when we get back up, we'll have only two blocks to walk through."

"Hmp, I guess."

"So, how'd you hear about the party?"

"Through my brother. How about you?"

"I kind of already knew about it."

"Oh…okay…"

"You thought it was stale, huh?"

"It was alright."

"Mmmmhmmm."

"It was…"

"Yeah, it was at least for everybody else."

"And me too, Lee."

"Naw…I can't quite say the same for you."

"Hmp, and why's that?"

"I don't know …probably because you weren't dancing…"

"Umm…okay and…"

"And so that meant that the party for you was stale…"

"Oh please, Lee, whatever!"

"Oh, c'mon Raine! You know it's true!"

"How is that supposed to tell you that I thought it was lame?"

"Well, uh…Let's see…for one you ain't get up and vibe not once for any of the music the DJ played there tonight! Not even for Serial Spittah!!"

"So! You know I can't vibe to Spittah's music! The man speaks too fast in his raps for me to understand what he's saying."

"Oh, please Raine! Spittah's style is sick! Plus, the song the DJ put on tonight was a slow jam type! Everybody was up and jamming, which means that you should've been too!"

"So, that still don't mean anything!"

"Bet you would have been up and dancing if J-Roc was there."

"J-Roc! Girl, what you mean?"

"I'm talking about your lil' crush. That's what I mean."

"Okay, so what about 'em?"

"That's what it was, wasn't it?"

"What? Him not being there?"

"Yeah. Admit it. You felt stood up, didn't you?"

"Hmmm, yeah he was on my mind a little bit."

"I know, and that's why the party for you was stale tonight."

"Well, the party is still going on."

"Don't tell me that you really believe that he's still coming?"

"But Lee, he did say he was gonna show up late."

"Please! After two hours, don't you think he'd show up by now?"

"Yeah…I guess…"

"Girl! What do you mean 'yeah I guess'? What you really ought to be saying is yeah of course."

"Yeah…of course."

"Look Raine, for the longest I've been out here, J-Roc and I been pretty tight, but right now, he's striking me like a gamer the way I see him coming at you. I don't know but I think you better listen to your brother and don't take 'em serious."

"Ugh! My brother can't choose who I should date!"

"Uh Raine, I don't think that's what he's doing…"

"So, you're sticking up for 'em because y'all have something going on between you too?"

"Wait, naw ah!"

"Okay then stay on my side!"

"Raine ding! I'm just saying Roc really ain't nothing to sweat about! That's all!"

"Lee, you're just saying that because he doesn't eyeball you the same way."

"Now, Raine, you know that ain't true."

"Hmmmm, I guess."

"It ain't! C'mon you be right there when I be checking out the other one he's always with."

"Oh, you mean his friend Vern?"

"Yeah him."

"Well, he does gotta pretty nose."

"Mmmm don't forget about his cute baby eyes."

"Yeah, I can't lie; he is cuter than J-Roc."

"Hmp, way cuter!"

"Yeah, but he's too soft!"

"Hmmm…you know what…Yeah, he is."

"I need someone who is a bit rough on the edge."

"Yeah, I feel you. Vern is just pretty."

"And lame."

"What about Rojo?"

"Hmp, he's like another, Vern."

"Hmmm, yeah but you liked him, though."

"Yeah, that's true."

"I think the only thing he needs to step up on is his English."

"Yeah, I say that's the only thing he is missing."

"When he speaks, I sometimes can't understand a single word he says."

"Wow! You too?! I thought I was the only one."

"I be seeing Tye, Lantino, and them with 'em sometimes and I be wondering how they know what he says."

"Shit, I ask myself the same questions sometimes."

"There come times where I just speak Spanish with him."

"Wow!"

"Yeah, it's like that sometimes."

"Girl, I don't blame you…Hmmm…what you think about Romelo?"

"You're talking about the boy we met after school at one of the programs?"

"Yeah…"

"Nann…Not my type."

"Mmmm, I think he's cute."

"Okay, I guess he's alright in my book because other girls I know says that he's gotta rap."

"It's true."

"Alright. Next."

"Big red."

"Heck, no!"

"Big boy get no love huh."

"Uh uh."

"Well, I know just one person who might have everything I need."

"Really?"

"Mmmmhmmm."

"You do?"

"Yep. Matter of fact, you've known 'em longer than I have."

"Wait, don't tell me. Is it Tyke?"

"Uh uh."

"Then, who?"

"Tino."

"Eeeeyuu! My brother?!"

"Yep."

"Yuck Lee! I can't check out my own brother!"

"I know Raine, I know. But if you could –"

"Ugh! Lee!"

"Alright let me stop."

"Yes, because you need to stop."

"Uh, sure."

"Hey…"

"Uh what's up…"

"Speaking of Lantino, what happened with you and him?"

"Ha ha…what's up between Tino and I, you ask?"

"Yeah, what's going on between you two?"

"Hmmm, has he told you anything?"

"Me? Uh no."

"What do you think so far?"

"Well, as of now I don't know what to say or think! That's why I'm asking you!"

"Okay I'll tell you what's going on…"

"Okay."

"Alright, we were seeing each other like that at first."

"You mean way before you went to Concrete?"

"Yeah…we had a lil' thing going, but right now, we're just laying things low."

"Like friends?"

"Yeah."

"But why? I don't get it."

"Well, since I came back, things just ain't been the same. I mean I stay with y'all, and he's cool, I'm cool, we all cooling and all but…him and I…just don't feel comfortable with each other like that anymore."

"Oh, so he feels the same way?"

"Yeah, because we both talked about it."

"I see."

"Hey, we tried to work it out though. I mean, at one point he and I were doing an open relationship."

"And that was a while after you came back, right?"

"Yeah."

"Too bad it ain't work out."

"Yeah, too bad. Our lil' fire seen its last days."

"So y'all just friends."

"Yeah, we think it's just better for us to keep it this way."

"Maybe it is…"

"Yeah…Hey, notice the wind stopped blowing since we came out through the subway?"

"Naw…I didn't even notice…"

"Yeah, it did. Since we came back on surface, I ain't feel any windblown pass us.

"Good, good. C'mon we should keep moving before it starts to pick up again."

"Just one block away, and we'll be back in your house."

With less than a block to go, both of them began striding, as Loraine suggested. As the entry to Loraine's building became more visible from walking distance, the girls come across a graffiti artwork in which they exchange a few comments on. It sat no more than ten feet away. On it, the girls noticed huge two-dimensional bubble letters that were done in red and white. Not all of the letters were completely filled in. However, they all spelled something that threw back a message. A message that a few people like the artist himself could grasp immediately…

"In the rough…," said Milleena reading out loud.

"Huh,"asked Loraine, who still hadn't figured out the letters. "What's that?"

"I don't know but that's what I'm reading on the wall he's tagging on."

"Is that what it says on there?"

"Yep. ."

"How do you know?"

"Raine, I do this stuff too. After all, that's what put me in boot camp for so long, remember?"

"In the rough… the hell is that supposed to mean?"

"I don't know."

"But you know how to read it."

"So…I don't know what he's tryna say. Since you so worried, why don't you go ask 'em."

"Girl, I don't even know him."

"Yeah, you do! That's Lantino's friend."

"Say who?"

"That boy that stays with y'all."

"Naw ah…"

"Ugh! Raine, you're starting to get on my nerves!"

"Is that really him?"

"Ugh! Yeah Raine! That's Tino's friend!"

"I ain't know he could do that…"

"Raine, you ain't remember I told you that Torris…Terres or Terrance…I believe that's his name…Whatever. Anyways, remember I told you that he could draw?"

"He could?"

"Ugh! Raine, you ain't listen to me when I told you that it wasn't Tino that sent you that letter, did you?"

"So, it wasn't him, huh?"

"For the last time Raine, NO…"

"Ding, he could draw…"

"Amp amp, I only told you that for the past 1500th time."

"Hey Lee, wait why's he stopping?"

"I think he's turning around."

The artist was wearing an all-black outfit, black baggy jeans, black belt, and a black leather jacket which belonged to Lantino. To guard his face against the fumes from the spray paint cans he used, he wore a cap and covered his mouth and nose with a red bandana. Just as Milleena thought, he turned around as soon as he stopped working on the graffiti artwork. He then quickly removed the bandana from his face, and his eyes began to widen as he stared back at Loraine and Milleena. "See, didn't I tell you that that was Tino's friend tagging on the wall," said Milleena as she confirmed that the artist was indeed Torence.

"Wait, wait!" said Torence. "Don't tell Ms. Tourez." He pleaded and dropped the spray cans unknowingly. "I found it like this! I promise!"

Hearing this, the girls paused and then took a glance at one another before they continued to look at him. He too stared back with his eyes and mouth still wide open. "Pl-pl-pl-pl-please d-d-d-don't tell Ms. Tourez," he said once more. Then he took off into the darkness.

"Terrance wait," said Loraine.

"Um, I think he heard you even though I know he ain't coming back this way," said a sarcastic Milleena.

"Why did he run?"

"Hmmm, I don't know, but he jetted that's for sure!"

"I think that's the first time I ever heard 'em talk."

"That's my first time seeing him so ALIVE."

"Yeah, I think that was my first time too."

"He's always so chill."

"And quiet."

"That too."

"Even though he ain't done, it looks good."

"Girl, who you're telling?!"

"I wish he could come back right now and finish it."

"Well, at least now I know who's been using up my spray cans."

"Maybe you could ask him for some pointers."

"HUH?"

"Hey Lee, I'm just saying."

"Anyways…You ready to go?"

"Yeah…"

"Good. Me too."

Hey, is that the same crescent moon and star I saw on my letter, Loraine thought. "Wait, Lee, there's some other stuff he tagged on the wall."

"Okay good, now could we go?"

"Um uh –"

"RAINE!"

"Uh, just gimme a minute."

"No! It's cold out, and this wind is starting to feel like a bunch of needles poking me in the face!"

"Just one 'lil minute –"

"RAINE!!"

"Whaaat, Lee!"

"I wanna go home, gosh!"

"Ugh! Fine! Okay! Let's go!"

"Don't forget he lives with us. So, you could have 'em put his autograph on your breast."

"Lee, I was just eyeing the tag. That's all."

"Yeah…uh huh."

From that point on, the subject of Loraine's conversation with Milleena on their way back centered around her supposed admiration for Torence's graffiti. The conversation went back and forth, and they carried it back through the ground floor to the elevators to Loraine's place. "I'm telling you I wasn't eyeing the tag," Loraine would say. And as a reply to Loraine's denial, Milleena would say "girl, please, go tell that to someone whose gonna believe that."

By morning, the conversation was done and over with for Milleena. Loraine, on the other hand, woke up thinking about it before starting her day. Thoughts leading back to her conversation with Milleena the night prior had stayed on her mind until she had reached the indoor shopping mall after school. It was then that her day finally began. Though it was mid-day, Loraine seemed to be having a good time as things suddenly turned around. She joined Milleena and a couple of girlfriends from school to window shop and tour around. The mall for now, seem like the new hang out spot till springtime emerged. A while later at the indoor shopping mall, Loraine and company ran into J-Roc who entertained them with his exaggerated tales about doing countless missions for the Vice Lords. He went on for several minutes, rambling about his experiences, and how it made him a "survivor." Sharing his stories and experiences with them also included expressing gestures, which his listeners found charming. However, Loraine, his main attraction, wasn't really tuned in to what J-Roc was saying. Apparently, her tuning into the stories really mattered to J-Roc as he continued to ramble on and make expressive gestures. Sometimes he'd even touch them as he'd talk about his experience.

Completely tuned out of what was being said, Loraine's focus was now set on a figure she noticed at a distance. Captivated, she kept a close eye on the figure which had shown up from the corner of the food court. Entering the scene, the figure was wearing an all-black outfit: a backwards cap, baggy pants, and a sweater. As he became more and more visible, Loraine also noticed that the figure had on Lantino's white sneakers which could only mean that it was Torence. While rambling away continuously with outlandish gestures, J-Roc all of a sudden just stopped what he was doing. "There goes my man," he said as he turned towards Torence's direction. "Hold on y'all I got some business to handle." Then he walked towards the sign by the food court, which is where Torence was posted and spoke to him for a few minutes. For every minute that passed, Loraine didn't take her eyes off Torence. Not even for a second. "Hey, Lee," she said.

"What's up," asked Milleena.

"That's him, ain't it?" said Loraine.

"That's who?" Milleena asked again.

"That's him!" once again saying, Loraine.

"Him who? Whose him?"

"It's him, Torance. Lantino's friend."

"You mean over there next to J-Roc?"

"Yes…"

"Ding Raine…You got some good eyes if you could spot 'em from there."

"What you mean? Lee, he ain't even –"

"Yeah, I know him," said Julisa, who cut off Loraine. "He's that boy that always stops by my house."

"Huh?" asked Loraine as she turned to her right to give Julisa a bewildered look. "You sure we talking about the same person?" she asked Julisa.

"Yeah, he sits in the park with us sometimes," answering an assured Julisa.

"Uh okay, so why's he stopping by your place?" once again asking a rather curious Loraine.

"Hmp, I don't know," answered Julisa. "He just shows up with your brother or other times he comes there asking for my cousin."

"He got kind of taller if you ask me," added Milleena. She sat there zeroing in on some details. "Maybe that's why I ain't notice him from here."

"Hmmmm, looks like they're done doing whatever it is that they're doing," said Julisa.

J-Roc, at that moment, folded up a piece of paper handed to him by Torence, carefully stashed it in his left back pocket of his jean pants and headed to where Loraine and company were sitting. This basically confirmed what was said by Julisa. While J-Roc was coming back towards Loraine and company's way, Torence left by the same way he entered. Just as he made his exit, he glanced at Loraine and her peers.

Thoughts ran through Loraine's mind as she examined everything that just happened. *That's weird; I wonder why he didn't come back with J-Roc to sit with us,* she asked herself. *Could it have been what I was wearing,* she thought. Feeling a bit conscious, she checked with Milleena for reassurance. "Lee," she said.

"Raine," Milleena replied.

"You gotta tell me something," said Loraine.

"Uh, okay. What?"

"Does my outfit look alright to you?"

"Uh, yeah Raine."

"You sure?"

"Um yeah."

"What about my hair?"

"What about it?"

"You think maybe if I had let it loose, he would've noticed me?"

"Raine, your hair is straight."

"Maybe I should have taken my jacket off, and then he would have wanna come sit with us."

"Raine, what are you talking about? With or without your jacket on, Roc will spot you. Here he comes as I speak."

Ugh…Not him dodo, she thought.

The day hadn't come to a complete turnaround for Loraine, though it ended better than it started. The next morning Loraine began her day in the bathroom where she spent more than two hours. Afterwards, she took over an hour to step out of her room. It soon became the story of the week as she turned this into a daily routine. Her daily routine also became unbearable for everybody in the house. Lantino was first to voice his dislikes towards Loraine's new ways of extended stays in the restroom. To add, he held no secrets about it either. Loriana also complained about Loraine constantly misplacing and wasting her perfumes or cosmetics. Milleena came last when she finally grew weary of Loraine consistently locking her out of the room. Torence seemed not to be disturbed about the complaints as he concentrated on his sketches for tattoo and graffiti designs.

On the dawn of February 14, Torence had made a stop at a local shop called the Roots. A few days ago, Lantino had told him The Roots made some of the best pizzas in town. So, curiosity had got the best of Torence that day. After finishing his third slice of pizza, Torence realized that the pizza shop was the perfect setting for him to concentrate on his drawings. Figuring that out, Torence closed his box and went back home. Later around noon, Torence returned with some of Milleena's art supplies to begin working on his sketches. He was able to work for about an hour or so. Away from everyone's complaints about Loraine's routinely times in the bathroom had Torence feeling like the pizza shop was a haven specifically made for him. Torence was one with his artwork, and the clerk working inside noticed that. He asked Torence a few times if he could get him something, but Torence shook his head "no" every time. A moment later, Loraine walked through the doors. Just seconds after stepping inside, the clerk assisted in placing her order. Once that was done, she leaned her back against the clerk's counter and sat comfortably on a stool. That's when she noticed Torence seated on a table near the bathroom at the far end of the shop. Within that very second, it was like she was back in that indoor mall again. Suddenly thoughts were running through her mind as she began to watch him. *Lee was right, I was into him that night he put up the tag on the alleyway,* she thought. *Oh, get a grip Loraine he ain't even my type. But I gotta admit, he's got this quiet confidence about him. And I like that...wait...but if I do...then...then could that mean that...I really do like him...I do...I guess I should probably go sit with him, so he doesn't feel so lonely sitting there by himself...Uh uh...let's see...Uh hey, Terrance I was just checking by to see if you wanted to grab a bite be-cause...uh uh I placed an order...Ummm...Nann. That sounds lame. Um hmmm...uh hey Terrance um...did you see my brother...uhhh_uh uh. He'll never buy that. Oh, here I know! I'll just say Lantino sent me to get some pizza! Yeah, that'll work.*

While Loraine was sitting by the clerk's counter deep in her thoughts, Torence was at the far end of the shop seated on a table that sat right next to a bathroom. Though he heard someone walk through the doors, his back was turned, and his mind was fixed on filling in one of his graffiti sketches. In spite of his back being turned he could tell that he was being watched, and he knew it wasn't the clerk. Nevertheless, he carried on and filled in his artwork. Right when he reached over to grab one of Milleena's colored pencils, he heard a voice, "Hi Terrance"."Hi Terrance," he heard once more. "Hi-Ter-rance," he heard for the third time. *Is this person talking to me?* He thought as he stopped what he was doing. "Ugh, Hi..." he heard again for the fourth time. *Yeah, yeah, this person really is talking to me*, he said to himself. He slowly turned around and saw Loraine.

"Oh hi, hello," she said rudely, "is your name Terrance?"

"Hmmm," Torence replied with a convoluted look all over his face.

"Yes, you!" said Loraine. "Boy, who else would I be talking to? Your name is Terrance, right?"

Staring back at her with a panned look now on his face, he corrects her with no sound of emotion in his tone: "My name's Torence, not Terrance."

"Ooops, uh...I know that..."

"You did?"

"Um...yeah."

"So how come you called me Terrance like three times then?"

"Uhhh..." She pauses.

"Don't sweat it."

Damn I feel like an ass, she thought. "Sorry...Is someone sitting here?"

"Naw...Just me."

"So, no one else is with you?"

"Nope...I'm the only one here."

"By yourself?"

"Yep."

"Sooo, what are you doing here?"

"Just needed to get away from the noise..."

"Ummm I'm lost...what noise are you talking about?"

"Back at Ms. Tourez house."

"Oh...you mean all the fussing and complaining that's been going on there?"

"Yeah, that."

"Oh...So that's why you left?"

"Yep...I needed a better place to concentrate."

"And so, you came here to a pizza shop?"

"Yep."

"Of all the places?"

"Yep."

"But this is a restaurant."

"And I don't hear any fussing."

"It is awfully quiet in here..."

"Yeah, and that's why I came here."

"Hmmm...Ain't know we were that loud."

"Yeah well, y'all are."

"Hmp."

"So, you ordered some food?"

"Oh me? Well, uh, I'm just here because my brother sent me."

"To pick up an order?"

"Yeah...that's all. Otherwise, I wouldn't have come here and run into you."

"That's weird..."

"What's weird about picking up food for my brother?"

"Naw, not you..."

"Then what?"

"Tino...I mean I thought I told him that I left a box for him in the fridge."

Ding, he caught me, she thought. "You did?"

"Yeah...I even remember seeing 'em eat a few slices before I left."

"Uh well...ummm Tino can sure eat." *Ugh, now I sound stupid for saying that*, she thought to herself.

"Yeah, had I known he was that hungry, I would've saved you the trip and got 'em some more."

Great. Now he just made me feel 'stupider' for saying that. "Oh really?"

"Yeah...Really..."

He's being such a smart ass...but it's ...cute. I wonder if he thinks I'm pretty. "Sooo..."

"Yeaah..."

"I have my hair tied back today?"

"Uh...okay..."

"So do you think it's cute?"

"Yeah...It looks pretty."

"What about when I let it loose? What do you think?"

"I think it's pretty."

"Yeah, but does it look better to you?"

"I-I don't know, but it's pretty though."

But not as pretty as that sketch you keep working on! Ugh! He keeps paying attention to his drawings! Don't I look good enough for 'em?

"What about my tank top? Do you think I should've come out here with this black one I have on right now?"

"Um uh…"

"I mean I have a red one like this back home. So, you think I should've probably brought that one instead?"

"Um naw…the black one."

"Here take a look for a minute and tell me what you think."

"Um…it-it-it looks…good…on you."

Ugh! Why won't he look me straight in the eyes?

"Mmm, you smell good."

"You like it?"

"Yeah…um…I mean…your perfume smells nice."

Hah! I knew it! He thinks I'm cute…could that be why he looks at me for five seconds. "Yeah well, it's my favorite. It's called Flirt."

"Hmmm…why is it called Flirt?"

"Because…Hmmmm…I don't know. That's just the name of the perfume bottle."

"So, it's called fffl-flirt?"

"Yes."

"Oh okay…So what is it?"

"What is what?"

"The name: Flirt."

"You mean like what does it mean? Is that what I think you're asking me?"

"Yeah. What is Flirt?"

"C'mon, you know what that is."

"I do?"

"Yeah. Everybody does."

"What is it?"

"You really don't know, do you?"

"Hmmm, what is it?"

"You know…it's like when two people are talking or something…wait a minute, no one ever flirted with you before, have they?"

"Umm, I don't know…"

"No one has, huh?"

"Uh maybe…"

She sighs, *Hmp, whatever.* "Anyways, what are you drawing?"

"Oh uh, this here's just a lil' sketch…"

"What about the other ones?"

"Oh…uh…they're just other sketches and stuff."

"Here, lemme see what you've got."

"Oh, uh wait –"

"Eww wow…Torence, this is really good!"

"Oh…yeah…"

"Damn you drew pictures of the dining area inside the pizza shop. Then you sketched out your own ideas for Roots. Ding and you even drew pictures of the pizzas!"

"Yeah, that's the one's I was eating earlier. Then gave to your brother."

"Damn…It looks so real!"

"I would've finish shading the bread crust, but I ain't want the pizza to get cold."

"Hey, is that a picture of me?"

"Oh that? Yeah, I had made a quick sketch."

"That looks like a picture of me on my thirteenth birthday."

"Yeah, I had looked off a photo Ms. Tourez had shown me back when you were at Concrete."

"Ding, you were able to do that today after only looking at my photo that one time."

"Yeah…It was the only new photo of you that Ms. Tourez had."

"Wow…"

"Here, Loraine, you could have it."

"You were the one who drew it, didn't you?"

"The tag on the wall…wait, I could explain. I-I mean I fo-fo-found it like that –"

"Wait, what?"

"Okay fine…But you won't tell your mom, will you?"

"Ugh! I ain't talking about that!"

"Huh?"

"I was talking about the picture in the letter."

"Oh…the letter…"

"You made it, didn't you?"

"Yeah, like a long while ago. So, you were able to get it?"

"Yes…"

"Do you still have it?"

"YES! It's folded up inside my room right now."

"Really?"

"Yes! I love it! Why didn't you ever say anything?"

"I never knew you had it. I didn't even think you'd ever get it."

After Torence said that, he took his eyes away from his sketches and finally made direct eye contact with Loraine. Once eye contact was made, not another word was said by neither of the two. Silence was in the air at that moment, and so was something else. A spark that neither of the two could deny. Torence's eyes began to get watery as he grew more and more aware of her beauty; he blinked constantly. He could feel a sharp pin poking his heart at every beat as his chest burned with nervousness. And the sweet scent of her perfume made it harder for him to breathe. Though Torence didn't say nor make a sound, he didn't have to because Loraine sensed his attraction for her. She smiled as she watched him struggle to cover it up. Clearly, Loraine was loving their moment together at Roots pizza shop. "Order number 190," shouted the clerk, "your food is ready!"

"Just sit it there, I'm coming!" said Loraine as she responded to the clerk. Directing her attention back to Torence, a question popped in Loraine's mind. "So, is someone meeting you here?" she asked.

"Hmmm, nope," he replied.

"So then why are you sitting here all by yourself?" asked Loraine.

"Beats me," again replying Torence as he quickly shrugged his shoulders.

"Um okay, well what are you doing later?"

"I'm a probably finish these sketches off later."

"Uh okay and then what?"

"I don't know; I'll probably get with someone who needs another tattoo sketched out."

"What about the dance?"

"What dance?"

"The dance at the concert tonight! Wait, don't tell me you didn't hear about it tonight?!"

"Uh nope."

"Really?!"

"Mmhm."

"Terrance-I mean Torence, what-what planet are you from? Everybody knows about the dance!"

"So, you're going?"

"Duh…"

"Oh. Okay."

"'Oh. Okay'…What do you mean 'Oh. Okay'? Do you have any idea what day it is?"

"It's…Saturday."

"But it's February 14th Torence!"

"I know…"

"Do you know what a boy does on this day?"

"Uh no…What?"

"He goes somewhere with a girl to have fun. He doesn't sit somewhere at a pizza shop."

"Oh."

"Ewww! Could you stop saying 'Oh'?"

"Okay."

"Ewww! You repeated it!"

"No, I said okay."

"Ugh! Whatever…just…don't say 'Oh'."

"Kay."

"So why aren't you going to the dance?"

"What dance?"

"Ugh! The dance at the concert. I just told you!"

"Oh, oh, oh yeah…that dance. Hmmm, cause I don't want to."

"But that's where everyone's gonna be at tonight!"

"Kay."

"That means you're gonna be all by yourself."

"I know."

Awkward…Hmmm, is he a virgin? "Hmmm, Torence."

"Yeah."

"Could I ask you something?"

"Sure."

"Have you…ever done it?"

"Have I ever done what?"

"Have you ever…done the thing?"

"What thing?"

"You know…the thing…"

Unfamiliar with the term associated with Loraine's question, Torence sat there completely unable to come up with a straight answer. "Don't hide in the bush," she said to him as he continued to look dumbfounded. Hearing her say that to him, Torence knew he had to come up with an answer quick rather it be right or wrong. "Um uh," he said as he got caught up trying to choose the right response. But then suddenly he was interrupted as the door opened. And just like that, their conversation was stopped by Milleena who happened to walk in. "Hey Raine," she said to Loraine, "you ordered my pizzas yet?"

"Yeah," answered Loraine, "why they're sitting right over there on the counter."

"Wait," said Torence, "I thought you said Lantino sent you to get some food for him?"

"Oh yeah, I did, didn't I?" answering Loraine.

"Raine, did you tell 'em that your brother sent you?" asked Milleena.

"Uh, yeah I did," answered Loraine.

"Now why would you tell 'em that, huh?" asking Milleena.

"Umm, excuse me Lee, but if you didn't notice, Torence and I were in the middle of something, ain't that right Torence," said Loraine.

"Um, yeah," replying Torence.

"Oh, oh well excuse me for barging in," said Milleena. "Hmmm what's going on here?"

"Um nothing," answering Loraine.

"Hmmm…more like something," said Milleena.

"Hmmm, like what?" asked Loraine.

"Don't play dumb," said Milleena. "If I ain't know y'all, I'd say y'all were on a date."

"Whatever Lee, it ain't like that," said Loraine.

"Not yet," again saying Milleena.

"Hey smiley, what you over there laughing about?" asked Loraine to Torence.

"Oh me? Uh nothing, nothing," laughed Torence.

"Nice sketches," said Milleena commenting on Torence's drawings.

"Yeah, thanks," replied Torence.

"Are those supplies mine?" asked Milleena to Torence.

"Oh, you mean these coloring pencils? Um yeah," answered Torence.

"I'm getting tired of you taking my stuff without asking," said Milleena to Torence.

"I was gonna bring it right back," said Torence.

"I know, but that's not the point," said Milleena. "Before you take something, you need to ask. I'm sure you've heard of something called common courtesy."

"Stuh! Girl please, he said he'll put it right back," said Loraine to Milleena.

"Hmp, anyways you ready to go Raine?" asked Milleena.

"Wait, right now? asked Loraine.

"Yes," answered Milleena.

"But I don't wanna leave him here by himself," said Loraine.

"Okay, well see if he wants to come," Milleena suggested to Loraine.

"Y'all could go," said Torence.

"It's okay," said Milleena, "you could come too."

"Namp," Torence declined.

"Let's go," said Milleena to Loraine.

"But wait," said Loraine to Torence, "are you sure?"

"Very," answered Torence.

"Oh, c'mon Raine," said Milleena, "you heard 'em. He said he's good. Now let's go. Julisa and the others are waiting for us. That's where I said we'd meet her at."

"But Lee he looks lonely," said Loraine.

"I'm alright," said Torence to Loraine.

"See he's good," said Milleena to Loraine, "now let's go. My pizza is getting cold."

"Alright then," said Loraine to Milleena.

"Bye," said Torence.

"Happy Valentines," said Loraine to Torence.

Chapter 16: Nights to Remember

Part 5: Tor'raine

On the dusk of February 14th, Lantino came back home from his date with Julisa and hung out in the living room for a little while before deciding to join Torence upstairs in the top floor. Making it to the top floor, he noticed that Torence was leaning forward against the bars on the balcony. When he reached the balcony, he did the same thing as well to enjoy the lovely view outside. "So, what's up," he asked Torence.

"Not much," answered Torence, "just enjoying this breeze."

"You too, huh?"

"Yep. So, what about you?"

"Ah, ain't much happen on my end either."

"How'd your day go with Julisa?"

"Hmmm, I guess I could say it was cool."

"What'd you do?"

"We saw a movie. Then after that, we went everywhere and stopped at the shopping mall. Couldn't take her to Roots because it was really busy there today."

"Oh okay…cool, so did she let you do it?"

"Hmmm, naw."

"Man, c'mon what did y'all really do?"

"Hmmm, I'm telling you that was it."

"Oh…Okay."

"So, anything happened on your end?"

"I heard there was a dance today."

"Oh yeah, there was. It was at a concert."

"Yeah, that's what I heard too."

"Did you go?"

"Naw. Did you?"

"Yeah, but I ain't stay out there for too long."

"Hmmm, how come?"

"Julisa told me that she can't stay out too long. She's on a curfew."

"Heard everybody was out there."

"Yeah, they were, but you ain't miss out on much."

"Hmp. Okay."

"Yeah, they do that every year for Valentine's Day."

"Hey you know what? That same person who told me about the dance said Valentines to me."

"You mean Happy Valentines?"

"Yeah...what does that mean?"

"Oh brother." Lantino laughs.

"What's so funny?"

"I forgot that there are still some things that you don't know about yet."

"Oh okay...So what's that?"

"It's a holiday for boyfriends and girlfriends to celebrate. It comes every year on the 15th."

"Naw, wait she told me it's on the 14th."

"Oh yeah, yeah they're right. It comes on the 14th."

"Hmmm...Okay."

"So, what's up?"

"Huh...Oh nothing."

"So, nothing else went down on your end today?"

"Hmmm, I finally went to that pizza shop you told me about. That's it."

"Okay...So what's UP?"

"How come you keep asking me that?"

"Cause it looks like you're thinking deeply about something, and I wanna know what's going on UP there. That's why I'm asking you what's up?"

"Actually, I am..."

"Hmmm, yeah I could tell."

"I have been thinking a lot these past few days..."

"Okay, talk to me. What's up?"

"It's about this girl..."

"A girl, man Torence that shouldn't be anything new, even for you."

"Yeah, yeah but this one's different."

"Different like how?"

"Hmmm, I-I don't even know."

"Who is she?"

"That's the thing I know her, but I don't know her like that."

"Okay so you know of her, but you don't know her?"

"Yeah, you get what I'm saying?"

"Yeah, yeah I getcha. So, so lemme ask ya this."

"What?"

"She looks good?"

"YES."

"Mmmm, how does she look?"

"She…she looks pretty yo…"

"Is she black, white, Puerto Rican, what? Tell me what she looks like?"

"Oh, she's black, but she's also mixed. Sometimes I hear her speak Spanish."

"Hmmm, okay. Go on."

"Um, she's light-skinned, short, and she's got long hair. Um uh, she likes to wear her hair tied, but other times she'll let it loose."

"When's the last time you seen her?"

"Stuh! Today."

"For real?"

"Yeah."

"When?"

"Like just an hour after I dropped off the box of pizza in the fridge. She was wearing a jacket with a black tank top underneath, and man she smelled good."

"Damn I wish I was there."

"Hey Tino…"

"Yo."

"This might sound funny to you…"

"What is it?"

"Hmmm, nann I don't think I wanna say it."

"C'mon what?"

"Hmmm, nann…"

"Oh, c'mon Torence just say it for crying out loud."

"Alright fine…I notice that same girl always smells like perfume."

"And you feel like she's always trying to get your attention with it, ain't it?"

"Yeah."

"That's cause she is."

"Huh?"

"I'm telling you, she knows what she's doing."

"But how do you know for sure?"

"I can tell based on what you just told me."

"You sure?"

"Trust me…"

"Hmmm, yo."

"What up?"

"You wanna know what else is funny?"

"What?"

"I can tell her eyes be on me sometimes."

"Whoa! For real? She be eyeing you too?"

"Yeah! Like the other week I was at the shopping mall near the north side."

"Oh, you mean Gurnee Mills, right?"

"Yeah, that one…"

"Oh okay, yeah…"

"Yeah so, I went there to meet up with J-Roc because you remember he wanted me to sketch the dices with bunny, right?"

"Oh yeah, he kept coming to our house about that tattoo design."

"Well on that day he gave me money for that, that same chick was there with a few more of her homegirls. I saw her sitting on the bench with all of her homegirls and man, let me tell you, she just wouldn't stop looking at me."

"Ding, how long was she staring at you?"

"Um, I say it had to be at least until I left."

"Ding, you sure her eyes were on you that long?"

"Man Tino, I'm telling you, I could feel them all over me."

"Hmmm, sure it wasn't Roc?"

"I'm sure Tino because there have been other times."

"Really?"

"Yeah, that wasn't the only time."

"Tell me about the other times."

"Okay like uh, there was one time where Tye and I were playing cue ball with Vern and some other people…"

"Wait, so y'all was at the Rec that day?"

"Yeah, yeah…"

"Okay so yeah, what happened?"

"Then she showed up and came through with two of her friends. One of them looked like Lee and the other one, I wasn't sure about."

"What did they want?"

"To hang out, I guess." Torence shrugged his shoulders.

"So, what did they do the whole time y'all were there?"

"Well, I saw Vern went to go talk to 'em, and Tye said a few things to 'em after we were done playing cue ball."

"Hmmm, what about you?"

"I worked on some sketch Tye was tryna pay me to draw."

"So, you ain't say nothing to 'em?"

"Naw…I just worked on that sketch while Vern and them talked to her."

"So, you just sat there and sketched out a design?"

"Yeah, but after I was done I caught her –"

"What? Eyeing you?"

"Yeah, just like that other time in the shopping mall. And all the other times."

"Hmm…"

"What? What are you thinking about?"

"Hmmm, you know what…I think…she likes you Torence."

"She likes me? Naw…"

"Yeah, she likes you Torence."

"Nann…It can't be that…"

"But it gotta be that…Naw, it is that."

"Yeah, but Tino how can you be sure?"

"From what I'm hearing, it's got to be that. Yeah Torence, that girl likes you."

"But I be seeing her talk to boys who got fresh clothes and they're taller than us."

"So…"

"So?"

"Yeah! Right now, she's got her eye on you which means that it's your chance to step up."

"Yeah but –"

"But what?! You scared of her?"

"Naw…"

"Is she ugly?"

"NAW…"

"Okay so she's hellafine, so what's up? What's holding you back?"

"Okay well, that time after I had caught her, she turned her head real quick and kept talking with Vern and them."

"That's cause she was trying to play it off!"

"Huh?"

"She got caught staring too hard, so she tried to make it seem as if she wasn't staring at you!"

"Hmmm…"

"C'mon Torence, can't you tell?"

"Hmmm…what about J-Roc?"

"What about 'em?"

"I always see him around her sometimes. You think that might be her –"

"What? Boyfriend?"

"Yeah…"

"You know what? Bump J-Roc!"

"Bump J-Roc?"

"Yeah, forget 'em. If anything, you'll find out from her."

"Yeah…Yeah…I'll find out…from her…"

"Yeah, yeah now you're thinking Torence."

"Yeah, but hey Tino."

"What up?"

"Hmmm, sometimes I notice that, hmmm, nann forget it."

"Man shoot it!"

"Hmmm…Sometimes, she looks at me as if she's staring right through me or something. I-I don't know how to explain it."

"Is that when you're talking to her or something?"

"Yeah, or when I'm by her."

"It's a deep stare, huh?"

"Yeah, and whenever I stare back for too long, I be feeling nervous."

"You feel like a needle's poking you in the heart, ain't it?"

"Yeah, yeah and my heart be giggling, man! Then I start blinking my eyes a lot because they start feeling watery!"

"Does your lips wiggle too?"

"Yeah, and I don't be knowing why."

"Stuh! I know that feeling."

"Oh yeah, you do?"

"Yeah, sometimes I could hear my heartbeat."

"Damn that's just like me."

"I know; I go through that too."

"Ding I thought I was the only one."

"Naw…You ain't alone."

"How do you cover it up because I be having a hard time?"

"You can't. You just gotta get used to it."

"For real?"

"Yeah, like me, I'm used to it. Though sometimes the feeling comes back to me when I talk to Julisa."

"How do you get used to it?"

"I don't know, but once you're used to it, you could control it."

"You can?"

"Yeah, and tell you what, never admit it to her that you're nervous."

"Ummm, why?"

"Just don't."

"I-I don't get it…"

"Look, just listen to me: Even if she can tell that you're nervous, never ever admit it."

"Okay, but what does it mean when she does it though?"

"What? You mean when she does the deep stare?"

"Yeah…"

"It probably means that she thinks you're interesting. Or, or maybe it means that you're just different, and you stand out."

"Stand out?"

"Yeah, yeah…You stand out, and so she wants to know more about you…"

"Is that what Julisa thinks when she does that to you?"

"Um uh…I don't know…"

Chapter 17: Tough Love

A couple of years had gone by and things in the area didn't necessarily change. However, the people residing within it did. It was spring, and the Windy City was experiencing its best time of the year. Though a cold breeze could be felt once in a while, Torence wasn't bothered by it because he had been living in Chicago for three years now. Working as a small-time artist and applying the required knowledge necessary to get around the city gave him enough reasons to call himself a Chicagoan. Although, he still had characteristics for mysteriously appearing out of nowhere and being aloof. His relationship with the Tourezes had become much better than where it started three years ago. His legal guardian, Ms. Tourez, who found favor in him from the start, now considered him her son; and her daughter, Loraine, finally warmed up to him over the years. In fact, they became more acquainted overtime.

On a nice sunny Thursday afternoon at approximately 5:17p.m, Torence was stepping out of a local tattoo shop to go to the park. There Loraine was seated at the spot which was once shared by Lantino and Milleena. After having gone through an experience such as the one in boot camp, Loraine had made progress in her behavior as well as her academics and never looked back. With her best friend, Milleena, getting ready to graduate this year, Loraine's now entering a pivotal time of her schooling. "Torence, where are you?" she asked as she waits for him at the spot. The wind coming from the breeze outside starts to pick up and blows against the leaves. She heard some sounds, which in her mind were sticks and leaves falling from the trees. She made a quick turn to find that Torence was right behind her. "Whoa, Torence!" she said as she took a deep breath.

"Raine babe, you okay?" asked Torence taking a glance above his right shoulder as he approached the bench.

"Ugh! Gosh!"

"What?"

"You! Ew!"

"What…what about me?"

"You're always showing up out of nowhere!"

"Uh, I do?"

"YES! And Torence boo, you need to stop doing that!"

"What do you mean? I just came from the other way."

"Keep doing that and I'm a start thinking that you're some kind of spook from that house at Ridgeway."

"But Raine babe, I just came from the other…wait…did you say house at Ridgeway? Wait you actually went?"

"Nan amp! Let's not even talk about that place."

"But Raine bab–"

"Na amp!"

"Ba–"

"AMP...Next subject"

"Fine okay…"

"Good boy…Sooo…"

"Hmmm, sooo…"

"Uh, did you leave something behind before you got here?"

"Leave something behind? Wait, I ain't leave…ooops yeah, that's right."

He reaches out and hugs her flirtatiously. "Mmhm, I better get my hug." Said a pleased Loraine.

"Mmmm, you smell very good."

"Thanks, boo."

"Is it Flirt you're wearing?"

"Yep. My favorite."

"I know."

"So, boo how do you like my hair today?"

"Mmmm, I like how you've got it tied back."

"You think I should've let it loose?"

"Mmmm, nann…it looks fine like this."

"Really?"

"Yeah…"

"Hmmm, why? What makes you say that?"

"Uh well, I like the way you have it right now…"

"Um…okay. Anyways, I have been thinking about adding a blonde streak on my hair."

"A blonde what?"

"You know, a blonde streak. I wanna have that run through my hair."

"Hmmm, Raine babe, I think you should keep it the way you have it now."

"Boo, you think I should?"

"Mmhm."

"Hmp, I guess you're right…So today I wore my pink tank top to school. Think it looks good on me?"

"Yeah, it looks right. Hey babe, how'd today go in that class?"

"Academic Prep?"

"Yeah, I think that's the class."

"Stuh! Stressful."

"What's bugging you out?"

"The SATs."

"What is it?"

"The test I told you about."

"Oh yeah, that."

"It ain't even that really."

"If it ain't that, then what is it?"

"Sta, don't ask…"

"Umm, babe what is it?"

"I'm thinking about graduating early."

"Okay, so do that."

"Boo…"

"What?"

"It's really not that simple."

"Hmmm, what's not that simple?"

"Graduating early…to do that boo, that means I gotta earn all of my credits by the end of the summer."

"Think you can do it, babe?"

"Yeah but…"

"But what babe?"

"It's gonna be a lot of headaches."

"Think you'll pass the test."

"Yeah, but I don't have to take it though."

"For real?"

"Yeah, that's only if I wanna go to college."

"Are you gonna take it then?"

"Well, Julisa already took it, and since Lee signed up to take it, I have been thinking about it. But I'm not sure yet."

"I heard Julisa's about to graduate."

"Who'd you hear that from?"

"Tye…"

"Oh, her cousin's badass."

"She is, isn't she?"

"Yeah, she is. I even hear that she's gunna go to college or she's trying to."

"Oh ding…I didn't hear about that."

"You know Milleena's graduating this year too."

"Damn, her too? Wow, I ain't know that, but now I do."

"She told me that she might get straight A's for the first time."

"Hmmm, babe, you think maybe that's why she ain't been by the house lately?"

"Hmmm, I don't know. I couldn't tell you because I don't know what's going on with her unless it's about school."

"Hmp…Seems like everyone's ch –"

"Torence boo!"

"Huh? Uh, what babe?"

"Sit up, sit up! I need you to sit facing my way!"

"Uh, uh okay…what's up?"

"Look at me in the eye…"

"Um…okay."

"I have some questions for you."

"Questions?"

"Yes, and I need you to answer them right away."

"Uh, right away?"

"Yes…That means no thinking in between to answer them, which also means that you better know the answer when I ask you my questions."

"Um…okay."

"So, boo you ready?"

"Um yeah. What's the question?"

"Torence!"

"What babe?"

"You better get this right!"

"Uh…okay…"

"You better not mess this up!"

"Uh…okay…"

"Alright, so my first question for you boo is…when did we first meet?"

"When did we first meet?"

"YES, boo…When did we first meet?"

"You and I met outside Ms. Tourez's building."

"HUH?"

"Well, I met you while I was standing outside. You were still inside the house, but you were looking through the window."

"You mean I was poking my head out the window."

"Yeah, yeah that's what I meant."

"You sure that's how it went boo?"

"Babe I remembered it like it happened a week ago."

"REALLY boo?"

"Yeah, that day Lantino and I were getting ready to go check out the Southside, but then you called him to come back upstairs because Ms. Tourez needed to talk to him real quick. So, waiting for him, I stood there, looked up, and saw you at the window."

"Hmmm, what did I say to you again?"

"Hmmm, I think you told me to wait outside because your mom only needed to see Lantino."

"I said that to you?"

"Yep."

"I did?"

"Uh huh."

"Awww…"

"Then you asked me what I was looking at."

"Boo, is that really what I said to you that time?"

"Yep."

"And you say that's how it all happened right? My meeting you?"

"Yep."

"Didn't that happen almost three years ago?"

"Yep. Uh huh."

"Ding and you still REMEMBER?"

"As if it happened last week…"

"Aww Torence…"

"Yep, I still remember."

"Okay so anyways that's just one question. I still have another one for you to answer."

"Okay…what's your next question?"

"My next question for you Torence….is…On what month did you and I finally decide to hook up?"

"April…"

"April?"

"Yeah, we hooked up in April."

"Sure about that?"

"Raine babe…I'm sure."

"Torence boo, I was about to SMACK you so hard if you ain't get that question right."

"So, babe, since I got both the answers to the questions right then, that means I get some sugar, right?"

"Actually boo, you got one of 'em wrong."

"Wait, wait whaaat?"

"The answer I wanted to hear on the first question boo was February 14th."

"February 14th?"

"Yes, now I know you remember that day! It was on Valentine's Day!"

"Oh, you're talking about that day you and I hung out at Roots?"

"Yeah…wait what you mean 'hung out'? You and I had a nice time there, remember?"

"We did…um yeah, uh I remember."

"It was Valentine's Day."

"Yeah, it was on Valentine's Day, wasn't it?"

"Duh, I remember the sketches you made. I'll never forget the one you drew of me."

"Yeah, I remember giving it to you that day. Hey wasn't there a concert going on that day?"

"Yeah, there was one that day. It was Valentine's Day concert."

"Hey babe wait a minute…"

"What happen boo?"

"You say that was the first time we met, but didn't we already know each other by then?"

"Yeah, we did, but that day at Roots was like our first time ever talking to each other."

"But we talked to each other sometimes, right?"

"Right, we did but we were like hi and bye like most of the time. For the longest, I didn't even get your name right. I just knew you as Lantino's friend. At one point, you had to help me get your name straight."

"Wow…I remember: It was like that at some point."

"Yeah, it was…But hey boo you know what, though?"

"What babe?"

"Because I liked how you were able to remember the first time you met me means that you earned a treat. Plus, your answer to my question was said without you having to take a second to think, which means that you deserve it."

She reaches down and kisses him. "Mmmm, you're…rewards…are good," said Torence.

"Mmmm, don't get too happy now."

"Mmmm, okay babe I'll try not to."

"Mmmm, good boy. So, boo you told my brother, right?"

"Uh, told your brother about what?"

"You know, about us."

"About us, you and I…Yeah, yeah."

"So, you talk to him right?"

"Oh him? Yeah, yeah."

"Sooo…"

"Sooo…uh yeah?"

"Did he trip or what?!"

"He tripped?"

"No, I'm asking you if he tripped out…"

"Oh, who him? Uh yeah…I mean naw."

"I'm sorry. HUH?"

"Naw, naw Tino ain't trip."

"You never told 'em, did you?"

"Huh? Wait, what do you mean?"

"You haven't told 'em a word."

"Raine babe I did."

"No you ain't."

"But I did."

"No you ain't."

"Babe…I'm telling you…I did."

"Boy, you better stop your lying."

"But I –"

"You know what I'm going home."

"Babe wait, wait-waaaiiit."

"No, no, no let go of me! I wanna go home!"

"Aw babe, c'mon…"

"C'mon let's go."

"Okay, okay fine. You're right, I didn't tell 'em."

"Hmp, I know."

"But-but-babe…You have to understand –"

"Ugh! Understand what! You said you were gonna talk to 'em last week!"

"Right, and-and I did, but –"

"But what! He's supposed to know by now! I mean, it's only been a while."

"Babe I know, but you see a lot is going on –"

"Ugh! Last time you told me that you weren't feeling right about telling 'em, and now you're saying that a lot is going on!"

"But babe, there is…"

"Okay, so a lot is going on, but my brother's gonna have to know about us sometime down the line."

"And babe, trust me, he will."

"Alright then, so what's holding you back?"

"Babe I'm-I'm gonna tell him."

"You still didn't answer my question."

"Ugh!"

"Hey! Look at me Torence!"

"OKAY."

"Good. Now again, what's the hold up?"

"Um…Something…"

"You ain't waiting on me to have your baby, right?!"

"Baby? Oh naw."

"Good because that's a LONG way from now!"

"Something…Something…came up last week when I talked to 'em."

"What? You scared of my brother? Is that it?"

"What?"

"That's what it is, isn't it?"

"What you talking about?"

"You're scared of Lantino?"

"What? No."

"Okay then, be a man for me and tell him."

"Raine babe, you already know why I ain't feel right about telling 'em. Remember, last time I told you that you're his sister and I ain't know how he would take it. I ain't wan 'em to feel disrespected?"

"Yes boo, I remember, and that was nice to know that you were trying to be respectful."

"Remember the things I told you that he told me when he thought that J-Roc was trying to run a game on you?"

"Boo, I never forgot."

"I would've told Lantino last week, but…"

"But what boo?"

"Something…happened…"

"Like what?"

"Something happened and now A LOT is going on."

"What's going on?"

"Something you don't wanna know."

"C'mon, talk to me!"

"Stuh…"

"Talk!"

Torence sits there without a word.

"Talk!"

He took a large gulp.

"Talk!"

"That's the thing; I can't."

"It has something to do with that fight y'all got mixed in, right?"

"Stuh…Raine babe, it does."

"Since then, he's been doing a lot of things different lately. He comes home late now. He's been coming home with more scars and bruises on his face. Sometimes he'll even step out with that big red leather jacket that I always see 'em wear. He doesn't even come to school much now. There are nights where he doesn't come home at all. I also notice that he doesn't smile. I mean, can you think of the last time you've seen 'em smile or laugh boo?"

"Hmmm, you know what…naw I can't."

"Okay, so it ain't just me then…"

"Hmp…"

"I'd say the weirdest thing about Lantino right now is when he doesn't say anything after mami fusses at him. I ain't realize that till the day mami brought it up while asking me about 'em."

"Wait, she's been asking you stuff about 'em?"

"Yeah boo…"

"Damn."

"He's in some kind of trouble, isn't he? Or he's causing some kind of trouble?"

"Babe…just …leave it alone."

"No! Tell me!"

"Stuh!"

"Look I wanna know what's going on! So, tell me!"

"I CAN'T!"

"Why? Don't you love me?!"

"Yeah, I do…"

"Okay so you shouldn't keep things from me!"

"But babe, telling you this would be like breaking the G-code."

"Huh?"

"The G-code…Pretty much, if I say something, then I'm basically putting his case out there. And I don't want that. That's why I can't tell NOBODY."

"Torence boo…"

"Ugh!"

"Just tell me…"

"I-I…can't –"

"PLEASE boo…"

"I-I –"

"For me…"

"Stuh…"

"Do it for me…"

"Ugh!"

"Boo…you don't have to tell me everything."

"Fine, but Raine babe…"

"What's up, boo?"

"You can't tell your mom this."

"Uh, I –"

"YOU CAN'T tell Ms. Tourez."

"Okay, okay…so what's going on?"

"Lantino leveled up in the gang –"

"Say what?!"

"Lantino's…down with the VLs. I mean it wasn't by choice…You see deep in the game things…Ra-Ra-Raine babe you-you listening…babe –"

"WHAT THE FUCK!!!"

Some weeks ago, several street fights took place within the Westside region. A fight led to a riot; the riot involved a bitter fight with the Gangster Disciples, their most hated rivals. Unfortunately, both Torence and Lantino, as well as their friend, Tyberius, all got tangled up in the riot. Since then, more and more Gangster Disciples have been showing up in the grounds in which the Vice Lords claim as their territory. Tyberius, who's always given his set a bit of an edge, has become more aggressive since his most recent encounter with the Gangster Disciples. Due to his admirable efforts in fending off the Gangster Disciples that day, Vice Lords from nearly every set have acknowledged him as their lead member. After the riot took place, Torence managed to stay low key. However, the same couldn't be said for Lantino. Since joining the gang at age thirteen, Lantino's primary place as a Vice Lord gangster was to be their look-out. This is a person stationed at a specific area to keep an eye out for any potential troubles while a function is in session. But with Tyberius now assuming his leadership role as one of the top hats of the Vice Lords, Lantino has been appointed as his scout. With the Vice Lords now being outnumbered by their rivals, the Gangster Disciples, Tyberius has turned to Lantino to find him new members to recruit. Under the pressure of trying to meet a certain desirable number of potential recruits every week, Lantino drops out of high school. Concerned about Torence's involvement in the gang, Lantino made sure he stayed out of it by recommending him as an apprentice at a local tattoo shop. Carrying out his new responsibility as Tyberius' scout has tarnished his relationship with Julisa and seemed to be creating a problem back home.

Back home, Lantino's relationship with the Tourezes seemed to be returning to where it started three years ago. Loriana, his legal guardian, is always complaining about him. So, to distance himself away from the negative energy back home, Lantino, as he did three years ago, spent his time elsewhere. He didn't have Torence to hang out with as much anymore because Torence's time was occupied at the tattoo shop. So, putting his motivation towards scouting pre-gang potentials, Lantino met, hung out, and got to know more people this way.

Friday afternoon had now marked the fourth week since the riot broke out. It was early May. The day started out at Stone Park, a territory which the Vice Lords by now had established as their main headquarters, and a mandatory hood meeting was taking place. Due to early release, an unusual amount of people had shown up to the meeting. The number of people present at the meeting included some that had familiar as well as unfamiliar faces. It was well over an hour and a half since Torence and Lantino left the tattoo shop to join Tyberius and the gang at the headquarters. Tyberius, who had arranged the meeting, was one of the speakers there tonight. "Weeks ago…We…sent a message! We…sent a message! Y'all wanna know what that message was? The message sent was that beat down we gave 'em weeks ago out here in our turf. You see y'all, we let 'em know that this here is our turf! VL turf!! What?! So they run things down South! And yeah, they got the East locked down! Oh, but they think they're gonna run us out our territory?! Stuh! How they gonna do that if not nann one of 'em can even whoop me?! How?! Let me tell y'all! It took almost four of 'em to put me down! Hah! And you know what?! Ain't nann one of 'em came close! Matter of fact, Five-O had to take me off them! Yeah, that's right! Five-O!! Five muthafuckin Oh! So, you see a GD can't take a VL out one on one, and they know that, that's why they ride out in packs. So tonight, after we spread out, I want y'all to hang tight. This is how we're gonna lock the blocks down. This is how I want all the blocks locked down! When they hit again we're gonna clap back mob deep! Hah, they won't even know what hit 'em...But hey if Five –O gives ya the business...then lemme tell y'all what I do...Blah say, blah say, blah say, questions, questions, questions and no answer...Questions, questions, and more questions. Questions this, questions that...Questions here, questions there, questions everywhere. Still, no answers because I don't know nothing about nothing. So, what this means is from now on no one's gonna rat on another nigga! From now on...No nigga is gonna rat on another nigga...Till then...ALL IS WELL!"

Once his message was delivered, Tyberius then stuck his index, middle, and thumb out from his right hand and raised his arm high in the air. Modeling after him, the rest of the members did the same thing all in unison saying, "All is well." The selected fingers raised are hand signals representing the gang's initials, VL for Vice Lords. Clearly, Tyberius had become the heart of the gang that night at the meeting. His demeanor, his attitude, and his choice of appearance seem to exemplify the ideal style of a Vice Lord gangster. Just the sound of his voice said more than his words that night at the meeting. His presence alone spoke volume to every member there, including Torence and Lantino. Both of them, who by now were on their way back home once the meeting was over, had a lot to talk about.

"Ding, did you see Tye out there tonight?" Asked Lantino.

"Yeah," answered Torence, "I see he's been pushing them caddies."

"Sta, Rence, who you're telling? It looks like it made 'em bigger!"

"Yeah, it did. Can't none of them GDs touch 'em now."

"Naw, ain't a single one of them wanna knock with 'em! He's got power, bread, and mad respect out here in the game."

"Yeah…The way he looked out there tonight, I'd say he runs the West now."

"Sta! Forget that! He could go anywhere in Chi town now."

"Not everywhere…Remember, the GDs are all over the Southside."

"Naw, he could show up down there too! There's a lot of us down there hiding."

"Hmmm, maybe he could step foot out there."

"He will when he wants to. Tye is strong, and he's got mad respect."

"Yeah, the VLs tonight showed mad love for him out there."

"Yep, his reputation out here is set. He probably doesn't have to throw up the signals or rock the star anymore when he goes to the other sides."

"Yeah, he probably doesn't…Hmp, remember when we started chilling with 'em more?"

"Yeah, that was like three years ago, I think."

"Ding, he got so hot."

"Sta! Tye always was. He wasn't that much different then."

"Hmmm…"

"Trust me, Torence; I saw the heat coming. He just needed something like that last fight to finally make 'em pop."

"The GDs better look out now…"

"Yeah, they do. Yo did you see how he popped Benito dead in the face?"

"You're talking about four weeks ago by the corner store?"

"Yeah."

"Uh huh, I was right there."

"Ding, ain't know Tye could fight that good."

"Yeah, me too. I think there were three people on him at that time."

"Yeah, there was."

"Damn!"

"Yeah, but you see, he got better after some time."

"Hmp, I thought Bear was our best fighter."

"Naw, Tye could take 'em."

"Hmmm, how about Train?"

"You mean Tye or Train?"

"Yeah, which one would you pick?"

"Hmmm, I don't know...I say it's a tie."

"So, you think Train would whoop Bear?"

"He could take him."

"But I've always heard that Bear's the best fighter, though."

"Naw...Y'all just think that because Bear is big. That's why everyone's always saying that none of the GDs would jump him because he's too big."

"True, he would be the last one they'd mess with for that reason."

"See, and that's why everyone's always saying that he's the best fighter. Otherwise, I know I could take 'em. Even you could take on Bear, Torence."

"Me??"

"Yeah, real shit!"

"Yeah, but what about the first time?"

"Man, he only had you because you were a lot smaller back then. Plus, your arms were too short to box with cuz."

"Uh yeah they were too short..."

"Too short. But things are different now that you got taller. Tell you what Torence..."

"What?"

"I say if you rush 'em like you did last time then you'll nail 'em."

"Hmmm, I don't know. I'll have to see next time we run to 148th."

"Hey, wait a minute, ain't that where the brawl happened at?"

"The last one we were in, yeah."

"Sta, ha ha ha ha! Rence, you stupid."

"Ha ha ha ha! I know…"

"Ding you know what? I ain't know how we were gonna get out of that boy…"

"Oh, you mean the fight?"

"Yeah, I mean, there were like five GDs you, Tye, and I were stepping up against."

"Yeah, I know. I was saying the same thing."

"Tye gotta a lot of heart walking across the street just to fight Nito and the Folks."

"Yeah man, he do…Say, what did happen after the cops cuffed 'em?"

"Well, because he's eighteen now, the cops pretty much locked 'em up."

"Hmmm, I know that, but what I mean is how'd he come back so soon?"

"Oh, well what I heard was that because of cases of self-defense, the charge on him was lowered to disturbing the peace."

"Oh…Hmmm, who'd you hear that from?"

"Julisa told me that."

"Uh…Oh okay. So, how'd she know that?"

"Well, they live together…"

"Hmmm, she probably would be the first to know."

"Something else she told me was that Tye's scheduled for another court date."

"Oh, for real? When?"

"Like in late May. Just days before Julisa's graduation."

"Damn…"

"I know right."

"Think he'll make it."

"Hmmm, I don't know. But if he can't, then I don't know who it'll hurt more: him or Julisa? I mean for Julisa, I hear that the graduation is gonna be a big day for her, and probably the best thing that's ever happened to her family. So for Tye to miss this…Ouch! That's gonna hurt."

"Ump, I think it's gonna hurt more for Tye."

"What about Julisa? I bet you, she'd wanna see her cousin there that day."

"Hmmm, with Nobles running things that day in court, I couldn't tell you."

"Nobles…Who's that?"

"Nobles…Kendrick Nobles…You don't remember the Sheriff out here?"

"Hmmm, naw…I mean they use to just say he was rough."

"Yeah, well that's him, and he's the new judge that Tye's gotta see that day."

"Oh, damn…"

"Yeah…Damn."

"Hmp, I hope all is well with 'em that day so that he could come."

"Me too."

"Hey well, you know Milleena's graduating too?"

"Straight up?"

"Straight up man! And you know what?"

"What?"

"I even hear that she's gonna get her name listed on the honors list or something like that."

"Di-di-ding! Did you say the honors list? Shit, I ain't know her ass was that smart!"

"What? The honors list means you're smart?"

"YEAH!"

"Oh…Well, uh okay…"

"Ding, I had no clue she was that smart…I mean, she wasn't dumb. I used to always let her do my work back when we had the same class. I just never knew she was that smart."

"So now what are they gonna do since they're finished with school?"

"Oh, Julisa told me that she's going to college."

"She really is, huh?"

"Yeah, like about three different schools wrote to her already."

"Ding, that's good to see someone out here made it."

"Sta! Even though I'm smart, you won't see me cram my head in those books like that."

"Naw?"

"Hah! Hell naw!!"

"But Tino, you should."

"Hmp, why?"

"Because Tino, once you're done with school, people are gonna come at you with more respect."

"Respect huh?"

"Yeah man. Ms. Tourez says it all the time. I mean hasn't she told you this before?"

"Yeah, she has…Maybe too many times, and you know what I think, Rence?"

"What?"

"I think school ain't NOTHING but a waste of time."

"Wait, huh??"

"Yeah, it is!"

"You think it's a waste of time?"

"Yeah, I mean, come on! Why should I be in there when I could be out here making some real money."

"Yeah, but Tino, Ms. Tourez says that after you finish, you'll have a better opportunity. An opportunity to be somebody in life. Don't you remember when she used to talk to us about this?"

"Yeah, but you see, that's where you gotta ask yourself a question?"

"What?"

"Is any of that shit she's telling us true?"

"So, you think she's been lying to us?! Dawg, Tino, Ms. Tourez loves us –"

"Rence, calm down! That's not what I'm saying."

"Okay then what?!"

"She's a nice lady…At least sometimes."

"Okay…"

"Yeah, and she probably means what she said."

"She do!"

"Yeah but if she's lying –"

"She AIN'T!"

"But if she is…Then that means that she's just trying to keep us away from being messed up."

"Hmmm, that ain't the point though, is it?"

"Naw…"

"Alright, so Tino where you tryna get at?"

"The point I'm trying to make is this NOTION, like my English teacher use to say. This notion…this notion about life getting all nice and cheesy after finishing school."

"So, you're saying that you don't think it's true?"

"C'mon Torence, you don't really think life is really gonna be that way after school?"

"But I'd like a better opportunity too…"

"So, you do believe in that shit then?"

"Yeah, I do. I mean this is what she believes."

"Please…I don't know if Ms. Tourez even believed what she said."

"What? But Lantino –"

"Ar-ar-ar-alright! Check it! If she does believe in that shit, then why ain't she ever finished school?"

"Hmmm, I-I…I-I-I…"

"I mean, if it's true then wouldn't she had done it a long time ago?"

"I-I…"

"You see, because you're home taught, you don't feel the way I do about school. But if you went there, you would have seen what I saw. And once you have seen what I saw and come home knowing what I know, you would have hated it too."

"Yeah?"

"Yeah! I HATE school!"

"Ding…"

"Why do you think Tye, Vern, and all of us never talk about it?!"

"Um, I-I don't know."

"Torence, imagine having to wake up at six something in the morning every day to waste the next 8 hours of your life."

"Oh damn."

"Yeah, that's what it feels like because out there, they ain't teach us shit!"

"Huh?! Naw, what about algebra?!"

"Algebra? Rence, what –"

"Square root of 45!"

"Square root of 45?"

"Square root of 45 is equal to the square root of 9 times 5. That's equal to 3 times the square root of 5."

"Oh ding…"

"In life…if something clicks with another, then there's chemistry."

"OKAY…"

"Like Loraine and I…We might be different, but there's science in the way we get things done. That's why she and I got chemistry!"

"Hah! Ms. Tourez taught you that huh?!"

"Yeah!"

"Ding she told me you catch on quick and boy, she wasn't lying that time!"

"So, you see, they taught y'all something!"

"Hah, if we had more teachers like Ms. Tourez, then I'd hop with you on that one."

"Huh? Wait, what you saying?"

"What I'm saying is most of the teachers ain't wanna teach. They just came for the money they're paid."

"Real..."

"Yeah, and that's why we ain't learn shit out there."

"Ding, ain't know it was like that."

"Yeah, well Rence man, there's a lot you ain't know."

"Ding…Like…Like what?"

"Sta! A lot of those classes we were in is boot classes! Classes that made kids wanna leave school."

"WHAAAT?!"

"Yeah man, and even some of the classes that weren't 'bootified' wasn't teaching me shit!"

"How come you weren't learning?"

"Because half the shit they were teaching had nothing to do with me!"

"But I don't get it. I mean I was always told that knowledge is like having…power, almost. Once ya got smartness, can't no one take that out away from you. I mean that's the teaching Ms. Tourez brought me up under. Hmmm, I know it may not make a lot of sense, but in some ways, it clicks. I guess that's why I wanted to –"

"Man! What's Socrates got to do with me?! He ain't putting bread on my table! He ain't showing me how to make money! When the GDs chase me back home, he ain't got my back! So, what's he got to do with me?!"

"Hmmm, I don't know. Nothing, I guess."

"Yeah! Nothing…Aristotle! The hell I need to know about him for? He ain't got shit to do with me! So, I don't wanna know jack about him! Shit, half the bull they try to teach me I don't even think is on point!"

"Hmmm, how?"

"Okay like Andrew Jackson. You heard of him, right?"

"Uh…Uh, uh…who's that?"

"It's that guy whose face is shown on the twenty-dollar bill."

"Oh, oh you mean that one."

"Yeah him."

"Oh, alright, so what about him?"

"Well, back in middle school I learned that he made this country win some states in the fight with the French."

"Damn, when was this?"

"Like a long time ago, I don't know. But anyways, I also found out that he had got a lot of help from the Haitians."

"The what?"

"The Haitians…"

"Ding, I don't think I ever heard of them. Who are they?"

"Naw they were some group of black people from the islands somewhere."

"And you said you learned that back in middle school?"

"Yeah at least about Andrew Jackson and his fight with the French."

"But what about them other people you said that helped Andrew Jackson."

"The Haitians? Man, they left them out."

"Huh? That's weird. Why'd they do that?"

"Stuh! I don't know, but you see what I mean about them not being on point on what they teach?"

"Yeah, yeah…I see…"

"I mean, if I'm a learn something, then I wanna know the whole thing. Not just half of it."

"Yeah, me too. So Tino, if they left them out, then how did you know about those people?"

"You talking about the Haitians?"

"Yeah…"

"Well, back when Ms. Tourez was going nuts about who was running for mayor, she was telling me that I could vote now that I'm eighteen."

"Oh nice!"

"Yeah, nice but I wasn't trying to do that."

"Hmmm okay. How come?"

"Well, same thing, like Socrates. The mayor doesn't know me, which means he doesn't care about me. So, with that said, I don't give a care about his ass either!"

"Okay."

"Okay, so I lived all my life out here in Chicago. I'm born and raised here in Chicago. I figured I might as well learn a little something about Chicago!"

"True!"

"True. So, trying to do that, I found out that this city was discovered by a man named Jean Baptist Point du Sable."

"What's his name?"

"Jean Baptiste."

"Hmmm…"

"And guess what?"

"What?"

"Turns out that he was Haitian."

"So, you mean that he was one of those people who fought the French people?"

"And helped Andrew Jackson win."

"Ding!"

"Yeah, it's crazy ain't it? But that's how I ended up knowing all that about the Haitians."

"Hmp, maybe you ought to run for mayor, Tino."

"Please…I'm a run this city my own way someday. In the meantime, this is how I'm gonna make money."

"Ding, so things are really hot right now, huh?"

"Yeah…Really hot."

"Did you see how many people showed up tonight?"

"Yeah…It was a lot. I mean, probably the most I've ever seen at one hood meeting."

"Yeah…Roc was there, Vern came out, Rojo, Lock, Rip. I even think I saw Lee there tonight, and she doesn't usually ever show up."

"I saw so many other faces I didn't know. Even cats from the SVLs came through, and last time I saw one of them was when the KCs were still around. Ain't even know we were still tight with them like that."

"Had to be about forty to fifty of us out there tonight."

"Naw, there was more than that. Way, way MORE than that."

"You sure?"

"Yeah…A lot more…I mean more than we could count."

"So, you think this count could hold off the GDs?"

"Look…I think we could take 'em. I mean, you heard what Tye said tonight."

"Hmmm, I don't know, Tino."

"Rence, all I gotta do is keep finding stronger people."

"Yeah, but look what it's doing back at the house."

"It's got Ms. Tourez yapping, huh?"

"And Loraine…most of the time."

"Ah like mother, like daughter. Stuh…"

"It's gotten so bad that you don't even wanna be home now."

"It's just like old times again."

"Tino man, let me help you find some people, and take some weight off your shoulders."

"Naw, naw, naw Rence! Stay out of it! I don't want you to get caught up in this!"

"But Tino think about it! If Tye sends me out there to find him some people, then do you know what that would mean?"

"Yeah, I know but –"

"That means that you'll stay out these streets less, come home earlier, and not have Ms. Tourez on your back as much."

"I hear ya Rence, I hear ya but –"

"So let me take one of the streets he's got you on!"

"Naw, last time Ms. Tourez blamed it on me when we found our asses in the mix!"

"Dawg, I know I could...WHAT?"

"Yeah, she blamed me for it..."

"But...we both know it wasn't your fault. I mean...We had to jump in."

"Naw it's okay...I took the heat."

"Why'd you do that?"

"Torence man, you don't see it but Ms. Tourez...she really loves you."

"Ding..."

"Yeah, that's why I don't want you to get in so deep. You're my boy."

"So that's what it's about?"

"Yeah, just stay out of this one."

"Naw Tino!"

"Ugh! Ding Julisa!"

"I can do this job. Ju-Ju-Julisa??"

"Yes! Ding it Julisa!"

"Wait, huh?"

"You starting to remind me of Julisa!"

"I don't get it...How?"

"I'm trying to tell you something, and you hear me, but you're not listening!"

"I just think it's a load for you."

"Look, for the last time! Stay out of it! I got it on lock Torence! You stay at the shop and do your thing. A week ago, I brought more people than Vern and Roc put together!"

"You did?"

"Yeah man, so I got it locked. And so what if Ms. Tourez asked about the keys I've got to the bakery. Like Tye said back there in the meeting 'blah say, blah say, blah say'…"

"…and no answer."

"Bingo!"

"You know what Ms. Tourez always said about the gang…"

"Look do your thing and let me do my thing! Most of all what I need from you –"

"…is that we're gonna go down if we fall in too deep –"

"Right now is to just STAY OUT of it!"

"…and that's…Huh…"

"End of discussion."

"Aright. Hey, you think we should take the bus the rest of the way back? I mean it'll get us back quicker."

"Yeah, I guess you're right. Let's take the bus."

"Okay. So…"

"Yeah?"

"Julisa be on you about this too?"

"Yeah…Like all the time. When she's not doing it, then it's Loraine and Ms. Tourez back home."

"Damn…"

"Yeah, but she ain't fuss at me these past few days, though."

"Oh okay, so then that mean she's cool now, right?"

"Naw…"

"What?"

"Naw she ain't …Between me and her, things are only getting worse."

"I don't get it…"

"What I'm saying is that she's doing this silent treatment thing with me."

"Aw ding, so she ain't been talking to you then?"

"Naw, not at all. She doesn't call, ask about me or say much when I'm with her."

"Hmp, ain't know it was like that."

"Yeah, that's exactly what's going on, and I know it is because of the new job Tye needs me to do."

"So, she doesn't understand?"

"Naw, right now how she sees it, is that all I wanna do is be a no good for nothing low life hustler for the V Ls."

"But Tino, haven't you told her that that's not what you're trying to do?"

"Yeah! What do you think I've been doing?!"

"Okay, so you told her, but she still ain't cool?"

"Naw, she ain't."

"I just don't get it."

"The thing is Julisa is not listening to that anymore. She's heard it one too many times, and now that I dropped out of high school, she doesn't wanna hear that completely."

"So, no matter what you say, she doesn't believe you?"

"Nope...I don't even think she's feeling me anymore."

"How do you know for sure?"

"Hmmm, tell you what, I don't know for sure, for sure."

"Then, what's making you say that?"

"Hmmm well, sometimes she brings up this boy who got this job at the detention center."

"You're talking about the one where they were holding Tye at?"

"Yeah...I hear his name is Jesus."

"Jesus...I don't think I know him."

"Naw, no one does except Julisa."

"Oh okay...uh hey, say is that the bus coming?"

"Yeah, that's it. Get your cash out."

"I got mine. You just make sure you have yours ha ha..."

"Please Rence, cash is outdated for me."

"Oooooh...Hah, you got your pass on you?"

"You know I'm always equipped with my itinerary."

"Yeah, so I see. Man, it ain't even feel like we waited that long."

"Naw, we didn't at all."

Choosing to save themselves another mile of walking home, both Torence and Lantino took the bus the rest of the way back. Throughout the whole day, gray clouds had covered the Chicago sky. However, not an inch of rain touched the ground. Streetlights were now turning on as the evening fully made its approach. The breeze in the wind never picked up, and stepping out the bus, Torence and Lantino immediately noted that down as a rarity. Making their way back to their floor, the issue with the Gangster Disciples came back into discussion. But after coming through their front door, the matters concerning their rival gang instantaneously dropped to the least of their worries. Ms. Tourez was home making a drink. Hearing Lantino make his entrance, she completely stopped everything she was doing and fixed her eyes on his every movement. Walking through the living room Lantino makes eye contact with her and immediately senses his unwelcome. From his peripheral vision, he can see that Loraine just stepped out of her room. Bending her eyes, she stares at him with the same look Ms. Tourez is giving him. Standing there next to her room door, she watched on anticipating something big to take place. Seated in the living room sofa Torence is also aware that something is rather different about the vibe in Ms. Tourez's place. Trying to ignore the feeling, he asks Lantino to have a seat. Instead, Lantino chose to stand, sending Torence an awkward reaction. Turning over towards Ms. Tourez, Torence tries to greet her uncomfortably. Unfortunately, there was nothing he could do to modify the intensity of the situation. The heated argument between his best friend and his legal guardian was inevitable.

"Hi Ms. Tourez," said Torence as he greets her.

"So, when were you going to tell me," said Ms. Tourez to Lantino as she dismissed Torence's greeting. "HUH?"

"Stuh…" replying Lantino while shaking his head and sucking his teeth.

"When were you going to tell me?" Ms. Tourez asked again with a bellicose voice. "HUH? I'd like to know Lantino!"

"I wasn't…" answered Lantino.

"Wasn't what?"

"I wasn't…"

"Wasn't what Lantino?! I want an answer!!"

"I wasn't gonna tell –"

"YOU WEREN'T EVER GONNA TELL ME, HUH?!"

"Umm…"

"WEREN'T YOU?!...WEREN'T YOU?!"

"Naw…"

"SPEAK UP, I CAN'T HEAR YOU!!"

"No, I wasn't!"

"OH, IS THAT SO! HUH!"

"Yeah, that's so because you ain't need to know!"

"HUH??"

"Yeah, that's right! You ain't need to know!!"

"AHH….AWW…UH HUH…"

"You ain't need to know shit because I knew that this was exactly what was gonna happen if I did tell you!"

"DID YOU REALLY THINK YOU COULD KEEP THIS FROM ME, HUH?!"

"Stuh!"

"HAH, OBVIOUSLY YOU DID! WHAT I REALLY WANNA KNOW IS, HOW LONG DID YOU THINK YOU COULD HOLD THIS BACK FROM ME?!"

"Uh um…"

"YEAH, I WANNA KNOW! HOW LONG DID YOU THINK YOU COULD KEEP IT UP?!"

Present in the living room, both Torence and Loraine watch and listen continuously to what's going on as they wait to hear a straight answer from Lantino. However, Lantino continues to stand silent and still with the look of a calm frown in his face. "Hey, she's talking to you!" Loraine cried out. "So, speak when you're spoken to!" she said again to Lantino. Turning to her direction, Lantino replies to her saying, "It was you, wasn't it? You told her didn't you?".

"Yeah, but Tino that's not the point −"

"LORAINE HUSH!!"

"Stuh, that's alright Raine…It ain't cool, but I'm okay…You know what, Ms. Tourez, I was gonna keep it from you for as LONG as I could."

"TIS, TIS, TIS, TIS, TIS, TIS...I SHOULD HAVE KNOWNED FROM THE START: THE RED OUTFITS, THAT BIG LEATHER JACKET, THAT STRIPED BANDANA, THE

189

MONEY YOU COME HOME WITH, THE BRUISES, THE SCARS!! I-YIE YIE!!"

"Man shit! So, what! I'm in the gang!"

"SO WHAT?! STUH! TORENCE, YOU KNEW ABOUT IT THE WHOLE TIME, DIDN'T YOU?!"

"I-I—" stuttering Torence as he automatically gets up on his two feet. "I-I-I was just —"

"DIDN'T YOU?!"

"Yes…and I'm sorry."

"Mami," said Loraine, "Wanna know something else? Lantino also dropped out of school!"

"AH HAAAAAH…IS THAT TRUE LANTINO? IS WHAT SHE SAYING TRUE?!"

"Stuh, yes..."

"YOU HEAR THAT TORENCE! LANTINO IS A HIGH SCHOOL DROP OUT!"

"Man, school ain't nothing but a waste of time!"

"I-YIE YIE YIE YIE YIE YIE YIE!!!! NO PUEDO CREER QUE DICE!! SIEMPRE QUIESE TENET UNA MEJOR OPPORTUNIDAD PARA USTED."

Lantino responded to Ms. Tourez in Spanish. For the first time in all the years Torence has lived with the Tourezes, he is actually hearing Lantino speak in a different tongue (something in which he never knew his friend could do till right now). Though he doesn't quite comprehend the language, he can sort of pick up what's being said in the argument between Lantino and Ms. Tourez. Based on Ms. Tourez's gestures and Lantino's facial expressions, he has a clear idea of what's going on. Again, there's absolutely nothing he could do to modify the intensity of the situation. However, he makes a second attempt at doing so. "Ms. Tourez," he said in a daunting manner, "try to understand. The teachers at Lantino's school aren't doing their job, and-and —"

"Naw ah!" said Loraine interrupting Torence, "Lantino is just plain lazy! He's been in the 9th grade for three years now!"

"But Raine —"

"Naw ah Torence! Don't stick up for him."

"THREE YEARS LANTINO! THREE YEARS!" shouting Ms. Tourez as she shifts her speech back to English.

"Stuh! Man, I hate school! They ain't teaching me nothing out there!"

"AFTER THE SUSPENSION, YOU ONLY GOT WORSE..."

But for real though, Ms. Tourez, is knowing the square root of forty-five really gonna make me any money in life? I mean half the shit they teach me I won't even need in life!"

"FINISHING SCHOOL IS GOING TO MAKE YOU SOMEBODY IN THE FUTURE, LANTINO!"

"Aww, please, I know you of all people don't believe in that shit Ms. Tourez!"

"QUE?!"

"If that's true, then how come you ain't finish school back in your days?!"

"CALLATE!!"

"If that's true, wouldn't you have gone back right now and finished to be this so-called somebody in life?!"

"FUCK YOU, Lantino!" said Loraine in retaliation.

"Hah, the truth hurts, don't it, sis?" asked Lantino.

"SO LANTINO, YOU'RE SAYING THAT THE GANG IS GONNA MAKE YOU SOMEBODY?"

"Ms. Tourez, I'm making some good money working for them."

"YES, BUT IT'S DIRTY MONEY, LANTINO!"

"Dirty money that's helping you pay the bills here!"

"WHY DON'T YOU MAKE MONEY THE NORMAL WAY...LIKE TORENCE!"

"You know that's not enough to help us Ms. Tourez! You know that!"

"IT DOESN'T MATTER. I WANT YOU TO EARN MONEY THE RIGHT WAY LAN–"

"The workforce is for SUCKERS!! Ain't no way they're gonna play –"

"GET OUT OF MY HOUSE!!!"

She then unexpectedly slaps Lantino. He can feel the hate that came with the slap as he received it across his left cheek. He looks back at her with a bit of a grin and licks his lips. "I've been waiting for you to say that," he said to her.

"GET OUT!!" shouted Ms. Tourez.

"On my way…"

"NO CRIMINALS IS WELCOMED IN MY HOUSE!"

"Please, it's not like you ever wanted me here."

"NO, I DID EVERYTHING I COULD TO HELP YOU DO RIGHT!"

"Lady, please! You never did like us!"

"THAT'S NOT TRUE, LANTINO!"

"My mother knew it from the get-go!"

"LANTINO, I HAD TO GET RID OF MONALISA. YOU WERE TOO YOUNG TO UNDERSTAND WHAT WAS GOING ON! SHE WAS NO GOOD!"

"She told me that no matter what, don't fall for it nor get close to you because you don't respect me. Those were her last words to me before you took her out of my life!"

"LANTINO, I ONLY DID IT BECAUSE I WAS DOING WHAT WAS BEST FOR YOU! I DIDN'T WANT TO SEE YOU END UP LIKE YOUR FATHER! IT'S TRUE!"

"Stuh! Just have my stuff waiting for me outside when I come back!"

Right there and then, Lantino made his exit and began making his way downstairs to the ground floor. Clouded with questions in regard to what was shared by Lantino and Ms. Tourez, Torence is unsure of what to ask first. Looking back and forth from the doorway to where Ms. Tourez stands, he then finds himself in utter disbelief to what's now transpiring before his very eyes. He tried to urge Ms. Tourez to go after Lantino but fails. "Ms. Tourez, he's leaving!" he said repeatedly, "aren't you gonna do something?! Call him back!"

He said the same line a few more times before finally giving up. Then he rested his forearms against the kitchen window to look outside. It's finally raining outside. Suddenly, that's when he saw Lantino walking across the street amid the light rain outside. "Tino!"

he shouted after seconds of opening the window. "Lantino!" he shouts again. "Lantino, WAIT!! Come back!" Sadly, Lantino chose to ignore his calls and continued his long walk. "I'm going after him," Torence decided. Already seeing that Lantino is far in his walk, he figured he'll have to stride if he wants to catch up. Just when he's about to leave, Loraine cuts his path to the door. "Let 'em go boo," she said to Torence. "Out of my way, Loraine, I gotta get 'em back!" Torence said to her. "No, no, no boo, I'm not letting you go out there!" Loraine insisted.

"Raine babe, you need to move!" said Torence. "Lantino's outside, and I can't let him be there on his own!"

"Uh uh boo, you're gonna get wet!"

"So will Lantino if I don't bring him back inside."

"Okay well, let 'em! If he's smart, he'll find a place to stay dry."

"Babe, you don't understand. Your brothers in the gang, and if GDs find him who knows what could happen. He's as good as dead."

"Boo, you are too if you go out there!"

"Stuh, sorry babe, but I gotta go get 'em!"

"Torence!!"

Torence moves her out of the way, stepped out to the hallway, but doesn't get any further than level two on the stairwells. Trying to talk to him while following him through the stairwells, Loraine somehow convinced Torence to stop while he's at it. "Let 'em go Torence," again, she said to him. "You don't really think you'll catch up with him now, do you? Especially right now…Tino's somewhere by now in that hard rain!"

"So that's it?... We're just gonna let family go like that?" asked Torence.

"Look boo, he'll come back," said Loraine.

"But…What if –"

"He'll come back."

"Sure?"

"Yes, he will. You know how many times Lee came back after she ran away from home?"

"For real? Lee ran away before??"

"Yeah."

"But babe, this is different. Lantino got booted out."

"Boo, don't worry, Tino's gonna be alright as soon as he cleans up his act."

"Oh…Kay…"

"C'mon, let's go. Come sleep in my room tonight."

Chapter 18: A Forbidden Love

Days and weeks came and went. In the month of May, Chicago experienced a lot of rainfall. By the turn of the new month, the big city was left looking soaked and wet. It was noon, but the day still had an early feel to it. It was almost as if the city hadn't fully woken up. There was no sound of sirens, there wasn't any heavy traffic. Neither were the sidewalks covered by pedestrians. Leaning against a pole on Broadway Street, Torence knew that it was only going to be a matter of time before everything outside became busy. Fortunately for him, he managed to stay all nice and dry.

Though it had been a long time ago, his mind was still plagued by his last memory of Lantino leaving his legal guardian's place on that dismal rainy night. Lantino's long and lonely walk away from the Tourezes, in a way, brought back memories of his rough trip here to Chicago. After jumping from one foster family to the next so many years ago, Torence developed this notion that he wasn't wanted and that no one could ever want him. He knew that this might've been exactly what Lantino was thinking when he left the house. That's why he was so adamant about apprehending Lantino that night.

Till this day, Torence often thought about what could have probably gone wrong. He remembered what happened that evening and a lot of questions came to him. *Who is Ms. Lopez? What was Ms. Tourez talking about when she said she had to get rid of her? She told me that no matter what, don't fall for it and I shouldn't get close to you because you don't respect me and you never will. Those were her last words to me before you took her out of my life.*

Leaning against the pole, Torence could hear the words of Lantino and Ms. Tourez playback as his mind reenacted the whole scene that night. Looking back, he evidently knows that his efforts weren't going to alter what transpired between the two that day. Still, Torence chose to delve deep into his thoughts. While amid his thoughts, he heard a whisper. For a second, he turned over to his left then his right to see where the sound was coming from. Then slowly, he began to drift back into his thoughts. "Speeeeee…" the sound went, and Torence heard it again. So again, Torence looked to his left and right. Finally, he heard "Yo" in a low tone of voice. Turning around, he then came to realize that it was Lantino, standing two to three feet away from him. "Lantino," said Torence as he gazed at him. "What up boy?" Lantino said as he reached over to embrace Torence.

"Chilling!" replied Torence. "Where you been at?"

"Ha ha ha ha, I been everywhere staying busy."

"Doing what, though?!"

"You know, finding people for Tye."

"Wow, I ain't seen you in a minute."

"Yeah, it's been a minute…Like almost three weeks now, right?"

"Yeah…Just about."

"How're things back at the house?"

"Everyone's doing alright. Lee's been showing up now."

"Well, that's good. Has she said anything about what happened?"

"Hmmm, you know what? I don't think Lee knows."

"Hmp, well I guess that's good too."

"So things are good but it just feels like someone is missing…that's all."

"Me, huh?"

"Yes."

"I know. I still think about Loraine…"

"I know you do."

"…and Ms. Tourez."

"Look just come back Lantino –"

"Naw Torence, I can't –"

"C'mon man, the door is wide open."

"You heard the things she said! You were right there when she called me a criminal!"

"Tino, I know you know that she'll take you back. Let Loraine and I get –"

"FORGET it, Torence! Ain't no way I'm trying to go back to a place I ain't wanted!"

"Stuh, alright…So how'd you manage to stay dry this past month?"

"Stuh ha ha ha ha! You got jokes huh?"

"I'm just saying…ha ha ha ha, it's been raining these last couple of weeks."

"Ha ha ha ha well since you wanna know, I have been staying with Tye this whole time."

"Oh, so you stayed at his place?"

"Yep."

"Yo you know what? That's funny because two Saturdays ago, Vern told me that Tye wanted me to come all the way out here to Broadway Street."

"Yeah, two days ago Tye told me to come out here too. I thought it was because he wanted me to find him some people here. But now that I know that he's meeting us here makes perfect sense."

"Okay, so if he wanted to meet us, then why out here? Why ain't he just have us come to the park like he always does?"

"Cause the courthouse is right up the street."

"Huh?"

"Remember his court date?"

"Yeah, he did have to go to court…"

"Yep, and today's the day."

"And it's sitting on Broadway Street?"

"Uh huh, just right up the street."

"I see…Ding, so did he tell you how long it's gonna be?"

"Aw ding, I forgot to ask Julisa that before she went to her graduation rehearsal!"

"Hmp, so neither one of us know how long the wait's gonna be."

"Gee, my bad Torence."

"You cool…Hey, so how's Julisa?"

"Um…she's alright. She's going to live in college."

"Oh snaps! She got accepted?"

"Yeah."

"Wow, she made it! I know Tye's gonna be so happy to hear this!"

"Yeah…He will…"

"Hmmm, wait how come you don't sound so glad?"

"Stuh, she broke up with me."

"Ding, sorry, I asked."

"That's alright. It was going to happen."

"Yeah?"

"Yeah, I saw it coming."

"You still going to her graduation?"

"Yeah, I am because she invited me."

"Oh well, then that's good because that means that she still got love for you."

"Yeah plus, it's nice to see that she made it."

"Yeah, it is."

"Hey yo Torence, you know her family throwing a graduation party?"

"Oh, for real?!"

"Yeah, man, real shit!"

"Damn!"

"Yo, and you wanna know what else?"

"What?"

"It's going down at a club somewhere."

"NICE!"

"Heck yeah!"

"So, when is it, anyway?"

"Like right after Julisa's graduation."

"Oh well, alright then. At least Tye can come to that then."

"Yeah…Hey Rence, you wanna wait here while I go snatch us something to snack on?"

"Yeah, yeah…I'll wait here."

"Alright then, so I'll be back."

"What do you think they're doing in there?"

"Hmmm, I couldn't tell you. But whatever it is that they're doing, Tye needs to tell 'em to hurry up."

"Ha ha ha ha, for real…"

Part 2: The Graduation Party

The night presented itself as one to remember for the ages. Loraine's friend Julisa walked elegantly into the evening with her long sleeveless red dress and gave the word "class" an incomparable description. In the night of the ceremonial event, she wore black metallic stringed earrings and high heels. Around her neck and cleavage area was a shiny gold necklace with a star and a crescent moon as the charm. It was a present given to her by her cousin, the Vice Lord, Tyberius.

She was young, petite, sociable, bright, and altogether just seemed to have a better tomorrow in the grip of her possession. This night was a proud moment for anyone who was associated with her. Of course, though, there were other Julisas present in the event tonight. They included Milleena, who was graduating with honors. Then there was Rose Lawson, the daughter of the school's principal, and the longtime acquaintance of Loraine. However, neither of the two could match with Julisa. She just somehow stood alone as the shining star. Clearly, it was her time, and the evening belonged to her.

Many names were called up to receive their diplomas. However, the event seemed like it only begun when Julisa's name was called. "Julisa Cross!" said the speaker, and a roaring sound of applause was heard at its highest volume. Camera lights flashed left and right as Julisa made it across the stage. Then, later on that night the speaker said "Milleena Moubay" which was followed by a loud burst of cheers by Julisa's supporting cast, Milleena's family, the Crosses, the Tourezes, and Tyberius, Torence, and Lantino who arrived late. A great memorable evening was the thought for many going into this event, and as expected, it turned out to be just that.

It was past 10pm, and the graduation ceremony was over. Though it was, the night wasn't. In fact, the ceremony's ending was only the beginning of the celebration. The celebration was basically carried over to a luxury location called Club Mansion. There, an after-party for Julisa's graduation took place. Making sure he didn't miss any minute of the party, Tyberius arrived on time. He showed up, stepping out of a red manually operated car with tinted windows. With him was Torence and Lantino, who kind of look alike despite the difference in their skin complexion. All three of them had on nice outfits and looked like a posse making their entrance to the party. Talking to Torence and Lantino, Tyberius filled them in on what occurred while he was at court. "Benito's punk ass tried to sue me," he said to them. "I saw him and all his peoples there," he continued. "The way I see it, his rep out here is done. Someone needs to snatch his G card."

"Damn he really tried to do that to you?" asked Lantino.

"Yeah," answered Tyberius, "but Kendrick let it go because Benito was throwing hands too."

"Hmp, well then at least that's good," said Lantino.

"Yeah hey, Tye what you think of the graduation tonight?" asked Torence.

"Man y'all, I'm just glad I was able to make it," answered Tyberius. "Even though we missed half of it."

"Yeah well, Tye that's because you were getting us lost."

"Aw c'mon Tino, don't start that again," said Tyberius.

"Hey but Tye it's true," said Lantino.

"Man, yo ass can't drive anyhow," said Tyberius.

"Aw naw don't try using that," said Lantino.

"Yeah Tye, I can't front," said Torence, "You were the only one who knew the way."

"Man, I told y'all that I don't know the way too well from Broadway street," said Tyberius.

"Yeah well, we still made it late Tye," said Lantino.

"Alright fine, I take it," said Tyberius. "But look we made it right?" he asked.

"Yeah-Yeah we did," answered both Torence and Lantino in unison.

"Okay and we here now, ain't it?", again asking Tyberius.

"Hmmm yeah-yeah true-true," again answering both Torence and Lantino in unison.

"Alright then, so let's head on inside and vibe. I mean it ain't all the time we get to do this, ain't it?" saying Tyberius.

"Hmmm…True-true."

"Okay so let's get in there and vibe. Oh, and yo, yo, yo when we vibe y'all…let's vibe ride. Not right. But RIDE. Y'all feel me!?" saying Tyberius.

"Yeah-Yeah we feel you!", answered Torence and Lantino.

"That's what's up!", said Tyberius. "Now c'mon. Let's ride. Oh, but just one more thing I gotta let y'all boys know before we slide through…", he added.

"Hmmm, what's that?" asked Lantino.

"Y'all boys, I love y'all for scooping me up by the courthouse today. I wasn't sure if Benito's boys were waiting to catch me outside," said a grateful Tyberius.

"You know we gotchu Tye," said Torence.

"Good looking out! I promise I'm a pay y'all back before things calm down! Word up!", said Tyberius.

The trio went inside and were met up by Vern, J-Roc, and Rojo. Later that same night, a few other members from Tyberius' clique made an appearance at the party. Every member had a pleasant time. Even their friends and other friends of a friend wanted the party to never come to an end. By the time Julisa showed up, the whole place was full. She had come through still dressed in all red, but this time in more casual clothing. With her was Loraine and the other high school grad, Milleena. And the three of them in their own way was like a posse of their own. They were all sitting in a very noticeable, isolated corner, not observing everybody else at the party, but instead attending to their own little business. It wasn't too long before Tyberius and company joined them. "Hey cuz," said Tyberius as he greeted his cousin. "Congrats!" he says while embracing her.

"Aww thanks Tye!", Julisa replied, "I'm so glad you and everybody else was able to come through! You don't know how much this means to me!"

"Hey, well, you know it's what family do!", said Tyberius.

"I appreciate your support so much!", said Julisa. "Honestly, you have no idea!"

"Well, cuz you did a good job," said Tyberius. "You earned it!", he adds.

"I appreciate the present you got me!", said Julisa.

"Aww thanks cuz, but it was nothing, you know," said Tyberius. "I just wanted you to know that you made it."

"Tye, I LOVE it!", said Julisa.

"Hmmm well, I'm glad you do cuz," said Tyberius. "It fits you."

"I think it's pretty," said Julisa.

"It's real nice to see my lil' cuz grow up and sprout out into the world," said Tyberius. "You're gonna make a good man really happy! I could already see it."

"For real Tye?" asked Julisa.

"For real! I'm proud of you cuz!" answered Tyberius.

"Awwww thank you, Tye!" said Julisa embracing her cousin.

"Anytime cuz!" replying Tyberius. "And I'm proud of you too, Milleena Moubay!" he says to Milleena as they made eye contact.

"Boy, I heard your voice all the way up in the stage!" said Milleena. "Yo loud ass ha ha ha!" she laughs.

"That's cuz I ain't know you were that smart!" replied Tyberius. "Yo ass never said jack!" he says.

"Well, thanks Tye," said Milleena. "I love you for the shout out!"

"Like I said! That's how family do," said Tyberius.

"So, when are you graduating, Lurraine??" he asked.

"Um excuse me!" said Loraine. "Now I know you ain't trying to crack."

"Hey, just answer the damn question!" said Tyberius.

"Hmmm, big question for someone who got booted out because he became too old for the 9th grade," laughing Loraine.

"A-a-a-ain't you still stuck in the nineth grade?" Tyberius asked jokingly.

"Boy, don't try me!" replied Loraine. "I'm about to graduate in December, so now what?"

"Huh?" asked Tyberius. "Since when the hell they start doing that?"

"They been started doing that, and as soon as I'm through with the SATs I'm a finish," said Loraine.

"Oh, so you're graduating early then?" asked Julisa.

"Yep, and I can't wait," answered Loraine.

"Hmp, Raine, I know what you mean," said Milleena.

"Yeah, so next year it'll be my turn," said Loraine.

"Girl, please," said Tyberius disparaging Loraine. "You ain't for real about pulling that off," he says.

"Oh yes, I am!" Loraine replies. "Ask Torence!!"

"A Rence, she for real?" asked Tyberius to Torence.

"Yeah, she's next," answered Torence.

"See I told you," said Loraine.

"Hmmm, we'll see," said Tyberius. "Anyways, Tino you got the camera on you?" he asked Lantino. Then everyone suddenly paused the minute they heard nothing but silence from Lantino. Looking towards Lantino, Tyberius repeats his question to him, and again no response. Looking at Lantino, everyone noticed that he seemed to have his eyes fixed on Julisa with a blank stare. "Yo what you thinking about," asked Torence as he shook Lantino's right shoulder.

"I'm cool," replying Lantino as he continued to look with a blank stare.

"You sure?" asked Julisa. In response, Lantino just nodded his head and continued looking at her with the blank stare on his face. "You wanna tell us what's on your mind, or you just wanna tell me?" she asked him. She then stared back at him.

"Oh snaps," says Loraine as she seemed a bit intrigued by what's going on. "Torence boo, you'll walk with me outside?" she asked Torence as she reached for his hand.

"Sure babe," replied Torence with a notable smile on his face. And like that, he and Loraine left.

"Hmp, okay Torence," said Tyberius. "I see you doing ya thang," he said while nodding his head.

Thing...what thing? Lantino thought as he turned away from Julisa to have a good look at Tyberius. "Tye, what you talking about?" he asked Tyberius.

"Huh?" asking Tyberius, who now drew a sudden bewildered look on his face.

"What you talking –".

"Julisa, you know where there's a restroom around here?" asked Milleena as she interrupted Lantino's question.

"Just go downstairs to your right," answered Julisa. "But good luck because there's probably a lot of people in there by now."

203

"Ump, well, I gotta go," said Milleena.

"Hmp, good luck," laughed Julisa.

"Yeah, later y'all," said Milleena as she made her way to the ladies' room.

"Tino, the camera on you or not?" asked Tyberius.

"Roc's got it on him right now," answered Lantino.

"Aw man, you know Roc can't take pictures, Tino," said Tyberius. "Ugh, why'd you give it to him?" he asked.

"Roc said he wanted to use it," answered Lantino.

"Ding, he's probably using up all the film!" said Tyberius.

"Well, he's still hanging out near the back where those girls were chilling if you still wanna catch 'em," said Lantino.

"Yeah, I'm a go check up on what Roc and them boys doing!" said Tyberius.

Once Tyberius left the two of them alone at that isolated spot, Julisa and Lantino were back at it again with the staring contest. It went on for about another two and half minutes till Julisa finally opened a conversation with a question to Lantino, asking him, "why are you looking at me like that?"

"Because I feel like it," replied Lantino.

"Ugh! Lantino, tonight I graduated from high school, so could you at least be happy for me?!"

"But I am."

"Um…Okay."

"Congratulations."

"Could you at least say it like you mean it? I mean, that would be nice."

"What, it doesn't sound legitimate enough?"

"No. Not even close."

"Well, hey I mean what I say."

"Okay…So do you want me to say thank you?"

"Hmp...Look, this is a little hard to get use to."

"What's a little hard to get used to?"

"You know, this going our separate ways shit."

"Tuh," She sighed. "Lantino...I'm glad you came out tonight."

"Yeah…Me too. Tye's right, you know."

"Wait, about what?"

"You're gonna make a good man happy someday. Just..."

"Just...Just what?"

"Just a little sorry I couldn't be him."

"I am too," she said swallowing a deep gulp. "Well, hey listen there's still a whole night left to enjoy the party. Why don't we head down stairs to where all the actions at."

"You go head on. That dancing stuff isn't for me."

"Hmmm, I think that's Flow Joe's music I hear them playing on the dance floor."

"Yeah, it is haha. What, you tryna egg me on?"

"What it look like to you?"

"Hmp, I preciate you trying," He chuckles, "but naw, I'm good up here. You go ahead on." Just as he said that, a new song came on and another guy showed up just in time to take Julisa's hand as an offer to dance. "Hey Julisa," he said to her.

"Oh, hi Jesus," said Julisa.

"Um, you wanna go dance?" asked Jesus.

"Sure, I would love to," answered Julisa.

As she took Jesus's hand and heads for the dance floor, she made one last eye contact with Lantino. Then off to the dance floor they went, and into the crowd they disappeared. Looking lonesome and isolated, Lantino just stood there, leaned back against the wall, and bopped his head to the music. Nodding his head to the music he somehow spots Julisa within the midst of all those people on the dance floor. He notates her moves as well as Jesus's. Then thoughts begin to run across his mind as he completely tunes out the music. *Hah, he ain't all that. Oh please, Julisa you're telling me that this is the guy who works at the detention center you met. Stuh, he wears glasses, and he doesn't even look tough enough to work there. Hmp, at least I ain't got nothing to be jealous –*

"Awww Tino," said Milleena as she automatically took him out of his thoughts, "you look lonely! You need a friend?"

"Um lonely…"

"Yes, Tino. You looking lonesome up here and you don't wanna look like that ha ha ha ha…"

"Stuh, I ain't lonely –"

"Boy, yes you are! Don't front!"

"Hmmm, if you say so…"

"You know she looks real pretty tonight."

"Who? Julisa?"

"Yeah, who else would I be talking about?"

"Well, Lee there's a lot of other pretty girls in here tonight."

"Boy whatever, you know who I was talking about."

"Yeah…"

"Look Tino, just be happy for her."

"Um but I am…"

"Hmmm, so you say."

"Ding, how come I keep hearing that tonight?"

"Um hmp hmp hmp."

"What you giggling about?"

"You ha ha ha ha …"

"Stuh, whatever!"

"Tino, you tripping."

"No I ain't."

"Yes, you are."

"Whatever Lee."

"So, everything alright with you at the house?"

"Hmmm naw…I'm trying to get my own place soon."

"So, you don't wanna be there no more?"

"Naw, I hate over there, and I'm just TIRED of Ms. Tourez."

"Ding, so she knows about the gang now, ain't it?"

"Yeah, she does…Let me guess, Loraine spilled her mouth to you too, huh?"

"No."

"Naw?"

"Uh uh."

"Torence?"

"Nope, I just could tell."

"Hmmm, how?"

"Stuh, by the way everything was going: Raine and Ms. Tourez fussing at you. You coming home late. Torence being invisible."

"Is that why you weren't coming by as much?"

"Duh, I had to focus on my classes. Those advanced classes were no joke."

"Ding, you know I-I never knew you were so smart."

"Well after I left boot camp, I made sure I left it for good!"

"Damn, you look…you looked…cool in your gold cap and gown."

"Tino, you a trip."

"Lee, how come you ain't tell nobody?"

"What? That I was smart?"

"Yeah…"

"Man, you know that better than I do, Tino! If you're smart, then you a nerd and people's finna clown on you."

"Yeah, that's true. It's a bad thing to be smart and do your work."

"My point exactly."

"Yep, you right. I can't lie."

"Even you know you're smart."

"Yep, but I dropped out."

"Yeah, you did and…that wasn't so smart."

"A well congrats Lee! I'm happy…for you too."

"Um hmp hmp, thanks Tino…So…"

"So…"

"You think there's still some fire left in our candle?"

"Hmmm…yeah."

"Good then. Now c'mon let's dance."

"Oh uh but Lee…"

"What?"

"I-I don't know how to dance."

"Boy quit being shy."

"Naw, naw it's true –"

"Well tonight you're gonna learn how to. Now c'mon!"

The entire place was on and rocking! The dance floor soon became the heart of the party. The lights became dim, and the level of the beat was now raised to its max. The sound of the sweet music moved through the speaker box, and the feel of a good vibration flowed as the dancers moved to it with such distinct harmony. Dancing with Jesus, Julisa suddenly lost control and caught the center of everyone's attention for an estimated six minutes. "Damn, she's sure busting the moves," said Tyberius, looking on from a distance.

"Ding, she sure is," agreed J-Roc. "Ain't never knew your cousin to be that sexy! Ump, ump!"

"Shut up!" said Tyberius. "Watch how you talk, when you talk about my cousin."

"Jeeze!" said J-Roc, "My bad, I ain't mean to pinch any…nerves."

"Stuhhh, my ass!" muttered Tyberius. Gazing on suspiciously at Jesus, a feeling of being protective began to grow on Tyberius all of a sudden. "A yo Roc," he says calling on J-Roc.

"Yo," responding J-Roc.

"Who that is over there on the dance floor?"

"You mean him with the glasses that's dancing with Julisa?"

"Yeah…Who is he?"

"Oh, that's some boy named Jesus."

"Nigga, I know what his name is!"

"Then, what you mean?"

"What I mean is, who is he? I don't know shit about 'em."

"Oh…Ha ha ha ha, you don't know? Why, that's Kendrick's boy ya cousin's dancing with over there."

"You mean like a kin?"

"Yeah nigga! And you wanna know something else?"

"What?"

"The judge hooked 'em up with a job at the tent…The same one they were holding you at."

"Hmmm…"

"What? What you thinking about?"

"You got the camera?"

"Uh yeah…"

"'Cool, let me see it."

"Huh?"

"Nigga, let me see it."

"Okay here…Um could I ask you why?"

"I wanna take a picture of the dude."

"Umm…Why?"

"Because I like this one for Julisa."

"Huh? Wait, what?"

"I feel that it's about time that my cousin found her a good boy."

"But Tye, he's linked to judge Nobles. He's connected with Five-O. I mean, it won't be too long before he turns into a cop."

"Yeah well, so what!"

"So, what huh…"

"Look I'm just glad she picked this one."

"Uh Tye…"

"Yeah…"

"I wouldn't say all that, especially right now."

"Why?"

"Look at the dance floor…"

As soon as Tyberius turned away from J-Roc to take a look at Julisa back at the dance floor, he came to find that she completely walked away from Jesus while in the middle of dancing with him. "Oh shit!" said Tyberius as he stared with his mouth wide opened. His eyebrows began to raise across his forehead as he looked, feeling just as shocked as the stranded Jesus. "I-I-I don't get it…What happened?" he asks J-Roc.

"Ha ha ha ha ha ha, I don't know," laughed J-Roc, "I guess she wasn't feeling 'em."

"Damn now that's messed up," said Tyberius as he shakes his head. "I wonder where my cuz is going?"

Chapter 19: A Forbidden Love

Part 3: A Gang from the Southside

By the time Julisa showed up, the whole place was full. With her was Loraine, and the other high school grad, Milleena. The three of them together were like a posse of their own. Hanging out at a very noticeable isolated corner, Julisa's posse would soon be joined by Tyberius and company. In the meantime, while that was going on inside, some unexpected guests were making their way through the parking lot. Showing up in a couple of metallic black cars with chromed rims, they were a party of eight. Their choice of appearance for the evening included an all-black outfit with flashing silver jewelry. Some chose to show up concealing their identities with Zorro like masks and black caps made of leather. Others came through with shades on. Among the unexpected guests was a young man named Romelo, who some knew better as just Melo. Out of the eight, he stood out as the only one with a good reputation. Enrolled in a magnet program, he earned three different scholarships under his name. He had already completed a few college courses, thus earning him some college credits. Also, he wasn't just accepted by one university. In fact, five higher institutions considered him as a student for their programs. Not to mention, he also participated in sports as a member of the school's track team. He's looked up to by many of the people associated with him.

A couple of days leading to the graduation, Romelo learned about Julisa's party while attending a graduation rehearsal. His lady friend, Rose, handed away her invitation to him, and then he passed the news on to his cousin, Benito, who in turn, had a few members of the Disciples gang tag along. Benito's family had filed a lawsuit against Tyberius after he gave him a fractured cheek bone. Romelo figured that the party would have been a good idea for taking Benito's mind off the claim against Tyberius, which was dismissed. Romelo had a few woes he too, was trying to overcome. His woes involved a few bad relationships. As for the rest, they were all simply ecstatic about the party they were showing up to. Once

Romelo's crew made their entrance, they instantly blended in with everybody else. They, as did many in the party, consumed their own share of drinks and danced continually to the sound of sweet music. Some of them later witnessed a dance contest take place in the center of the floor. As a matter of fact, it was Romelo's best friend, Mauricio. Benito needed to grab something out of his car, and so Romelo offered to do it for him. Unfortunately, he missed out on his best friend's dance contest as he became too occupied to return. However, there was someone else in the party who didn't miss out.

Observing from a distance, Tyberius was moved by Mauricio's performance at the dance contest and became even more captivated by his cousin's moves on the dance floor. "Damn, she's sure busting the moves," he said, standing next to J-Roc. "Ding, she sure is," agreed J-Roc. "Ain't never know your cousin to be that sexy! Ump, ump!"

"Shut up!" said Tyberius. "Watch how you talk when you talk about my cousin," he said, warning J-Roc.

"Jeeze!" said J-Roc, "My bad. I ain't mean to pinch any...nerves."

"Stuhh, my ass!" muttered Tyberius. Gazing on suspiciously at Jesus, a feeling of being protective began to grow on Tyberius all of a sudden. Curious, Tyberius begins to drill J-Roc for some background knowledge on Jesus. Informed by J-Roc about Jesus's kinship to the honorable Judge Kendrick Nobles, his growing suspicions died down as well as his curiosity. He then goes on to express his approval of Jesus once he comes under the impression that he's good. "I feel it's about time my cousin found her a good boy," he says to J-Roc while nodding his head.

"But Tye, he's linked to Judge Nobles. He's connected with Five-O. I mean, it won't be too long before he becomes a cop," replying J-Roc.

"Yeah well, so what! He's doing his thing!"

"His thing huh?"

"Yeah! I'm glad she picked this one if you ask me!"

"Uh Tye..."

"Yeah..."

"I wouldn't say all that, especially right now."

"Why?"

"Look at the dance floor…"

As soon as Tyberius turns away from J-Roc to take a look at Julisa back at the dance floor, he came to find out that Julisa completely walked away from Jesus while in the middle of dancing with him. Tyberius' jaw nearly dropped to the floor as he stared in shock. J-Roc shakes his head, smirks, and looks on with a bit of a grin on his face. Jesus, for a few seconds, glanced in a swivel. Then the crowd slowly began to close in on the center of the dance floor.

"I-I-I don't get it. What happened?" asked a bewildered Tyberius.

"Ha ha ha ha ha ha I don't know," laughed J-Roc. "I guess she wasn't feeling 'em."

"Damn, now that's messed up," said Tyberius as he watched Jesus making his way slowly off the dance floor. "I wonder where my cuz is going?" he asked.

"HEY YO TYE!", said J-Roc.

"Huh? What's up!" replied Tyberius.

"YOU SEE 'EM OVER THERE!"

"See what over where?"

"HIM!"

"Yeah man I see Jesus walking off the dance floor –"

"Naw I could give a less about Jesus! I'm talking about over THERE!"

"OH SHIT!"

"YEAH, YA SEE WHAT I'M TALKING ABOUT!"

"YEAH, I SEE WHAT YOU SEE ROC!"

"So Tye, let me know what's up! What we gonna do?"

"I'm a fuck 'em up! That's what I'm gonna do!"

"Just him? What about the rest? How do we know there's not more than one of 'em around?"

"Damn! That's right, GDs never travel alone!"

"Hey yo Tye, it's your call on what you wanna do."

"Check this out! You're gonna go get everybody else."

"Okay…so…and then what?"

"Then y'all gonna find out how many of them GDs are really here!"

"What about you?"

"I'm a keep an eye on his ass!"

"After that you're gonna fuck 'em right?"

"FUCK YEAH! I'm a fuck all of 'em up!"

"Wait but Tye, you might not wanna do that."

"Say what nah?"

"Think about it…Your uncle put up a lot just to get this all together."

"Yeah…He did…"

"C'mon…Nice party…Happy people…and then your pretty cousin."

"Ding…"

"Yeah ding…Oh and Tye, don't forget Julisa went through a whole lot just to talk your uncle into letting you in. Remember that…"

"That's right; I don't wanna mess up Julisa's night…"

"So Tye, what you're telling me is that we're basically gonna stand here, let GDs come all the way out here and try us at your COUSIN's party? Like what the fuck?"

"Man, shut up!"

"Tye look! I'm just saying, what you gonna do? I mean, it's your call."

"Roc, you let me worry about that! In the meantime, you make sure you pass the word out and get everyone together, so these niggas can't leave! Iyite!!"

"Iyite…I gotchu…"

Soon a mess looked like it was going to be painted in the picture with all due to just one slight disturbance amid the surface. With Vice Lords and Gangster Disciples at the same place, at the same time, the appearance of the unhappily ever after was only inevitable. The expected between these sworn enemies was just a matter of time.

As the vibe inside seem to be moving towards a more unfavorable transition, everything outside, on the other hand, became rather calm. The view outside somehow seemed to be drawing back a more soothing reaction out of the few who was present, especially for Romelo, who now was using this moment alone outside to reminisce. He sighed as he dwelled on his own personal issues. "I-I wonder what went wrong?" he asked out loud. "How come…Rose bailed out on me in the last second? Why? I don't get it…I mean, we finished school, we were still talking and all. Plus, she gave me a ticket to come out here tonight…I mean…what happen? Could what Mauricio said to me earlier be true?"

Doing Benito the small favor was completely behind him as he continued to delve and talk to himself about his own current events. Little did he know that someone nearby was listening to him. "Ding, I guess Mauricio was right then," said Romelo. "Maybe –" Romelo suddenly comes to a halt at the sound of a female's voice. The dialog of the female's voice to Romelo was, "Um, excuse me, but who are you talking to?" Following the direction in which the voice was heard, Romelo leans back and slightly tilts his head to the left. He then widened his eyes and made a full turn to have a clear view of what he saw. Gazing back at the female standing before him, he immediately read this person as someone who is a whole-hearted individual. That there alone amplified his attraction to her. It was Julisa he happened to run into at that instant. However, Romelo was unaware of who Julisa was. Though, she had a very familiar face, he thought. At the same time, he couldn't seem to put it all together. Now staring back at Romelo awkwardly, Julisa again asked, "Um, who are you talking to?".

"Uh, umm…You didn't hear all that, did you?" Romelo responded.

"No but I heard quite a bit."

"Hmmm, how long you've been standing there?"

"Hmmm, not that long. I mean, I stepped outside to have a look out here from the balcony, but that's when I noticed you sitting here making all these gestures."

"Stuh, you saw me?"

"Yeah, and I heard you, so that's when I went to thinking that you were talking to someone. But when I came to realize that you were all by yourself, that's when I asked myself, *who is he talking to*".

"Um, uh…ding."

"Is that all you did out here tonight?"

"Naw…I was inside earlier with my cousins."

"Oh, so you're here with people then?"

"Yeah, I brought my cousin out here just to help him get some issues off his mind."

"Did something happen?"

"Yeah, he got in a pretty bad fight with someone several weeks ago. I forgot the name of who he told me it was but yeah, he tried to press charges against him."

"So did he win?"

"What? Who? My cousin?"

"Yeah, did he win?"

"Naw, the judge denied his claim, and it's been bothering him since. So, someone I know gave me her invitation to come out here, and since I know he likes to party, I figure I'd bring him along."

"Aww well, that was real sweet of you."

"Yeah, I had to help him get it off his mind."

"Okay, well has it helped?"

"Oh yeah, my cousin's in there and loving it right now."

"Well, that's good. So why aren't you in there?"

"Oh, me?"

"Yeah, you ought to be in there having some fun too."

"Hmmm, nann. That's my cousin's kind of scene, and besides, I like the way it feels out here."

"So, what you're saying? My party is lame or something?"

"Your party?"

"Yeah, my party."

"Wait a minute, your party?"

"Yes, my party. Everyone I've checked tonight's enjoying the party. Everyone except you."

"Wait a minute, so this is your party?"

"Yeah, I'm the one throwing this party."

"You're the girl whose name I saw posted up on the banner when I came here tonight?"

"Yep."

"It read 'Congrats Julisa.'"

"Uh huh, that's my name."

"You're her?"

"Uh huh."

"Well…ding…"

"Um, what?"

"Oh nothing, nothing."

"Then what?"

"I just wanted to say congrats to ya."

"Oh well uh…thanks, I guess."

"So, what are you gonna do after school?"

"Wow, you know how many times I've been asked that?"

"A lot?"

"Yes, and right now, you've made the hundredth person to run by me with that."

"Uh, okay…So now what?"

"I'm thinking about going to school here in Chicago, but then again I wanna try going somewhere out of state."

"Hmmm…Okay well, if you decide to stay here for college, don't go to Kendall or Malcolm X, you'll see the same people you remembered from high school, at least I did."

"Hmmm wait, how do you know all this?"

"Sta, because I went there."

"You're in college there?"

"Naw, I just took a few general classes there to get some college credits."

"Oh, I see…But wait, how were you able to do that if you're still in high school?"

"The school's magnet program enrolled me in some of the courses."

"Hmmm, I wish I'd known about that."

"Yeah, I don't think many people knew about it."

"What high school you went to?"

"Hah, the same one as yours?"

"Hmmm, you ran track, didn't you?"

"Yeah, but only one year for varsity."

"Okay, and did you know a girl named Rose?"

"Mr. Lawson's daughter? Yeah, she was the one who invited me out here tonight."

"I thought that's who you were. So how come I hardly ever seen you around? You got all quiet around the third and fourth quarter."

"That's because I graduated early this year."

"Hmmm, well look at you."

"Look at me…"

"Yeah you. I see you and your quiet lil' self is doing some big things."

"Aww shucks, that ain't nothing."

"Boy, please, what you mean?"

"It ain't."

"Boy, you better stop that."

"I mean, it's not that big compared to what I'm really trying to do."

"Hmmm…So what else you got going on?"

"Well, right now, there are two things I'm trying to do."

"Hmmm, okay…Talk to me (like what)."

"Okay, one of them right now is college. I got in three different ones, and I'm not sure which one I'm trying to go to. On top of that, they're all not in Chitown."

"Hey well, that's good."

"Yeah, so that's just one thing."

"Okay so, what about the other one?"

"Well, the other thing I'm trying to do is help my best friend open his own business out here."

"Ah really? What kind of business is it?"

"He said it's for income tax and stuff like that. My cousin told him that the Westside's a nice spot to stretch his business."

"Does your cousin know about running income taxes?"

"That I ain't sure, but what I can say is that he's been out here for a while, which means that he could get our boy some clients. I figured I could probably do the same thing before I leave for college."

"Yeah, why not."

"Yep, so after tonight, I'm a do that first thing tomorrow. As a matter of fact, why don't you take this business card."

"BOS –"

"B.O.S Financial Services."

"Oh okay…Hey, wait a minute."

"What happened?"

"The address on this card is like right up the street from Stone Park."

"What? You go there?"

"Like all the time."

"Well, hey maybe we could meet up there sometimes then."

"Yeah, we should do that sometimes."

"Wanna go tom –"

Suddenly, a loud, jarring sound broke through the glass doors of the balcony and interrupted the conversation between Julisa and Romelo. Thankfully, it wasn't the result of two opposing gangs. The discordant sound instead was the boisterous tone of Milleena, who Romelo now had his eyes fixed on. "Do you know this person?", he asked Julisa.

"Oh gosh," answered Julisa. "Yes, she's one of my best friends," she said, shaking her head.

"I think she's trying to tell you something," said Romelo.

"Yeah, she is."

"Well, you should probably go see what she wants."

"Yeah, well then good night."

"Alright, so tomorrow at Stone Park?"

"Yeah…Hey…"

"Yeah?"

"I never got your name."

"I'm Romelo, but the Folks know me as Melo."

"Hmp, the Folks huh?"

"Yeah…"

"Hmmm, well alright Melo, I'm Julisa." As Julisa headed back up to the balcony, she turned back towards Romelo, and waved at him. Then through the glass doors, she went. Watching her as the glass doors closed shut behind her, Romelo looked on practically mesmerized. He returned inside to find his cousin, Benito.

Somehow their parting ways momentarily for the night, in a way, signified the end of the party. Romelo and company made an early exit to avoid the heavy traffic. Julisa considered this night to be better than her own birthday celebration. She and her posse stayed behind to make sure everyone else enjoyed the night immensely. Everyone felt the same way she did in the end. Everyone except her cousin, Tyberius. At this point, Tyberius stood still next to a window. It was through that window he watched the Gangster Disciples leave the parking lot. From his exterior, he appeared unusually calm. Internally however, Tyberius was filled with outrage. His contempt for the Disciples that evening was such that it spread on to his clique and carried over to the following days.

Part 4: A Gang from the Southside

On the dawn of the second day that followed the graduation, Tyberius summoned every member of his clique to stop by his cousin's place. Ten of them had already arrived, but there were still others who were on their way. Still infuriated about the unwelcomed guests who crashed in Julisa's party, Tyberius wasted no time trying to arrange a meeting at the park. Upon arrival to Julisa's place, Torence and Lantino noticed some unusual characters lounging around in the front porch. Among them were Vern and J-roc. Everyone was aware that there was word going around about the Gangster Disciples crashing the party. To worsen the case, word had it that Tyberius did absolutely nothing about it. Lantino suspected that it was J-Roc who was fueling Tyberius' mind with the rumors. It was very early in the day, yet everyone was trying to find shade. The temperature was hot outside, but the day was only heating up. Waving his black cap, Torence tried to create his own fan. That's when he unconsciously opened up a new subject outside of the main issue of everyone's discussion. "Ding, I thought we usually had hood meetings late in the day," he said.

"We do," replied Vern. "But today, Tye wanted us to come out here."

"About the GDs?" asked Torence.

"Mmmm hmmm," answered Vern.

"I saw one of them there that night," said J-Roc.

"Tye said he saw one of them at the dance floor," said Vern.

"Yep, that's the same one I saw," said J-Roc.

"Damn, so they were really there?" again asked Torence.

"Uh huh, about eight of them, I heard," answered Vern.

"Where's Julisa?" asked Lantino.

"I think she went out on a date with Kendrick's boy," answered J-Roc.

"With who?" again asking Lantino.

"The police officer…" answered J-Roc.

"Oh…stuh, Jesus," said Lantino.

"Yeah him…" said J-Roc. "Remember, she's not your girlfriend anymore, Tino."

"Man, bump Julisa, I'm trying to figure out when Tye's gonna come down here," said Vern. "It's hot as hell!"

"He might still be waiting on a few more people," said Torence.

"Shit why, we already have enough people as it is," said Vern. "Roc, I thought you said Rojo got a lock on the GDs trail."

"He does," said J-Roc. "The message got to the SVLs as soon as the party was over."

"So Tye's still waiting on word from Rojo," asked Vern.

"Pretty much," answered J-Roc.

"That can't be all he's doing up there," said Vern.

"I wonder what else he might be doing up there?" asked Lantino.

"Stuh," replied J-Roc, "who wants to –"

"BOOM!" sounding the door as it suddenly bursts wide open, cutting off J-Roc's response to Lantino's question. With the door now open, Tyberius walks through the front porch with a rather temperamental demeanor. Silent, the entire clique can already tell that he's hotter than the temperature outside. He then goes on walking back and forth from the porch to the front yard endlessly rambling on about what he might have done if his uncle wasn't present on the night of Julisa's party. He seemed very irritable at the present moment, so not a word was said to him by anyone. "Y'all brought the bats like I told y'all to, right?" he asked everyone. And in response, they all in unison nodded their heads. "Aright, cool, all is well," said Tyberius.

The next several minutes consisted of the clique's listening to Tyberius' monologue. "Motha fuckin' Rojo," he said in a bellicose expression, "while I was upstairs just now told me that them GDs tagged the main parking lot that night at Julisa's party! Stuh, ain't that some shit! Yeah, that's what I said the minute he went to telling me this! Hey, but check this out, though. Motha fuckin' Rojo also told me that one of Benito's cousins stay out here in the Westside, and that she runs by the name of 'Ice.'"

Lantino suddenly begins to bend his eyes and somehow tuned everything out. *Ice, hold on...didn't I use to know an Ice,* he thought. *Wait, Tye and everybody else out here used to know her –.*

"Yo Tino," said Tyberius.

"Yeah, what up," responded Lantino as he snaps back out of his thoughts.

"Them rooks, you sent me ready?" Tyberius asked Lantino.

"Trust me, all is well!" answered Lantino.

"Aright, we all-mighty then," said Tyberius. Directing his attention back to everyone else around him, he completed the rest of his monologue saying, "I will see to it that them rooks don't go soft on the job at all! It's been one day, two nights, and we still ain't snatch them Disciples off our turf yet. So, we gonna bring Benito's kin the business now. Remember, it's a sister of the struggle, and the name we're looking for is Ice. Y'all boys spread out but keep it tight! Tino, Roc, and y'all boys roll out with me!"

Once Tyberius closed that sentence off, they all in unison threw up the VL hand signal. Next, they all headed to their own cars and began clearing the scene at Julisa's place. With the cars packed, bats loaded, and music blasting, they all rolled out into their own destinations. Each of them is led by a common goal. A common goal to find that link to the gang from the Southside.

The car Tyberius was riding in was on its way to somewhere near Stone Park. Around that same area, Romelo and Mauricio were just stepping out of a room in a building they had leased for a business they were getting ready to start soon. Drained from all the work he had put in, Mauricio figured that he had just about enough and was ready to call it a day. With a little more work, he had hope that business would be ready by tomorrow. As for Romelo, he had only spent a few minutes inside with Mauricio. In fact, this was his first time seeing his best friend since that night at Julisa's graduation party. Unlike Mauricio, Romelo seemed rather innervated and unusually at ease with himself. Walking with Romelo towards his car, Mauricio automatically read the vibe even when they were both in the office. "So, where have you been, Romelo?" he asked.

"Oh, you mean today?" asked Romelo.

"Naw, today and yesterday."

"Well, yesterday, I was just vibing it out with my homegirl."

"Oh…you mean that same one who invited you to that party we went to but ain't even show up."

"Naw, Rice…another one."

"Hmmm…Wait, you sure we ain't talking about the same one you've been trying to get at for over seven years?"

"Trust me, it ain't Rose."

"Yeah…Uh…Okay."

"And today, her and I chilled again. So that's when I decided to let her meet Laurence."

"Laurence?"

"Yeah, you know Laurence. He works with Mr. Nobles."

"Oh, you mean one of my cousins from the courthouse. The same cousin who by now probably disclaimed me?"

"Yeah, yeah him…."

"Oh okay. Hey, but wait…"

"What?"

"What were you doing hanging out there by the courthouse?"

"Aw c'mon Rice, you know Laurence and I are tight."

"Mr. Laurence if I'm right, is a notary."

"Okay, so that's what he do?"

"Is there something you ain't telling me, man?"

"Aw c'mon Rice, do we really gotta talk about this?"

"Um…Yeah because it ain't like you to go missing in action."

"Oh please, I always go M.I.A on y'all man."

"Yeah well, not like that. You always let me know where you be."

"Alright, alright I admit it. That's true."

"Okay, so I'm right."

"Yeah, you are, now could we hop in the whip and ride out?"

"Yeah…but let me drive."

"Here, take the keys."

"Alright, cool."

Mauricio starts the car, and off to another zone, the two go. The temperature outside had only increased now that time moved on into the height of the day. Though somehow it didn't seem to bother either Romelo or Mauricio. From the time they left the office building up until they reached their third traffic light, they drove with the A.C on low the whole way. Making the stop at another red light, Mauricio opened a question out to Romelo. "So, Melo, you wanna share that one something?" he asked.

"Uh what?" replying Romelo while looking out at the window.

"Do you wanna share that one something?"

"What one something? Mauricio, what are you talking about?"

"That one something you're holding back from me."

"What? About the notary?"

"Yeah, don't try and play dumb."

"Aw c'mo –"

"'Aw c'mon…NO…Melo, I've known you since we were born –"

"Don't you mean since when we were kids?"

"Naw. Since when we were born."

"Born?"

"Born. Yeah, that's right, we go way back like that. Too far back for you to hold things back from me now. So, talk and tell me what's up."

"Alright, Mr. Laurence and I are pretty tight like that."

"Yeah, all of a sudden."

"You're an asshole…But yeah, he told me he could help me set something up for the court wedding."

"Court wedding…For what? Who's getting married?"

"I am…"

"Who?"

"Me…"

"Uh okay…To who?"

"This girl I met at the party."

"The party you brought us out to a couple of days ago?"

"Yeah."

"Wait, do I know this girl?"

"Naw, none of y'all do."

"Neither do you."

"Wait but Rice something is different about this one! I'm telling you Rice, I feel a connection –"

"A connection? Boy, you crazy."

"I'm telling you I feel like this chick could read my mind and all. It's almost as though I knew her from another life or something."

"Melo…You sure about this?"

"Rice, listen to me, man! This girl can sense my presence and all. Like the other day when I was stopping by her spot to pick her up, she told me she could hear my heartbeat from almost five blocks away."

"Melo, did you just heard what you told me?"

"Yeah-yeah but Rice, check this out. How about I had a dream that she and I were back at that same party we all went to the other night."

"For real?"

"Yeah, I saw her in my dream last night, and I'm telling you Rice; I saw her almost as clear as I see you now."

"Hmmm, what happened?"

"It was like we were back in that same spot, but then again, it ain't feel like we were at a party. I mean, the whole vibe was so different. The mood was all dark, but yet there was still daylight outside. Oh yeah, it also rained too."

"Did something happen?"

"Yeah, something did, but I wasn't sure what. I was too worried about her. I was too ecstatic, and she felt it."

"Huh?"

"She could feel me…"

"Okay…what about her? What'd she do in the dream?"

"I saw her standing this time, and she was wearing this jewelry I ain't see on her the first time at the party. She wasn't alone, though. Someone else was with her?"

"Who?"

"A light-skinned Chinese girl, I think. It may have been one of her friends. Anyways, she was standing at a distance, and she ain't seem too friendly when I was around her."

"So, it ain't sound like a good dream then."

"Well, I don't know what to say, really. All I know is that my girl was happy to see me just as much as I was happy to see her. It's like we were stuck together."

"Damn, that's funny."

"Shit, that ain't even the funny part."

"Hmmm?"

"You wanna hear the funny part about it?"

"Yeah, what happen?"

"She told me what I had on in the dream, what I smelled like and all."

"What the fuck!"

"Yeah…That's what I wanted to say."

"What's her name?"

"Her name?"

"Yeah…I need to know her name so that way, we know who you're with in case we don't see you."

"Her name's Julisa."

"Okay, Julisa what?"

"Julisa Montgomery."

"Shame, you don't even know her full name Melo. Ump, ump and yet you trying to marry her."

"Naw Rice, I just think you heard enough."

"Ah okay…Let's stop over here by the park."

"Hmmm…Why are we stopping out here at Stone Park?"

"Well, this where we been coming at after we close shop, but ya see you been M.I.A for so long that you don't even know that now."

"Oh Rice, get off my back about that already."

"Hey, but is it the truth?"

"You know what? You're an asshole."

"Guess, we'll just keep it moving."

"Right on…So this all y'all been doing these past few days?"

"Yeah well, we just trying to know the West side a 'lil better."

"It don't look like y'all been doing much lately."

"That's easy to say when you been going –"

"Hey, is that my cousin and the rest of the crew?"

"Sitting there at the Gazebo? Yeah."

"Ding…"

"What? You thought I was just talking?"

"Rice, you a clown –"

"Hey yo cuz!" shouted Benito from the gazebo Mauricio pointed out from a distance. "BRING YO ASS OUT HERE!"

"Is that Benito making all that noise?" said Romelo as he approached the gazebo.

"WHAT YOU MEAN IF IT'S ME?" again shouting Benito. "OF COURSE, IT'S ME! CUZ, IT'S ALWAYS ME! AND YES, I'M TALKING TO YOU MR. COLLEGE BOY!"

Shaking his head, Romelo reaches over and embraces his cousin, Benito, and in turn, he greets the rest of his friends. "Hmmm, so now I'm 'Mr. College' boy?" he asked the group jokingly.

"Naw, more like Mr. California Berkeley," replying Mauricio as he slaps hands with Benito.

"Oh my goodness, y'all some clowns," laughing Romelo. "I told y'all that I'm thinking about going there."

"Naw, Melo you told me, you got in that school last time I asked you," said Mauricio.

"Alright, yeah and I did," replied Romelo.

"Wait, last time I checked, I thought you were already in a college," asked Benito.

"Ugh, I don't know how many times I gotta say this: I already am, but those are just my prereqs that I'm taking," answered Romelo.

"Say what?" asked Benito.

"My prereqs," again answering Romelo.

"Yo Rice, where'd you find my cousin?" asked Benito to Mauricio.

"Stuh, I didn't," answered Mauricio. "Your cousin found me at the office today just before I was about to leave."

"So Rice, you told 'em what he's been missing?" asked Benito to Mauricio.

"Naw, I figured I'd bring him here," answered Mauricio.

"Wait, what's going on?" asked Romelo.

"You wanna tell 'em Rice, or should I go ahead?" asking Benito to Mauricio.

"You go right on ahead," answered Mauricio.

"Okay…Yo cuz," said Benito to Romelo.

"What's up?" asked Romelo.

"You'll never believe who was at that party we went to the other night," said Benito to Romelo.

"Uh…Who'd you seen at the party?" asked Romelo.

"Not me," answered Benito, "but two of us: Smoke and Black-n-mild."

"Who was it?" again asking Romelo.

"That same bitch ass nigga who clocked me across my face a while back," answered Benito.

"The same one you took to court?" asked Romelo.

"Him…" answered Benito.

"Ty-Ty…" stuttering Romelo.

"Tyberius," said Mauricio.

"Damn…but what was he doing there?" asked Romelo.

"Because he's the one who threw the party," answered Benito.

"Yeah, which means that the VLs put the party together," said Mauricio.

"Which I find crazy," said Benito to Mauricio.

"Why is that?" asked Mauricio.

"Because I ain't never know VLs to have money like that," answered Benito.

"Stuh, me neither," agreed Mauricio.

"Ump, ump, ump," said Romelo while shaking his head.

"'Ump, ump, ump', what?" asked Mauricio to Romelo.

"Y'all," answered Romelo, "I thought y'all told me that y'all was trying to move away from all that."

"We are," answered Benito. "We just gotta get this business started, that's all."

"Don't sound like it to me," said Romelo, "I mean, I still hear all this talk about VL this and that."

"Relax, Mr. Lover boy, we got it all covered," said Mauricio trying to assure Romelo. "Now that we are trying to expand up here on the Westside, we should be alright."

"Hey, hey, hey wait," said Benito, "what's all this about uh… 'Mr. Lover boy'?" he asked.

"Nito, our boy Melo here's wifing a new chick now," said Mauricio.

"Ahhh… Is that so Melo?" asked Benito, "You finally let Rose go?"

"Yeah, that's why he's all jolly," said Mauricio.

"Hmp, well it's about time," replied Benito.

"Look y'all," said Romelo, "I'm just wondering who's gonna keep y'all out of trouble after I'm gone?"

"Hmmm, you know what cuz that's a really good question," said Benito.

"Well, hey who's gonna get you into it?" asked Mauricio to Romelo.

"Hmmm, even better one Rice," commenting Benito.

"Stuh, y'all some clowns," said Romelo.

"Out here won't be Chitown without ya Melo," said a sincere Mauricio.

"You know he's right cuz," agreed Benito. "It won't."

"I'm a miss you too," said Romelo to Mauricio as they embraced again. "I'm a miss all y'all."

Out of nowhere the sound of burning rubber against concrete was heard way across the park from where Romelo's company was hanging out. A red two door manual car with dark tinted windows could be seen driving awkwardly from a distance. It's not too long before it came to a full stop. The doors on each side of the vehicle opened and five individuals stepped out. Out of the five of them,

Benito has his eyes completely fixed on one in particular. That same one, in particular, happens to be Tyberius, someone he had a previous encounter with. Evidently, the mood in the park became more tense. Everyone paused as they watched Tyberius and his followers make their way towards the gazebo. "Is that him?" asked Mauricio to Benito and Romelo.

"Yep," answered Benito.

"In the flesh," adding Romelo.

"Hmp, y'all weren't lying when y'all said I'd know him the minute I saw 'em," said Mauricio.

"Let me handle this," said Benito as he takes the initiative. "I wanna see what he wants."

With hot air blowing through his flaring nostrils, a prideful and furious Tyberius opened his conversation to the Gangster Disciples saying, "BENITO! I see clocking you on your right side just wasn't enough! Maybe I need to clock you again on your other side if that's what it's gonna take to get the message across! Across that thick skull! Yo ass ain't welcomed in my turf!!"

"Hmp, what turf?" asked Benito in a calm manner.

"My turf," answering Tyberius.

"This?" again asking a relaxed Benito. "You mean this here?"

"Yeah, you call this your turf," interrupting Mauricio. "This garbage?" he asked Tyberius.

A bit bewildered, Tyberius stared back at Mauricio with a suspicious facial expression. "Who are you?" he asked Mauricio.

"I'm Rice," answered Mauricio to Tyberius. Tyberius' suspicions about Mauricio began to grow. Turning towards Benito, he questioned him. "Who the fuck is he?"

"No one you need to know," answering Benito.

"You should feel proud knowing that we even give a less about you," said Mauricio taunting Tyberius.

"Say what!?" replying Tyberius.

"Word has it that your court ain't even yours till it gets dark," again said Mauricio.

"Yo Nito, whoever the fuck he is, he's talking a lot of mess," said Tyberius to Benito. "Maybe I ought to clock him upside his head one time, like I did you. But then that'll probably have Mr. Nobles knocking at my door again. Won't it Nito?"

"If it makes you happy, it'll just be a whole bunch of us times ten," said Benito to Tyberius.

"Yeah, bring it!" replying Tyberius. "We right here!"

"I thought it would make you happy," said Benito.

"You know it's one thing when you cross me," said Tyberius to Benito. "It's another thing when you do dirt on my turf. But crashing my parties, now that's personal!"

"Where's the wrong in doing that?" asked Benito to Tyberius. "I mean last time I checked, weren't we all having a good time?"

"Naw, fuck that!" replying Tyberius. "That party you showed up to was my cousin's party! That wasn't just any ole party!"

"So, is 'sorry' what you wanna hear now?" asked Benito.

"Hmp, I see your fuckery has no boundaries…" said Tyberius.

"I'm sorry for crashing at your cousin's party and having a very…very…very wonderful time there that night," said Benito.

"Not half as sorry as you about to be!" replied Tyberius. "As a matter of fact, I'm a make you feel worse than sorry! It's only right that I do after dissing my peoples like that!"

"Who gives a fuck about your damn cousin anyway?" asked Benito.

"I-I-I don't believe it…" said Romelo. "Julisa…Julisa and you…wait y'all can't be –"

"Wait, who are you?" asked Tyberius to Romelo. "…and what the fuck you know about Julisa?"

"She's my girl too," answered Romelo to Tyberius.

"Whoa, whoa hold up! What?" replied Tyberius.

"Wait, cuz run that back at me again?" asked Benito to Romelo.

"You mean to tell me that, that's his cousin you-you-you seeing?" asked Mauricio to Romelo.

"Ding, I should've known from the get-go," said Romelo. "She was rocking the five-point star…but something –"

"Hey wait, where I know you from?" asked Tyberius, interrupting Romelo.

"Me?" responding Romelo back to Tyberius.

"Yeah you," answered Tyberius. "I know I've seen you from somewhere."

"Listen, I don't know you, man," said Romelo to Tyberius.

"That ain't the point," replied Tyberius. "The real point of the matter is, have you been fucking her?" he asked.

"Huh?" Romelo replies.

"You heard me, mother fucker!" said Tyberius.

"It ain't what you think," answered Romelo. "What we got going on is deeper than that. What we have is REAL –"

"Have you been fucking her?" Tyberius asked again.

"Oh shit, my dawg!" said Benito. "Mi primo got him some big cajunas!"

"Ugh…It's not like that Nito! I'm really feeling her…" said Romelo.

"Huh?" replied a bewildered Benito. "Hey, he said that like he really meant it y'all…"

"I LOVE HER," said Romelo to Tyberius.

"That's not what I asked you now, did I?" shouting Tyberius. "Are you fucking her?! Yes, or no motha fucka! Answer the question!" Romelo paused and stared back at Tyberius without saying a word. "Alright, for the last time, have you been fucking my cousin?" asked Tyberius to Romelo. Silently, everyone waited for an answer from Romelo, and watch him with a lot of anticipation. Weary of the suspense, Mauricio shined the spotlight on himself: "That pussy was good" he says to Tyberius. "It was real good," he said repeatedly out loud, and just like that, everyone gets on with the action. A rumble is taking place at Stone Park between a small band of bitter rivals.

Between the Gangster Disciples and Vice Lords there was nothing but pure hate. Just utter hate in the air. Only hate everywhere. At Stone Park, hate existed there for the moment, and it moved violently. It grappled swiftly, dodged punches, swung haymakers, drew blood, and taunted endlessly. Hate for that time being was in the flesh, and it was ugly. Amid the fighting, it took the form of steel and produced the sound of a gunshot. At last, it paused in the presence of the bitter rivals.

"What the fuck was that?" said Benito as he gasped for air. "What the hell just happened?" he asked.

"Rice…" said Romelo as he noticed Mauricio lying lifeless on the grass. "Maurico!" he calls again, but no response.

"Oh, shit Tye, you smoked 'em!" said J-Roc of the Vice Lords.

"Man shut yo monkey ass up before I blast you too!" replied Tyberius.

"Mauricio…" again Romelo said.

"You did this…" said Benito to Tyberius.

"This our turf," shouting Tyberius.

"Hey Tye look, he's moving!" said Lantino to Tyberius. Both Benito and Tyberius took their eyes off each other to watch Mauricio slowly get up. Barely standing on his own, he nursed his left midsection and immediately starts dragging himself back towards the same way he parked his car. While Romelo instantaneously runs to Mauricio's aide, Benito and his remaining Disciples slowly and silently make their exit. Leaving the scene, Benito's last words to Tyberius is: "Now you done really fucked up…"

"VL HERE!" shouted Tyberius.

"Yo Tye, he's alright now; let's go!" said Lantino to Tyberius.

Tyberius shoves his Glock pistol back in his belt and turns to Lantino to tell him that the park is the heart of their territory. "Tye, if Five-O catches you again, Kendrick's gonna lock you up for a good amount of time," said Lantino to Tyberius. "After what just happened out here, we can't lose you! You hear me, so let's go!"

Chapter 20: A Forbidden Love

Part 5: Heat in the Streets

Mauricio, the longtime associate of Benito's Disciples, is dead. The message from the Westside gangsters has been received. With that said, Benito has retreated to the Southside: the old main headquarters of the Gangster Disciples. There the words of a new recruit could be heard as he pledged his oath to the ways of the Six: the creed of the Gangster Disciples.

Evidently, a street war had been provoked with Mauricio now dead. Romelo's anger had tripled and now was equivalent to that of ten men. Watching him from afar, a close relative of Benito could only shake her head with the thought of disgust. Standing near her, Benito held cannabis in his right hand, inhaling its fumes as thoughts began to run across his own mind. "Sherray, why you keep shaking your head?" he asked while flicking the cannabis out the window. "Nito, you should already know why," answered Sherray.

"If I did, then would I be asking you?"

"You know what I'm going to say."

"No, I don't, and that's why I'm asking you."

"Ugh...You're the one who caused all of this."

"What...What you mean? I ain't mean —"

"Had you listened to me the first, second and third time, this shit would've —"

"So, you trying to tell me that this is all my fault, huh?!"

"Yes! It is!"

"Stuh..."

"I don't know about Smoke or Black, but I know about me for sure. I ain't tell you to stop messing with this Tyberius? I ain't tell you that?"

"Stuh..."

"I told you to quit playing around with this Tyberius cat, but you wouldn't listen."

"Sherray —"

"Remember when I told you that Ice and I fought one of them at Concrete? You remember?"

"Yeah…"

"I know you do because I told you that she was just one…A VL! Them right there are just fucking loko!"

"Yeah Ray, I remember."

"Yeah, I know you remember, and I know you remember when I told you them VLs love to fight. That's all they good for."

"Yep…"

"We with the Folks. So, what we do is big business. They ain't got it like us: money, developments, executives. So, they ain't even worth the sweat. You know that!"

"All…"

"But yet you wanna toy around, and waste time on Tyberius. Now look at things. He left you with a mark next to your eye, plus Rice is dead, and now everybody else gotta get mixed in your bull shit."

"You know Rice was the one who was gonna open the branch on the West to hold down the back-door transactions there? So, he wasn't just someone else."

"I know, but he's dead now…You know very soon your schoolboy over there is gonna join 'em."

"Melo ain't got nothing to worry about. Tyberius can't touch 'em."

"That's not what I'm worried about."

"Hmmm?"

"Nito, I'm worried about him trying to touch Tyberius."

"Sherray, you know he and Mauricio go way back. They were best friends, so how can he not feel what he's feeling right now."

"See, there you go again, not listening to me."

"You really think he's –"

"He's gotta nine on his strap, Nito."

"WHAT?"

"Stuh, you still not listening. I don't know why I'm wasting my breath."

"Okay, hold on Ray…Romelo gotta gun?"

"Mmmm hmmm."

"Wait, but I ain't give 'em no gun."

"I know…"

"Because the Master Don did…"

"He pledged this morning…"

"Call Ice."

"Ice can't talk to 'em now. She's back in the Northside now."

"She's still on that Martin program shit."

"I told you she bought into it."

"Who's he gonna listen to?"

"You."

"Me?"

"Yeah you."

"Naw, he ain't gonna wanna hear what I have to say…He's too hot."

"Next to Ice, you might be the only person who could talk some sense to him."

"I don't know…"

"Nito, you better go over there and talk to him, before he kills himself."

"I-I –"

"For once, just listen to me."

Pausing for just a moment, Benito notated his visual of Romelo. Benito can pick up the dark mood crowded around Romelo's surroundings. Watching him just a little longer, he can feel the dark thoughts clouded in his cousin's mind. It was almost as though Benito was looking at a total stranger. A pure negative energy had completely consumed Romelo and it suited his attire as well.

He sat alone in the room, leaning back against his chair. Wearing Mauricio's black hoody, he looked like a dark hooded figure just sitting without a word or sound. Nodding his head as he watched Romelo, Benito said "Okay" to Sherray, and proceeded at possibly attempting to apprehend his cousin. Hearing Benito's footsteps as he made his way in the room, Romelo spoke out, saying

"Let me guess, you're gonna try and talk me out of this, huh?" he asked.

"Oh, you heard us?" replied Benito.

"Of course, you guys spoke like I wasn't even in the room."

"Look cuz, I think we need to talk about –"

"Talk about you talking my head out of this! Hell NO! My mind is made up!"

"Cuz, before you do –"

"Naw, I'm a fry him the same way he did Mauricio!"

"Cuz…It's been a minute since your folks heard from you. I mean I appreciate you coming down to the Southside with me but pledging –"

"Look, Nito, if you ain't gonna help me, then I'll just find him and smoke him myself!"

"Hold on cuz! Hold on for a second!"

"Shit!"

"Look, just try and chill for a minute, alright. I know ya feeling hot, but I really need ya to chill fa a minute!"

"Ughhh!!"

"Look, I feel ya Melo! We all did!"

"He shot him…"

"Yeah, he did and trust me if we really wanted him –"

"…and killed Rice. I'm-I'm…"

"…look, we could have got him by now…"

"…What?"

"Yeah, we could have got 'em that same day, but the Folks figured they'll get 'em after some time. Probably in a couple of weeks from now…"

"Why in a couple of weeks?"

"You see that's the thing; we wanna let 'em think that he's hot. After two weeks go by, he'll probably figure that the heat died down, so that's when we'll snatch 'em up off the streets. Right there, we'll really show 'em how evil we are. So be easy and just chill for a minute."

"Stuh…Alright…"

"Just chill for a minute and know this, 'All ain't well.'"

"Because all is one."

"And one is all."

That night Benito made a believer out of Romelo as he spoke like a true seer of tomorrow's world. His words on how the next days were going to play out seem to be coming into reality. Within two weeks, the Westside saw a bit of a lighter mood. Though, Tyberius' main circle would still walk around with a third eye open every now and then. The tattoo shop had become everyone's new hangout spot, and Tyberius could always be seen stepping out with one of Torence's latest designs on his arms. By now, the Gangster Disciples were back in the Westside region. This time they were out to even the score with the Vice Lords, as Benito predicted. Lurking like something wicked, they did day in and day out.

Driving in a metallic black car with chromed rims, they followed a red two-door manual operated car to a street just four blocks away from the tattoo shop Torence worked at. In that street sat a local food store in which the red car pulled up to. Coming out, the passenger side of the red car was the Gangster Disciples' primary target, Tyberius, who could be seen approaching a bench. Accompanying him were two other Vice Lords. The store was closed, but a dim light from a sign on its glass door shined on the bench. The scene was still soaked from the rain that came down earlier that evening, and everything else in the surrounding area that extended beyond the light's border appeared pitched black. Making their way out of the metallic black car unnoticed, four shadowy hooded figures crept into the scene with their arms raised forward. Finally, noticing the Gangster Disciples, Tyberius stood tall with dignity. By then, bullets had already pierced through the surface of his body, and he along with his two other Vice Lord warriors, came crashing down to the concrete floor. Right there and then, Tyberius knew the face of death and immediately embraced it. Blending back in with the darkness, the Gangster Disciples exited the scene without barely making a sound.

It was somewhere around the early morning hours when the store owner came and found the bodies lying down on his development. He, in turn, instantaneously notified the proper authorities, who then sent the Chicago police and paramedics on the scene. By sunrise, the street was flooded with people who were trying to figure out what was going on. Tyberius' body had been removed by then, and the other two vice Lords were now recovering in a nearby hospital. After the investigators finally cleared the scene, they concluded that there's a connection between the two murders that took place and that they're gang related. To further the investigation, detectives went questioning any possible suspects, including the victims' families.

Overall, nineteen hours had gone by since the death of Tyberius. At this point, all but one member of the Cross family was still unaware of the incident that transpired the night prior. Young, petite, bright, and sociable, Julisa altogether just seemed to have a better tomorrow in the grip of her possession. She was loaded with infinite potential and a beautiful personality to match her physical description as a character. Returning home from a day spent mainly over the phone with her lover, Romelo, she now joined her father in the living room.

"Hey daddy," said Julisa as she greeted her father,

"Hey, princess," her father replied.

"I got your message about the family meeting," said Julisa.

"Yeah, well, good because we have a lot to cover."

"Where's mom? I thought you said she'd be here soon."

"She will, but she's still by your aunt's grieving with the others."

"Grieving? About what? What's going on?"

"Does anything come to mind when you hear the names Jimmel Jones and Vernon McGee?"

"Hmmm...Jimmel Jones and Vernon Mc-who?"

"Vernon McGee."

"Um...No. What about them?"

"Okay, so you don't know neither of the two?"

"No...Who are they?"

He sighs, "Thank God, that means you don't have no real link to the other bodies found this morning."

"Wait, daddy, what's going on? What are you talking about?"

"Did you hear anything about the homicide that took place this morning?"

"Oh that, yeah…I'm sure that's all over the news by now."

Her dad sighs again, "Well, princess, this won't be easy for me to tell you."

"What happened? Was it someone you knew that got killed?"

"Yeah…In fact, it's someone we know, Julisa."

"Wait, who?"

"Tyberius…Your cousin. My nephew, Tyberius, is dead."

"No daddy –"

"The police found him shot to death this morning by that food store."

"Naw ah…"

"Yeah…"

"Are you sure it was him? How do you know all this?"

"I got word from the Chicago Police sometime around mid-day. So, I left work to confirm if it was Tye I saw in the body bag."

"It was him?"

"Yeah...He was all shot up. Cops said that the bullets on his chest were shot from close range, which means that the kill was intended."

"Oh my God, Tye is dead."

"There were two others found near Tye's body."

"They got killed too?"

"No…Both of them are recovering at the hospital."

"Who are they?"

"The names I mentioned earlier: Jimmel Jones and Vernon McGee. Two gangsters from the Vice Lords."

"How'd you find out about them?"

"Your guy friend, Jesus, stopped by to give me some more details about the murder."

"What did he say? Does he know who did it?"

"He believes that Tyberius' death may have been gang-related. He said that a couple of weeks ago someone by the name of Mauricio Nobles was shot and killed by Vice Lords. So, shooting Tyberius might have been in result of retaliation."

"I know Tyberius was in the gang but –"

"Princess let's not beat around the bush. What happened to your cousin has been coming for him. He wouldn't give up that kind of life. But with his death being gang-related that means more trouble is gonna come knocking at our door Julisa. This means that you have to sign up for school and live there to get the hell away from this mess."

"But daddy wait, I just can't move out and leave, I gotta –"

"Damn that, Julisa, now's the time! I lost him to bull shit; I'm not losing you too!"

"Daddy, I haven't even made up my mind on what it is exactly I wanna do with school!"

"But...wait, HUH?"

"Anyways, does Jesus know who killed Tye?"

"He suspects that it's the Disciple's Gang...He also brought one more name that might have ties to the two murders."

"Who might that be?"

"He said the name was Romelo Montgomery..."

"Romelo...Montgomery..."

"Yeah, he says this guy's been missing since the death of the first victim, and his folks haven't seen 'em in over two weeks. He's now wanted for questioning."

"Hmmm..."

"Where this gets interesting to me is that this guy was friends with the Mauricio victim."

"Daddy, I know that guy."

"You said what?"

"I said I know him."

"Aww shit!"

"What daddy? He's not a bad guy! I told you I know him."

"He's a link to your cousin's death, and yet you think he's good!"

"Daddy, trust me, Romelo didn't kill Tyberius."

"Then why is he hiding from the police if he didn't kill anybody."

"Daddy, I'm telling you he didn't do it! He's innocent!"

"Like Lantino, huh?"

"No, this is different."

"You said that about Lantino and look how he turned out: a high school dropout and a young no-good for nothing gangster!"

"Daddy, I'm not with Lantino anymore!"

"You should've never been with him, to begin with!"

"You don't know him like I do! You don't know a single thing about Lantino!"

"Stuh, that's not my problem! Wait…Is that what it is? You're seeing this guy too, huh?"

"Well, uh –"

"Am I right, you're seeing him too, huh?"

"What if I am?"

"Stuh…Unbelievable! Julisa, what is with you and bad boys?"

"He isn't a bad boy…Not my Romelo."

"Stuh…First, a low life gangster and now a wanted killer of your cousin!"

"Daddy, for the last time, Romelo did not kill Tyberius!"

"Julisa, why not a guy like Jesus?"

"What about Jesus?"

"I thought there was something between you and him!"

"Daddy, I don't want him. There was never anything between us."

"But Julisa for Christ sakes, he's a cop, and not just that, he's kin to Judge Kendrick."

"So…"

"Okay, well, why not consider another guy. I mean if it can't be Jesus then at least another who has a future."

"But daddy, that's the thing Romelo has a future –"

"Princess, you don't understand. You broke the cycle. For the first time, a member of this family has graduated from high school and is moving on to a better life in college. If you marry a man like Jesus, Judge Nobles may offer you a possible full ride through college! Do you understand the name you could make for your family and me?"

"What about what I want, daddy? For all my life, I have been trying to keep you pleased! Haven't I done that long enough? Isn't it about time I get to do what I want?"

"Princess, I was young just like you once, and use to think the same way you did. I believed that I could change things and save someone, but that's not how the world runs!"

"If that's how you think, then Tyberius was right to feel the way he did about you."

"I did whatever I could to keep that boy alive, Julisa! He's lucky he got to see nineteen!"

"You're too absent-minded. I see why he never claimed you as his uncle."

"What?"

"Now, I see…"

"You know what, if joining your cousins is the route you've chosen, then you could forget about the financial support you're gonna need from me to aide you through school!"

"What?"

"You can go ahead and be with your killer, but you're not gonna bring him under this roof."

"But daddy –"

"Since you want to do what you want, then go ahead on! I won't have any part of it!"

"Daddy!"

"Come to your mother about the funeral arrangements."

Part 6: Heat in the Streets

Tyberius, the heart, soul, and ideal figure of the Vice Lord gangsters, was dead. With him out now, operations in the Westside could run accordingly for the Gangster Disciples, meaning that the development of an extended branch could be established. The message from the gang of the South was sent. A funeral took place days after the incident transpired. Present at the funeral were the Crosses, the Moubays, the Tourezes, and every other associate of Tyberius. The funeral occurred during the day though oddly; it felt as though it were 10 pm. It was a rainy day and that added more emotional drain.

Julisa began the ceremony with a speech that was well delivered. Afterward, a few relatives of the Cross family went up to express their woes. Then came Loraine's eulogy, which was written by Milleena. When the casket was being lowered, Torence finally found the heart to share a few of his last words, after Loraine pushed him. Lastly, came Lantino, who, with some quiver in his voice, kept his farewell short and simple. J-Roc surprisingly made an appearance there as well, though it didn't lighten up the mood at the setting.

Once the service ended, everyone met with the Crosses at a luxury hotel to show their condolences. Tyberius' Vice Lords covered the reservations and payments. Like the graduation party that took place weeks ago, there was once again an uninvited guest amid the memorial service. And this time, the uninvited was well-groomed and dressed in casual dark black formal clothing. With his face sealed by his shades and attire matching with every other male in the room, he walked around, looking relatively invisible among the people there.

However, Julisa recognized him and directed him to one of the building's rear exits. She was dressed in a jet black sleeveless mini dress with the same metallic black stringed earrings she had for her graduation day. She also wore the jewelry her cousin, Tyberius, gave her along with black heels.

"Romelo, you could come out now," she said to the uninvited. Removing his shades as he steps on the scene, Romelo takes a look around, making sure the coast is clear. "Come over here," Julisa commands. "I wanna see you closer."

"You sure no one knows we're here?" asking Romelo.

"There's only one other person here, but she's watching us from the balcony," answered Julisa.

"Oh shit! Who?"

"Milleena."

"Who?"

"Don't worry about her."

"I told you no one could know that I'm here trying to see you."

"Melo, it's okay. She's only there trying to make sure I'm alright. That's it."

"You sure she's cool?"

"Yes, now can you stop looking back at her like a fugitive."

"Ugh…okay."

"And take off those ugly shades."

"Ding…Sorry, baby."

"Look at me, so I could see your eyes."

"Okay."

"I should slap you for not telling me that you hadn't been back home for a while…"

He took a deep sigh. "Baby, I didn't know how to tell you –"

"When I asked you 'is everything alright,' why didn't you just say it right then! Instead of sealing it away from me."

"Everything was happening so fast, and I didn't think you'd understand –"

"What?"

"I mean, even I didn't understand."

"I hear you been gone for a while."

"After my friend died, it's like things just changed. I couldn't go see my people right away. I needed to stay away from everyone because I was different for a second."

"Are you talking about Mauricio?"

"Yeah…I mean when Rice died I-I-I –"

"You wanted Tyberius –"

"YES…Damn bad…Baby, I didn't do it."

"I know."

"That boy they had the service for –"

"You mean Tyberius?"

"Uh…Yeah um, him…Was he really…your…cousin?"

"Yes…He was."

"Wow…stuh…"

"Romelo, you gotta understand that no matter what he was to you, I loved him."

"I understand."

"Were you there when your friend died?"

"Yeah, in fact I saw everything –"

"You don't have to tell me."

"That's crazy…"

"What's crazy?"

"Where I'm from, I used to always hear that the Lords were a crazy bunch, but it wasn't too often I'd hear about 'em."

"I don't really know much about them myself unless you were to ask me about my cousin. He's practically the closest thing I knew next to the Lords.

"I think it was up until that street fight when I started hearing about the Lords a lot. My cousin told me everything I know now about them after coming back from court."

"He's the one who filed the lawsuit, right?"

"Yeah…man, you really are Tyberius' cousin."

"You're one of them too, aren't you?"

"A Disciple?"

"Yeah…"

"Well, my Folks did whatever they could to keep Rice and I out of it. Even though, it was the Disciples who got me in the magnet program and covered my expenses out here in the West. With that being said, I guess you can call me one of them."

"I'm really sorry about your friend."

"Baby, I'm sorry too. I wish your cousin ain't have to go out like that."

"Come here and let me wrap you in my arms."

"I miss you."

"I miss you too, Melo."

"Baby…"

"Yeah…"

"I wish we could just stay like this."

"Like how we are now?"

"Yeah, just stuck together."

"Me too…Mmmm baby…"

"Yeah?"

"I love that cologne you have on."

"Yeah? You smell it?"

"Mmmm hmmm."

"Thanks.

"You're welcome Melo…You know something look different about you today."

"Oh yeah?"

"Yeah."

"Well, something seems different about you too."

"Hmmm…yeah?"

"Yeah, but that's okay."

"Why is that okay?"

"Because if you were to come my way, I wouldn't let anything happen to you."

"Mmmm, you're stupid, but that was cute, though."

"So baby, tell me."

"Okay, what."

"Even though you knew that something was wrong with me, how'd you find out that I wasn't around for a while."

"Melo, everyone knows about it, but I found out from my dad a few nights ago. And he found out from the police who want you for questioning."

"Hmp…"

"So, you're gonna go back to your peoples?"

"Yeah, I'm ready to see them now."

"What are you gonna do about the police."

"I'm a just tell them what they need to know in hopes that I could get my scholarships back."

"Wait, so you're really going to Berkley then?"

"Yeah…"

"It's obvious you ain't have me on your mind all day?"

"Now baby, you know that's not true!"

"Then why have you been thinking about it all day?"

"Because Julisa, you know why!"

"Ugh!"

"C'mon Julisa; you read my heart rate better than my doctor, so you know it's true, even if you call me a liar."

"I don't wanna hear it, Melo."

"Look…Julisa; the Disciples are no joke."

"Neither are the Lords!"

"Baby, I know! But I'm telling you this situation's getting out of hand, and I don't want you getting caught in it."

"So, after the Lords hit back, you think the Disciples may try coming for me?"

"Yeah, they will if they can't get someone who's marked for death!"

"Maybe you're right."

"You know I'm right, baby. Let's face it, it's a street war, and until things calm down, I can't risk endangering your life."

"Melo…"

"Yeah, baby."

"I love you."

"I love you too…Hold on…"

"What…"

"Wait a second…"

"What's wrong baby?"

"I remember this…"

"You mean out here?"

"Yeah, it looked just like…this! Your friend from a distance
—"

"The balcony?"

"Yeah, and then outside looking soaked and the sun going down. This is what I remember telling Rice about."

"You told 'em about this."

"Yeah, and you-you were standing just like that in front of me."

"I guess this is the part where you hand me my jewelry."

"Yeah, that's what you had on that I ain't see on you yet."

"Pull it out so I can see it."

"Here you go baby. This is for you."

"It's a charm."

"Yeah, it's one of my favorites because this one was actually passed down to me from other generations in my family. It's like a symbol of my folks, but since I'm giving it to you, I want you to think of me when you wear it."

"Wear it…"

"Yes, baby I want you to keep this because I'll come back for it."

"Okay, I'll make sure I hold this for you."

"Good. Muah."

"I should probably head back to my friend now."

"Yeah, you should."
"And you better get going."
"Yeah, you're right."
"Bye Melo."
"Bye Julisa."

Chapter 21: Reflections

Once the service ended, everyone met with the Crosses at a luxury location to show their condolences. While Julisa was sharing a few words with her lover, Romelo, at one of the rear exits, Torence and company stayed visible at the building's common areas. Minutes later, he checked on Loriana, who for some unknown reason, isolated herself. Approaching her near the building's main entrance, he kindly greeted her, "Evening Ms. Tourez."

"Buenos papi," replied Loriana.

"Are you alright?" asked Torence.

"No…No, I'm not," answered Loriana as she shook her head.

"I know…Today has been really hard to get through."

"Si papi…It has…"

"Today might be the saddest day I've ever seen since I've been here."

"Yeah?"

"Yep."

"What was his name again?"

"Tyberius."

"And how old was he again? Eighteen?"

"Naw…nineteen."

"Wow…nineteen…"

"Yeah."

"He was just a baby."

"Hmmm…"

"Papi, did you know him as one of your friends?"

"Mmmm hmmm…He used to love coming by the shop. He was probably the best customer I had."

"Really?"

"Yeah, he showed up more than any other person I knew, and some people said that if I weren't there he wouldn't come or stay at all."

"So, he was killed?"

"Yeah, by gangsters."

"And the other two that were with him?"

"They're still alive. Matter of fact, one of them I heard was at the funeral."

"I yie yie!"

"Ms. Tourez, do you need a napkin?"

"No papi."

"You sure because I can run and get some."

"No papi, just…just stay here."

"Okay."

"Look, papi…"

"Yes?"

"You and Loraine have to get your brother out of the gang."

"Out…of the gang?"

"YES, or else he's going to end up like your friend."

"Shot up and killed?"

"YES, I FEAR for his life!"

"Ding…"

"Lantino's going to end up in jail, hurt in the hospital like those two boys or worse: DEAD!"

"Stuh…"

"Please papi, you have to try. You're probably the only one who can reach him because he won't listen to anyone else."

"Damn!"

"What papi?"

"I-I…ugh…Just forget it."

"No Papi; talk to me."

"Why-why-why did you let 'em go?"

"Papi…That night, Tino had already made up his mind."

"You mean when he left?"

"Si papi…When he walked through the door and out into that rain that night, he made his choice."

"But I don't get it…I mean I-I don't understand…"

"Papi, what don't you understand?"

"After you…you –"

"After I yelled at him? Is that what you're trying to say?"

"Um…yeah…"

"Okay, what about it papi?"

"You told him to get out…"

"Papi, don't you see? He needed to go…"

"Go?"

"Si…Papi, Lantino is LOST. You heard him that night in the living room. He really believes that he's walking with a purpose serving the gang."

"So why let him go now? Why, after all this time?"

"I didn't make that choice papi. He already did when he decided to drop out of school. He already did the minute he joined the gang. He knows how much I hate them. He knows what I think of them. You've even heard me when I said that they're no better than CRIMINALS."

"Yeah, I remember when you'd say that."

"Like I said that night, 'no criminal is welcomed in my house.'"

"Ding…"

"But papi…"

"Yes?"

"I will let him back in. But until he leaves his new life, he won't dare step foot in my door."

"But Ms. Tourez, you know he might die if he tries to leave."

"He's gonna die if he stays in now. Like, like your friend…"

"Tyberius…"

"Ugh…Oh papi, why couldn't he be more like you?"

"Like…Me?"

"Yes…You've always listened and never gave me trouble."

"Hmmm…"

"From the time I first met you, I knew something was different."

"Really? You did?"

"Yes, and don't ask me how…I…just knew from the way you spoke and how you were. You were always so calm and quiet. And that's what I liked about you because you weren't like any of the other friends Lantino brought home. Even Loraine said the same thing."

"She did?"

"Yes, papi…"

"What were his friends like?"

"Trouble…But you papi…was good. I know this is why I always wanted you two together."

"You mean Lantino?"

"Yes, I know standing next to you Lantino had a chance."

"Huh?"

"Papi, what I'm trying to say is that you're everything I wanted him to be like, and everything I'd want in a son."

"You…You really mean that?"

"Si, papi."

"Thank you."

"No really, you're everything anyone would want in a son, and now that you're all grown-up, Loraine has the special thing that I never had…"

"What's that?"

"A good man…"

"Hmmmm…"

"I think you're the reason why Lantino is eighteen today. In some way, it seems like you kept all of us together"

"What about…Lantino?"

"Lantino…You two are like…like night and day. You both are so different. Yet you both look alike and kind of seem alike especially when you're together. But if only he'd just listen…He's become more and more like his father."

"Did you know him?"

"Yes papi, I did. In fact, Caesar and I were once in love."

"You mean…Lantino's father?"

"Si papi, si…"

"So, what happened to him?"

"He was in too much trouble…But there was a charm about him that no woman could resist. That's how we had Loraine…"

"Loraine..."

"Si papi…"

"Did he…die?"

"Die? No Papi. Trouble chased Caesar away before it could finally catch up and kill him."

"Ding…"

"He really loved me…But Lantino's mother became envious of me once she saw that he favored me over her."

"You mean…Monalisa?"

"Yes, papi…Her…You remember when I shouted her name out?"

"Yeah…I-I remember when you-you said that you had to get…rid of her…"

"Wow, you remembered that papi?"

"Ms. Tourez, did something happen between you and Lantino?"

She sighed, "Yes…Yes, papi something did."

"Wha-what-what happened?"

"Some time ago, after Caesar ran off from Kendrick and the police, Monalisa and I had a custody battle for Lantino. The courts sided with me because Caesar left me with the parental rights after he and Monalisa separated. Plus, she had dirt under her name, so it made it easier for the judge to decide who gets to take Lantino."

"Ooooooh…"

"Even though Lantino isn't my son, I wanted to take him under my wing because he was so young, and I didn't want him to know the kind of life his mother and father came out of. I wasn't born here, but my family (the Tourezes) taught me that education was the way to the good life. That's why I strived to show you things you know now. This is what I wanted for Lantino. I only did it because I wanted what was best for him."

"I know you did, Ms. Tourez."

"Thank you, papi."

"So Ms. Tourez, what happened to Monalisa after she lost?"

"She was deported for not having the right documents to stay here."

"Whoa Ms. Tourez…Did all that really happen?"

"Yes papi, it did."

"So, you feel like this is why he gives you a cold shoulder?"

"Yes, this is exactly why, and I know that after kicking him out, he hates me now."

"Ms. Tourez, I'm sorry all of this happened."

"I am too papi…"

"Stuh…"

"Papi, that night before he walked out and said to me that the workforce is for suckers, he sounded just like his father. It hurt me to have to see him leave."

"Do you really believe that he hates you, Ms. Tourez?"

"Papi, I know he does."

"That's not what he tells me when we talk."

Milleena's Place

Loriana clearly felt apprehensive about Lantino's role in the gang and wasn't looking forward to potentially sharing an estranged relationship with him. After hearing what Torence said to her as opposed to what she thought, she then seemed rich with optimism. Appreciating his efforts to comfort her, she embraced him. Then they left the main entrance to join everyone else back in the common areas. The day came to an end, and along came several other days. Before Torence knew it, a whole week had gone by since the funeral took place. Nowadays, he was spending more time with Loraine. He had taken some time off from the tattoo shop to catch up with Lantino, who he didn't see very often anymore. He didn't touch base with the Vice Lords as much as he did now that Tyberius was gone. In fact, nearly everyone he knew distanced themselves from Tyberius' associates on account of the last events that occurred. Even Julisa kept her distance from the clique. Lantino now seemed to be the only exception. Days after the funeral, he continued to be present in the hood meetings and remained very active in the streets, especially around the late hours.

During the day, Torence would sometimes run into Lantino during his walk with Loraine somewhere. At times, both he and Loraine would stop to have a word with Lantino as an attempt to have him come back home. But Lantino insisted, and soon the feelings of concern began to grow on Loraine as time passed. As a means to alleviate Loraine of her concerns for Lantino, Torence one day took her out to one of her favorite hangout spots: Milleena's place. Though it was Torence's first few minutes at Milleena's place, he already seemed fond of the Moubays' hospitality. He only sat in one place, which was the living room. However, his eyes traveled all over the interior of the home. It was his first time being inside a triplex building. "Boo," said Loraine, who was seated right next to him.

"Huh, oh yeah babe," respond Torence.

"You looking for something?" asked Loraine.

"Me…uh naw," answered Torence.

"Then why you looking like you missing something?" again asking Loraine.

"Oh naw…I just never seen a house set up like this one," explaining Torence. "I mean, it looks like a three-story house on the outside, but yet when you're inside, one floor is only for one family," he adds.

"Yeah, I know, and the stairs is the only way up to the second and third floor," said Milleena, who had returned one of her items to the living room. "Yeah, it took me a while to get used to that back when we first moved here. Most of the buildings here are set up this way around this side."

"You're the only one home?" asked Torence to Milleena.

"Naw, Bree's inside my mom's room," answered Milleena.

"Hmmm…where's everybody else?" asked Loraine to Milleena.

"Tuwan went to work, my mom went somewhere, and the other two are upstairs at the neighbor's house," answered Milleena.

"Oh okay," replied Loraine. "So girl, tell me what's going on with you these days?" she asked.

"Shit," answered Milleena. "The most I've been doing is stopping by Julisa's place. But today I ain't feel like stepping out once the rain came down. Until you two showed up, sleeping is really all I did today."

"You've heard from Julisa," asked Loraine. "Eww, tell me, how is she doing? Is she alright?"

"Hmmm, I'm not sure. I hear she's moving to New York," answered Milleena.

"Wait, but I thought she was going to college, though," said Loraine.

"Oh yeah, she is," replying Milleena. "Except it's gonna be over there."

"Hmp, way out there," said Loraine.

"Mmmm hmmm," answered Milleena.

"Hmp, well I really hope she's alright," said Loraine.

"I hope so, too," said Milleena. "Okay new subject: so, what's going on with y'all two love birds over here?" she asks.

"You mean me and my cutie here," replying Loraine.

"Yeah, I see you've got your legs across his lap like you're trying to mark your territory or something. Okay Raine, I see you," laughed Milleena.

"Oh please, Lee, you need to go sit down," said Loraine.

"Hmmm, so he's your cutie now, huh?" asked Milleena.

"Torence is my boo," answered Loraine.

"Hmmm, I see. So, he went from Lantino's weird friend to your boo now?" asked Milleena. "Ump, ump, ump Torence, I gotta hand it to you," she says to Torence.

"Oh, whatever Lee," replied Loraine.

"No, for real because most guys weren't able to keep up, but you have so far, which means that there's something you're doing right, to everything they're doing wrong," said Milleena to Torence.

"Um, okay," replied Torence.

"Please…Lee, you need to stop," said Loraine to Milleena.

"Uh huh…" laughed Milleena.

"And Torence, you better not be feeling big-headed right now," said Loraine to Torence as she leaned forward to tap him on his cheek.

"Raine babe, I ain't say anything," said Torence to Loraine.

"Hmmm, so tell me," said Milleena. "Y'all finally got it together now? Y'all love each other or should I expect any breakups again? Hmmm, naw you know what? I shouldn't even ask Loraine this because you never give me a straight answer."

"Ugh," replying Loraine.

"Better yet, let me ask Torence this question," said Milleena.

"Me?" asked Torence to Milleena.

"Yeah, this question is for you, Mr. Cutie. I wanna hear it from your mouth: y'all got it together now?" laughed Milleena.

"Uh…Yeah," answered Torence.

"Yeah? Hmmm, you don't sound too convincing, Mr. Cutie," again laughing Milleena.

"Look, he's my husband, okay," said Loraine to Milleena.

"OH, OH…Okay…It's like that now huh," replying Milleena. "It's got to that level."

"Yep, it's exactly that," Loraine said.

"Hmmm, does Lantino know anything about this?" asked Milleena.

"Um, uh…He will…" answered Torence.

"Um, uh he will…wait boo, what do you mean?" asked Loraine.

"Raine babe, he doesn't know yet," answered Torence.

"What do you mean? He should've already known by now," said Loraine.

"And he will babe –" said Torence.

"No, that's what you told me last time, and the last time before that," said Loraine interrupting Torence.

"Well, babe how you expect me to tell him when he's been like a ghost these past few weeks," replied Torence.

"Hey, you know what, that's true," Milleena agreed. "Torence does have a point. When do you ever see Tino these days?"

"You feel me?" asked Torence to Milleena.

"Yeah, I do," answered Milleena, "I mean the last time I remember seeing Tino was at the funeral."

"Ugh! I swear he's the next one to go after Tyberius," said Loraine to Milleena.

"Uh, excuse me," replied Milleena. "You said what? I ain't catch that last part," she said to Loraine.

"He's a dead man walking out in those streets," replying Loraine to Milleena.

"Wait, what's going on?" asked Milleena.

"Stuh, Lee…What's going on is that Tino is in real deep. It ain't like you and me where if something goes down, we gotta show our face if the top hat summons for peeps. Tino's at a point now where the box is his only way out," explaining Torence to Milleena.

"Boo! Don't talk about the box!" said Loraine interrupting Torence.

"Raine is tripping out because Tino may very soon end up like Tye. Especially now with the war going on," again explaining Torence to Milleena.

"Have you talked to him?" asked Milleena.

"Yeah…I have," answered Torence. "I mean…I've tried to."

"Lee, we've all tried, but Tino won't listen to anything we say!" said Loraine to Milleena.

"Because he can't leave," said Torence to Loraine.

"Why not?" asked Loraine.

"Because he'll die if he tries," answered Milleena.

"Boo is that true?" asked Loraine to Torence.

"Yeah…stuh…" answered Torence.

"Wow…Well, couldn't he just move somewhere else?" asked Loraine.

"It wouldn't make a difference," answered Milleena. "The VLs will find him and kill 'em."

"Yeah, and even then, where would he move to?" asked Torence. "Who would he be able to trust."

"Ding Tino…" muttered Loraine.

"It ain't his fault," replied Torence to Loraine.

"Yeah, it ain't," agreed Milleena. "Hey, wanna know what I heard a couple of days ago when I went to see Vern back in the hospital?" she asked them.

"What?" answered both Torence and Loraine.

"I hear since Tye is gone, J-Roc is supposed to hold it down for the set, right," said Milleena.

"Okay," replying Torence this time.

"Well, not so," said Milleena. "Word has it that the rooks ain't showing any respect to Roc. That means the seat for top hat is still open,"

"So you think Tino can hop on it?" asked Torence to Milleena.

"I think the clique want 'em to," answered Milleena.

"Hmmm, but what makes you so sure?" again asked Torence.

"That's the thing," again answering Milleena, "while I was there, someone said something to me about a light-skinned dude with a red bandana tied on his head."

"For real? Wait, who?" asking Torence.

"Someone Vern must know. But that light-skinned dude sounds a lot like Tino that he was talking about," answered Milleena.

"Yeah, it sure did," agreed Torence.

"You know what this could mean if he's the top hat?" asked Milleena.

"But Tino, hasn't even got through all of his ranks yet, Lee," replying Torence.

"I know, but think about what that could mean," said Milleena.

"Y'all, I don't care. He needs to get out of this!" said Loraine.

"Yeah he does," agreed Torence. "The problem is where's an easy place to find 'em?" he asked.

"Well, I usually see 'em near the train station," answered Milleena.

"Raine and I sometimes run into him on our way somewhere," said Torence.

"Hmmm…On your way here, was it still raining outside?" asked Milleena.

"Hmmm, naw," answered Torence.

"Why?" asked Loraine to Milleena.

"I don't know…You guys feel like going somewhere?" Milleena asked.

"What place you have in mind?" asked Loraine to Milleena.

"Hmmm, I don't know, answered Milleena. "Just anywhere but here."

"I guess," replied Loraine. "Torence boo, what you say?" she asked Torence.

"Uh yeah," answered Torence. "I don't think it's wet outside anymore," he says.

The Park

Torence's thought on how things looked outside were accurate. It had stopped raining, and everything outside was finally drying up. An hour or so had gone by since Torence, Loraine, and Milleena had stepped out. By now, the breeze in the air was starting to pick up again. After having gone nearly everywhere desperately trying to find something to do, the three of them came across Stone Park and decided that they'll stop there. Going to the park was something that became very seldom for them especially for Loraine. It was uncommon to find even the Vice Lords there since the shooting of a rival gang member happened there. Walking Loraine and Milleena towards the gazebo, Torence said "Right here…"

"Right here what?" asked both Loraine and Milleena.

"Right over here," Torence said. "This is exactly where it all happened that day when that boy got shot."

"Wait, you mean you was actually there?" asked Loraine.

"Yeah…" answered Torence. "It was me, Tye, Tino, Roc and Vern that was there when it happened."

"I thought you told me that you heard this from someone else," said Loraine.

"Babe, I ain't want you to know what went down," answered Torence. "It was the first time I had ever seen anyone shot up, so I was tripping out. Shoot, we all were."

"Who shot 'em?" asked Milleena.

"Well, Tye was the last one I seen fighting him," answered Torence. "But I'm not that sure. I mean everything was happening so fast," he said.

"What do you mean?" asked Loraine to Torence.

"I'm talking about when the rumble happened," Torence replied. "Everybody was caught up in the heat of the moment. It was like an all-out hate fest!"

"Just like the first street fight?" Milleena asked.

"Yeah," said Torence. "It was hardly any different."

"You think maybe that's why the GDs killed Tye?" asked Loraine.

"Yeah, that's exactly why," Milleena replied. "It all makes sense now."

"I ain't all too sure though," said Torence. "I mean all I know is that everybody was throwing fists and then the next thing I heard was BANG! Just like that," he explained.

"Then what happened," asked Milleena to Torence.

"Then everybody just stopped moving, and that's when I heard Roc shouting 'Oh shit, Tye! You smoked 'em!'"

"So, what did you do?" asked Loraine.

"I took off scared like everyone else after I saw what happened," answered Torence.

"Damn, all that went down?" asked Milleena.

"Yep," answered Torence. "It was crazy and right here is where it all happened," he said.

"Ew, c'mon y'all let's keep moving," suggested Loraine.

"Yeah, y'all wanna go check out the spot?" asked Milleena.

"Yeah, let's go," answered Torence.

The Spot

Just like that, they walked away from the gazebo area, and headed towards their new destination. Making their way towards the old hang out spot sparked their memories, which overall opened up a new conversation. "Wow, coming here feels funny to me somehow," said Loraine.

"Stuh, I thought I was the only one," agreed Milleena.

"Yeah, I remember when we all use to come out here a lot," said Torence. "Ding, it's been a long time. Wait, how long has it been?" he asked.

"I don't know," answered Loraine.

"A long time," said Milleena.

"It's still the same but yet it feels so different somehow," said Torence.

"Yeah I know right," agreed Milleena.

"Hey boo, it looks like someone's sitting in our spot," said Loraine to Torence.

"Yeah, there sure is somebody at our spot," Torence replied.

"Do any of y'all know 'em?" asked Loraine.

"Uh…naw," answered Torence. "But whoever he is, he's gotta move."

"Hey, wait y'all," said Milleena.

"What's up Lee?" asked Loraine.

"That's Tino," answered Milleena.

"Tino? You sure?" asked Loraine.

"Yeah, I don't know about all that," said Torence.

"I'm telling you that's Tino over there at the spot," again argued Milleena.

"Hmmm," thinking Loraine.

"That's your brother Loraine," replied Milleena.

"Um, okay but Lee what if it ain't?" asked Torence to Milleena.

"You know what, let's just walk there," again argued Milleena.

From where the three of them stood, they could see a figure seated comfortably on the bench in which they once normally hung out at. Observing him from the distance, Torence could already tell that this wasn't just another individual. According to his knowledge, a person posted up at the park around sunset hours usually meant that they had a reputation. Loraine figured the same thing based by the seated figure's attire. His dress code included an all-black outfit, big puffed-up jacket and baggy jean pants. On his head was a bandana in which he wrapped up distinctly. He appeared to be the same size and height as Torence. Moreover, he gave them the impression that he was around their age range. As they walked closer it became more apparent to them that he surely was someone they knew indeed. Hearing their voices and footsteps, the figure looked over his shoulder immediately noticing Milleena, who by now had approached him. "See! I told y'all it was Tino sitting here this whole time!" she said.

"Okay, so you were right Lee," replied Loraine.

"TINO!" greeted Torence.

"RENCE!" Lantino shouted.

"Ain't think I'd find you out here," said Torence as he slapped hands with Lantino.

"Ain't expect to find you out here either," replying Lantino as he embraces Torence. "I see you brought Lee and my sister with you," he said.

"Yeah, we were just bored trying to see if there was something to do," replied Torence to Lantino. "So, we figured we'd swing out here," he said.

"Where'd y'all came from anyway?" asked Lantino.

"Um…Where did we come from?" asked Torence as he thinks back.

"Shoot, we came from everywhere," said Milleena.

"Everywhere?" Lantino repeated.

"Yeah, like I said we were bored trying to see if there was something to do," answered Torence.

"I feel you on that tip," replied Lantino.

"So, is this all you did today?" asked Loraine.

"What? You mean hang out here at the Spot?" asking Lantino.

"Yeah," Loraine replied.

"Naw, I did a lot of things before I came here," said Lantino.

"A lot of things, huh?" asked Loraine.

"Yeah…A lot of things," answered Lantino.

"A lot of things out in the streets!" Loraine said annoyingly.

"What you trying to say?" asked Lantino.

"You're slinging rocks!" shouted Loraine.

"Raine chill," said Torence to Loraine.

"You're slinging rocks!" Loraine shouted again while interrupting Torence. "Aren't you? Aren't you!? You might as well come out with it, Tino!" said Loraine.

"So, is that what you came out here to do?" asked Lantino. "To fight me on this subject again?"

"Yo Tino," said Torence as he came between Loraine and Lantino, "Gimme a second, lemme try and talk to her real quick," he said, pulling Loraine to the side for a brief moment. With his back to Lantino and Milleena, he faced Loraine and leaned toward her. Placing his hands on her shoulders, he whispered to her in hopes of giving her better advice on persuading Lantino. "Babe," he said to Loraine, "I know you're one hundred percent worried about 'em and all but try not to yell at 'em because he ain't gonna listen to you if you do that."

"Ugh!" said Loraine. "He needs to listen to us, though!"

"Babe," replying Torence, "I know that he will if we come at him nice and strong. But going off on him is only gonna make him walk away from us."

"Ugh!" Loraine said. "I feel like bopping him in the head!"

"Babe," said Torence, "Can you at least try not to argue this time?" he asked her.

"Ugh!" responded Loraine in disgust.

"For me please," begged Torence.

"Fine, okay!" answered Loraine while rolling her eyes.

"Alright, good," says Torence as he turns back to Milleena and Lantino.

"Hmp, so y'all gonna try talking my head off again about leaving my job?" asked Lantino to both Loraine and Torence.

"Naw," answered Torence, "We just want you to think about –"

"Boo, it's okay. I'll handle this," said Loraine interrupting Torence.

Boo...Hmmm, that's interesting "Oh, you'll handle this, huh?" asked Lantino facing Loraine.

"Yes, I will because you need to leave this shit, you're doing out here on these streets," answered Loraine.

"Oh, and you're gonna make me, huh?" Lantino asked.

"Lantino, can't you see what joining the gang has done to you? It's changed you, and you don't even know it," said Loraine.

"Okay…" replied Lantino.

"Lantino, we're worried about you!" Loraine said. "Especially my mom –"

"You mean the same lady who kicked me out and told me to get the fuck out of her house? Just like she did to my mom when we were kids," responding Lantino.

"Lantino, that's not true!" Loraine shouted.

"The hell it is, and you know it!" Lantino shouted back.

"Lantino, she worked hard to keep a roof over your head!" Loraine said.

"Please Loraine! The only reason why she ain't have me out in the streets yet was because I was too young to take care of myself, and now that I'm grown, she saw the perfect moment," replied Lantino.

"What?" shouting Loraine. "Lantino, you owe her a lot more than that to be talking this mess!" she said.

"Why?" shouting back, Lantino. "She never wanted me there, to begin with!" he argues.

"Yes, she did, Tino!" shouted Loraine. "Otherwise, she would've given you up for adoption a long time ago."

"I don't know why," said Lantino. "It's not like she ever liked me," he said.

"Lantino, not liking you has nothing to do with you being Ms. Lopez's son!" said Loraine. "C'mon get it through your thick skull!!" she shouted.

"Man, please, I ain't buying that!" said Lantino.

"First of all, ain't nothing to buy because I ain't got nothing to sell," replied Loraine. "Secondly, what she ain't like about you is how you keep messing up," she said.

"Messing up huh?" asked Lantino.

"YEAH," answered Loraine. "First the suspension, then the bad grades, next you dropped out, and now you're a Vice Lord!! Damn, I could see why Julisa dumped you!" she attacked.

"Loraine, shut up!" said Lantino.

"What?! It's the truth, ain't it!" shouted Loraine.

"What about what I've done to make it up?" asked Lantino. "Doesn't that count?" he argued back.

"What you mean?" asked Loraine.

"Ms. Tourez told me to quit bringing people over, and I did! When she needed someone to put food in the table, who stepped up?! That's right; it was me! When our lights got cut off, and we had to use candles to see our way around the house for a week, who bailed us out, Loraine? That's right, again it was me! Or how about the time when the eviction notice came at our door! Who showed up that time and saved everyone from getting assed out?! Uh huh, yeah…Me! Me, me, me, me, me! It was up to me to grow up fast to become the man around the house!" he said.

"But Tino, you know she hates the Lords! Why couldn't you make money the normal way?!" said Loraine.

"Fuck Loraine! Making money off McDonalds and Burger King wasn't gonna keep the lights on or bring food to the table! After busting my ass, sweating and smelling like burgers and fries, I ain't even have enough to treat myself. Shit, the way I see it, they're just robbing me like an all-out dumbass! That's why I say the workforce is for suckers! A nigga ain't gonna make it in the real world through that!" explained Lantino.

"But Tino, any longer and you're gonna end up like Tye!" shouted Loraine. "Shot up and dead or like Vern, laying up in the hospital bed."

"Man, so what!" Lantino shouted back. "It's my life! What the fuck it's got to do with you?" he said.

"You see; this is what my mami hates about you the most: your guts!" shouted Loraine.

"My guts, huh?" replying Lantino. "You know what, hearing what's wrong with me, me, me is all I ever hear about! What about what's wrong with her? Let's hear about that for a change!" he said.

"Ugh!" said Loraine while shaking her head.

"Shit! She's always giving me this bad look like I just robbed a store or something!" explained Lantino.

"She ain't always doing that," says Loraine.

"Yeah, she is!" shouting Lantino, rudely interrupting Loraine. "It's like she ain't appreciate a thing I tried to do! When I ain't around, I know damn well that she's talking shit about me behind my back!"

"Tino, you know that ain't…"

"Raine, you could stay on that bull shit all you want, but at the end of the day, you know as well as everyone else over here that it's true!" said Lantino as he again interrupts Loraine.

Soon an on-going slur of provocative words were exchanged between the two as Torence and Milleena continued listening to what was being said in the dialog. Lantino's tone of voice continued to rise as it matched with Loraine's intensity. The conversation shifted into a heated argument, and now seem to be only seconds away from escalating into a physical confrontation. Milleena's eyes began to widen while Torence started shaking his head in disgust. *Ugh, here we fucking go again! It's like they'll never learn from back then,* he thought as he watched the two argue with one another. Festered up with emotions, Torence, at that point, got up and put an end to the argument. "MAN, FUCK!! STOPPPP!!" he shouted. "BOTH OF YOU NEED TO SHUT UP!!! JUST SHUT UP! SHIT!!" he shouted again.

"Look at you two…both brother and sister…yet y'all both sound like a straight up mess! The VLs. The VLs. The VLs…seem more like a family to me at the meetings than both of y'all! And the sad part is that ain't nan one of them blood! Damn, what does that say to y'all…ugh! Here, I have one person who believes that she's better than her brother! She looks down at him like he's a bad apple and overlooks his high points! Also, I have this person here feeling like he needs to prove a point to his family to really feel like somebody! Yet, he about ready to lose his head and his peeps pushing him to it! Y'all so stuck on y'all views that y'all lost sight of what really matters! Tino, do you have any idea what I would do just to talk to my own sister?" Lantino paused, allowing Torence's question to go unanswered. Torence shifts his attention towards Loraine, who like Lantino, completely stopped everything she was doing to hear his words. "Raine babe, do you have any idea what I would do just to talk to my own brother?" He asked her, and again, his question went unanswered. "You two don't have a clue what I'd do just to talk to my real family…" he said, staring up to the sky.

"Yeah Torence, you tell 'em because they both need to hear this," said Milleena. "You know what I know just how you feel because –" she said.

"PLEASE LEE! DON'T COME AT ME WITH YOU KNOW HOW I FEEL!" shouting Torence as he interrupted Milleena. "Your family stays just right down the street from theirs! At least you can always come running back to them after you're done running away from home! They'll always be right there when you leave Raine's house or whenever you just choose to come back! So, don't tell me that you know how I fucking feel because you don't know a single thing about how I feel," he shouted.

"Oh…damn," Milleena said, as she moved over to stand near Loraine and Lantino.

"RAINE, TINO," said Torence. "At least y'all have a father! At least y'all know something! Something about him! I...I don't! I have the slightest clue who he is or what he even looks like! And then Lee...at least you know who all your brothers and sisters are. You know who your mother is! You see but me...I don't. I don't even know if I have any brothers and sisters! Matter fact, y'all here are like the closest thing I have to brothers and sisters! Ms. Tourez...she's like really the only mom I have...ugh...how sad is that? I don't know my family...I don't have no family...I don't have nobody," he said as he closed his monologue, and he left the area. Now watching him as he went, the three of them were left feeling pretty stunned by Torence's unexpected outburst. Despite clearing the scene just momentarily ago, the three were left without a word to say to one another. Pondering to a bit further extent than the others, Loraine decided that she's going to follow her boyfriend's trail, but Lantino apprehended her suggesting that another time will be wiser. Finally, breaking the mood and silence, Milleena says to Loraine and Lantino that Torence went light on her. "Hey, I don't know about y'all, but I feel like I got off easy," she said. "Phew, I really thought that he was gonna go hard on me after he heard me say 'that I know how he feels.'"

"Yeah, he was real P-O'd," said Lantino.

"Yeah, I-I never knew he could get like that," said Loraine.

"Hmp, I think that's the second time I ever heard the boy speak out," said Milleena.

"Shit, honestly, I knew he could be mad but not like that," said Lantino.

"I-I never thought I'd ever see that from my baby," said Loraine.

"Baby," said Lantino.

"Yeah, me too," agreed Milleena interrupting Lantino.

"In all the fights I've seen Torence got in, this was the maddest he's ever looked," said Lantino.

"Shit, he ain't even have to knock someone out," said Milleena.

"Did you see his eyes?" asked a dismayed Loraine.

"Hell yeah!" answered Lantino.

"Yeah, he looked so, so fucking focused," said Milleena.

"Shit, what about his voice?" asked Lantino.

"Yeah, I heard that too," answered Milleena.

"Yeah, he almost sounded like someone else," said Loraine.

"Hmp...almost..." said Milleena.

"Damn, it's crazy because he's always so cool," said Lantino.

"And so sweet," Loraine added.

"Yeah, he is," Milleena agreed.

"Yep, up until just now," said Lantino.

"Yeah...Yeah, I know," said Loraine.

"But y'all, you know he's right though," said Lantino.

"Hmmm, what? About cussing and going off on us?" asked Milleena.

"Naw, about the family part," answered Loraine.

"Yeah, there was some shit he said that really made me think yo," said Lantino.

"Yeah, he was right about some of the things he said," said Loraine.

"I feel like-like we haven't touched base on what really matters," said Lantino.

"Yeah, it's like we're wrapped up in our own right that we went blind on the things that really, really mattered," agreeing Loraine.

"Yeah...Just like he said," said Lantino.

"Ding, he's been sitting on the outside looking in at us this whole time," said Loraine.

"Yeah, he has plus, it's no wonder he been breaking us up every time we got hot," said Lantino.

"Yeah...Yeah, he has," agreed Loraine.

"Ump, ump, ump, and I thought my peoples had some issues," said Milleena. "Y'all really gotta look things over because like Rence said 'y'all a mess,'".

"Look, sis; I'm sorry for calling your mom a sucker," apologizing Lantino. "Matter of fact, sorry for most of the things I said about her. She probably thinks I hate her now that I left, but...I don't. And if you all are worried about me, then I'm a see what I can do about making money the normal way," he added.

"Tino, look I know I have been acting like such a bitch about you and the gang business and all," said Loraine. "But that's 'cause you're the only brother I have. As funny as it may sound, I really care for you! But knowing what I know now vs. what I ain't know before about leaving the gang…I guess I take back a lot of the things I said to you before," she added.

"Stuh, don't sweat it," said Lantino as they both embrace.

"What about some of the other stuff he said," said Milleena.

"Like having no family…" said Lantino.

"Or not knowing his family," said Loraine.

"Yeah, that's whoa," said Milleena. "Is that really true?" she asked.

"I-I…You know what, I really don't know," answered Loraine.

"Um, tell you what, I never really liked to talk about it with him," said Lantino.

"I remembered you always saying that his family let him sleepover or something," said Loraine. "But I knew damn well that wasn't true, Tino."

"Does he have any family here?" Milleena asked as she faced Lantino.

"Well, when we were kids, I remember him saying something about Sheffield somewhere," answered Lantino.

"Sheffield…What the heck?" said Loraine.

"Is that where he's from or is that where his real family is?" asked Milleena.

"I think that's where he said he ran away from," answered Lantino. "But I ain't sure about the family part."

"What did he say to you when you asked him?" asked Loraine.

"That's the thing. He'd close that topic real quick," answered Lantino.

"But-but why?" again asking Loraine to Lantino.

"Beats me," answered Lantino. "I just tried not to ask 'em too much."

"He made me think about some things when he was saying all that about no family and stuff," said Milleena.

"Yeah? What you thought about?" asking Lantino to Milleena.

"It made me look back at the times I used to run away from home," answered Milleena.

"Yeah, I remembered those days about you, Lee," said Lantino. "That's what put you in camp for a minute."

"Yeah, and it really hit me when he said that I'm a still have people to come back to," said Milleena. "I felt real bad for him."

"Yeah, I know me too," said Lantino.

"Y'all, it's starting to get real late," said Loraine. "Where do you think he went?" she asked.

"Um…I think I know where he is," answered Lantino.

"Really? Where?" Loraine asked eagerly.

"He's at his spot right now," answered Lantino.

"And where might that be?" asked Milleena.

"It's on the top floor of Ms. Tourez's building," Lantino asked.

"Ding, he probably feels so lonely," said Loraine.

"Naw, he's just chilling out now," said Lantino.

"Well, let's go y'all. Out here is dead," said Milleena.

"Yeah it is," agreed Lantino. "Let me walk y'all back," he said.

Chapter 22: Reflections

Part 2:

For everyone who knew him well Torence, was known as a laid-back character. To some extent, he at times could be pretty mysterious in his own way though he wasn't aware of it. He had a unique confidence in which Loraine found most intriguing about him. Over the years, Torence had developed the kind of personality that drew a lot of people to him. However, he also had an unpredictable anger that had finally been exposed to his best friends that evening at the park.

Just moments after shouting at Loraine and Lantino, Torence cleared the scene and took a nice long walk alone as a means of clearing his mind. A concerned Loraine tried to follow his trail shortly after he left, but Lantino apprehended her, suggesting that a better time would be wiser. Just as Lantino thought, Torence had gone up to the top floor of Ms. Tourez's building. However, that was sometime long after he had left the park. He went up to the rooftop to enjoy a better view. He continued to delve deep into his own world while the breeze blew against his clothes. To capture the view of the cityscape, Lantino joined him "Hmp, I see why you came up here," he said to Torence.

"Yeah? And why is that?" asked Torence as he lifted his left cheek to grin.

"Because out here's the best view," answered Lantino.

"Stuh, yeah, it is."

"So, what's up?"

"Ah, nothing…"

"So…You cool now?"

"Yeah, yeah, I'm straight."

"Alright, cool. So, you wanna head back down?"

"Naw, I'm alright up here, but if you want to, you could go."

"Um, yeah?"

"Yeah, you should go get your rest."

"Naw, I think I'm a stay here too."

"Look, Tino, you ain't gotta be up here to check on me. If you wanna go to sleep, then you can go."

"Naw, naw Rence, trust me, I'm alright up here."

"Um…Okay…So, how'd you know I was here?"

"Well, I looked everywhere else and didn't see you, so I figured I'd find you up here."

"Oh…Okay. Um, does Raine know where I am?"

"Yeah and I told her that I'd find you because I already knew where you went."

"She was real worried?"

"Yeah, but I don't think she told Ms. Tourez anything, though."

"Did she say anything to you about me?"

"Yeah, she did. On your way out, she even tried to call you."

"Wait, she tried to call me?"

"Yeah, didn't you hear her?"

"Naw, I didn't hear anything after I left."

"Yeah, she tried to follow you after you walked out too."

"Ding, she did?"

"Yeah, Rence…She was that worried."

"Ding…"

"On the way back, she asked about you a lot."

"Like what?"

"Things like who are your people and stuff."

"Hmp…And what'd you say?"

"I don't know… That's all I could say."

"Because we don't talk about that…"

"My point exactly."

"Hmp…"

"You know that's got to be the most worried I've ever seen Loraine."

"Real talk?"

"Yeah, I don't ever think I've seen her stress over someone else the way she did for you tonight."

"Hmmm…"

"Come to think of it; you two seem real close now. In a way, she seems closer to you than she does to me somehow."

"Tino…Raine and I…Are real tight now."

"Yeah?"

"Yeah, I mean, I have been meaning to tell you this for a minute, but I just couldn't find the right time."

"Sounds like she really warmed up to you, Rence."

"Tino man, I love your sister."

"Well, I'm glad to hear all this after all this time because I know you remember way better than I did on how cold she used to treat you."

"Uh yeah…I remember those days."

"You know what I'm talking about?"

"Stuh, she was real spicy back then."

"Please, Loraine still is, but I'm glad you're on her good side now."

"Yeah, it's a good thing."

"Hey, but Rence, you know what?"

"What?"

"Don't feel like it was just you. She had a personal thing against everyone she came across."

"Hmmm, but why is that, though."

"I don't know. Loraine is just bitchy like that. Pretty, but snaps on people, and then it rubs off everyone the wrong way because she seems stuck up."

"Yeah, she seemed that way at first."

"My thing is that I think because our dad took off, she felt like this is how all men were. So, maybe that's why she was like that around everyone I brought over. That's the only thing I could say."

"I remember the times she'd make me feel like I couldn't say anything to her."

"I used to hate it when she'd put you on the spotlight in front of her friends."

"Yeah, I remember those days too. Sometimes, I felt like I couldn't even look her way."

"You know why I think it took so long for her to warm up to you was because of how you handled her."

"Uh, what you mean?"

"Like when she'd say shit to you, you just looked and ain't say a word. And I think it threw her off because she wanted to see you say something like J-Roc and everyone else."

"Ooooh…"

"Yeah, but you know what Lee told me one night while we were still at the Spot?"

"What?"

"She said that Loraine liked you."

"Well, it sure ain't seem like it back then."

"No, I mean like, like you…like you in that way, Rence."

"Lee told you that?"

"Yeah, and I just shook my head."

"Hmmm…"

"What's up?"

"I probably shouldn't have said all that to her tonight."

"You mean back at the park?"

"Yeah."

"Stuh, I'll never forget that."

"What? When I went off on y'all?"

"Yeah, I mean, you let us have it tonight…"

"Stuh…damn."

"Ain't think I'd ever see that part of you, Rence. "

"Stuh, she probably doesn't wanna talk to me anymore. Shit, I probably wouldn't know what to say even if she did."

"Naw, you know what, you right for going off on us the way you did."

"Yeah?"

"Yeah! And Rence, you know you were…"

"Hmp, and what makes you say that?"

"Rence, you touched on the one thing that hit us all deep when you spoke your mind! FAMILY!"

"Family?"

"Yeah, Rence…I mean, you really broke it down."

"Hmp, I guess I really did huh?"

"Yeah, Rence…You did. I mean, I'm not promising that you'll never see us fight again."

"Tuh ha ha…"

"But I can guarantee it'll be a while before Raine or one of us starts fussing. And I mean a long while…"

"Hmp, well then that's good."

"Yeah, no more fussing for a while is really good. No more fussing…especially about who's better than who…"

"Wait; what?"

"No more of this talk about who's wanted more…"

"Wait, is this about Loraine?"

"Yeah, and the fights you used to break up…"

"Stuh, I figured…You know I'll never forget about your fights with Loraine."

"Ha ha ha ha…"

"But is that what they were about?"

"Yeah, she used to get me hot all the time talking about she's better than I'll ever be."

"But why? What was that all about?"

"It was about him…My dad."

"Her dad too?"

"Yeah, our dad, Caesar…tying the knot with Ms. Tourez…"

"And not your mom…Mona, Mona, Monalisa, right?"

"Yeah…Because my dad gave Ms. Tourez the legal rights to have custody of me after him, and my mom separated; it made Loraine always feel like her mom was truly loved. Loraine used to always say that if it hadn't been for my mom, dad and Ms. Tourez would've been together."

"Damn…How'd that make you feel?"

"Like shit! How else you think it made me feel?"

"Yeah…Raine sure can hit one pretty hard."

"Yeah, she can…"

"So, anyways is that who Ms. Tourez was talking about?"

"You mean that night she kicked me out?"

"Yeah."

"Yeah, that was my mother she took out of my life."

"I don't get it. What happened?"

"What happened…A custody battle between my mom and Loraine's mom is what ended up happening. Then after that, she got deported, and that was that."

"So, you ain't heard from her since?"

"Naw…Ms. Tourez cut all ties with her and her side of the family. So yeah, that was it…"

"Ding…"

"I always think about her: what she probably looks like now or what she's doing…Sometimes, I even wonder if she's thought about me over the years…"

"What about your dad? He ever comes to mind?"

"Sometimes…But Ms. Tourez has old pictures of them together, so I don't go to wondering about him the way I do about my mom."

"I can see why…"

"You feel me?"

"Yeah…"

"Anyways…I just miss her."

"At least…You knew what happened to her…I still don't know anything about mine…"

"Hmmm…what do you wanna –"

"Hey, look over there…"

"Um, uh where?"

"Over there near that third sign…You see where I'm pointing?"

"Oh yeah, there. That's the way we take to get to the tattoo shop."

"Yeah, ha ha ha…"

"What about it?"

"I don't know; I just thought it was cool how I was able to point that out from right here."

"Hmmm, that is a pretty good night vision. What, you have cat eyes or something? How were you able to tell from right here?"

"Beats me, I guess from all those other times we stood on the balcony."

"Hey, speaking of the tat shop, ain't it you who is supposed to unlock the doors today?"

"Yeah, but lucky for me, it's a slow day, which means I'm a probably open the shop a little later today."

"You know what, that's true Rence, for some reason, clients don't come through the doors on this day as they do over the week."

"You'd think more would come through over the weekend, but they don't."

"Why's that, though?"

"I don't have the slightest clue."

"Hmmm…I wonder what else they probably do if they ain't at the shop…"

"Hey, that's true; what is everyone else up to when the shop is running slow?"

"You think Price might be posted at the train station?"

"Ha ha ha ha naw there's gotta be a day where he hops on one of the trains."

"You know what…Yeah, let's go with that."

"Ha ha ha ha…"

"Hmmm…what about Ms. Tourez?"

"Hmmm…Probably cooking…"

"Or cleaning…"

"Before she starts cooking later…"

"Is that all she ever does? I mean, how bout when she's not just doing that? What about when she's outside the house?"

"She's probably grocery shopping."

"Oh yeah…She was always bringing food home back when I was there."

"Lee's probably gonna swing by the house tomorrow."

"Yeah, but that's if she ain't already there by now."

"Think the twins will come too?"

"Hmmm, nan. They're probably gonna go to work and do their own thing later after they get off."

"Wait, they got jobs now?"

"Yeah, I thought you knew that already?"

"Hmmm, naw, I didn't. Ding, come to think of it, I lost touch with almost everything they do."

"Hmmm, let's see…What about Rojo? What do you think he's up to tomorrow?"

"Hmmm…Rojo, Rojo…He got bigger since the last time I saw him."

"So, you're saying you think he'll be hitting the weight room tomorrow?"

"Well, I know he won't be at the shop, so…"

"If Tye were here, he'd probably be there with Rojo and the SVLs pumping weights."

"Ding, you see how things got crazy?"

"Yeah, and it only seems to be getting crazier."

"Stuh, if only Tye were here…"

"Things might've been a little different."

"Part of me still can't believe he's gone."

"I know…me too. It's like he was just here yesterday at the graduation party."

"And then you wake up the next day to learn he's gone."

"Yep…Just like that. He's gone."

"You know what Rence, I never saw him back down to no one. Not even the cops…"

"Hmp, yeah…Tye was a strong dude, and…a crazy motherfucker."

"Yeah, ha ha ha…Tye sure could get a lil' crazy sometimes."

"You remember the time he walked across the street to thump with those GDs."

"Yeah, there were five of them and three of us, right?"

"Yes, and they were all posted up by the gas station on 148th."

"Oh yeah, I remember…Tye had a lot of heart stepping up to them boys the way he did like that."

"I don't know how we got out of that one."

"You too huh."

"Yeah…"

"Well, hey we had somehow and I'm glad we're able to talk about it. I mean, looking back now made me realize how crazy that shit was."

"That had to be the biggest rumble I had ever been in."

"Naw, a riot is what that was Rence."

"A riot…damn. When Five-O showed up, I was shocked that he stayed…It's like it ain't faze him…at all."

"You think maybe he ain't heard me when I shouted at him?"

"Hmmm, maybe…But I heard you as clear as I hear you now."

"I yelled out to him just like this: 'A yo Tye, Five-O, Five-O! C'mon let's go, let's go! What you doing?'"

"Yeah, I remember you shouting at him to split. Not sure what you said, but I remember you shouting."

"And he just carried on…unpassed."

"I know…He showed a lot of heart, and word got out about that real quick."

"Hmp, Tye always had a lot of heart going way back. Remember when we first started hanging out with him."

"Yeah…I don't know about you Tino, but things started getting better."

"No, no, you're right. Getting around town got much easier for us once we got to know him."

"You two met in school, right?"

"I ran into him several times in school, but it wasn't there where we met."

"Wait, so then how did you two meet?"

"You remember the first time I brought you out to the park?"

"Oh yeah, you mean around the time you were suspended from school, right?"

"Right, well pretty much that very moment in the gazebo was how we met."

"Ooooh okay...So hold up…If Vern and J-Roc were already in, then how come you couldn't just jump in through them?"

"That's the thing Rence, those two were stalling and running game on me. Weeks before I got suspended, I was hanging out with them a lot. But hanging out with them led to my getting jumped like every single day."

"But ain't that part of getting in the book?"

"Yeah, but not if you're talking about J-Roc. You see, Roc would hit up Vern and his boys in the clique and arrange the whole thing. They'd all meet up somewhere at a junkyard and then jump me. Rence, half the time, I ain't even know it was gonna go down like that. If we weren't at the junkyard, then we'd be at an alley

280

somewhere. And you know how beating someone in is supposed to be about five minutes?"

"Don't tell me they'd go over?"

"It's either they did, or those were the longest five minutes of my entire life, shit. It wouldn't just be alleys and junkyards; sometimes it'd be at the playgrounds too."

"Playgrounds?!"

"Yeah, we'd play basketball sometimes and I'd usually get jumped after we lost. Vern, J-Roc and those same fools would always gang up on me. Then, there came times where we'd win, and I'd still get jumped. It finally dawned on me that I wasn't one of them this whole time and that ganging up on me was all fun and games to them. Once it got to that point, they weren't doing it as much. But that's only cause I wasn't chilling with them like that as much now. Once that fight with security happened, it's like respect completely shifted my way. Everyone went to thinking that I was a VL; Tye, and I clicked, and Roc's boys now had my back."

"I still remember the few times Roc and his boys used to chase me down these blocks. Almost every day I was running from them just to get home. Till one day one of them cut me off."

"Are you talking about that one day you came home telling me that you got thrown in the trash by VLs?"

"Yeah, it was that day…J-Roc and his scum Lords finally got me."

"As much as I ain't want to, I knew I had to get you in the book. Especially after you told me about Vern and how he touched you."

"Yeah, Vern stuck me a couple of times in the face, but I still kept wrestling to get loose."

"Hearing that got me real hot, and I knew I wasn't gonna be able to get 'em for you. Not without fighting Roc and his other punk-ass niggas. So, I figured the only way was by getting with Tye on seeing how I could get you in. I knew once you were in, neither of them could fuck with you then because they know you'd turn to Tye or another up line being that you're one of us."

"Yeah, after that day, I wanted in so bad."

"I know you did, and I wanted you in too, but…Here's the other thing I ain't tell you, Rence."

"What?"

"I kind of stalled on getting you in the book because I already sensed that Ms. Tourez liked you from the jump. Plus, you had just walked in our lives, and I ain't want her to think you'd be another one of my thug friends I brought over the house."

"I feel you, Lantino."

"Getting you in was my last option."

"So…What'd you end up saying to Tye?"

"You mean to get you in?"

"Yeah…How'd you do it?"

"Well, something I knew about Tye when we first started hanging out was that he'd take someone with heart over someone who could fight really good. And when you told me that you were still trying to get loose even after Vern stuck you twice in the face, I knew that was all I needed to see if I could get you in real quick and easy! I knew I couldn't let you get beaten up because I ain't wanna let Roc and Vern get a second shot at roughing you up. Getting you in quick, I knew meant that you were gonna end up having to fight a few people to see if you could really take hits."

"Okay, so what'd you say to him?"

"I told him straight up: I know someone who could take hits as hard as he can throw 'em."

"Ding, you worded it like that?"

"Uh huh, just like that, and like that, Tye was ready to see you. I mean, he was hooked to my every word for the next, I'd say, five to ten minutes. After that, he just cut me off and said 'You know what bring 'em out here. Tell 'em I wanna offer him a job or just say whatever you can to get him here'."

"And that's when you scooped me up to meet up with Tye at the park."

"Yep…All was well, because everything was already set up for you to get payback on Vern's punk ass."

"Hmmm…Did you tell Tye about what happened with Vern and J-Roc?"

"Ha ha nope…I just said all the right things to make that night happen for you."

"I won't lie to you, but after we got there, and I was standing there in front of Tye and the clique, I felt nervous."

"I know you did. I could tell. That's why I told you to just be cool because I knew he was gonna come at you hard to really see where your heart and mind was at. That fool wanted to see if you had what it took."

"He had some hard stares, and I know he was around our age, but somehow he seemed so much older."

"Kind of like a man, huh?"

"Yeah."

"He had to act hard because he was around the other Lords."

"That's funny though, when he first looked at me, I saw disappointment in his eyes."

"Tuh ha ha ha Rence, I think everybody was expecting to see Rambo come through the park."

"I know, that's what it seemed like. I can tell 'jitty bug' is what he was thinking after his first look at me."

"Ha ha ha ha!!"

"For real, I was small, no taller than you, and my arms were too short to box with any of y'all."

"He was sizing you up the whole time too."

"Yeah, I remember…While he was circling and talking to me, he'd give me the hard stares and flinch at me several times. Next, facing my profile, that's when he stopped and said:

'I see you been chilling with us for a minute or two lil' nigga. Ya boy Tino here tells me that you heard about the dices, the niceness, the sips from glasses, and all that comes well with the Chitown privileges… I heard that you want in…well, you know what? It takes the strong to get in. Whether or not you are, we're gonna find out…You want in, huh? Well, let's see how much you really want in…'"

"Yep, he said it just like that, Rence. Then after having said that, he stepped away from you and started shouting at everyone else."

"Yeah, he yelled out saying, 'Don't nann one of y'all go soft on him! Y'all hear me! None of y'all!' Then he called out Vern to step out and fight me. Right there, I got Vern back for what he did."

"Yeah Rence, you punched his lights out. The look on Tye's face changed after you whooped Vern."

"I know, but then Tye called out Bear…"

"That's cause he couldn't believe that it was you who just laid Vern out like that on the floor. So being that Bear at the time was our best fighter, he called him up."

"Damn, Bear was so tall and big. No one wanted to step to him."

"And I keep trying to tell you that it's because he's too big. Otherwise, you could've taken him."

"He dropped me like three times."

"But you kept coming right at him with those hard licks. I'm telling you, you hung with him, and that's what Tye wanted to see."

"A lot of people there had to hold me back."

"Yep, and that was really the only way to end the fight. For a minute, we couldn't get you to be still."

"I know…It was crazy."

"Yeah, it was but hey, you got Tye's respect though. As a matter of fact, Rence, I think everyone at the park that night gave you props."

"Yeah…Before we left that night, Tye asked me what's my name, and after I told him, he said to me, 'Yo Torence, from now on around these hours, you could come out here…and then he flashed the VL hand signal.

"Yeah, if Tye wanted to know your name, then that means you definitely left an impression on him."

"After that happened, Roc and his boys never chased me back home again."

"Rence, sometimes I think it should've been J-roc and not Tye that got killed by the GDs. Roc is just a gamer, and sometimes I wondered whose side he was on: us or the GDs."

"That's true; I did ask myself what's he on our side for."

"I think he might've cut a side deal with the GDs to take Tye out."

"He could've probably but what makes you say that?"

"Okay well, around the time when Loraine was in boot camp, and you were out somewhere with Ms. Tourez, Roc, Tyke, and I were on our way to chill with Vern and some girls. In route to Vern's hang out spot, we stumbled upon a couple of GDs. So, you know the deal: we got in a fistfight with one of them who couldn't outrun us in a foot race. Just when I thought we were gonna finish him, J-Roc pauses the whole thing and throws a deal at him!"

"What did he say?"

"His exact words to the disciple were, 'We gotchu cornered and at this point, I can hear your heart beating against the concrete. But I'll tell you what…I'll let you go if you fuck one of them up for me. Hah, I may just even help you, help me fuck one of them up for me. How you like the sound of that?'"

"Wait, why'd he do that?"

"He told the disciple that Tyke and I have an attitude problem, and we talk too much shit. By then, Tyke had already taken off, which now left me alone with Roc and the disciple."

"Oh snaps! So, what ended up happening?"

"I probably should've taken off like Tyke, but I stayed for the result and boxed with both they're asses for a short while. The GD finally took off running scared after I picked up a pop bottle. Now the odds were even, but at that point, I sized Roc and just walked away."

"He ain't try and pull another stunt?"

"Stuh…Naw. With his hands up and a crooked smile, the trick just kept saying 'Lil Tino, I just wanted to see y'all spore real quick, that's all,' but I wasn't trying to hear any of that."

"This is why you always told us not to trust J-Roc."

"Yeah, he's a gamer. He'll sit there and run mind games on you all the time. You can't trust him because he'll twist the truth around."

"Yeah, I remember you telling Raine and I that."

"You know there's been a lot of stories like mine about J-Roc?!"

"Yeah, I think Lee told me a few like that she heard about from the SVLs."

"Yeah, it's true, I heard this plenty of times with the rooks I helped get in the game. The same way he'd gang up on me when I was trying to get in, is what he was doing to them. Why do you think he showed up with the fewest potentials?!"

"Hmmm…Word had it that the rooks and SVLs ain't showing him the same respect they had for Tye."

"Ain't surprised…Those same rooks I got in the book were the ones he kept beating up on before they got in. I'm telling you right now Rence; Roc will be the reason why the gang splits back up into cliques."

"You sure?"

"Very! At the end of the day, Rence, people won't respect someone who doesn't respect them. It's as simple as that."

"So, his rep is no secret to everybody. Yet, my thing is why did Tye keep him around?"

"Rence, what did I teach you? Remember, part of being in this game is to keep your head in the streets. Doing that, you're most likely never gonna lose."

"Because I'm a step ahead of the game…"

"Right!"

"So, I have to analyze…"

"Yeah…As bad as J-Roc is, Tye only had him around because he's as good as the rest."

"Huh…"

"C'mon think about it. Back when we were fighting off KCs, who was setting them up in dead ends?"

"Roc…"

"Exactly…He set the whole thing up. Another thing about Roc is that he keeps our rep up as the hardest gang on the Westside. I mean, Tye's the baddest member ever known, but J-Roc spreads the fear and respect around. By setting random people up and jumping them, builds this perception about us not only on this side but on the other sides as well. I'm sure that's gotta be why Tye kept him around."

"Hmmm…That makes sense."

"You see what I'm saying?"

"Yeah…"

"The last thing I could think of is knowing how to throw, but he wasn't even all that. He does what I call tactical moves. And while he fights, he gets into your head."

"Damn, I wouldn't be able to concentrate."

"Yeah, he's the only person I know that does that."

"I never did like him."

"Neither did I…I can't tell you how many times I wish I could knock that crooked smile out his face."

"Y'all must've fought several times."

"Actually, only a few times. That time back in the alley with the disciple, to name a few. And one other time at the Rockwell Gardens projects. All the other times were really nothing. He'd just say something to get under my skin and then walk away with the crooked smile."

"Tell me about the other time at Rockwell Gardens…"

"That whole thing was about Loraine. You remember when my sister was going through this phase where she spent all day trying to get all pretty for him?"

"Yeah, she was driving everyone crazy."

"Yeah, well, J-Roc as you probably already knew, was trying to take advantage of that, and of course, you know I wasn't having that. So, to make the long story short, I eventually visited him by his spot at Rockwell Gardens to settle this once and for all. It was either he was gonna back off and stop playing games with my sister or deal with the repercussions."

"Okay, so what ended up happening?"

"Oh, you want me to go into details?"

"Yeah, tell me everything."

"Alright, so this is how it went down: I knew he lived on the third floor but wasn't sure which door. So, my gut instincts just told me to call his name out, and surely, he creeped up out of the cracks he came from. The moment I saw him, arms went flying left and right. I gotta lot of licks, but it ain't seem to faze him at all. He just kept running his mouth the whole time. I couldn't hear nor make out what he was saying even if I wanted to."

"You probably should've just hit 'em in the mouth. That would've shut him up."

"Yeah, you right, I should've but…Anyway, I took a moment to breathe, and by now we stood near the edge of the main area on the third floor. Standing by the rail, he opened his mouth one more time talking about 'I'm a start macking up on Julisa after I'm through with your sister'."

"He said that?!"

"Yeah, and I heard everything word for word. So, you know that made me hot!"

"So, is that when you bust him in his lip!?"

"Naw…I swung, and that's when he caught and twisted my left arm, putting me in some kind of lock hold."

"What'd he do? Some kind of karate shit?"

"It wasn't karate, but whatever it was, must've been some tactic he'd been working on…Anyways, while on the lock hold, I remember thinking this nigga's crazy!"

"You said crazy?"

"Yeah! You wanna know what he said to me?"

"What'd he say?"

"This what he said: 'Yeah, Tino, take a good look at how high you are from the ground…If I really want to, I could push you over the rail right now. That's if I want to…But then, that means you might die.'

'Yeah, and if you don't then we'll only go right back at this beef shit all over again!'

'You know what, you're right…Perhaps, maybe I should push you over this rail after all.'

'Ugh! Well, nigga what are you waiting on?!'

'Good question…Someone might've seen us (duking it out up here) because someone definitely heard us. I can't do it like this…'

'Then loosen up your grip on my left arm!'

'Yeah, I better do that…Besides, Lil' Tino, I may need you to whoop some of Nito's Disciples for me.'

'Know your limits Roc…'

'Tuh, know my limits, huh…'

'That or learn ya lesson. You choose.'

'Whoa, whoa Lil' Tino…You need to calm down with all that. I wouldn't ever hurt your sister in any way. Above that, keep this in mind: we both work for the same employer, we rock the same star, so if anything, it should be cats of the Folk nation we ought to be pounding and throwing over balconies…Not us…Not each other…'

'You know what, fuck you! I'm outta here!'."

"Ding…sounds like it's all a game to Roc from what you just told me."

"That's cause it is."

"Tis, tis…You know I can't tell you that stepping up to him was a good thing even though I understand why you did it."

"Hmp, I can only guess that I did some good stepping up to him because I ain't hear about him messing with Raine since then. I guess that Raine probably found her a new boyfriend."

"Yeah…she did."

"Oh okay, well then that confirms. Say, you feeling sleepy yet?"

"Hmmm, nann…Why?"

"I don't know; I was saying why don't we take a walk."

"Where to?"

"Anywhere around the neighborhood, I guess. I mean, the sun still ain't out, and my legs are starting to feel like they need to move after standing for so long over the rooftop."

"Hmmm…I know a spot I don't think you and Raine saw yet."

"Okay, lead the way."

Chapter 23: Reflections

Part 3: Street Credit

In the weeks leading up to what Torence and Lantino recalled as the street riot, sightings of Gangster Disciples in mass numbers around the west side region were stirring up conversations about whether or not smuggling heaters into the area was going to be necessary. At the same time, while that was being considered, other options were also being explored by the Vice Lords. One of the first and foremost options that was usually among the topics of being implemented was the recruitment of new members to help fortify the Westside headquarters. Being that everything at the time was shaping out to be pivotal for anyone involved, Torence, Lantino, and a few others got together at the park to further discuss the matter in what one could call an informal hood meeting. "Tino! Rence!" shouting J-Roc, "Ain't expect to see y'all here."

"Hah, it's funny you say that," replied Lantino. "Because we weren't expecting to find you here either, although we heard you were coming."

"Hmmm…who'd you hear this from?" asked Vern to Torence and Lantino.

"From Rojo," answered Torence.

"Yeah, he told us about this," adding Lantino.

"Hmmm, speaking of Rojo, where is he?" asked Tyke. "Wasn't he supposed to be here."

"Well, he didn't say anything to us about that," replied Torence, "but tell you what, that is a good question, though. I mean, where is he?"

"As a matter fact, where's everybody else?" asked Lantino. "Shouldn't there be more people?"

"They're all probably at 148th," said J-roc.

"True, that could be the case," said Tyke, "or they're probably not here because of Rojo…"

"Maybe, I don't know…" replied J-Roc.

"Hey, you know what? I hear Rojo and the SVLs beat in a new member a couple of nights ago," said Price.

"What? Again?" responded Vern.

"Yeah, isn't that like the third time someone got beat in this week?" responded J-Roc.

"Yeah, but you know times are serious if snatching rooks is all they been doing for some time now," replied Price.

"Yeah, he's right," agreed Tyke, "and I say we need to get Tye to jump on that ASAP."

"So, then it's true…GDs are making moves up this way," asked Lantino.

"Yeah, it is," replied Price. "Why do you think I'm up here and not the train station?"

"Naw, what we really need is some heaters!" suggesting an outspoken J-Roc.

"To smoke these fools out our turf!" said Vern.

"Vern, J-Roc try and paint the scenario together," replying Lantino, "You bring heaters out here, start smoking fools, and now they're blasting back. This ain't the KCs. These are GDs were dealing with here. So, bringing heaters is only gonna drop our numbers below zero, feel me!"

"So, you're saying snatching rooks is our best option, Tino?!" asked J-Roc.

"Yeah, as much as we can…" answered Lantino.

"Please…the rooks here don't even have potential to hang," replied J-Roc.

"That's cause half the time, you're out somewhere beating up on them," said Lantino to J-Roc.

"Y'all let me tell you what," shouted J-Roc to everyone else, "I hear one of them rooks the SVLs beat in was a female! The fuck you call that?!"

"Hahaha, SOFT," Vern laughed.

"Exactly!" said J-Roc.

"Y'all gonna listen to that?" asked Lantino to everyone else.

"Please, they sure hell ain't gonna listen to your bullshit, Tino," replied J-Roc to Lantino.

"Yeah, well, I guess we'll just have to take this up with Tye then, won't we," said Lantino to J-Roc.

"Tuh, Tino, you really think Tye is gonna listen to you?" asked J-Roc. "To you…A look-out…"

"What you're trying to say?" asked Lantino.

"What I'm saying is you don't have enough street credit, Tino," answered J-Roc.

"Why don't you throw your set up and find out how much street credit I have," replied an offended Lantino.

"Whoa, whoa y'all calm down," said Tyke, who stepped in between Lantino and J-Roc.

"Yeah Roc, you're kinda pushing it a 'lil," said Price.

"What?" J-Roc responded, "But it's true, isn't it!? Tino, hardly got any street credit. Tino's just a look-out…A look-out…Tye ain't gonna listen to no damn look-out."

Everyone paused and turned back to Lantino to hear him deliver a response. However, he continued to stand and stare with the look of a frown on his face. That then allows J-Roc to continue his verbal assault.

"You've been a look-out for how long? Too long, if you ask me. By now, you should've been moved up a notch. But yet, you're still a look-out after all this time. A look-out…A VL with no rank…"

"Stuh…" Lantino sucked his teeth.

"Tye, would listen to me before he ever decides he'll listen to you," said J-Roc to Lantino. I got enough credit going way back when I first got in the game…You see, after I got beaten in, I was still standing, and you can ask Vern if you don't believe me!"

"You talk too much," said Lantino while shaking his head.

"Well, hey when you got credit to back you up like that, then you can talk all you want. Anyways, from there on in, I did missions left and right. That's why today, I'm right behind Tye in line to be the top hat," replied J-Roc to Lantino.

"Tuh ha, never that…" muttered Lantino.

"Oh, you'll see…" replied J-Roc.

"Naw…naw I won't," said Lantino, "not as long as Tye's around. C'mon Rence, let's bounce."

"Right behind you," said Torence to Lantino.

"Hah, leaving already Lil' Tino…" said J-Roc to Lantino.

"Ain't no point in wasting my breath nor time bumping with you Jay…" replied Lantino.

"You're just a look-out! Know that! And a broke-ass one too!" said J-Roc.

"And know this before I go, Roc…Jumping these rooks in the game is our best option, fool!" said Lantino.

"Our best option, huh? You know what, your 'lil buddy man has more street credit than you do. You know what, wait just a moment Tino…" yelling J-Roc.

"Stuh, what?" asked Lantino.

"I think it's real amusing to me how you keep saying beating new members in is our best option…which brings me to this next question for you: Have you ever jumped any in??"

"What?"

"Just answer the question…"

"Uh…uh…"

"Yo…come to think of it: Have you…have you-have you ever been jumped in?"

"I-I –"

"You never have, haven't you?"

"Um, uh…I…"

"Shit, you really ain't!"

"Yeah, I have…"

"Oh yeah, when?"

"By…by you at the junkyard."

"I don't remember. Plus, I ain't even ranked to knock you in. You know that…"

"I…uh, um…"

"When were you ever jumped in?"

"I…don't know…"

"Shit, haha wait till Tye hears about this."

"Bitch wait, where are you going?!"

"If I were you, I wouldn't be so worried about me right now. After all, it ain't me who's gotta answer to Tye about this."

"Damn…"

"Peace…"

As Vern and J-Roc exit the park, Lantino tilts his head sideways and looks on, knowing that they're more than likely on their way to 148th or other areas Tyberius was known to hang out at. Turning back facing Torence and the two remaining in the park, Lantino shakes his head in dismay because he's well aware that the odds of Tyberius learning about his status as a Vice Lord isn't going to be in his favor. Oddly enough, his mind isn't the only one clouded with questions and concerns regarding the possible consequences.

"Yo, Tino," says Torence, "that's not true, is it?"

"Yeah, is it?" asked Tyke.

"If it is, my biggest wonder is how'd you manage to keep that hidden, for so long?" asked Price.

"Look, none of that matters right now!" replied Lantino.

"Y'all he's right," agreed Tyke. "The real question of the matter is, what the hell are you gonna do?"

"Yeah, what are you gonna do?" asked Price.

"Hey, wait, can't he just get beat in like all the rest of us did?" asked Torence.

"But Rence, I don't think it works like that," said Lantino to Torence.

"Oh, hell naw," said Price.

"Tye is gonna see that as a disrespect," said Tyke. "Tino, I think you should just go ghost for a while because I don't like what I think is coming next."

"I could have you hop on a train for the low," said Price.

"Yeah, but then Roc knows who set that all up, and if he can't get to me or y'all then he's gonna come knocking at my people's door," replied Lantino.

"Yeah, Tino's right," agreed Torence. "Roc will do that."

"The best thing for me is to just wait," said Lantino.

"What? Wait?" asked Tyke. "Wait for what?"

"Just wait and let everything play out," answered Lantino.

"You sure about this, Tino?" asked Price.

"It's not like I got a better choice," answered Lantino.

"Maybe…he was bluffing about going to Tye," said Torence.

"Maybe…" replied Lantino.

"Naw, that wasn't no bluff," said Tyke, "he's on his way."

"Well, hey…true or not, ain't much he could say to prove Tino ain't never been jumped in before," said Price.

"Hmmm, okay," replied Tyke, "letting things play out might be best, but…I still don't like that idea. Just letting y'all know that right now."

"Hey well, Rence, Tino, y'all be well," said Price.

"Alright, likewise," replied Lantino to both Price and Tyke. Everyone had part ways, and for once, the park was closed at sunset. It was apparent that Lantino and the small band of Vice Lords had forgotten what they initially came to the park for. Instead, it now seemed like an entirely new problem arose, and Lantino was sitting in the pit of it all. There now stood a huge uncertainty moving forward, and Lantino knew it was only a matter of time before he'd go face to face with Tyberius and the Vice Lords about the issue at hand.

A couple of days had gone by nearly as fast as the second-hand ticks on the clock. Lantino laid low and waited for the situation to play out just like he said he would the other evening back in the park. Yet, ironically, he still hadn't heard back from Tyberius. It wasn't till Torence came home early from the tattoo shop that he finally received word about Tyberius' summon. Though then again, Torence seemed rather tranquil in his delivery of the message, which suggested that perhaps "all was well" after all. *Perhaps J-Roc was really bluffing*, he thought as he was walking with Torence on his way to Tyberius' place.

"Tino, you alright?" asked Torence, "You look like you're thinking hard."

"Yeah, I'm straight," answered Lantino. "So, you sure Tye said it was his place we were going to?"

"Yeah, that's what they said back at that tattoo shop."

"Who's they?"

"I don't know; I have never seen them stop at the shop before. Tuh, I have never seen them anywhere around here, to be honest."

"What'd they look like?"

"Well, they were big like Tye. Two of them. They had a lot of tats on their arms. I saw martini glasses on one of them too, which meant they knew Tye."

"They're one of us then."

"Yeah…You think this about you, ain't it."

"It is about me."

"We don't know that for sure, Tino."

"I don't know Rence…Something's up. Look Rence; I'm a need you to stay out of this no matter what happens."

"Say what?!"

"Look, don't argue with me! Just do it, okay!"

"Tino…"

"All c'mon Rence, why are you looking at me like that? C'mon, don't give me that look!"

"Tino…You really need to lighten up. It's probably not what you think."

"And what if it is?!"

"If it is, then Tye will get you out of this."

"Rence, Tye is a top hat!"

"And…"

"That means he's more than a VL now!"

"Yeah…well, we know him, Tino. He ain't just another top hat."

"True, but Rence, you know as well as I do that he could be another person, especially around the VLs. I mean, you've seen 'em."

"Yeah, I have."

"That's why I need you to stay out of this, no matter what happens."

"Shit…"

"Look Rence; if I can't count on you to do that, then you might as well turn around and head back to the house!"

"Alright…fine, I'm a stay out of it."

"No matter what…"

"No matter what."

"Alright, cool…This next corner leads into Tye's street, right?"

"Yeah…"

"You ready to go?"

"Yeah, you?"

"On vicious spaghetti. C'mon let's go!"

With Torence right behind him, Lantino bravely made the turn to the corner that brought him right into the street in which Tyberius resided in. From the moment Torence and Lantino first stepped foot on the scene, they immediately noticed that the street was crowded with Vice Lords. Ones they had never seen before. There was no Vern, Tyke, and shockingly no sign of J-Roc, who they were expecting to see. However, Lantino was able to mark out the two big guys Torence mentioned earlier from the tattoo shop. They were standing near Tyberius' front porch. And lounging at the front porch was Tyberius himself, who still hadn't notice Lantino from afar. As Lantino slowly made his way through the mob of Vice Lords, there was no denying the mood at the present time. The place he and his best friend had often call their second home all of a sudden seem like a hostile environment. He, as well as Torence, undoubtedly knew what this was about. And once Tyberius stood and roared "TINO," that completely dismissed any hope that Torence had regarding the outcome. Right there and then, Lantino paused and quietly whispered to Torence, telling him, "Remember what I said, stay out of this no matter what." Responding, Torence calmly nodded his head and wisely chose not to follow Lantino any further. As for the mob of vice Lords, they were each in their own world. But once they all heard the shout from Tyberius, they cleared the way, automatically creating a path for Lantino to walk through. "Get ya ass over here nigga!" once again shouting a belligerent Tyberius, who slowly stepped away from his front porch. With his red vest sitting on his porch, the infuriated Tyberius stood shirtless before Lantino with khaki pants and black tennis shoes. Bulging his fists and flaring his nostrils immediately communicated to Lantino that an altercation between the two of them was imminent. Looking at Lantino repeatedly from head to toe, Tyberius kept the suspense going by opening a conversation saying, "You understand we need to talk?"

"Yeah, I know."

"Word has it that you ain't never been beat in…"

"I'm guessing you must've heard that from J –"

"Don't matter who I heard that from. The bottom line is that it's a disrespect…which also means that all ain't well. Only one who's been jumped in has the right to walk with the almighty G card. So Tino, before we move on…I needed to hear this from you myself…Is it true? You ain't never been jumped in?"

From that moment, Lantino is asked the question by Tyberius; the loud pounding sound of his heart against his chest is all he could hear. So loud that he could barely hear himself think nor breathe. It takes a minute or two, but with a slight delay in his speech, he responds ecstatically saying, "Naw, nigga!" Staring back at Lantino sideways, Tyberius raises his left eyebrow replying, "Say what?"

"Yeah, you heard me nigga!" again shouting Lantino. "My ass ain't never been jumped in, and ain't need to get jumped in to show I could take real licks! Bitch, my track record will show you that I'm way harder than the rest of these fools you brought out here to your crib! Bitch, the fuck wrong with you! I fought a man, the security guard of our school! I fucked up way more people than you got out here right now on this ground! Got fucked up by a gang of niggas twice the size of the bunch out here now, and what! My nigga! I'm still standing! Let anyone of you fuck niggas know that I'll take on GDs mob deep by my own damn self! I don't need nann one of y'all niggas!"

After he finished his loud and dramatic outburst, he found himself instantaneously surrounded by twenty other Vice Lords. Looking before him, he can still see Tyberius positioned in the middle of the front yard. Using his peripheral vision, he noticed Torence has been caught in a headlock by one of the other Vice Lords just right across the street.

"You done?" asked Tyberius. Lantino nodded his head communicating yes to Tyberius. With a few fingers from both hands, Tyberius signaled to the other Vice Lords that everything was fine. Next, he walked up to Lantino and uncharacteristically told him in a calm voice to swing by a specific address in three days from now exactly at 8 pm. Finally, he signaled to the Vice Lord across the street to release his lock on Torence.

"Yo, Tino!" he shouted, just as Lantino was leaving. "Don't be late."

Replying, Lantino nodded his head. Then he walked away, following Torence back to the same corner they both came from. "Bet," said Tyberius as he watched them exit the scene from his front porch.

The Present

Two and half months later, Torence and Lantino were en route to a supposedly new hang out spot, but while on their way there, they made a quick stop towards memory lane. Reflecting on the events that occurred at what used to be Tyberius' residence brought in a lot of closure once thoughts were shared between the two of them.

"Yo, Tino, all I could say to all that was whoa."

"Tuh, tell me about it…"

"Tye seemed like a-like a-like a different person…"

"Yeah…this whole place that day felt different."

"I know right, and what's weird is that there wasn't another time it felt like that, except that day."

"It's like…Tye set that moment up for us."

"I know he ain't see that coming when you told him off."

"Shit, I ain't see it coming neither. You know like twenty other VLs stepped in my face by the time I was done?"

"Whoa…To think he still let us walk."

"I know…"

"So, I heard him say to you, 'Don't be late.' What was he talking about?"

"Before he let us go, he told me to stop at this hideout: 2015 W. Warren blvd. I was made clear that I had to be there in three days, 8 pm sharp."

"So, you showed up?"

"Tuh, it's not like I had a choice."

"Okay, so you showed up. So, what happened after that?"

"Okay well, you know how there's getting jumped in?"

"Yeah…"

"Well, that night I found out that there's another way to get in the gang."

"Another way?"

"Yeah, another way that ain't done too often."

"Hmmm, so, so how did this go down?"

"After a couple of look-outs checked me for weapons, they walked me around the side door, where I met up with Tye."

"Wait, Tye was there?"

"Yeah, he was there, and the first thing he said to me was 'Sup Tino…Glad you made it on time'."

"Did he-did he bring up what had happened earlier that week at his place?"

"About the violations? Yeah…He brought that up right away. As a matter of fact, this is what he said, 'That was quite a show you put on back there, Tino. Tuh, at that point, I wasn't sure what was gonna happen next. But look…I understand why you did what you did back there. I mean I came off too strong. But c'mon Tino, on the real, did you really have to try me like that in front of them boys…Okay, I was too strong but, but c'mon Tino, you know me better than that. I wasn't about to let something happen to you…Not, after all, the years we have been through. You and your brother been coming by my place for a minute. You know I love having y'all around. Shit, even my cousin loves you! So, you really think I'd let something like that take y'all out of my life? C'mon, Tino, you know me better than that…You out of all people should know that I gotta play my role when I'm around the peeps…I'll tell ya what…I'm just glad you ain't touch me because then the peeps would've had to beat yo ass, and then, I'd really feel some pressure cause I wouldn't know how to get you out of that. Anyways, we passed that, and we're here now, so c'mon in, let me show you inside…A but just one last thing I wanna add: It takes more than street credit to do what you did, Lantino…What you did there takes a lot of heart. A lot of heart'."

"Tino, weren't you nervous going in?"

"Kinda because I ain't know what the hell I was walking into. But after he mentioned you, the vibe felt good.

"Hmmm...What'd he say about me?"

"Well, while following him inside, he stopped for a moment just to say 'Oh uh, hey Tino...Uh, tell your brother I hope we're still cool after what happened. Ain't mean to keep him on the headlock so long'...and I just told him that all is well."

"Oh, okay. So, tell me more about the hideout. What it looked like?"

"On the outside, it looked like some old shack. There was no fresh car, no fine dime females, none of that. It looked like the last thing you'd expect any thug lord to hold meetings."

"For real?"

"Yeah, but on the inside, it felt like a different place...I mean it was so...it was so...it was so spacious, but yet everything was kept so low key."

"Hmmm..."

"Yeah so, I followed Tye inside, and he led me to the basement saying that he wanted me to meet the boss Lords of the almighty VL nation. Tye told me that because it wasn't easy setting this all up, only three out of the four was able to show up."

"And this was to get you in the book?"

"Yeah...It was a good thing I had served as a look-out for some time because that made them consider me as a junior member, which meant that three top-ranked Lords could initiate me."

"Oh okay, so because you weren't just some peewee off the street, it was easier to put you in."

"Yep...Bingo. So that night, Tye introduced me to one of the originators and a couple of supreme chiefs, Big Willy, Lord Mert, and Lord Sweetz."

"What'd y'all end up doing?"

"Nothing really...they just had me repeat this pledge. Then we talked and had dinner for the rest of the night."

"So you got sworn in?"

"Yeah, that's how I got in...You wanna know something else, Rence?"

"What?"

"One of them told me that I looked like someone they used to know."

"Who? Which one of them?"

"Sweetz…He told me that I look and sound a lot like this guy called Ceeze, and when he said it, you couldn't help but notice the sound of ze…Anyways, the name sound familiar but nothing ringed a bell."

"Did you ask him what the guy look like or something?"

"Yeah, and Sweetz told me all he could. He even told me that this guy, last time he heard, went running off with his girlfriend from Puerto Rico somewhere. Then, he told me that I look like I could be his son."

"Damn, that's weird…"

"Yeah, and he had me thinking for a bit until he told me that he thinks this guy had kids or at least one he might've known about."

"Hmmm…Ceeze. Um, naw nothing comes up."

"Hmp, that's what I said."

"So, with Tye gone, who's gonna recruit the new breeds?"

"I know someone needs to wear the top hat."

"Yeah…I mean; it's just sitting there."

"I know, and it's been a while now."

"Tino, have you thought about making a run at being the new top hat? I mean…I hear the rooks really respect you after helping most of them in."

"Hmmm…Top hat…Uh maybe. But wait, where did you hear that?"

"What, you mean the part about the rooks? Uh, I don't know…the tattoo shop, I guess. You know the lady Lords talk a lot."

"Lil' chicken heads…"

"Hahahaha, yeah…So say, have you heard anything yet?"

"Um, naw, but I know Roc was one of the prospects."

"You think he'll last long being our top hat?"

"No…I don't think he'll make it to this rank: I mean, no one likes him, and the rooks from what I know, ain't showing him any respect. Not the same way I remember with Tye."

"What about his sidekick?" He laughs.

"Tuh ha, you mean Vern?"

"Yeah, you think maybe he'll be a top hat?"

"That clown, please…With his rep, I don't think he'll ever move up another rank."

"Oh yeah, that's right; the whole crew knows he's a dirty fighter."

"Yeah, ain't no one's gonna respect that. Plus, he's a better trash talker than he is a brawler, so naw (hahaha)."

"Hmmm…You know; the only time I ever see him is when J-Roc's around. It's like he was stapled to Roc or something."

"Stuh, he was one of those fools who'd take Roc's word over Tye's."

"Yeah, I know…Hey, you remember when that almost got Roc in some heat with Tye?"

"You're talking about the time when Vern was supposed to deliver something somewhere to Price at Ridgeway but end up doing something else Roc told him to do?"

"Yeah!"

"Oh yeah, I don't think anyone ever forgot about that. That whole mess got settled at the park."

"Yeah, they almost fought."

"Naw…Tye almost whooped his ass."

"Yeah, that's pretty much what was gonna happen, had Tye not changed his mind."

"Tye looked at Roc and asked him, 'Should we do what you wanna do J-Roc? I thought it was I who was left with the job of handling the street operations for the clique. I mean, everyone seems to know that but you…Perhaps, maybe we should find out who runs the set then, Roc'."

"Roc looked scared at that point. I saw it in his eyes."

"And that's why he backed down. Tye made it known that day not just only to Vern and J-Roc, but to everyone that he's the man."

"J-Roc wouldn't have had a chance."

"Hell no, not against Tye."

"Tye, you will be missed."

"Yeah…Gone…"

"But not forgotten.
"Rest in peace."

Torence's New Getaway

From the rooftops to the street of Tyberius' old residence to a
relatively remote location was where Torence and Lantino now
stood. Before them flowed a smooth murky lake. From afar, they
could see a bridge in which traffic ran through. Around them was
nothing more than a plain, open field of grass. Now and then, they'd
hear the sound of a soothing breeze blow against them and their
surroundings. Following Torence towards the edge of the lake,
Lantino took a look around the area. *Pretty quiet*, he thought as he
took a moment to rest his legs on the grass comfortably. "So, this
your new spot, huh?" he asked Torence, who he was now seated
next to.
        "Yeah, this is it Tino," replied Torence. "This is my spot."
        "Hmp, must be a lot easier for you to think."
        "Yeah…a lot easier."
        "So, how often you come out here?"
        "Hmmm, that's the thing. It's too far."
        "Tuh, you telling me…"
        "Yeah…I come out here only when I can."
        "To think?"
        "Yep…and that's it."
        "What's on your mind now?"
        "Hmmm…Vern."
        "Who? Vern?"
        "Yeah…"
        "Rence, I was getting ready to sink my feet into something
so deep but –"
        "Hold, hold, hold on for a minute. Let's talk about Vern for
'lil bit."
        "Okay…What about him?"
        "What do you know about Vern?"
        "Huh?"
        "Like, tell me some things we know about Vern."

"Uh…well, it's like we were saying back near Tye's place. He's always with Roc. You don't see him unless you see Roc. He's a dirty fighter…he clowns on niggas, and…that's just about it for the longest I've known Vern."

"Hmmm…Now notice anything different about him?"

"Hmmm…Kinda. Why? What about you?"

"Yeah, I've seen some changes from the time he got out of the hospital up until now."

"Hmmm…like what?"

"Well, for one, he hasn't been around Roc like that lately. Two, he's been quiet the last few times I've seen him."

"Hmmm, yeah…It's not like him to go M-I-A, and you're right, he's been very quiet as of late. It's like he's on lockdown or something."

"Yeah, he's always been the jokester of the set."

"But now, he's acting differently which is weird…You think there's something he knows?"

"About Tye getting shot? Hmmm, maybe…Or maybe Tye's death probably hit him hard. Maybe everything's finally breaking him down."

"Hmp, maybe…"

"One can only wonder…"

"I still remember the first time I met him."

"I remember the time I met him too."

"Hey Rence, you still remember the time we first met?"

"Haha, I never forgot."

"How old were we at the time? Like thirteen, fourteen years old, right?"

"Yeah…Like four years ago."

"Wow, feels like such a long time ago."

"Yeah, but if you think about it, it really hasn't been that long at all."

"Rence, didn't it feel like we were out of breath all night long?"

"Yeah, but that's cause we spent the whole night trying to outrun the GDs."

"Tuh, oh yeah…that's what we were doing. No matter how much we ran, it felt like it just wasn't fast enough."

"I know right…But I'll tell you what, at the time, anything for me was better than the orphanage or group home. There was no way I was going back!"

"Tuh, you've been saying that since day one."

"I know…"

"Ha ha ha…So, who bumped into who that night: was it I or you?"

"Stuh, we both did Tino."

"Hmmm…Wow, yo Rence, doesn't today feel like that night we met?"

"Yeah, I was just thinking that. It's funny, you asked."

"Ha ha ha ha…You remember the time Tye first met Tyke?"

"Are you talking about the time Tyke looked like he got bum-rushed by a gang of people?"

"Yeah, but turns out it was just one dude?"

"Tuh ha ha, yeah…Tyke got fucked up."

"Yeah, his nose was leaking like a faucet and all."

"I remember…Tye helped him get up."

"Yep, and then that's when Tye said 'I once stood where you are now'…You know I used that same line for every rook I helped get in?"

"So, that was like your pick-up line?"

"Yeah…I mean, I liked how Tye said it and how it made Tyke feel like he was somebody. I guess that's what I wanted those rooks to feel like."

"Tino, I'm sure it did, the same way it did for Tyke that night he met Tye…Hmmm, speaking of Tyke…I think that was my first time meeting him too."

"I was just about to say that Rence…"

"Yeah, before that, I don't think we ever saw him around the block."

"Wait, no…Hadn't we seen him at the train station?"

"The train station?"

"Yeah, like around the time, Loraine was still in boot camp."

"Naw, you're talking about Price. It was him we met that time."

"Wait, but wasn't Tyke with him that time too?"

"Did he have a red skully on?"

"Yeah, that was Tyke, ain't it?"

"Oh naw, naw, naw but I know who you're talking about. That boy stays way out at Ridgeway, that's why he was probably with Price. Plus, I know Tyke always has on a skully, and that's why you're getting the two mixed up."

"Oh yeah, that's right! Tyke's skully is black."

"Yeah, whoever he was, wasn't Tyke. That was just Price and a Ridgeway Lord."

"Yeah, now I remember…Hmmm, you know what?"

"What?"

"Tyke is really the only one out of our crew that runs if we're outnumbered."

"I know, he's always the first one to dip."

"Shit, I can't blame him."

"Tuh ha ha ha ha ha!!"

"Huh?"

"Ha ha ha ha ha ha ha!"

"Tuh, what's wrong with you?"

"Price, ha ha ha ha!"

"Okay, and what about 'em?"

"I just thought about something, ha ha ha!"

"Tuh, okay I wanna laugh too."

"Okay, okay, okay…Notice Price always wears that same trench coat?"

"Ha ha! Rence, you just figured that out after all these years?"

"Ha ha ha ha!"

"Yo, Price wears that like every day. I think he even sleeps with that on or showers with it."

"Damn, ha ha ha!"

"Ha ha I'm for real! I bet you he'd wear it on his grave too. I put five on it!"

"Ding, you make the man sound like a junkie ha ha…"

"Well, I'm just saying Rence…"

"How'd he ever get his name anyway?"

"Oh c'mon, don't tell me you don't know that either?"

"Well, I'm asking you ain't it?"

"Tuh ha ha…Think about it: he puts a price on almost everything he does for you…"

"Uh…Oh, I see…"

"C'mon, Rence really…"

"Hey, I said I see, right…"

"Tis, tis…"

"So, did you ever see him in your class?"

"You mean Price?"

"Yeah."

"Naw, Price wasn't in our school. Now come to think of it…I never had a class with any of them except Rojo."

"So, wait, y'all all went to the same school and ain't have not one class together? At least one?"

"Hmmm…Well, Tye and Lee were older than me. Isis wasn't in our clique, ain't really know Tyke like that then, and Vern and J-roc were only in my class sometimes because they were skipping."

"You never seen Raine or Julisa?"

"Yeah, I saw Julisa in my class once, but then I got switched out after I came back from suspension. And then Raine, believe it or not, was in all the smart classes."

"Hmmm…So you ain't see them much in school then?"

"Not in class, no. But everywhere else, most times, yes. Before I dropped out, I started running into Bree a lot at Saturday school."

"You're talking about one of the twins?"

"Yeah, Lee's sister. Otherwise, Rojo was really the only one who had my classes. I still remember the first day I met him."

"What happened that day?"

"Well, he was a new student, and he had just transferred from ESOL classes to regular classes."

"Wait, what is ESOL?"

"It's a class for kids who only speak in their own languages."

"Oh…Oh yeah, that's right, he has an accent in his slang."

"Yeah, so anyways, kids in the back used to crack jokes on his English. Now that he had the same class with them, he started talking about them to me in Spanish."

"Hmmm…What did he say to you?"

"Stuh, ha ha ha…he was talking to me about how he was gonna beat them up after school."

"Oh shit, ha ha ha ha…"

"I know, having him around was fun."

"Ha ha ha, I still remember the first time he'd ever spoke to me."

"Shit, I remember too ha ha ha! Your first words to him was, 'YOU SPEAK ENGLISH?'."

"Tuh ha ha ha ha! Look, I just wasn't expecting to hear him speak in English. I mean, when he was around us, he'd either speak Spanish or not speak at all."

"Tuh ha ha ha ha ha! Even the SVLs were cracking up!"

"Stuh, my bad Rojo ha ha…"

"It's all love, Rence."

"Hey, you know our boy is a funny guy."

"Yeah, I know what you mean: he's always talking in English when he's calm."

"But when he's all hyped up, you'll know it because he's always talking in Spanish."

"Yep, and he always looks all tense."

"Tuh ha ha ha…funny guy. You know, even when it's cold, he rocks those tanks."

"Yeah, and that's how he showed up to school too."

"For real? Even in school?"

"Uh huh, in tanks and khakis."

"Hmp, damn."

"Rence, you know what, he's our best link to the SVLs."

"Yeah, for real."

"Lee always said it."

"Said what? What you just said about Ro?"

"Yeah…And she was right."

"Hmp, did we talk about her yet?"

"I don't know, maybe…"

"Well, anyway she seems to know more…a lot more than she says…or show for that matter. What do you think?"

"Not sure what you mean, Rence."

"Hmmm…Okay, picture back in the graduation party."

"Uh huh, okay, yeah…"

"Okay, so remember when you, Tye, and I found out she was graduating?"

"Oooooh, okay yeah, now I see where you're going…"

"You see what I'm saying? Lee knows more than she lets out."

"Yeah…Yeah, naw you're right on that one…."

"Tuh, she's like a diamond in the rough, if you think about it."

"Yeah…something special…that ain't been found."

"Hey, you know if it weren't for her always tagging up walls, I probably wouldn't be at that shop today inking tats."

"Word Rence?"

"Word up. I don't think I would've ever moved the pencil like I do today."

"Well, I'll tell you what, you've definitely got Lee on tagging, sketching, and all that. I mean, both of y'all do it with a different intent. You tag like you're writing a message; Lee is all street. You can tell what she wrote off rip cause its just simple letters. Plus, it's always in one color."

"Yeah, sometimes she puts symbols up, and then she'll write on almost anything."

"I know…I hear this why Tye, Roc, and them let her in the clique. She was basically our unofficial artist. She repped and marked our turf more than any of us did, shit."

"I see Lee ain't about that anymore…"

"Naw…Ever since she came back from boot camp, she started doing it less."

"Now she doesn't do it at all…"

"Hmp, I guess she ran out of paints in those spray cans."

"Tuh ha ha…So…if she ain't doing that, then now what is she doing?"

"Stuh…I think Tuwan, last time I heard, told me that she's around here and areas in the Northside performing live."

"Performing, doing what?"

"I don't know, like rhyming, spitting licks, and stuff."

"Hmmm…We'll have to catch her one of these nights."

"Hmp, well I hear this underground jazz club be her spot now. So, you might wanna go check out there."

"Where's that at?"

"I don't know…You'd have to talk to Wan about that."

"Hmmm, well even though Lee is hardly ever around, at least it's good to know that she still is around…unlike Tye's cousin."

"Aww c'mon, don't feel like that, Rence."

"But Tino, she's never around."

"I know, I know, but you gotta remember too Rence, Julisa's going to college."

"Yeah but Tino, even you gotta admit it, ya girl just coasted without a word."

"Ding…Ain't know you was really feeling like that, Rence."

"Tuh, it's not like it matters now."

"Rence…Just try to see things from her view."

"You're just telling me that because y'all use to have a thing together."

"No, I'm not Rence; I'm really trying to make you see things from a different angle. Now if you'd just hear me out…"

"Ugh! Okay, go ahead and let me hear it."

"Okay, just try and picture if it were you, and you just found out about me dying…Wouldn't you wanna change your scene too?"

"Hmp…Okay, yeah I probably would've too."

"Probably…Naw, you would've."

"I guess you're right."

"I know…I mean think about it: a lot of people quit coming out to the park, they stop swinging by the shop, and in Julisa's case, she just moved to New York."

"Adios, Julisa."

"Ha ha ha ha…Yep, so long girl…I ever told you that she was in my class?"

"Super smart and pretty, Julisa, yeah."

"You know that's how we met, right?"

"Really, you and Julisa?"

"Yeah, right there in that one class…The only class we had together."

"Hmmm, what class was that?"

"Poetry shop, one of the few classes I actually passed. In fact, I made a better grade than her in that class."

"Ding…You just made me think of Loraine when she says you're smart but lazy."

"I felt like I was really taking something in there that I could use for the rest of my life. It wasn't just 'cause of Julisa…"

"Hmmm…I wish I could've taken that."

"You would've liked it. I know I did. Besides suspension, I don't think I missed a day."

"Damn…"

"Hmmm…You know what still cracks me up?"

"What? Tell me…"

"She was real smart…"

"Who? Julisa?"

"Yeah, I'd hear about her a lot, and yet there she was sitting in the same class with a D.O.P student."

"What's D.O.P?"

"Dropout prevention…"

"Hmmm, an advanced student and a D.O.P student.

"Opposites attract."

"Hmp, yeah…Now come to think about it, I notice my grades around the time we were together was decent. I made a lot of C's and C minuses."

"Well, that's good. Tell me what happened that time at the graduation party? I mean, Raine took me downstairs, and I missed out on everything else."

"Ha ha ha ha, you still remember that moment at the VIP section, huh?"

"Yeah, yeah what happened with all that between you and Julisa?"

"Hmmm, ha ha ha ha…Well, there were some things we hadn't close."

"Huh?"

"At the time that she and I broke up, there was still a lot of things, a lot of doors that was left open."

"Like what?"

"It's complicated; it's something only her and I'd understand. That's why everyone cleared it so we could just talk it out."

"So, what'd y'all end up saying?"

"Rence, we just talked. I don't remember what was said. But what I will say is that we, for the most part, I guess closed things on a good tip because she asked me if I wanna dance."

"Look Tino, you don't have to tell me if you don't want to."

"What do you mean, I just told you we talked. Then she asked me to dance, but I told her no. So, Kendrick's boy showed up out of nowhere and took her downstairs to dance."

"Hmmm…"

"I'm telling you, that was it. That was the end of her and I ever being together."

"When you say Kendrick's boy, you're talking about Jesus?"

"The police officer, yeah."

"Whatever happened to him?"

"He ain't cuff her, that's for sure."

"Oh yeah, that's right; he was the one everyone thought Julisa liked."

"Naw, he was the one Tye wanted for her because of his rep with Kendrick Nobles."

"Yeah, yeah that's right! I heard even Tye's uncle actually liked him."

"Yeah, I heard that too several times from Tye himself."

"Well, Tino, I'll tell you what, I think Tye liked you with Julisa too. Although, he may not have said it as much."

"Thanks, Rence."

"It's true. Otherwise, he would've been tripping like he did when he learned about the GD Julisa was messing with the whole time."

"Oh yeah, I almost forgot about Benito's boy."

"I think everybody was shocked. Even the boys from the other side."

"Oh yeah, it wasn't hard to tell because they had their mouths open."

"I think it was him everyone was looking for after Tye got killed."

"Oh yeah, for a while, Chi town police was on his case heavy."

"Seems like it died down now. I wish I could say the same for this street war."

"Me too, Rence…Me too."

"Julisa was right to go to New York. I hope she does something real special with her life."

"She will Rence. Just like you're doing something with yours right now."

"Right now…Tuh, I'm not sure about that, Tino."

"What you mean? What you're doing is way better than what I've got going on."

"That's the thing Tino, I don't think what I'm doing's enough."

"What are you saying?"

"I'm saying that I'm not pleased with what I've got as is…A part of me wants more."

"You're not happy with the tattoo job?"

"I'm not saying I ain't, Tino. I just feel like that's not all there is to me. I think I could gain more. I believe I could go to New York too or somewhere and do something special with myself."

"Hmmm…"

"Tino, I believe you can do this too! Gang life ain't where the road ends for you!"

"Hmmm…I don't know, those shoes sound too big for my size, Rence."

"Remember when you told me that someday you're going to be the king of this city? Remember that?"

"Ha ha ha…Yeah, you still remember, hah."

"I don't know about you Tino, but I'm a do more than just inking tats on people."

"What are you gonna do?"

"Shit, I'm a write and spit flows and shit, like Lee. I'm a tag up places and everything…"

"Did you say spit flows, Rence?"

"Yeah, and you're gonna do it with me."

"Naw, I don't know about that…For now, I gotta hold it down for Tye."

"No, you don't! Tino, that was Tye's life!"

"Rence, he looked out for me and now it's time I rock on for him."

"Naw Tino, you see, he did that for you for as long as he could, and now that he's gone, it's your chance to walk and make your own path!"

"Rence, you said that as if Tye set this all up."

"He did, Tino! He did even though I don't know how, but he did…Just like the time he got you in the book, or the other time, he had us scoop him up at the courthouse."

"Hmmm, you know what that's true…But what about the VLs? I just can't…you know that."

"I know…"

"I mean, this is what's bringing bread to the table."

"What are you gonna do?"

"I'll find a way."

Chapter 24: Poetic Lee

From the east comes the breeze,
to the west as far it blows,
thin air there it goes,
exposed yet somehow unknown by those who roam in its mist
all fixed by the twist of depicted intellect
which thus brings two in the mix,
seated on the trenches, ditches, disguised as benches, here in
the sphere of the given imagery of our greenery, in turn
comes an exchange of toe to toe, type a blow for blow, tone
for show
while in an iller zone…

"Hmmm…So Lee, first tell me, how long you've been doing this?"

"Um, excuse me; that's Poetic Lee to you, Mister Tino."

"Oh, oh my bad Miss Poetic Lee."

"Thank you…anyways, I have been doing this for a while now. Now that one you just heard, I started literally like last night."

"Hmmm, well it sounds dope."

"Yeah?"

"Yeah, and by the way, the flow is on point too."

"Well, that's what's up. Glad I got that down, ha!"

"Yeah, so is that it? Or you got some more rhymes for me?"

"Naw, that's it for now boo, but hey, since you're feeling my flow, that means you're gonna come out tonight, right?"

"Come out where?"

"To my show?"

"Your show?"

"Yeah, I'm hosting an open mic tonight at the Joint."

"The Joint? Hmmm, what's that?"

"You know what Tino, just come out there tonight and bring the fam with you too."

"Alright, I'll be there."

"Tino, when's the last time you've actually been out?"

"You mean like, have a life? Is that what you're asking me?"

"Yeah…"

"I don't know, tell ya the truth. I mean, I've been real caught up lately."

"Let me guess: work?"

"Stuh, yeah…"

"You look tired."

"I'm good."

"No, I mean, you look tired of doing this job."

"Tuh, actually…I am. Told Rence the other day that I'm thinking about hanging it up."

"How you plan on doing that?"

"Tell you what, I'm a set up a meeting with the high ranks, and I figure I'll pay them."

"How much are we talking about?"

"I don't know…I guess it's on whatever's owed to me in tax time."

"You told anyone else this?"

"Besides you, Torence is really the only other person who knows."

"I see…Look Tino, I don't think it's a good time to leave, especially with the street war going on right now."

"Stuh! You got one bunch talking all in ya ear saying 'Tino, you gotta leave, leave, leave the gang,' so, I figure yeah I'm a do that and now I'm hearing 'Naw, naw, stay, stay in the gang'."

"Look Tino, I know you ain't like what I just said, but I feel like I need to tell you this!"

"Stuh!"

"And listen! I got some more stuff I feel like you need to hear before you decide to take this gamble! So, ready to hear what I'm 'bout to tell you, Tino?"

"Go ahead, I'm listening."

"Okay…Now Tino, you won't like what I'm about to say, but just hear me."

"Okay, well say what you gotta say."

"Boo, I know why you wanna leave, but…here's why I think what you're getting ready to do is a bad idea. One, the street war: for you to just bounce when tensions are high…Hmmm, I don't think so. Two, there's a story out about one of us who tried to leave."

"Please Lee, I know how that story ends. The member either gets killed or beat."

"No, no, no…Did you hear the recent story about the one guy who tried to hang it up and call a quits?"

"Did you say recently?"

"Yes. Did you hear about it?"

"Naw, tell me. What happened?"

"Okay yeah, not too many of us know about this, but that's just because the gang doesn't want that story to get out to everyone."

"Ding…Like what happened?"

"Well, recently, I say like a week or so after Tye died, this one guy just like you met with one of the LTs talking about he wanted to leave."

"So…"

"So, hearing that one of the LTs took out a Glock pistol and busted a cap on his legs."

"Damn…"

"Yeah, and he told the guy to come see him again if he has any second thoughts about leaving."

"Shit…"

"Now he gets around in a wheelchair. You can see him now and then by the train station."

"Who was that guy?"

"You mean the one who got shot?"

"Yeah."

"His name is Bear."

"Nah ah…"

"Yes."

"BEAR…"

"Bear."

"BEAR…"

"Isn't that just now what I said?"

"Oh shit! The same Bear we know? The biggest member on our set?"

"It's shocking news for me too. He was the last person I ever expected to get capped. Especially, with how long he has been serving the gang."

"Now, it all makes sense why I hardly see him around."

"Like I said, you can always catch him by the train station."

"I wonder if this would've happened if Tye was around."

"Probably not…That's just one story, though. Did you ever hear about the SVL that went missing?"

"Uh naw, what happened with that?"

"I'm surprised how someone with your rep doesn't know that yet."

"Why? What happened?"

"Well, you remember that one guy from the SVLs that was always flashing signals?"

"I think so."

"You knew him; he was like their best English speaker."

"Oh him. The translator! Yeah, what about him?"

"Well, he went missing out of nowhere."

"Did something happen."

"Yeah…What happened is that he was trying to leave, so word got to the SVLs about it, and since then, no one's heard about him. Not even his family."

"No one knows where he is?"

"Nope but then again, no one's asking. Not his girl, his peoples, no one."

"But they all know it has something to do with the SVLs?"

"Yep…So are you still gonna buy your way out?"

"Tuh, I really don't know. I, I don't know what to do. All I just know is that I'm tired of this job. I'm tired of getting up so early to go to this meeting and that meeting to be a look-out for this one set or another one down the street. Tired of coming home late, tired of fighting other cliques over territory that was never ours, to begin with, and even the nightlife is getting old to me now."

"Are you still scouting new members in?"

"Naw…Tell you what…"

"What?"

"I actually regret getting all those rooks in."

"Why?"

"Because all I've heard is them laying up in the hospital or being locked up in jail since joining the gang. As a matter of fact, I found out that two of them got killed. That broke me down because both of them looked up to me. One of them reminded me of Torence when he had first moved here."

"Tino, it's not your fault."

"Hmp, maybe not, but I feel like shit right now. Lee, I was just trying to help these boys out, and now it seems like all I did was make things worse."

"Aww boo, don't feel like that. Remember, it was a job to bring in new members."

"I know, but I can't help it."

"Well, keep in mind that you looked out for your brother."

"Hmp, that's true. Hey, you know him, and I spent the whole night talking."

"Are you talking about that day he went off on us at the park?"

"Yeah."

"Oh, you actually found him that night?"

"Mmmm hmmm…he was hanging out alone in the rooftop."

"Was he alright, I mean, how's he been?"

"He straight. He just needed to clear his head, that's all."

"Oh…Okay well, what'd y'all talk about?"

"Tuh, everything and everyone, going back from day one till now."

"Hmp, if I didn't know y'all, I would've thought you two were really brothers."

"Ha ha ha ha ha ha…"

"Oh, you laugh?! I'm telling you…you two really do seem like brothers."

"Lee, that's cause we are."

"Hmmm…Missed me with that bull shit."

"Lee, I'm telling you, Rence is my long-lost brother."

"Oh yeah, tell that to Raine and hear what she says."

"To hell with what anyone says, that's my brother!"

"No…your adopted brother. Moreover, your best friend."

"Brother."

"Okay…Anyways, how'd Ms. Tourez manage to get everything to work out?"

"You mean for adopting Torence?"

"Yeah, do you know?"

"She did it through an agency and some connections."

"Hmmm, but like how?"

"Now that only Torence could tell you because she used to always take him with her to the home study meetings."

"Wait, home study? What's that?"

"Tuh, a long process he and Ms. Tourez had to go through to keep Torence with us. Like you remember, the times Torence would step out with Ms. Tourez, and they both wouldn't come home till late in the day?"

"Uh, naw…"

"Oh yeah, that's right, you and Raine were still in boot camp at the time. Well, anyway it was a long process, and because Torence was a runaway from a group home, it made things even longer."

"Like what were the meetings about, and why'd it all take so long?"

"Hmmm, investigations, signing Torence up and shit like that. It was hectic, but with connections, Ms. Tourez sealed the deal, and Torence was able to stay with us."

"Ohhhh, okay…"

"Yeah, for a while, we had to call him Rence Tourez because that was his adopted name. But once the judge gave Ms. Tourez the birth certificate, we all went right back to calling him by his real name."

"Well, I bet you were real happy."

"Tuh, you got that right!"

"Aww, well tell you what, I'm glad it all worked out too."

"Yeah, we all were…everyone except Loraine; she was still the same after it was all over."

"Hmp, that doesn't surprise me a bit. I remember when she was so nasty to him."

"Yeah, I don't think any of us ever forgot except her. She seems closer to him than she does to me."

"What? Too much brotherly love going on at Ms. Tourez's place? Ha ha ha…"

"Uh yeah…"

"Well, you know they're a lot closer than that?"

"What do you mean?"

"Hmmm…Remember back when I told you that I think your sister likes Torence?"

"Hmmm, that was back in the spot, right?"

"Yep, like three years ago."

"Lee, I know where you're going with this. Look, Rence told me on our way back somewhere that one night: he and Loraine like each other."

"Yep and looks like I was right."

"Ah whatever…So, anyways, how long this been going on?"

"Stuh, like a while."

"Like what's a while?"

"I don't know! You can't put no time frame on those two because they got this on and off thing going on!"

"Wow, I've always known my sister to be strong, especially around boys…"

"Oh, she's not like that around Torence."

"Hmp…And Rence, is so quiet and laid back…"

"Yeah he is…I can see why she likes him."

"Hmmm…"

"You gotta admit, there's a spark between the two, Tino."

"Hmp, I always thought she was the sister he never had."

"Boy, you'll get used to it."

"I guess."

"Hmp, hmp, hmp, hmp, hmp."

"So Lee, let me ask you this: How'd you get out?"

"Get out of what? The gang?"

"Yeah."

"I didn't. I'm still in."

"How's that so? I mean, I hardly see you at the meetings, nor do I ever see you flash the colors."

"That's the thing; I stayed low key. I found people to take my place."

"Like, what do you mean?"

"What I mean is, I used replacements. I made my own set of peewees and schooled them on how to tag up walls and shit."

"Wait, so once they figured how to do everything you taught them, the clique ain't really need you like that."

"Right, because I had them in place to do my job now. I mean yeah, the pay ain't much, but then again, it wasn't much to begin with when I was out there tagging shit."

"When'd you come up with this?"

"Stuh, as soon as I realized that I was tired of it all."

"Hah, if only I could do something like that."

"Hey! You know what Tino, maybe you can!"

"What? Find rooks to take my spot?"

"Yeah! Why don't you just do that!"

"Naw, I ain't trying to scout and jump rooks in this trap life anymore."

"To hell with trying to find new members! Take the ones you got in! Set up your clique and school them on everything you know."

"Hmmm, you really think that'll work, Lee?"

"Yes, you're smart and probably the best look-out here in the westside. Plus, those rooks respect you, Tino. At least, way more than they do J-Roc. Tino, those peewees look up to you."

"Hmmm, maybe I can pull this off…"

"Tino, you will, and on top of that, you'll still be getting paid even after they took your spot!"

"Hmmm…"

"You should do it Tino, even if you don't think this plan will work out."

"Yeah, yeah I'm a think about it."

"And then after you're done, you know what I want you to do?"

"What?"

"I want you to do it."

"Ha ha ha ha okay, okay I'm a do it."

"I'm for real."

"And I am too, Lee, chill."

"Okay, good."

"So, before your show tonight, what else are you doing?"

"Hmmm, I don't know. Say, you feeling hungry boo?"

"Hmmm, a little bit."

"You wanna grab a bite at Roots?"

"Uh yeah, okay."

"We'll both share a box."

"Yeah, that's cool…Hmmm, you know that reminds me…"

"What?"

"I heard one of the rooks found him a job at a pizza shop like Roots."

"Which pizza shop?"

"The one near Gurnee Mills Mall."

"Oh good, so he could hook us up."

"Not so…I heard he had to quit working there because someone from the GDs recognized who he was."

"Oh wow, ha ha ha ha."

"Yeah, I just shook my head to that."

"Well, you see why you need to do what I just told you about."

A Blizzard (of Words) by Poetic Lee

From the east comes the breeze,
to the west as far it blows,
thin air there it goes,
exposed yet somehow unknown by those who roam in its mist
 all fixed by the twist of depicted intellect
 which thus, brings two in the mix,
seated on the trenches, ditches, disguised as benches,
here in the sphere of the given imagery of our greenery,
in turn comes an exchange of toe to toe, type a blow for
blow, tone for show while in an iller zone, drawing two
minds,
a couple of membranes tirelessly connecting dots,

attempting to discuss what's undeniably a must
in relevance to what's in place,
regarding all at stake,
with a means to reach, seize, resolute, and exceed surpassing
a midrange,
going ghost, coast to coasting in terms of an endpoint.

Chapter 25: Rence and Raine

On an early Friday in the Fall, the pissy preteen, Loraine woke up to what she thought was going to start as a quiet morning. Stepping out of her room into the living room, she automatically noticed that the bed Lantino and his new friend shared was fixed back into a sofa. It was almost as though they had done it specifically for her, according to her own thoughts. There was no school today, and with no one present, she instantaneously embraced the silence. The soothing calmness made her look onward towards the weekend. However, the comfortable silence in the living room was short-lived due to her mother, who happened to be coming out of the restroom. Joining Loraine in the living room, Loriana wore a bathrobe, and her hair was wrapped in a shower cap. With a few high hopes and eagerness, Loriana said to her, "Oh, Mother Mary, thank goodness you're up. Your brother and his friend just stepped out. I don't think the elevator is working, so they're still going downstairs. If you hurry Loraine, you could catch them!"

"Huh?" replied Loraine with a convoluted look in her face. "Mami, wait, say what now?" Loraine asked while seated on the sofa. "Ugh, bebe, there's no time to explain," said Loriana, "Just hurry downstairs and tell your brother I need to have a word with him! Hurry, go!"

"Right now, mami? Can't you talk to him later?"

"I won't have time, and who knows when he'll be back. Now go, go, go, go! Get up out of the couch bebe, c'mon!"

"Why can't you go get him?"

"I can't catch him with this on plus; I'm too slow anyway. But you're fast, now go!"

"But mami, I'm still in my pajamas."

"Okay si, si and your brother is still downstairs. Now here, put on your tennis shoes!"

"Are you sure? How do you know he hasn't left?"

"Loraine, you know, it's not like you to talk back to me. You're starting to act like Lantino and his roughneck friends. The same lokos who got him suspended from school."

"So, you think I'm hanging out with them?"

"Well, are you?"

"NO, mami! I'm always here cooped up in this house."

"Okay, whatever! That's enough! Go get Lantino and bring him back here. I'll be in the bathroom blow drying my hair."

"But mami, what if he –"

"Tell him its urgent."

"But mami…"

"Iyee!!"

"But –"

"LORAINE, what did I say?"

"Ugh, okay…"

In the meantime, while her mother is fixing herself up in the restroom, Loraine reluctantly gets up from the sofa and slips on to her sandals because she didn't want to waste any time trying to locate where she might have placed her other pair of tennis shoes. Seeing her mother's long sleeve shirt near the kitchen window, she reaches over for it, figuring she'll put this on to feel warmer while she's outside. Just as she grabbed it, she spotted two figures outside within seconds of glancing through the kitchen window. Staring a little longer, she visually notated the following details, one of them has on baggy clothes and a red striped bandana while the other is dressed casually in black jeans and a red sweater. From her view, she can tell they're around her age group. Right there, she concluded that it's her half-brother, Lantino, and his new friend, Torence standing and hanging out in front of their building.

Being that it's her first time ever having a good look at Lantino's friend, Loraine decides to observe him closely. *Hmp, black usually goes with anything yet, he looks like he's mismatching*, she thought as she zoomed in on Torence's outfit. *Hmp, I know it's a 'lil chilly out, but that's probably the last thing he needs to worry about,* again Loraine thought as she watched Torence converse with Lantino. Standing before the kitchen window, she continues watching the two of them converse without realizing several minutes had gone by. From that point, she begins to delve and ask herself exactly what they're talking about. But then, Lantino drew a gesture that indicated that it's time for both of them to move on. Right there,

Loraine snaps back into reality and slides the kitchen window up. With every bit of her breath, she shouts on top of her lungs yelling, "LANTINO!" Everything for the moment seems to come to a sudden stop as her voice echoes through the streets. Both Torence and Lantino pause and turn towards one another. Shouting again, Loraine yells out, "LANTINO!" a couple of times. Now clearly hearing his name being called out loud, Lantino tilts his head up and finds that its Loraine calling him from the high rising building. Just the very sight of Loraine begins to create an irritable sensation on Lantino, and staring back at Lantino, Loraine can immediately feel his mood as she watches the change in the expression on his face. "Yeah nigga, that's right, I'm talking to you," she says to him.

"Man, what do you want?" he asked her.

"Um, excuse me but don't you 'what do you want' at me. You need to remember Tino; this is my house, my momma gotchu staying in so, you need to come at me correct."

"Stuh, whatever…What you need?"

"What I need…No, I don't need ANYTHING from you. More like, what mami needs from you."

"Man, I'm on my way somewhere right now, and you're holding me up. So, spit it out."

"Mami said she needs to see you."

"Okay…"

"Like right now."

"Right now? For what?"

"I don't know. Maybe that's why you need to come up here and find out."

"Stuh, I'm doing something right now. My friend and I gotta head somewhere."

"I don't give a care to what you or your lil' friend gotta do. You come up here right now and talk it out to mami."

"Stuh…damn."

"Hurry up; she's waiting for you!"

"Shit, I'm on my way! Can't you see I'm walking."

"Tuh, you need to get a step on it, already!"

So, with a bit of reluctance, Lantino made his way back inside the building to meet with Loriana, his legal guardian. Not too far behind him, his new friend Torence followed his trail. Watching Torence from the kitchen window, Loraine took the opportunity to introduce herself bringing him to an immediate halt. "Um, hold on 'lil boy!" said Loraine to Torence, "but did anybody ask to see you upstairs?!"

"Uh…No," replying Torence as he slowly shook his head.

"I didn't think so," said Loraine. "Which probably means you have to wait."

Torence stood silently still as he's stopped on his track by the pissy Loraine. Looking back at her from where he's standing, their eyes connected, and as this is happening, a sensation begins to come upon him. It's as though he's going through a state of hypnosis. "Do you gotta eye problem?" asked Loraine. Unaware, Torence didn't respond to her question right away. "Hey, you…" Loraine said, as she tried to get Torence's attention. "Um, yeah you…Do you gotta eye problem?" she asked once more. Shaking his head, an embarrassed Torence looked away to the floor. Poking her head back inside, Loraine shut the kitchen window. So, while Loraine got her day started, Torence continued to keep his eyes on the floor till Lantino stepped outside several minutes later. "So, I see you met my sister," said Lantino as he approached Torence.

"Hmmm, is that who she is?"

"Yeah, that's what I deal with every day."

"So the lady who called you up…Is she your –"

"Mom? No."

"Huh, wait, then how is she your sister?"

"We have the same dad. And that's it."

"Have you ever seen your dad before?"

"Yeah…Before he left."

"What about your mom?"

"I don't know where either of them is but one thing's for sure…"

"What's that?"

"They'd never let me stay here with them."

"What makes you say that?"

"Because nobody wants to live in a place they're not wanted."

"Oh yeah…I know what you mean."

"Yeah…"

"So, is your sister always like that?"

"Tuh…All the time. She never has a good day."

"Not even one?"

"Not even one. Trust me, if she's mean to you, don't take it as a personal thing. Everyone that's come over felt the same way. She's just like that, and…you'll get used to her. I did."

"Well, at least she's pretty."

"Yeah, well, it's too bad the rest of her ain't."

"Yeah…Hey, what did her mom need to talk to you about?"

"Stuh, nothing. Just a whole lot of questions."

"I feel like it was about me."

"Naw, you're good. Trust me, Ms. Tourez is gonna like you once she gets to know you."

"You sure?"

"Yeah, trust me. Don't worry your head so much about that. I got it."

"I just don't wanna go back to the orphanage."

"You won't, Torence, I promise."

"Okay…"

"You ready to head on out?"

"Yeah, I am."

"C'mon let's go."

Pissy and Gripped

It had only been a couple of weeks since Torence came into the Tourezes lives, and yet somehow, he had already sealed a place in their hearts. His connection with Lantino was evident, and his developing a relationship with Ms. Tourez was inevitable. Ms. Tourez had pretty much become really fond of Torence, just like Lantino said she would. Unfortunately, the same couldn't be said for the pissy Loraine, who had become increasingly hostile towards Torence. At some point, she'd act hostile towards Lantino, and practically anyone she'd come in contact with. But once her hostility had reached its max, she was sent to boot camp, where she spent quite some time.

Fortunately, after her return, the change in her attitude was apparent. Since her return, her popularity had grown to a great extent. Her popularity was centered around Lantino's fight with their school's security guard and the fact that she was related to him. She was well known among the older crowd. Boys had become particularly fond of her looks. Above all, she seemed to possess the type of personality to match her appearance. Her focus was more on those who were older as far as her interest in boys was concerned.

So again, the change in her attitude was apparent. However, it remained the same when it came to Torence. Although at times, she'd have a few instances in which she'd show concern for him if he weren't present throughout the day. On days Torence wasn't anywhere to be found, usually meant that he was out marveling in creativity. Spray painting was practically all he was doing on days Lantino wasn't with him. He'd often venture out into other settings now that he was becoming more comfortable. However, at the same time, he didn't try to get too complacent when he was alone. Given the fact that Lantino, as well as Tyberius, had supplied him with some knowledge regarding their rival gang, he considered the possibility of them lurking around.

On one very windy February evening, Torence was up on the top floor of the balcony. After having spent most of his time there throughout the afternoon sketching ideas, he decided to wrap his evening up by spray painting one of the alleys nearby where he lived. It was one particular area he had wanted to work on for quite a while and figured tonight was the perfect opportune moment being that the wind was blowing pretty hard. It was starting to get dark, and although he wasn't cold, he concluded that the freezing temperature outside was going to keep everyone inside. With that, he decided not to wait any later.

Within a matter of twenty minutes, Torence now stood before a solid brick wall of the alley. He had on an all-black outfit: black baggy jeans, black belt, and a black leather jacket which belonged to Lantino. To guard his face against the fumes from the spray paint cans he stole from Milleena, he wore a cap and covered his mouth and nose with a red bandana. And just like that, Torence began spraying the brick wall for the next several minutes. Using red and white as his primary color scheme, Torence sprayed what appeared to be a thick two-dimensional bubble letter of words, scribbled in abstract form. Not all of the letters were completely filled in. However, they all spelled something that implied a message. A message in which only a few could grasp immediately.

Working under the impression that no one was going to be out in this freezing, windy weather, Torence paced himself as if he had all the time in the world. Suddenly, he began to hear what sounded like footsteps striding to get to a particular destination. Being on the alert, he used his peripheral vision to see what may have been coming from the sidewalk, just outside the alleyway. So, using his peripheral vision, he caught what he ended up believing to be the breeze shuffling against a bunch of leaves and old newspapers. After all, the wind was blowing pretty hard, he thought. However, the sounding of footsteps continued and seemed to only pick up in volume. He glanced over his right a few more times before finally dismissing the sounds. Then he heard what now sounded like chattering, but again, he opted to tune it out. Finally, the wind knocked over one of the spray cans he placed on the ground. Thus, he turned around to reach over for it before the wind could blow it away. Just as he was doing that, he quickly removed the bandana from his face. Beyond that point, he paused as his brain finally registered the fact that those sounds, he heard were indeed the voices of people. Two people in which he happened to recognize: Loraine and Milleena. "Wait, wait!" said Torence. "Don't tell Ms. Tourez," he implored as he dropped the spray cans unknowingly. "I found it like this! I promise!" Hearing this, the girls paused and then took a quick look at one another before they continued to look at him. He also stared back with his eyes and mouth wide open. "Pl-pl-pl-pl-pl-please d-d-d-don't tell Ms. Tourez," he said once more. Then he took off into the darkness. He ran as if he was being pursued by someone. After retreating to the top floor's balcony, he took a moment to catch his breath. *Ding, they're probably gonna tell Ms. Tourez,* he thought. *Shucks! Just when things were going good...Why couldn't it be someone else who caught me? It could've been anybody...Anybody but her (Loraine). I hope she won't tell Ms. Tourez...Who am I kidding? She hates me. So, of course, she's gonna tell Ms. Tourez about this. Then I'm a get sent back to the orphanage and never see another good day in my life again.*

All sorts of conclusions were being drawn in Torence's mind now that Loraine and Milleena knew about him writing graffiti on public surfaces. However, little did he know that telling on him was the last thing on Loraine's mind. In fact, Loraine was impressed by his graffiti because she recognized some of the same symbols that were drawn in her letter back in boot camp. Overall, she was aroused with curiosity regarding Torence.

Moving forward, Loraine tried to make attempts to draw Torence's attention. She often wore a particular scent, styled her hair in a distinct way, wore specific outfits, tried to make eye contact, or even make several gestures to communicate interest to him. However, all of her efforts proved unsuccessful. Apparently, Torence was still in the stage of the oblivious. Moreover, when it came to possibly anything concerning Loraine, he was at a point in which he thought she didn't want him around. Above all else, Loraine knew about him marking graffiti on public places, so he tried to avoid her by all means necessary. Given the fact that she could've exaggerated any story about that night to his legal guardian at any given time or day, Torence was precautious when he was around her. They both lived in the same place. Yet, somehow, someway, Torence usually always managed to stay out of her sight. Ironically, this only incited Loraine's curiosity about him even more. So, for necessary reasons, Torence kept his distance, but again, they both knew the same group of people. Altogether they were both part of the same social network. All and all, they were bound to run into each other at the various spots their friends liked to hang out at.

The Rec

Hanging out indoors seem to be the new thing for everyone to do till the emergence of spring. The weather in Chicago around this time of the year was frigidly cold, and no one wanted to turn into a popsicle stick. So, everyone stayed indoors. However, hanging out in malls or meeting up in populated areas wasn't typically something Torence would do. Torence was a pretty low-key individual, but this time was an exception. He was summoned to come by the recreation center, which was where he was heading. A while ago, he had sketched out a tattoo design for J-Roc, and ever since then, Tyberius, who was waiting for him at the recreation center, had become particularly fond of his drawings. In fact, Torence's name was slowly, but surely starting to get around, and being asked for was something that became common.

So, on his way to the recreation center, Torence was suited with more layers of clothing. He made sure to bring along his sketchbook and he packed at least three pencils before his trip to the recreation center. Because it was so cold outside, he didn't waste any time trying to find the recreation center's exact location. When he made it through the front entrance, he immediately noticed Tyberius, who was sitting down inside the game room area, signaling for Torence to come join him. "What's happening, young lord," greeting Tyberius as he slapped hands with Torence. "I'm straight," replying Torence as he nodded his head. "Anybody else here?" he asked.

"Vern is."

"Where is he?"

"In the bathroom. He'll be coming back. Say, where's Tino?"

"I thought he was at your place."

"No...Oh wait a minute, that's right, Julisa did say he was on his way to our place."

"Oh, okay...It's not that thick in here."

"Yeah, a lot of people must've got frozen on their way here."

"Ha ha ha ha, then I'm glad I was able to make it."

"Ha ha ha ha, yeah man, me too. So anyways, Roc tells me you know how to sketch tats. Is that right?"

"Oh yeah?"

"Yeah, matter fact, that's the word out right now. I mean, the whole clique's been talking about it."

"Well, yeah I can sketch something together."

"You think you can do something for me?"

"Yeah, I mean whatever you want."

"Can you make something like what you did for Roc?"

"Yeah…How soon you need it?"

"Whenever…Just one thing, though…"

"What?"

"Add a pitchfork in there this time."

"I gotchu…"

"Cool, so what your bout to go do right now?"

"Uh…Nothing, probably work on another sketch somewhere else."

"Why don't you stay out here and shoot some cue ball with Vern and me. That's what we bout to do now."

"Nann, I ain't all that good."

"Well, then stay here for a minute and get better, shait."

"Ha ha ha ha…"

"I mean, why not, right?! If anything, your local fan club is probably gonna come looking for you out here at the rec."

"Ha ha ha ha ha, naw, you right."

"Shit, I'm just saying. You seem so quick to head right on out to the north pole. Might as well, wait and let the ice melt first before you do that."

"Ha ha ha ha true…So, wanna shoot first?"

"Oh naw, you go right ahead, lord."

So, a rather courteous Tyberius racked the cue balls up, and by hitting the white ball against the rest of the balls, Torence started the game off. Handing his pool stick over to Tyberius, he noticed that his friend was dressed unusually casual. He wasn't rocking any of the gang's colors in his attire, which in a way meshed with the mood of the recreation center. The atmosphere felt laid back, and though Torence was knocking in more cue balls than Tyberius, they both seem to be enjoying their friendly competition.

By the time they practically forgot about Vern, he returned out of nowhere. He was just in time to enjoy the suspense of seeing who was going to knock the last cue ball in one of the pockets. But suddenly, all the suspense seems to shift away from the pool table and towards the other side of the game room. On the other side of the room was a bench in which three girls were sitting on. The boys were able to make out who the one in the middle was but weren't necessarily too sure about her friends on the side. One thing they were all certain about was the fact that everything, for some unknown reason seemed to gravitate towards them from the moment they entered the room. "I know y'all see that, right?" asked Vern.

"The one in the middle, right," answered Torence.

"Yeah," replied Vern.

"Don't you mean all three of them," said Tyberius. "Because I see one…two…three of them sitting over there on that bench."

"Well, yeah that too," replying Vern. "But what about that one in the middle?"

"Yeah, I see her too," said Torence.

"Isn't that Tino's sister?" asked Tyberius.

"Yeah, that's her," answered Torence.

"Oh yeah, that is her, ain't it," said Vern.

"Yep, her 'lil spoiled ass," said Tyberius.

"Ding, she looks really pretty," said Torence.

"Stuh, she just tryna show out," replied Tyberius. "Say, I wonder what she's all dressed up for?"

"Hmmm, I'oin know, but she looked right," replying Torence.

"Shoot, I wouldn't stare too hard jit," said Vern. "That's J-Roc's girl that's sitting over there."

"Please!" replying Tyberius, "J-Roc just tryna claim."

"Wait, so she gotta boyfriend?" asked Torence.

"Yeah, and Roc don't like it when other niggas be eyeing his girl," answering Vern.

"Man don't listen to that shit lord," said Tyberius to Torence.

"Oh…alright now," replying Vern.

"What about the one to the right?" asked Torence.

"Ain't that, that one black Chinese girl that be with Lantino," answered Vern.

"Yeah, kinda…" replying Tyberius.

"Yeah, I thought that was her too," said Torence.

"Hmmm well…Maybe it is, maybe it isn't," said Vern. "What about the white chick on the left?"

"Hmmm, I don't know," answered Torence. "Tye, what about you?"

"Hmmm, I don't think I've ever seen her around here or anywhere," answered Tyberius.

"Well, I'm a go see what's up with the 'blackanese' on the right," said Vern.

"Wait, hold on, you might wanna slow ya role homeboy," said Tyberius to Vern.

"And why's that?" replied Vern.

"Because Lee likes Lantino, last time I checked," said Tyberius.

"Well, Tino ain't here now, is he?" replied Vern.

"Hey, just trying to save you from wasting your time," said Tyberius to Vern.

"Yeah whatever," replied Vern to Tyberius. "Just worry about the one in the middle."

"Tino sister? Hell naw!" replied Tyberius. "I'm a pass and say what's up to the one on the left. Yo peeps, you could have that."

"Naw, I won't mess with another boy's girl," replied an honorable Torence.

"Hmmm, I don't know what Tino's been telling you, but he's obviously doing something right," replied Vern to Torence. "It's wise shit like that, that's gonna make you hang for a long time out here. Ain't it, Tye?"

"You know what, just step fool," replied Tyberius to Vern."

"But I'm right though, ain't it Tye? Ain't it?" asked Vern.

"Just head on over there for I knock you with my pool stick," again replying Tyberius to Vern. "Yo lord, stick around. We'll be right back."

So again, from the moment the girls entered the game room and sat down on the bench, everything concerning attention began to gravitate towards them. Hanging out inside the recreation center is one answer someone could say if one were likely to ask exactly what the girls wanted. But aside from hanging out, what else did they want, is what the boys were pretty much looking to know. So, Tyberius and Vern went to find out while the younger and more reserved, Torence returned to his sketches. As he moved his pencil across the paper, he could kind of make out what was going on using the corner of his eyes. He could tell there was a lot of giggling and stories being told based on the gestures he saw from the interactions between his buddies and the girls. Adding more detail, he decided to focus on the sketch but realized he wasn't able to tune out his surroundings. Suddenly, he began to acknowledge the change in the mood of the atmosphere. A mood that made him feel subdued and singled out. It was almost as though this spotlight was shining loud and bright on him. *It's her,* he thought as he stopped moving his pencil. *I could feel her eyes on me,* he thought once more. Figuring that he was being watched, he took a moment to look back towards Loraine's way while tilting his head. There, his eyes connected with her eyes and wallah…a contact was made between the two. As Torence began to lift his head, Loraine instantly turned away, realizing that he caught her staring at him. The stare between the two that took place for but only a few seconds and felt like everlasting minutes, suggested something utterly new to Torence. Something which really contrasted with the thoughts he had about Loraine prior to coming to the recreation center. *She can't stand me*, he thought. "But how come…It seems like she…wants to talk," he whispered as he slowly placed his pencil down. Debating on what he was going to say to her, he closed his sketchbook and gets up. However, when he turns towards the direction in which Loraine was sitting on, he noticed she, along with her friend and Vern, has left the bench to head upstairs. The third girl that came with her isn't present, and neither is Tyberius, who was last seen talking to her. "Hmmm, where's everybody going?" he asked as he continued watching Vern head upstairs with his new company. Opening his sketchbook, he looked meticulously at his drawing and realized he wasn't pleased with what he had come up with so far. "Hmmm, well, I guess I might as well see if I could touch up on it a 'lil," he said as he returned to his sketch.

After the next fifteen minutes, Torence figured that he did enough and was ready to go. That's when he also came to find Tyberius standing over his shoulder with his head sideways. "Ding Tye, ain't know you were standing there the whole time," said Torence as he crouched his body while turning to look back at

Tyberius. "You ain't heard me when I was coming in?" asked Tyberius with his head still positioned sideways.

"Uh…Naw. How long have you been standing there?"

"Tuh, not long at all. I pretty much just got back."

"What happened with that girl I saw you talking with?"

"Nothing, really. We just walked around the rec for 'lil bit; then I lost her after I came back from the bathroom."

"Or you mean she lost you, ha ha ha ha."

"He he he he, ya got jokes today, huh?"

"I'm just saying."

"Whatever. Where's Vern?"

"I saw him going upstairs with those two girls, but he ain't never come back."

"'Lil sell out. He left us."

"Hmp, I guess."

"So what'cha got there, lord?"

"That same sketch I made for Roc that you wanted."

"Damn, it's banging! I gotta have Tino see if he could buy you an ink gun."

"For real?"

"Hell yeah, we gotta set that up real quick."

"Anyways, you ready to get out of here?"

"Yeah, let's head back to my place and see what's happening with my cuz and Tino."

"Yeah, bet."

February 14th

On February 14th, Loraine began her day going back and forth between the room she shared with Milleena and the restroom. It was a daily routine that Loraine had practiced. Everyone in the household had grown sick of it because it was starting to become uncomfortable for them. Lantino was first to voice his dislikes towards Loraine's traditional extended stays in the restroom. Next, was her mother, Loriana, who complained about Loraine constantly misplacing her perfumes/cosmetics. Milleena also said she is growing weary of Loraine locking her out of their room consistently.

Milleena banged on the door with utter frustration. "Hold on, hold on, I just got in here!" said Loraine.

"Just got in here?" replied Milleena. "Oh, please! Just open up this damn door already! It was locked when I came out of the bathroom earlier, and it's locked now."

"Okay, just hold on! I'll be right there!"

"Ding it, Raine! It's been more than what… like twenty minutes. What'chu doing in there anyway?"

"Ugh, fine! Here Lee, it's open! You happy now?"

"Ugh, about time, shoot! J-Roc gotcha way too worked up about this dance night. So worked up that you forget that you're staying home with everyone else too ya know.

"Hey, is that what everyone's been talking about in here?"

"No Raine, we're all just tired of being tired of you and your 'lil rituals."

"Oh c'mon, am I really that bad?"

"Hmp, like every single day! And if I'm fussing about it now then, you know it's got to stop."

"Okay, ha ha ha ha ha…I'm sorry, Lee. As of now, I won't lock you out of the room."

"And…"

"And I won't be in the bathroom for so long."

"Good."

"But just to clear one thing, J-Roc does not have me all worked up about some Valentine's Day dance.

"Then, who?"

"What do you mean 'who'? No one's got me worked up."

"If it ain't Roc, then it's gotta be some boy because I ain't used to you acting like this."

"Whatever Lee, I'm a let you believe what you wanna believe."

"Look, would you just tell me, and stop trying to hide it."

"Tell you about what? What are you talking about?"

"You know what I'm talking about, now tell me."

"No, I don't Lee."

"Who is he, Loraine?"

"What? Who?"

"Your crush. Who is it? Is it Roc?"

"No Lee, I just told you that I don't like Roc like that."

"Okay then, who is it?"

"He ain't nobody.

"Nobody…wait, do I know him?"

"Yes!"

"Yeah?"

"I mean, no…"

"See, I knew it! You're hiding something."

"I don't have a crush on him."

"You don't have to tell me, but I'm a find out anyway. Point him out to me tonight at the concert."

"Stuh…"

"Now, I'm mad at you, Raine."

"Fine, I'll tell you one thing about him."

"Yeah, at least do that. Like, tell me if he's cute?"

"Yeah, he is, but he's younger…"

"Hmmm…"

"What? What? Say it! Tell me!"

"Now I kinda see why you felt shy to tell me. It's because he's younger than you."

"YOU BETTER NOT TELL ANYONE LEE!"

"I won't, but you better point him out tonight at the concert."

"What time's the Valentines' Day concert?"

"This year, it's at eight."

"So, what are we gonna do first?"

"Well, everyone's gonna meet up at Julisa's place, and then we're gonna head out there."

"I hear Tye's gonna bring a car."

"Funny you say that because I heard that too."

"Well, whatever, I guess we'll just see."

"Yep. Oh, by the way Raine, stop by Roots to pick up the pizza Julisa ordered."

"Why can't it be you? Why it gotta be me?"

"Well, Julisa's the one setting things up at her place, plus Tye is sliding through with a car. Then you have me trying to scoop our other girlfriends up from the rec to meet at Julisa's place. So, I figured while we're all out doing whatever, this is where you'd come in and pick up the pizzas."

"Hmp, girl. I guess. Hmmm…Did you hear something?"

"A sound coming from the living room?"

"Yeah…Did Tino get up?"

"Naw, that's just that boy that's staying with y'all."

"Oh him…"

"Mmmm hmmm…I think he just left, though."

"How do you know?"

"When I saw him walked in, it looked like he was dropping off some food.

"Him?"

"Yeah…Hey, if you hurry, maybe you can catch up with him to tell him happy Valentine."

"He he he he, you trying to be funny."

"Um, no I was just saying Raine; after all, he did make that picture on your letter, remember?"

"You know what, I'll see you later at Julisa's."

"Oh okay, I might swing by the Roots after the rec."

"Okay well, bye."

"Oh, and Raine…"

"Yeah?"

"You ain't happen to see my color pencils around, have you?"

"Uh no. Sure you ain't leave them at your mom's house?"

"Yeah, I'm sure. You know I'm starting to think someone's taking my stuff. Probably that boy, Terrance."

"Terrance?"

"Yeah, because that night we caught him tagging up the wall; he was using my spray cans."

"Yours?"

"Yeah…Anyways, order 190. Remember that."

"Wait, you said 190?"

"Yeah, pick up order number 190."

"Okay…Bye."

Loraine stepped out of the house dressed relatively inappropriate for the weather. However, she was fine with her choice of attire, knowing that she could add on more layers of clothing later when she got to Julisa's place. In addition, it was only mid-day, which for Loraine, meant that the weather outside was warmer at least till the sun went down. With that, she had on a red thick layered hooded jacket on, long blue fitted jeans along with black boots. Underneath her thick jacket was a black tank top she wanted to show off, and some bracelet like earrings. Her hair was wrapped up in a ponytail, and she made sure to spray herself with her favorite perfume. Despite all the arrangements she made with her friends, she wasn't in a hurry to do anything related to the concert because everyone might not come on time. So therefore, she decided to make several trips around the area. Her first stop started with Torence's graffiti, which was literally just a block away from where she lived. She took a moment to admire the graffiti he never finished making.

About an hour or so had passed, and Loraine had finally made a stop at a local pizza shop after all the sightseeing around the city. Just seconds after walking inside, the clerk assisted her. Once that was done, she leaned her back against the clerk's counter and sat on a stool. That's when she noticed Torence sitting on a table near the bathroom at the far end of the shop. Within that very second, it was like she was back in the mall again. Suddenly, thoughts were running through her mind as she began to watch him.

While Loraine was sitting by the clerk's counter deep in her thoughts, Torence was at the far end of the shop seated on a table that sat right next to the bathroom. Though he heard someone walk through the doors, his back was turned, and his mind was fixed on filling in one of his sketches. In spite of his back being turned, he could tell that he was being watched. Nevertheless, he carried on and filled in his artwork. Right when he reached over to grab one of Milleena's colored pencils, he heard the sound of a voice that had mispronounced his name. It took a while, but he eventually turned around to find that it was Loraine. "Oh hi, hello," she said rudely. "Is your name Terrence?" she asked condescendingly. Torence initially looked back at her with a convoluted look all over his face. However, that soon changed after she repeatedly mispronounced his name. Staring back at her with a panned look now on his face, he corrects her with no sound of emotion in his tone. For a moment, the roles are switched, and for once, it's Loraine now feeling like she's all vulnerable and subdued. While Torence, on the other hand was feeling like he's confident.

Throughout the opening of their conversation, Torence, to his surprise, was rather comfortable. It wasn't until Loraine began to communicate interest to Torence, is then when he dwindled back into that quiet/reserved character she knew. His responses began to create a bit of confusion for Loraine, as he avoided eye contact. Fortunately, that all changed when the conversation moved towards the letter he made and sent to her while she was away in boot camp. At some point, he took his eyes away from his sketches and finally made direct eye contact with Loraine. Once eye contact was made, not another word was said by neither of the two. Silence was in the air at that moment, and so was something else. A spark that neither of them could deny. Torence's eyes began to get watery as he grew more and more aware of her beauty. And like that, his eyes began to blank constantly. He could feel a sharp pen poking his heart at every beat as his chest burned with nervousness. And the sweetness of her perfume made it harder for him to breathe. Though, Torence didn't say nor make any sound; he didn't have to because Loraine sensed his attraction for her. She smiled as she watched him struggle to cover it up. Clearly, Loraine was loving their official meeting together at the local pizza shop. "Order number 190!" shouted the clerk. "Your food is ready!"

"Just sit it there, I'm coming!" said Loraine as she responded to the clerk. Directing her attention back to Torence, she broke the ice and pretty much opened up a new conversation between the two. According to Loraine, the concert was supposed to be the main highlight of the day. However, it seemed like the concert was right here at the pizza shop. There was no predicting how long she was going to carry away in a conversation with Torence. The store may have closed, and they'd still sit and converse. But then, she as well as Torence heard movement from the doors as they opened. And just like that, their conversation was interrupted by Milleena, who happened to walk in the scene. "Hey Raine," she said to Loraine. "You ordered my pizzas yet?"

"Yeah," answered Loraine, "why they're sitting right over there on the counter."

"Wait," said Torence, "I thought you said Lantino sent you to get some food for him?"

"Oh yeah, I did, didn't I?" replied Loraine.

"Raine, did you tell 'em that your brother sent you?" asked Milleena.

"Umm, excuse me, Lee, but if you didn't notice, Torence and I were in the middle of something, ain't that right, Torence," said Loraine.

"Um, yeah," replying Torence.

"Oh, oh well excuse me for barging in," said Milleena. "Hmmm, what's going on here?"

"Um, nothing," answering Loraine.

"Hmmm…more like something," said Milleena.

"Hmmm, like what?" asked Loraine.

"Don't play dumb," said Milleena. "If I ain't know y'all, I'd say y'all were on a date."

"Whatever Lee, it ain't like that," said Loraine.

"Not yet," again saying Milleena.

"Hey smiley, what you over there laughing about?" asked Loraine to Torence.

"Oh me? Uh nothing, nothing," answering Torence.

"Nice sketches," said Milleena sending her comments to Torence.

"Yeah, thanks," replied Torence.

"Are those supplies mine?" asked Milleena to Torence.

"Oh, you mean these coloring pencils? Um, yeah," answered Torence.

"I'm getting tired of you taking my stuff without asking," said Milleena to Torence.

"I was gonna bring it right back," said Torence.

"I know, but that's not the point," said Milleena. "Before you take something, you need to ask. I'm sure you've heard of something called common courtesy."

"Stuh! Girl please, he said he'll put it right back," said Loraine to Milleena.

"Hmp, anyways, you ready to go, Raine?" asked Milleena.

"Wait, right now?" asked Loraine.

"Yes," answered Milleena.

"But I don't wanna leave him here by himself," said Loraine.

"Okay, well see if he wants to come," Milleena suggested to Loraine.

"Y'all could go," said Torence.

"It's okay," said Milleena, "you could come too."

"Namp," Torence declined.

"Let's go," said Milleena to Loraine.

"But wait," said Loraine to Torence. "Are you sure?" she asked him.

"Very," answered Torence.

"Oh, c'mon Raine," said Milleena, "you heard 'em. He said he's good. Now let's go. Julisa and the others are waiting for us at her place. That's where I told her we'd meet at."

"But Lee, he looks lonely," said Loraine.

"I'm alright," said Torence to Loraine.

"See, he's good," said Milleena to Loraine. "Now let's go. My pizzas getting cold."

"Alright then," said Loraine to Milleena.

"Bye," said Torence.

"Happy Valentines' Day," said Loraine to Torence.

You're Everywhere

On the dusk of February 14th, Lantino came back home from his date with Julisa and hung out in the living room for a little while before deciding to join Torence upstairs in the top floor. Making it to the top floor, he noticed Torence was leaning forward against the bars on the balcony. When he reached the balcony, he did the same thing as well to enjoy the nice view outside. Shortly, a conversation between the two began. A conversation which reflected on all the highlights of the day that they recorded. For Lantino, the day was just another day that had gone by. Torence, on the contrary had questions that were lingering all over his mind. Some in which his best friend, Lantino, was able to answer. At the same time, the rest was left to him to figure out on his own. After their interesting conversation on the night of February 14th, a couple of days had gone by. Things seem to only get more interesting for Torence beyond this point. After his official meeting with Loraine that day at the Roots pizza shop, he was pretty much convinced that she wasn't going spill anything to his legal guardian. With that said, he felt more comfortable, which resulted in her seeing him around at home more often.

Loraine was surely beginning to lighten up on Torence. However, the two of them were only saying hi and bye to each other for every time they were passing by. It was almost as though they both had returned to their worlds after their moment together at the pizza shop. But that inevitably changed; over the next several weeks, they both started running into each other nearly everywhere they went.

The weather in Chicago in the days of winter was frigidly cold, and no one wanted to turn into a popsicle stick. So again, hanging out indoors seems to be the new thing to do till spring emerged. However, that wasn't the case for Loraine and Milleena on this one day of late February. The two had decided to meet up in the early evening to hang out. For the most part, the day was interesting, but things took a turn towards the more interesting after they both came across one of Milleena's graffiti. They both discovered that someone tagged Milleena's graffiti. While Milleena's eyes were fixed on the tag, Loraine's mind was lit up with loads of thoughts. *Torence, you're really getting good at this*, Loraine thought as she figured who had spray-painted over Milleena's graffiti. "Lee, can I ask you something?" Loraine said as she looked towards Milleena.

"Go, head, girl," replied Milleena.

"Has this ever happened to you?"

"What? Someone tagging my shit? Maybe…I'oin know."

"No, I mean, have you ever ran into the same person over and over again?"

"You mean, like no matter where you go, that same person's always at the same place you be at somehow?"

"Yeah…Has that ever happened to you?"

"Hmmm, nope. Why? Is that what's going on with you?"

"Hmmm, sort of."

"Well, I know something you can do."

"What?"

"Tell 'em to quit stalking you, ha ha ha ha!"

"Very funny. But no, this is different."

"Wait, you mean you like him following you?"

"No, no…"

"Okay, then what are you saying?"

"Well, I keep running into this person, but I know he ain't following me. Nor am I following him. Which is weird…"

"That is weird, Raine…Like where y'all be running into each other at?"

"Stuh, everywhere…"

"Hmp, well, think you'll run into him again tonight?"

"Now Lee, how the heck am I supposed to know that?"

"I'oin know, I'm just going with what you're telling me that's all, ha ha ha ha…"

"No, you're just a smart-ass, Lee."

"So, what happens when y'all bump into each other?"

"Uh…Nothing."

"I knew you were gonna say that."

"Well, he says hi to me and all."

"And that's it? Y'all talk or do anything else?"

"Well, no cause, I hardly know him like that."

"Hmp, seems like you think he's cute. So, why don't you try and get him to talk to you."

"Like how?"

"Raine, you don't remember what I taught you?!"

"Hmmm…"

"You know, like smiling at him or licking your lips one time while you're looking him in the eyes. You gotta have him come to you, Raine."

"I know, but something's different about him though, Lee."

"Girl, please. Look, you said he says hi to you and all, right?"

"Yeah…"

"And you tell 'em hi back, right?"

"Right…"

"Okay, so, next time when you see your lil' friend again, just smile and do all the other stuff I told you to do, and y'all be good."

"Okay, fine, whatever."

"Just do it, Raine. Oh, and try not to look all mean, haha. You wanna make 'em feel like you wanna have a convo."

"Wait, you saying that I scare boys away with my look?"

"Yes, you do, ha ha ha ha."

"He he he. Whatever…Anyways, you ready to go?"

"Yeah girl, where are we going now?"

"I wanna get out this cold."

"Oh so, now you're ready to stay inside?"

"Yeah, let's see if we could catch Julisa and my brother at the movies somewhere."

"Hmmm, okay…Nann, wait, you know what, I'm starting to feel hungry. You wanna stop at Roots to grab a bite?"

"Lee, can't we just eat at the movies?"

"Girl please, I ain't trying to eat just popcorn. I want something that's gonna fill me up with a soda on the side."

"Okay, well I guess there's no talking you out of it, so I think I'm a wait for you by Gurnee Mills, and then when you're done, you'll meet me at the theaters."

"Okay, so we'll get back together there?"

"Yeah."

"Okay…Sure you ain't hungry?"

"I'm sure."

"Alright then, later."

"Later girl."

While Milleena went to grab a bite at Roots, Loraine decided to make a trip to the mall. It was now 6:40 in the evening, and the weather was setting at thirty degrees; snowflakes were starting to come down. Fortunately, for Loraine, a city bus happened to pull up to a bus stop she was nearest to. It was pretty crowded inside and although, there were a few empty seats, Loriane chose to stand on her feet. En route to Gurnee Mills Mall, Loraine had hoped to run into a few of her friends. Though, she had a feeling that this hope wasn't going fall into her favor, she, at this point, just wanted to stay out of the cold for a while.

A while had gone by, and the bus had pulled up at a central terminal, where Loraine was getting off. Just as Loraine was stepping out, she coincidently happened to run into Torence, who was just getting ready to come in. He was standing amid a crowd, who like him, was also waiting to come on in. Watching him, she could tell he was counting how much coins he had in his hand. He had on khaki pants along with Lantino's black leather jacket. Underneath his jacket was a thin layered hoodie which gave him a different look. A look that made Loraine want to touch her hair. With her eyes still on him, she began to notice that he's taking his attention away from his coins and is now casually waiting in line with the others in front of him. Slowly moving his head in a swivel, he has a glance of his surroundings at the bus terminal. Once he stopped turning his head, he then recognized Loraine, who's smiling right at him. He smiled back at her and signaled to her to come talk for a moment. She then walked towards an empty bench and followed him. As Torence approached her near the bench, she tilted her head and said to him, "Ugh, you're like everywhere now. Why is that?"

"Stuh haha, I don't know. You tell me," laughed Torence.

"Boy, I'm for real…I'm running into you here, there, everywhere…It's starting to creep me out, but…It's kinda cute."

"Ha ha ha ha…this now makes like the third time I saw you today."

"Wait, where else did you see me today?"

"Well, there was this morning when you were passing by Tye's place, and the other time by the rec, when you were with your friend, Lee. I saw y'all upstairs, but I don't think you recognized me."

"Oh yeah, we did pass through the rec earlier, but wait, I don't remember seeing you there…"

"I had on a skully, and I was by the vending machine."

"When Lee went to get some snacks?"

"Yeah."

"Oh, you mean that was you..."

"That was me."

"So, if you saw me earlier, then why ain't you come over and say hi?"

"Oh, um uh, well, I saw you with Lee. So, I ain't wanna disturb y'all or anything."

"Hmmm, you still should've said something. I mean, it's not like I wouldn't say hi to you too."

"Hmmm."

"Right?"

"Right, I guess."

"Bighead...So, anyway, what are you doing right now?"

"Hmmm, I don't know...I just wanted to see where this bus was gonna take me."

"Right..."

"I was..."

"Right, right..."

"Well, anyways...what are you doing out here...so late?"

"What you mean so late?"

"I mean like_like where are you heading to?"

"Oh...Okay. Well, I'm on my way to the mall."

"The mall? It's still open?"

"Um, yeah..."

"Oh...I didn't know. Hmp, well, the bus is gonna leave Raine so, I better hop on."

"Oh, uh well...um, I'll see ya later."

"Um yeah, later."

"Hey, Torence um, wait up."

"Huh?"

"Um, listen, why don't you come with me to the store somewhere?"

"Um, the store?"

"Yeah, there's one down the street from here."

"Wait, I was just down –"

"You coming?"

"Well, I gotta hop –"

"Come walk with me. It'll be real quick, c'mon."

Wrapping her arm around Torence's left arm, Loraine basically stapled him on to her and ultimately had him miss his bus ride. Walking together, they both mingled and strolled around the neighborhood for a couple of miles before finally making a stop at a small store. There Loraine picked up her favorite perfume and pretty much had Torence carry it for her on their way back home. What was supposed to be 'real quick', according to Loraine, had taken well over an hour. It was now a quarter after eight, and the couple was less than a block away from their building. By now, their conversation had died down, and the two were just ready to call it an evening. Oddly, Loraine still had her arm wrapped around Torence's left arm, and this time, her head was resting against his shoulder. Noticing this, Torence cracked a smile and just carried on as they were passing the alleyway near their building. Staring at Torence's graffiti art put a bit of a smile on her face as well. Thinking, she then told him that it was him who spray-painted over Milleena's graffiti. Torence denied it, but she insisted and right there, a whole new conversation opened up between the two of them.

"Raine, I'm telling you I didn't tag that wall."

"Oh, yes you did."

"Naw, I didn't. I haven't tagged any place since that day you and Lee caught me."

"Oh, stop lying. I know how you tag."

"Wait, you do?"

"Oh, yeah…"

"Shit."

"What?"

"Stuh, alright."

"Alright, what?"

"Alright fine, I did it. I-I did tag up that wall y'all saw earlier."

"Stuh! I know that!"

"Yeah."

"My thing is, why'd you try to lie to me?"

"I ain't try to –"

"Yes, you did."

"No, I –"

"Yes. You. Did."

"Okay, yeah I did."

"Yes, you did, and why?"

"Why…"

"Yeah, why'd you try to lie to me?"

"Uh…hmmm…I'oin know."

"You know what, let's stop here for a minute."

"Wait…Why?"

"Because I still wanna know why you tried to lie to me."

"For real?"

"I'm still waiting."

"Um…"

"C'mon, talk."

"Um, uh…"

"Talk."

"Hmmm…"

"Talk."

"Ha ha ha ha."

"What's so funny?"

"You and how you're looking at me…"

"Boy, I should make you carry me upstairs."

"Um…right."

"C'mon, let's go."

"Upstairs?"

"Yeah, let's go."

"Okay, but what about the elevator?"

"What about it?"

"Why don't we just go up the elevator."

"Because…We're gonna take the stairs."

"But…why?"

"Because I like walking with you…"

"Oh…"

"Okay?"

"Okay."

"Good. Now hush."

Up the stairway, they went, and through the front doorway they came, marking an end to a late February day. Taking off his hoodie, Torence shut the door while Loraine switched the lights back on. Loraine wasted no time going to her room and doing whatever she needed to do. Torence, on the other hand, took his time getting comfortable. He placed his hoodie on the coat hanger, removed his shoes, and sat down on the living room sofa. Next, he slouched back and turned on the television. Using the remote, he flipped through every channel there was but didn't find anything on television to watch. So, he closed his eyes and just rested his head back. Loraine soon joined him in the living room, saying, "Boy, that must be your favorite jacket." Opening his eyes, he tilted his head towards the direction she was standing, replying, "Oh, yeah, but this is actually your brother's leather jacket, Raine." Nodding her head, Loraine responds saying, "Boy, I know that." Next, she walks to the sofa to sit next to him. "Here, move over some," she said a couple of times to Torence. Sliding over a little to his left, Torence instantly noticed that Loraine is sitting really close to him in a tucked seated position. Another detail he captured was that she's wearing a tank top and now has on pajama shorts. Moreover, she smelled like the perfume she had on back when they were at Roots a couple of weeks ago. Thus, the sweet scent began to make him feel a bit uneasy. Sensing it, Loraine looked a little over to her left. "Are you okay?" she asks him. "Who? Me? Uh, yeah, yeah…just fine," Torence denied. "Oh…Okay," said Loraine as she slowly turned away. Both of them now have their eyes fixed on the television for the next couple of minutes. However, neither of them seemed to be tuned in to what they're watching, and suddenly, an uncomfortable silence began to linger around the air. "Um, Torence, what are you watching?" asked Loraine, as she broke the silence. "Uh tuh, I'oin even know," he replied. "Here take the remote," he said handing it over to her. "Let's see what's on TV tonight," she said while flipping channels. "Hmmm, you know it's awfully quiet in here," she said to Torence. "Is anybody else home?" she asked.

"I don't think so. But everyone's usually home around this time."

"Hmmm, I guess they're all coming home late tonight."

"Hmp. Probably…"

"Torence…"

"What?"

"You're crazy."

"What do you mean?"

"What were you wearing?"

"What do you mean what I was wearing? I was wearing clothes."

"It was freaking cold as hell. Like twenty degrees."

"I didn't feel that cold."

"Hah, don't know how you do it."

"What, you felt cold?"

"Yea-ah."

"Ha ha ha ha but how so…You were all bundled up in that big ole jacket of yours."

"I don't know."

"Well, you know what? Next time, you could wear Lantino's jacket ha ha ha ha."

"Wow look who's got jokes."

"Ha ha ha ha…"

"So, he walked around with a hoodie and goes to thinking that he's Mr. Hot to trot."

"Wait, Mr. Hot to who?"

"Hot to trot."

"To trot…wait, what's that?"

"You don't know what that is? Ugh, you know what…just-just forget it."

"Tuh…um, okay."

"You and your hoodie."

"Hey, what about my hoodie?"

"Why'd you walk around with a hoodie?"

"Uh, because it was cold."

"Really? You're getting smart?"

"Raine, what else you want me to say?"

"Tuh, forget it."

"What? You don't like my hoodie?"

"It just gave you a different look."

"Okay…like how?"

"Don't worry about it."

"Okay, you ain't like my hoodie."

"That's not what I said."

"Okay, then what are you saying?"

"Creo que es lindo."

"Huh? Wait, what does that mean?"

"He dicho que es lin da."

"I_I don't understand…"

"Es lindo."

"Oh, I see. You're not gonna tell me…Alright, then."

Loraine began to draw a smirk on her face seeing that Torence is a bit irritated. Her statements and responses were so broad and out in the open that it literally had Torence feeling like he's sitting in the dark. A straight answer was really all he needed to put everything in his world back in the light. Using the corner of his eye, he looked at Loraine, and the expression on her face was making him feel irritable. So, laying his eyes on the television, he tried to zone everything out. That's when Loraine out of nowhere reached over and kissed him on his right cheek. Torence's eyebrows at that moment begun to move way above his forehead. His eyes also began to widen as he took a quick intake of breath. Seeing that, there's a bit of disturbance in Torence's peace; she looks slightly over to her left and asked him if he's okay. Surely, he denied it by nodding his head. Finding it a bit amusing Loraine giggled and then asked him "Ain't it your turn now?". With his peripheral vision, Torence looked to his right, replying "My turn?". Loraine, who's now got a big smirk on her face, responded saying, "Uh, yeah…". With his eyes now back on the T.V screen, Torence paused for a moment. "To do what?" he asked Loraine. "You know what," replying a smiling Loraine, "stop beating around the bush." As Torence lifted his right eyebrow, he looked towards her way and fixed his eyes on her lips. He then moved his tongue across his lips as he got ready to make his next move calmly. "Wait, do that again," Loraine said to him.

"Do what again?"

"Lick your lips again."

"Tuh," sighing Torence as he licked his lips for Loraine. Reluctantly, he squeezed his lips and pushed them out. Closing his eyes, he leaned forward to kiss Loraine on her left cheek. But at the last minute, she caught him by surprise, turning face to face and kissing him mouth to mouth. Torence opened his eyes widely and instantly started to hold his breath. Trying to concentrate, he could feel her tongue moving wildly across his tongue. Opening his eyes, Loraine then came to a sudden stop. That then brought the two to a moment in which they're just staring into one another's eyes. Without a word, it seems as though both of them are saying 'I see you.' Tilting his head to the side a little bit, Torence began to smile and lick his lips. He tried to hold back from smiling while staring into Loraine's eyes for some reason and failed at doing so. Trying to play it off, he moved his eyes back on the television screen. Using the remote, Loraine turned the television off. Slowly redirecting his eyes away from the television, Torence's eyes again met Loraine's. Slightly bending her eyes, she right then and there told him, "Let's do the same thing we were doing, but this time, I want your tongue to touch mine for a while before our mouths meet." Liking the idea of their next move, Torence nodded his head. As they both leaned toward one another to try this as Loraine suggested, they instantaneously came to a sudden halt. They paused due to the movement they heard from the front doorknob. As soon as Loraine turned over to her right, her mother, Loriana, came barging through the front door. "Buenos nochas Torence and Loraine," she said as she was making her way through the living room, and then that's when she paused. With her head positioned sideways, she stared back at Torence and Loraine with the look of a huge question on her face. "Did I miss something?" she asked Torence and Loraine. In unison, Torence and Loraine looked at one another and then looked right back at Loriana with no response. Standing near the kitchen area, Loriana gently placed a sack of groceries on the table. Again, staring at them sideways, Loriana, this time said, "Si…I did…I did miss something." Looking away from Loriana, Torence stared back at Loraine, who then taps him on his shoulder. That indicated to Torence, that Loraine wanted an answer to what her mother is saying, but he just simply shrugged his shoulders. "What are you talking about mami?" asked Loraine with an irritated tone of voice.

"Bebe, don't play dumb with me. You two know what I'm talking about," answered Loriana. Hearing that both Torence and Loraine began to cringe to the thought of being caught in the act. Tying everything together, Loriana began to smile and nod her head endlessly. "Ah hah, I know what's going on here…" she said. "You two are finally starting to get close."

"Mami, it's not like we were doing anything," said Loraine.

"Ah ha ha ha…Mmmm hmmm," replying Loriana.

"What do you mean?" asking Loraine.

"Don't play dumb with me Loraine, I know exactly what's happening here," said Loriana.

"I don't know what you're talking about," Loraine said.

"Hmmm, well I bet your pookie knows everything that I'm talking about," replying Loriana.

"Wait, and who's my pookie supposed to be?" asked Loraine.

"Oh, he knows who he is," said Loriana. "Why don't you speak up," she said to Torence. Blushing, Torence licked his lips and giggled a little bit. Tapping Torence on the shoulder, Loraine told him to clarify everything. "Well, Mr. Pookie, you think maybe you can speak up to set things clear."

"Oh, naw, this is between y'all," Torence responded.

"Oh, c'mon Torence, really?" said Loraine to Torence.

"Bebe, it really is nice to see you two getting close," said Loriana.

"Ugh! Whatever!" said an irritable Loraine.

"Hey Ms. Tourez, did you want me to shut the door?" asked Torence. "I noticed you left it open."

"Oh no, no papi, that's okay," replying Loriana. "Lantino, should be coming through the door any minute now with the rest of the groceries."

"Wait, mami, did you say 'Lantino'?" asked Loraine.

"Si, bebe, your brother," answered Loriana.

"The same pain in the ass Lantino that's always pissing you off?" again, asking Loraine.

"If you want me to answer you in English then 'yes' bebe, that one," said Loriana to Loraine.

"Hah, wow now that's a first," responding Loraine as she shook her head. "It must be way too cold outside if mami and Tino are working together."

Suddenly, out of nowhere, Lantino comes barging in with a hand full of bags. "Yooo," he says as he dropped the bags near the living room sofa. "Now Tino, is that where my groceries go!" asked Loriana to Lantino. "Oh, c'mon Ms. Tourez, you've gotta give me a break," replying an exhausted Lantino. "That freaking elevator broke again, and I ended up having to carry all these bags up the stairway."

"Why'd it take you so long to come up though?" asking Loriana to Lantino. "You were right behind me."

"I got stuck waiting inside the elevator," answering Lantino, "After like ten minutes, it finally let me out but on the first floor!"

"Aw damn…" replied Torence reacting to Lantino's issue.

"Yeah, like 'aw damn,' that's what I said too!" replying Lantino to Torence. "I'm telling you, they need to fire that handyman who worked on the elevator."

"Yeah, seems like there's always something wrong with that elevator," said Torence.

"Yeah! It's always broke!" saying Lantino.

"Well, okay now you're here, and you made it, which means you could shut the door and help mami put the stuff away," said a snotty Loraine.

"Well, hello to you too, Loraine Soulberg," Lantino replied to Loraine.

"Oh, um no, for your information, that's Tourez," replying Loraine to Lantino. "Ms. Loraine Tourez, honey, get it right."

"Yeah well, remember he's your father too," said Lantino.

"Please…He ain't here is he?" asked Loraine. "Okay, so nann."

"Tuh, whatever," replying Lantino.

"Yeah whatever," again saying Loraine.

"Yeah…Hey, you know…You two are awfully close," said Lantino as he noticed Torence and Loraine sitting so comfortably close to one another. "Hmmm, I wonder what's that about?" he asked. Hearing that across the kitchen, Loriana jumped right in the conversation shouting "Hah, that's what I said!".

"Look, we were just sitting here together on the sofa, that's it," again Loraine said.

"Mmmm hmmm…" responding Loriana to Loraine.

"Stuh…" sighing Loraine.

"Tuh, whatever…Anyways, it's about time you warmed up to Torence, Raine," said Lantino to Loraine. "Hmp, but what probably could use some real warming up is old man winter outside," he said once more as he returned to putting the bag of groceries away in the kitchen. Handing the remote back to Torence, Loraine got up saying "It's getting late and that means I'm going to bed." Heading to her room, she and Torence made one last eye contact. Reading her stare told Torence that there was going to be more moments like those to come. Once her bedroom door closed shut, he decided to set up the sofa bed.

Chapter 26: Rence and Raine

Part 2

The year had now moved over to the month of March. Around these days, it seemed as though the weather had warmed up. The temperature in Chicago was usually sitting in the 40's. Although, when the wind blew, everything felt like it was back in the 30's. At times, it still felt like February. Nonetheless, the freezing temperature outside wasn't keeping Torence on the indoors. In fact, he was en route to find Lantino's school. He had been there quite a few times but seemed to be having trouble finding it this time on an early Thursday afternoon. "Wait, hadn't I already come on 99th way?" he said to himself as he tried retracing the correct route. Walking up towards a streetlight, he noticed a school bus driving south, pass the street he was on. Right there, he decided to follow the direction in which the school bus came from. He walked further up and noticed more school buses coming from that same direction. At this point, he pretty much knew he was headed the right way. However, that didn't matter once he heard Loraine's voice calling him across the street. "Hey you over there!" Loraine shouted. She stood near the main entrance where the school buses and cars arrive. Waving and signaling for Torence to come join her, she shouted once more saying, "Hurry, traffic is starting to pile up!". Hearing that, Torence wasted no time crossing the street to join her. "Hey Raine," greeted Torence as he approaches Loraine.

"Hey dodo," replying a pissy Loraine.

"Dodo? Uh, okay…"

"You wanna know why I'm calling you a dodo head?"

"Um…No…"

"Uh…You wanna know why I'm calling you a dodo head?"

"No…but why?"

"Because I had to come way out here to meet you after I told you to meet me at the student parking lot."

"But Raine, you told me to meet you at the parking lot, and that's where I was going…"

"You were walking towards the faculty parking lot."

"The facul-what?"

"Ugh…faculty."

"Well, it's a parking lot."

"But I said student parking lot, which is around the backside, Torence."

"Well, Raine, how do I know the difference between the two parking lots?"

"You should've known because it was in the directions I gave you this morning when you walked with me."

"What directions?"

"The directions."

"What directions?"

"Hun, my directions this morning was to come around either side of the school, and you'd see me at the student parking lot (which is on the far end), ugh!"

"Okay well, Raine, I'm here now, so…"

"Yes…You are…"

"So, what now then?"

"C'mon, follow me."

"Wait, follow you where?"

"Would you just c'mon."

"Where we're going?"

"I don't know. Away from here, I guess. Let's just beat the crowd."

"Oh, I see, okay now I'm following you, Raine."

"Yep…So, ask me about school today."

"Like what?"

"I don't know anything. Just ask me."

"Uh, okay…Um, uh so how was school today?"

"Tuh, boring, but the good thing is that we got to go home early today because it was early release day."

"Early release?"

"That's when school end early and lets everyone out."

"But why?"

"To heck do I know. All I care about is the fact that we're getting out early."

"Hmp okay…So, what are you doing the rest of the day?"

"Well, since you asked, I was thinking maybe you should come with me to a party later tonight. What do you say?"

"A party…Uh, where at? And who's throwing it?"

"Someone Julisa knows is throwing it somewhere by the rec. I want you to get to see what that's like. So, you wanna go?"

"Uh, maybe…"

"Okay, well do you know something fun we can do?"

"Um, why don't we check out the park. Maybe there's something we'll do there."

"Like what?"

"I don't know yet."

"You're boring. We're going to the party."

"But…"

"But what?"

"What if I don't wanna go?"

"Honey trust me; it's gonna be a lot of fun."

"Hmp, you sure?"

"Yes…You see, too much hanging out with Lantino got you missing out on some real fun."

"Real fun?"

"Yeah…You need to do something more than tagging up walls because you're always alone. Plus, it is cold out, and I know you're freezing your butt off. So, hang out with me, and you're gonna see."

"Tuh, okay."

"Watch, people are gonna be there, and you won't have to be so by yourself all the time."

"What time's the party?"

"Like another 6 hours from now. So, we have time."

"I think I wanna go home."

"Right now?"

"Yeah, it's starting to feel cold out here."

"But the sun's still out though."

"I just wanna go."

"Okay, fine we'll take the subway back. Was mami home when you left?"

"Yeah, she just went back to sleep before I took out the dump."

"Oh okay…Did she say anything to you about that night?"

"You mean that one night where she walked in on us?"

"Yeah."

"No. Did she mention anything to you?"

"Nope."

"Hmp, well I guess that's good then."

"You think she knows anything?"

"I don't know. I couldn't tell you."

"Let's just keep it moving then."

"Yep, keep it moving…"

"So, Torence…"

"Yeah?"

"What's it like being home taught?"

"I think Ms. Tourez is showing me a lot. With her, I don't think someone can ever stop learning. But I wonder sometimes…"

"About what? What do you wonder about?"

"Sometimes, I wonder what it's like to be at a real school like yours and Lantino's."

"You do?"

"Yeah…I do…Sometimes."

"Well, it can be rough if you're someone like Lantino. But if you're someone like me, then it could be a lot of fun."

"So, every day you have fun at your school?"

"Pretty much. Almost every day…Except today because it was really boring, but good thing we had an early release."

"Wish I could be at a real school."

"I wish…Come out to the party tonight."

"Will anyone we know be there."

"Yeah, there'll be some, and a lot of kids I know from school will be there too."

"Maybe…"

"Say yeah."

"Yeah?"

"Yes. Tell me; I'm gonna see you out there tonight."

"Hmmm."

Loraine, for a while continued to insist on getting a favorable response out of Torence. Torence, on the other hand seems to be at a halt and can't quite utter out his initial response to Loraine. Instead, Loraine ultimately swayed him into saying "yes" after she reached over and kissed him. Torence, who's now smiling and staring back at Loraine, nodded his head continuously, signaling yeah, he'll show up to the party. Slightly bending her eyes, she right there and then said to him "This time, I want your tongue to touch mine for a while before our mouths meet." Being that he's fond of their next move, Torence drew a grin on his face. As he came closer to Loraine's face, he noticed that she's wearing her favorite perfume again. There, at least for the fleeting moment, he began to wonder when she sprayed it on because he didn't recall her having it on when they were walking together earlier this morning. Trying to keep his poise, he calmly placed his hands on her hips. Wrapping her arms around Torence's neck, she closed her eyes and moved in on executing the kiss. Closing his eyes, Torence tilted his head sideways a bit and followed along. As their tongues moved in and out of their mouths, the warmth from within suddenly began to feel more like a current moving across their body. Their lips gradually locked into one another. However, as soon as it does, Loraine for some odd reason, began to pull back, which made Torence opened his eyes. Looking at her, he had a completely convoluted look on his face. "Torence, are you...are you okay?" Loraine asked him. "Um yeah," replying a bewildered Torence.

"You sure?"

"I said yeah. Now let's get back to it."

"No, you don't seem too good at this."

"Wait, huh?"

"Sorry, but I think you might need more work."

"Tuh okay...Well, Raine I think we better head downstairs to the subway if we wanna hop on one of these trains."

"Tuh ha ha okay."

Part of Torence had felt as if he'd been pushed off a cliff after hearing Loraine say that to him. At the same time, another part of him didn't believe her. At least, he didn't want to believe her despite how credible she sounded when she told him. On their way down to the station, Loraine made a stop to purchase a metro card. While she was doing that, Torence used that time to delve deep in his thoughts about what transpired momentarily ago. However, his mind didn't journey too long nor too far in this personal abyss of disappointment. A loud jarring sound burst his cloud of thoughts. It started from the stairways on which he and Loraine came from and seemed to echo its way around the station.

As it turned out, it happened to be a couple of girls causing all the ruckus and somehow Loraine knew them both from school. "HEYYY!" shouting an ecstatic Loraine waving at her two school mates. "Raine, um, who are they?" whispering Torence as he watched the school mates make their way towards him and Loraine. "These are my girls from fifth hour," answered Loraine as she spread her arms wide open, ready to embrace them. "From where?" asked Torence, who's unfamiliar with the term, fifth hour. "From school," again replying Loraine. "They're girls from my school," she said. "Oh, I see," said Torence, whose mood now dwindled away from disappointed to the more disappointed. Slowly shaking his head at Loraine, who at this point isn't really paying him any mind, he asked her a question saying, "Will we see them at the part –"

"Oh my gosh, Torence here they come!" said Loraine interrupting Torence's question. "Listen up. All I'm a need from you right now is to just stay suave and go with the flow," she said to Torence. "If they ask you any questions, just answer, but please keep it short and simple…Or matter fact, just let me do the talking." Initially, Torence wants to respond with a smart remark but instead replied saying "So, you got this, huh?". Nodding her head with absolutely no awareness of an irritable Torence, Loraine's answer is basically: yeah, she'll handle everything. Shortly after she replied, she along with her two school mates embraced one another, and a new conversation among the three of them begins. "Raine girl, what you doing way out here?" asked one of the school mates. "We figured you of all people would probably be somewhere at the rec by now," she said to Loraine.

"Hmmm, that's funny," said Loraine. "You think there's people there this early?" she asked. "Girl, YES!" answered another one of the school mates with her eyes wide open. "Before we left the school today, someone else told us your 'lil crush, J-Roc was heading there," she said to Loraine. "Oh my gosh, we should probably be heading on our way then," said Loraine to her school mates. "But wait, if a whole bunch of people is over there, then what y'all doing way out here," she asked her school mates. "Girl, we were actually on our way the minute we left the school, but thanks to this 'lil ol' eating machine right here, we ended up stopping at one of the Chinese food joints up the street," answered one of the school mates. "Oh, okay I see," said Loraine. "So, who's your friend, Loraine?" asked another one of the school mates. "Yeah, is he supposed to be your date tonight?" asked the nosey school mate. "Oh, uh…him," responding a slightly embarrassed Loraine. "Uh naw, this here is just my friend," she answered. "Matter of fact, he's really one of my brother's good friends, and child, we were just walking to who knows where ha ha ha…" she explained to her school mates. Rudely observing Torence from head to toe, one of the school mates greeted him with a bland tone of voice, before exchanging a side joke about him. Torence quietly stared back at them without saying a word. His silence, in some way, sent back an odd reaction to them. Turning their attention away from Torence, they invite Loraine to come with them by their place to try on a few outfits. Feeling pretty dismissed, Torence spoke up saying, "Yo, Raine –"

"Torence, I'm a go with them somewhere right now, but we'll catch up," said Loraine. "Meet me by Julisa's place tonight before we go, okay," she said as she headed back up the stairway with her two school mates. Shaking his head, Torence rolled his eyes and walked away towards the subway in utter disgust. "Later friend," said one of the school mates to Torence.

Thinking long and a little too hard about how the day was turning out so far led to Torence missing his stop a couple of times. He eventually got home, but a lot later than he anticipated. Unable to rid his mind of being dismissed earlier, he was now trying to debate if he should even show up to the party or not. *Hmmm, I told her I was coming,* he thought. *Plus, she told me to meet her at Tye's place, but she dissed me pretty bad,* he said in his thoughts.

"Hmmm, perhaps things won't go so bad at the party. Alright, just for you, I'll come out tonight," he said as he began dressing up.

Figuring that his dress code might've play an important factor on whether or not, Loraine will enjoy his company; he chose wisely for his outfit. It took more than a while, but after looking endlessly through Lantino's wardrobe, he stepped out of the house feeling warm and confident. Heading to Tyberius's place, Torence kept thinking about what he was expecting to find once he arrived at the party. *Exactly what was he going to do or say once he met most of Loraine's friends? What was Loraine going to think once he arrived? Was Lantino going to be there?* He sure hoped Lantino was going to stop by even if he was staying for a second.

So, the day made a turn for the night, and the time now sat within an hour before the party started. By now, Torence had made it to Tyberius's place just like Loraine told him to. With less than an hour remaining, Torence figured he'd relax and lounge around in the living room area until Loraine showed up. However, he waited for a couple of hours with no sounding of a doorbell ringing nor a knocking on the front door. Torence pretty much concluded that Loraine stood him up.

Part 3: Rence and Raine

In comparison to last winter, Loriana seemed to be enjoying this winter fairly well. Her daughter, Loraine, wasn't in boot camp. Lantino, aside from other issues, wasn't getting suspended for a lengthy period of time. With all of her documents submitted and approved, she was pleased to know that she can claim Torence as her adopted son. She strongly believed that Torence was the reason behind why Lantino was staying out of trouble. Moreover, seeing Torence and Loraine together made Loriana overwhelmed with excitement. Although, she often wondered what transpired between the two of them to see Loraine warm up to Torence suddenly. When or how it started wasn't making any sense to neither her nor Lantino. However, unlike Lantino, Loriana wasn't oblivious to what was happening before her. Intrigued, she observed them closely and remained conscious of walking in on them at times when they were alone.

A couple of days before the emergence of spring break, Loriana happened to be home one evening, fixing a hot plate. She'd often be home alone around the evening when everyone was out. She had grown quite used to it and wasn't necessarily worried about where everyone was. With school getting ready to be closed for about a week or so, Loriana was hoping that perhaps everyone would be home to have a supposed family get together type of thing since that wasn't really common. Everyone just seemed to be really tied up in their own worlds, and like everyone, Loriana soon cruised into her own world once dinner was ready. Just as dinner was ready, someone happened to knock on the door. "Who is it?" asked Loriana turning her attention to the doorknob which was moving. "Ms. Tourez, it's me," answered the person outside. Pausing for a moment, Loriana tried to register the sounding of the voice to her head. "Me, who?" she asked suspiciously. "Ms. Tourez, it's me, Rence," says the person outside. "Hmmm, where's your key?" again asked Loriana. "Ugh, I know I left it inside my book bag and forgot to take it with me," said the person at the front door, who turned out to be Torence. "I'm sorry about that, Ms. Tourez."

"That's okay papi," replied Loriana as she walked over to unlock the front door. "But remember to always take your key because suppose none of us are home? Then how would you get in, papi?"

"Yeah, thanks Ms. Tourez. You're right; I gotta remember to take it with me."

"Which is funny because you don't usually forget to take it with you, papi."

"I know; I know…I just forgot."

"Yep, and you might not be so lucky next time."

"Ha ha yeah…What'd you make tonight, Ms. Tourez? The food smells good."

"Well, papi you're welcome to have a look."

"Mmmm mmmm…"

"Hmmm, papi."

"Yes?"

"Uh, you forget something?"

"Um, I did?"

"Uh, si."

"Oh yeah, that's right: muah and muah."

"Mmmm, gracias. Okay, now go eat."

"Could I have Milleena's plate if she doesn't sleepover tonight?"

"Si, papi si."

"Bonito!"

"Haha haha...So loko."

As Torence headed to the kitchen and made his own plate, Loriana pulled out a glass of water and sat it on the table for him. Putting the jug of water away in the fridge, she couldn't help but notice that there's a bit of uneasiness lingering around the presence of Torence. A rare and noticeable gloominess that's crying out loud. In addition, she recognized that a lot is awfully different about him tonight and figured that she should have a talk with him. "So papi," she said to Torence as she grabs a chair to sit down. "Are you doing anything else tonight?" she asked.

"Hmmm...No. Why?"

"Oh well, I'm just asking because I see you still have on your big red jacket."

"Oh, you mean this Chicago puff jacket. Oh yeah, I must've forgotten again, but don't worry, I'll put it up now on the coat hanger if you want."

"Oh no, no, no, don't worry yourself papi. Eat, sit down."

"Oh...Okay."

"Hmp. I've never seen you wore that jacket before. Did Lantino get that for you?"

"Oh naw...This is actually for a friend we both know named Tye. He let me use it tonight."

"Hmp, but papi, you and your brother have jackets here."

"I know, but my homegirl wanted me to put this jacket on because it matched with the red outfit she had on."

"Oooooh, you have an amiga, ah? Well, tell me, how did things go?"

"Hmmm, it...went well."

"Well?"

"I mean, it was alright, I guess."

"Papi…talk to me if something is troubling you."

"I just feel lost…"

"I can tell because you haven't picked up your spoon at all."

"I mean one day she's got me feeling like, like I'm special. Then the next minute, I feel like a piece of trash. And now…I'm just lost, and I'm angry for feeling that way."

"You said she makes you feel special? Who's she? Is this the amiga?"

"Yeah, my homegirl makes me feel good and then bad the next minute. Ugh!"

"Hmmm…Like how papi?"

"It's complicated."

"Okay, so make it not complicated…Talk to me papi. Tell me what's going on.

"Well…It all started late last month_ _Well, actually way before last month, but I'm a start with last month."

"Okay, Febrero…"

"Well um, we were at her mom's house. Alone in the living room, just talking. Then we started kissing…"

"Uh ha, okay…"

"Hmp, and then that's when she walked in on us."

"Who? The mami?"

"Yeah…I think she caught us…well, might've caught us. Tuh, whatever, it was funny and ever since then, we been hanging out more and more, going anywhere and everywhere together."

"So, you two like each other."

"Yeah, something like that."

"Ewww, Torence papi."

"Tuh…But…"

"Uh oh. But what papi?"

"She's always trying me too."

"What does she do?"

"Well, when she gets around her friends from school, she acts like she doesn't know me."

"Hmmm, okay but why?"

"I think she feels embarrassed to be seen with me when her friends are around. Like as if I'm out of her league or something."

"Hmmm…"

"That's not all…"

"Oooooh…"

"Sometimes, she stands me up. Or other times, we could be talking, and out of nowhere, she'll leave our conversation and hop in on a new conversation when one of her friends shows up. It's really messed up."

"Si, that's no good."

"These last few days, she's been trying to change the way I dress too. Stuh, she says she's only trying to give me a dress code."

"Papi, you need to talk to her."

"But Ms. Tourez, I have, and you know what she'll tell me?"

"What?"

"She'll tell me sorry and then turn around and start doing it all over again."

"So, this happens a lot?"

"Yeah, sometimes. No, really like all the time this whole month."

"Ump, ump, ump…Well, papi here's this…"

"What?"

"She either fixes up her act, or you'll go. Simple."

"Hmmm…"

"Si, it's either that or you'll go. No fix, no papi. Easy."

"Ms. Tourez, are you sure?"

"Ooooh si, papi, I'm sure. It's time you tell her now or otherwise, you'll never get respect."

"Hmmm yeah, I guess you're right."

"Ooooh trust me, I am papi. After all, a girl would know."

"Okay, so I guess that's what I'll do the next time I see her."

"Si, do that papi."

"Yeah…Hey Ms. Tourez, you think I can save this food for tomorrow?"

"Alright, that's fine. If you're not in the mood to eat papi."

"I'm a take this jacket off. Don't worry; you won't find this on me again."

"Ha ha, it was looking too big on you."

"Yeah, it was hahaha…Hey, Ms. Tourez."

"Si, papi?"

"Thanks for listening."

"Denada papi. Anytime."

"Okay."

"Oh, um papi."

"Yeah?"

"This chica came by looking for you earlier. I told her you were not here and wasn't sure when you'd be home."

"Who was it?"

"I didn't catch her name, but she had on glasses."

"Oooooh, that must've been Tequesta...I'll catch up with her."

Despite going to bed with a full mind and an empty stomach, Torence slept well. Talking with and listening to Loriana provided some closure for him. Moving forward on to the week of spring break, Torence wasn't hanging out with Loraine as much. In fact, he seems to have returned to the things he usually did before hanging out with Loraine. However, as anticipated, he eventually ran into Loraine on his route to someplace around the area.

It was Thursday evening, and most of the streetlights were coming on. Loraine, who had just finish picking up her favorite perfume, was stepping out of a local beauty supply store. That's when she noticed Torence casually walking down the street. *Hmp, he probably ain't doing anything,* she thought. With that in mind, she figured she'll walk with him somewhere. "Hey, you over there," she shouted while waving her hand. Torence heard her calling from a distance but continued walking towards his destination. Assuming he probably didn't hear her, Loraine shouted several times. Again, Torence carried on down the street. Now striding, Loraine caught up with him just before he could turn the corner. "Hey, you, hey you, hey you," she said to Torence, grabbing his left wrist. Staring back at Loraine with a panned, blithe look on his face, he nodded his head one time at her. "Okay..." said Loraine as she picked up an odd signal. "Aren't you gonna talk?" she asked.

"What's up," said Torence with an unusually carefree expression on his voice.

"Um, nothing…I just noticed you down the street and figured I'd say what's up."

"Okay. So, what's up?"

"Uh, nothing. Um, I was actually gonna stop somewhere to get my hair done. I was wondering if you wanna come?"

"Uh, naw."

"It'll be quick, trust me."

"Okay, then go."

"Wow, you ain't gotta be all mean."

"Wasn't trying to be, but if that's how ya feel then too bad."

"Fine, just walk me home."

"Raine, I'm headed somewhere right now, and you're holding me up."

"Oh, well what you up to?"

"I'm going to Tequesta's."

"Where you're going?"

"It don't matter; you don't know her."

"Oh okay, well fine."

"Ight…So, can I be on my way now?"

"You know what, why are you being so mean?"

"Tuh…"

"Is something wrong? Did I do something, or are you just having a long day?"

"Tell you what: You did, but it's too bad you don't see it."

"Okay, you wanna tell me what I did since I don't see it."

"Okay, like how about when you stood me up that one night you and I was supposed to go to this 'stupid' party, you invited me to."

"Okay, Torence, that was only one time. Get over it."

"Please Raine, that was one out of the many."

"Alright, so I stood you up a few times. So what?"

"How about when your friends come by, you wanna act like I'm nobody to you, and the funny thing is I told you about that a few times."

"Okay, well they go to my school, Torence."

"So…"

"It's complicated."

"No, it ain't."

"Yes it is. And if you were at my school, you'd understand."

"Raine, how come we're always doing all the shit you like to do?!"

"What you mean?! This is what everyone's doing, Torence; you gotta keep up or else you're gonna get left behind and have some kind of reputation."

"Raine, I can't click with your 'school' friends like that. They don't like me because I'm different from them!"

"Torence, just give it time."

"And what's up with trying to give me a dress code!"

"Rence, I'm trying to help you fit in."

"You see; this is exactly what I mean! You just don't get it! I'm out."

"Hey! Heeeey! Torence! I know you hear me!"

Calling Torence, Loraine shouted out loud several times, but Torence just ignored her as he continued his route. Watching him walk away and give no response boiled Loraine's blood pressure. Right there, she decided to follow him a few yards and blow off some steam. "Oh okay, fine just ignore me if that's how you feel!" She shouted. "It's not like you're even in my league! In fact, boy you're way out of my league! You ain't got your own place! You should feel good to know that I even gave you out of all people the time and day! Better believe you won't find another like me, boy! Yeah, that's right, just keep walking! Ugh!"

It all seemed as if everything had been thrown out the window that night. After Torence confronted Loraine about some particular issues, she completely overreacted out of emotion. While Torence went one way, Loraine eventually went the other and moving forward towards spring break, the two basically returned to where they were at the beginning. Except for only this time, Loraine wasn't as hostile towards Torence. After getting to know a little more about him, she couldn't deny the fact that she still felt some kind of interest for him.

The days had now mounted onto a week since Loraine had lashed out her anger on Torence. Yet, she was still holding on to some hard feelings. Part of her knew that she was wrong after saying some of the things she had said to Torence that night. However, being too proud and stubborn kept her back from trying to reach out to him. So, as time passed, the guilt lounged on her consciousness like an itch she couldn't scratch. Though, Loraine, like everyone else, took full advantage of the spring season and stayed outdoors more often. With that said, she was able to overlook any thought or guilt she may have had regarding Torence. However, on one fairly warm day, she planned to meet up with friends, Loraine, in the last minute, decided to stay home. It was an early day and a rather beautiful one at that. There was still a light breeze, but the sky was clear of clouds, which drew plenty of room for the sun to shine bright over the city. Again, it was a fairly warm day, but for some unknown reason, Loraine was still in her pajamas. Tired but not sleeping, she laid down on her right side. Facing the now-folded up letter Torence sent her a while ago when she was away in boot camp, she grabbed hold of it. Unfolding it, she gazed at the detailed picture Torence sketched out for her. Admiring the time he put in to make this for her, she began wondering about him. And with the thoughts soon came the feelings she couldn't ignore. *Hmp, it's funny how I hardly see him around*, she said while in her thoughts. *Hmmm, I wonder what he's up to*, she asked herself. Then suddenly, she heard knocking coming from the front door. Interrupted by the sounding of the knocks, Loraine got up out of bed, feeling a bit agitated. Walking up towards the front door, she figured that it might've been Torence now. However, when she answered the door, it turned out to be a girl about her age and size standing before her. She had on a sporty black sleeveless shirt, along with black long tight leggings and tennis shoes. Pretty much everything on her rivaled what Loraine would tend to wear. Staring her down from head to toe, Loraine then tilted her head saying, "That's funny; I never seen Lantino with this one before."

"You said who?" asked the girl at the front door.

"Lantino," Loraine answered. "Isn't that who you're looking for?" she asked her.

"Um, no," answered the girl at the door.

"Oh, well, I'm sorry, but you must have the wrong door," said Loraine, interrupting her.

"No, but wait," said the girl at the door, "he told me it was this door right here on the third floor."

"Wait, who told you?" asked Loraine.

"The boy. You know, the one who knows how to draw," the girl replied to Loraine.

"The boy who draws…wait, Torence," Loraine said.

"It's okay Loraine, she's coming to get me," said Torence rushing out of the bathroom. Turning back towards Torence, Loraine then tilted her head the other way, asking the girl at the front door "You're here to see him?". Nodding her head while smiling, the girl replied back saying, "Yes, that's who I'm talking about."

"Tequesta, just hold on for a minute," said Torence to the girl at the front door. "Lemme find my black book real quick," he said while searching for his sketchbook.

"Hmmm…Tequesta huh," said Loraine as she stared back at the girl in particular.

"Yeah, that's my name," replying Tequesta.

"Well, Tequesta, I'm Loraine," replying Loraine to Tequesta.

"Oh…Never knew he had a sister. Hmp, but then again, he never said he had one," replying Tequesta to Loraine. Taking that as a form of disrespect, Loraine bends her eyes at Tequesta. "What are you trying to say?" Loraine asked.

"Found it!" shouted Torence directing their attention to him. "I found my black book Tequesta. C'mon let's go," he said as he walked through the door. Shoving his sketchbook in his rear side, he said, "I'll see ya later, Raine." Walking by his side down the hallway, Tequesta turned her eyes away from Loraine saying, "Yeah, later."

'Yeah, later,' said Loraine, mimicking Tequesta as she watched her walk down the hallway with Torence. Closing the door shut, Loraine could begin to feel the emotion of jealousy crawling in. Thinking about Tequesta, questions like who was she and what exactly was she to Torence began to sit in her mind. Stepping back inside her room, Loraine took a look at herself in the mirror. *Oh wow, she must've thought I looked bad*, Loraine thought as she stared at her reflection. She felt conscious, knowing that her hair wasn't nicely combed nor washed, and she was still on her pajamas.

Suddenly, Loraine felt like she didn't want to sleep in for the day. Instead, she felt moved and anxious and figured she'd try to catch Milleena and the others at the park.

So, moving past that earlier part of the day, Loraine was now at the movie theaters. Milleena and Julisa joined her. The three of them together were trying to debate on whether or not if they should wait in line. Julisa was trying to persuade them to borrow her cousin's car to watch a movie at a local drive-in theater. While Milleena suggested that they should just watch a bootlegged version at her place. Loraine argued that they might as well just wait in line since they already showed up. The girls went back and forth about the issue, but at the end of the day, it seemed as if Loraine got the final word on what the three of them were going to do for tonight.

The trio waited in line for quite a lengthy period. It got to a point in which Loraine's eyes began to wander elsewhere around the theater. Looking from a distance, she happened to notice a couple coming down from the escalators. Fixing her eyes on them, she could tell they were pretty much on their way out. As they were headed towards the exit doors, Loraine recognized Torence, which didn't necessarily surprise her at all. She was practically used to seeing him everywhere she went. However, it was the girl he was walking with that caught her attention. Watching her as she walked with Torence, Loraine noted the tattoo design on her right upper arm. That told Loraine that this wasn't the same girl she met earlier that day at the house. Loraine found it awkward because she looked very similar to the other girl in height, size, and attire. As they walked through the exit doors, Loraine wondered about where they were going. Thinking about them, she also realized that they weren't holding hands or anything. Nevertheless, it made Loraine uncomfortable seeing Torence putting all of his attention on another girl even if it wasn't the same one she met earlier. Thinking about what she or any girl may have potentially seen in Torence reminded her about why and what she liked about him.

Despite the long wait, the trio did end up catching a movie at the theater. However, they didn't sit through the entire movie to catch the ending. Instead, they took a long road home to Julisa's place, which is where Loraine and company basically wrapped the evening up. On a much warmer day of spring, Loraine had just come home after volunteering at her school for community service hours. Sitting her backpack on the living room sofa, she noticed Lantino was occupied, fixing a meal in the kitchen. After sending her greetings to Lantino, she then realized how quiet everything was. Torence and her mother, Loriana wasn't home, and for some reason, it seemed like they hadn't been home all day. *Hmp, where they been*, she asked. *Well, my brother's been home all day, perhaps maybe he'd know*, she assumed. Seated comfortably on the sofa, Loraine leaned back on it a bit while facing Lantino. "Hey, Tino," she said to Lantino, who for the moment still seemed too occupied. "Lantino," she said again as she projected her voice. "Sup," answered Lantino.

"Where is everybody?"

"How the heck I know."

"What you mean 'how the heck you know.' You were home when they left, right? So, you should know."

"Well, I don't know. But since you're so worried, why don't you go out and find them."

"I just got home, and you're already giving me an attitude."

"Well, Raine, can't you see I'm trying to eat? I feel like you're taking me away from my meal every time I hear your voice."

"Okay, well sorry, but I'm only trying to find out."

"Hmmm…I don't know. Ms. Tourez said something about looking for a new job at the workforce place."

"Oh, okay…I guess that makes sense if I don't see her and Torence doing the home school thing."

"Yeah, that's true. They didn't do that today."

"Well, what about Torence?"

"Hmmm, I saw him left with some girl this morning."

"Some girl? Wait, who?"

"Hmmm, a chinga I saw somewhere by 148th. Hmp, he must be sketching tats again because I see him picked up his black book when he was leaving."

"Did she look cute?"

"Hmmm, yeah, I guess. I don't know. Wasn't really looking at her like that."

"Hmp, when he started talking to all these girls?"

"Tuh, it's been a while, but then again, a lot of people have been asking for him. Like just the other day, this girl was looking for him. If I remembered right, I think she told me her name was Tequesta."

"Tequesta, huh…Yeah, I saw her before."

"She's the only one I remember being that she came here the most."

"Torence, what kind of girls are you talking to?"

"Raine, I'm telling you, it's the sketches he makes. Everyone's starting to know about him now."

"But about these girls that he's hanging out with. Do you know if he's talking to them like that?"

"Probably the one that comes to him a lot about them sketches."

"Tequesta?"

"Yeah, that one…But then again, how the heck do I know."

"Tino…"

"What?"

"I want you to keep an eye on him."

"Who me? Keep an eye on Torence?"

"Yes, watch after him, and when he's around these girls."

"Why?"

"Because they're no good."

"Who's no good? What are you talking about, Raine?"

"Tequesta! The hoes that's coming here!"

"Wait, how are they no good?"

"Because they ain't, but Torence doesn't know that! So you know what, you need to talk to him!"

"No, I don't."

"Yes, you do."

"No, I don't, and no the hell I won't."

"Tino, would you just do it!"

"Why? Torence is making some money off these clients. It's not much, but it's something. A lot better than the way I make mine. I know Ms. Tourez likes that."

"Okay, but –"

"But what? If you're all worried about him, then why can't you talk to him?"

"But I don't want to."

"Then, there's nothing to worry about, right."

"Ugh! I mean, I can't."

"And why not?"

"Ugh!"

"You see, now you're confusing me, which probably means that it's time to get back to my food."

"Tino, he's our adopted brother. I think it's right that we look out for him."

"He's good."

"No, he is not."

"You know what, hold up just a minute…Loraine, tell me something: you used to put this boy on the spotlight and go out your way to make 'em feel like dirt. Why suddenly now you start worrying your head so much about Torence? Why?"

"Because…Because…"

"Because what?"

"Stuh, because…I can!"

"Because you can, huh? Okay, you know what? I'm done."

"But, Tino…"

"Nan amp amp!"

The West siders of Chicago saw a much warmer month in April, which they enjoyed. While it was still windy and chilly out, the snow wasn't piling up on the streets and walkways as it did in the winter. So, with warm changes to the weather, Torence, like everyone else in the household, was wearing lighter layers of clothes. Now that the summer was around the corner, Torence wasn't having early sessions of home school as often. With that said, he'd often find himself sleeping on the living room sofa in the early part of the day. However, on one particular morning, he woke up, nearly falling out of the sofa bed. Sitting up and rubbing his eyes, Torence looked around to find the source of the noise that caused him to wake up. Widening his eyes, Torence came to find an irate Lantino looking through his wardrobe. Getting up out of the sofa bed, Torence also noticed the front door, which Lantino had barged right through, was left opened. "Lantino," said an emaciated Torence. Dismissing Torence's call, Lantino continued scorching through the closet like as if an explosive had been planted inside. A bit dismayed by the utterly incensed Lantino, Torence called his name a second time, but with a lowered tone of voice. Pulling a hoody jacket out of the closet, Lantino throws it at Torence, demanding him to put it on immediately. "Hurry up Rence," said Lantino. "What's going on?" asked Torence as he rushed to get dressed.

"These fools outside are talking shit!"

For real? Wait about what?!"

"Just c'mon, ain't no time to explain!"

"Where we going?"

"Follow me! We're gonna whoop these niggas ass this morning!"

"Uh okay…Lemme, just make the bed real quick."

"Naw, damn that! Let Ms. Tourez fix it!"

"Uh, you sure?"

"Yeah, I'm sure, now c'mon! There's no time!"

"Okay…"

Putting his blankets down, Torence then left the sofa bed the way it was and decided to start making his way out the door. Walking behind Lantino, Torence shut the door and followed his trail. Trying to keep up with Lantino's pace while in the hallway, Torence's mind was clouded with confusion. Where were they going, and who or what could've caused Lantino to be this unpredictably temperamental? For it was something Torence wasn't used to seeing from Lantino. But whatever the case, he was surely going to find out once they got to wherever Lantino was walking them.

It seemed as if the day wasted no time moving to what was now the evening. After a bunch of fistfights and foot races got recorded, the streets became clearer of traffic, and the streetlights were dimming on. With a clearer pathway, Loraine found her trip to the store rather painless. She had just picked up some triple A batteries for the flashlights Milleena brought home a couple of hours ago. Feeling like she wasn't in much of a rush to come back home,

Loraine decided to take her time. But then, that's when she realized that she forgot to pick up a lighter for the lanterns that were kept in her mother's bedroom. So turning around, she strode to make another stop at the convenient store. That's when she coincidently noticed Torence walking right through the front doorway. Stepping out, he seemed to be casually minding his own business. He seemed also to be heading the opposite direction, but like Loraine, he came to a halt the moment he noticed her. Right away, they both knew that they apparently missed one another's company. Not a word had to be said because the signals were just that apparent. "Hey, you," said Loraine, with a big smile on her face. "Hey, Raine," replied Torence, who tried to seal his smile under his hoodie.

"Where are you coming from?"

"Tuh, nowhere. What about you?"

"Hmmm, I was just coming from the house to pick up some stuff from this store. I forgot to get us a lighter."

"Who else is home?"

"Just Lee, who's waiting on me to bring the batteries."

"Stuh haha, since when did you need batteries?"

"Like today, after we came home and found out the lights got cut off."

"Cut off? For real?"

"Yep. Mami, ain't pay the electric bill yet. So, we're gonna be sitting in the dark for a while unless I put these batteries in the flashlights."

"Damn, things must really be getting hard for Ms. Tourez."

"Yeah well, anyway, I better get us that lighter for the lanterns mami keeps in her room."

"Oh uh, yeah, okay."

"You're heading to the house?"

"Hmmm, maybe…Why did you want me to wait up for you?"

"Oh no, bebe, I'm good."

"Sure? I mean, I can wait."

"I'll see you in the house bebe."

Dismissing Torence, Loraine walks right through the door of the convenient store. She immediately picks up the item she needed but then hesitates to take her eyes off a few items on the next aisle. Minutes later, Loraine is at another aisle looking through fashion magazines. Little does she know that Torence is watching her through the glass window. When she finally noticed him, she's startled, and nearly dropped everything she's carrying on her hand. Amused by the surprised look on Loraine's facial expression, Torence cracked a smile and shook his head. Wondering why he's there, Loraine spread her arms out, and then made several gestures at him. Unable to hear her, Torence began to laugh, and he shook his head continuously. Having enough, Loraine finally stepped outside the store to join Torence for a conversation. "Oh my gosh, you actually waited?" she asked. "Yeah," answered Torence.

"Okay, but why? Especially if I told you, you ain't have to."

"Because I wanted to. Plus, I don't have anything to do at the house."

"So, you just waited here?"

"Uh, yeah…So, what? You ready to go?"

"Oh shit, no! I forgot my stuff inside! You see what you made me do!"

"Me?"

"Yeah, you!"

"It wasn't me who told you to come outside, ha ha ha."

"Eww, I can't stand you."

"So, you're going back in to buy that lighter?"

"Yes, that's what I came to get in the first place."

"You know what, let's just go, Raine."

"Stuh, you can go if you're tired of waiting. Just know, I told you, you ain't have to wait."

"Raine please, you can get that another time. Let's go somewhere else."

"Wait, you're not talking about the house?"

"No, I'm talking about hanging out somewhere else."

"Wait, first of all, where?"

"Anywhere…I don't know. Now would you just c'mon."

"Hmp, I'm good."

"Ugh, Raine, tell me something…"

"Oh boy…Okay, like what?"

"Why's it so hard to do what I want us to do?"

"Stuh..."

"I mean like why? You know, it would be cool if we did that sometimes."

"Because! Becau...Cause..."

"Because what?"

"Cause...um..."

"Because I'm too lame, and you're not?"

"Just forget –"

"The look you gave me minutes ago when I came here told me you miss being friends. I can tell by that look in your eye, but...but Raine, being friends with you hurts. I'm out."

"Wait, wait Torence, wait, don't leave."

"Stuh..."

"Wait! Torence! I SAID, WAIT!"

"Okay...What?"

"I said wait. I wanna come...with you."

Pleased by what she said, Torence turned back and slowly stuck his right hand out. Reaching for it, Loraine grabbed hold of his hand with her left. And together, they strolled around their neighborhood for quite a while. The question of where they were going was still being asked at the back of Loraine's mind. Although, at the same time, Loraine was excited by the suspense of not knowing. So again, both of them strolled all over town till they finally had a stop by a corner store that sat just off the borderline of the city's north/west side region. Torence could tell that it had just recently opened. A particular interest was drawing Torence to the store, and Loraine could tell by the look in his eyes. "So, why are we stopping here, boo?" she asked Torence. "There's something I need to get from inside," answered Torence, who's still got his eyes on the store. "Like what?" again, asking Loraine. "Something...You know what, just wait here," said Torence making his way towards the store.

"Wait, I'll come with you."

"Naw, just wait out here. It'll be real quick. I promise."

"Ugh, fine, go head."

"Real quick."

So, while Torence is inside grabbing what he needs, Loraine waited on him outside. Waiting on him, Loraine immediately started feeling a bit agitated. Rolling her eyes and shaking her head, she asked herself if this was really what Torence had in mind about hanging out tonight. "Hmp, I guess this is what I get for letting him do what he wanted us to do," she said. Suddenly, within a moment of waiting, she's distracted by the commotion coming from the corner store. *What's going on*, she wondered as she kept her eyes fixed on the front doors. Next thing she noticed was Torence bursting through the front doors and shoving several witnesses out of his way. Running towards Loraine, Torence shouted "RUN!".

"Wha-what's going –" asked a convoluted Loraine. "RUN!" again shouting Torence, blowing pass her like a speed of wind. Not wanting to be left in the dust, Loraine too began to run as fast as she could. Following his trail, Loraine tried to keep up with his pace. However, she became too winded to keep up and shortly, stopped to catch her breath. As she slowly feels the air coming back in her lungs, she realized that she's lost and doesn't know where she is exactly. Moreover, she has no clue where Torence may have gone. *Shit, he lost me*, she thought as she looked around her surroundings. Then that's when she heard a voice spoke to her saying, "Hey, I'm over here." Looking towards the direction in which the sound of the voice came from, Loraine responded asking, "Who said that?".

"Loraine, it's me," again, saying the voice, who actually happened to be Torence. "Me, who?" asked a paranoid Loraine. "It's me, Rence," answered Torence.

"Torence, is that you?"

"Yeah, I'm right here."

"Where are you?"

"I'm up here like right in front of you."

"In front of me…"

"Yeah, look up to your right on the balcony."

"Oh, I see you…Wait, how'd you get up there?"

"The doors to the building were open."

"Torence, get down here before someone catches you."

"Raine, it's okay, no one's gonna know we're here."

"Torence!"

"Raine, just come on up."

"Ugh!"

"It's okay, I come here all the time, and no one's caught me here, not once."

"Hmmm."

"Just c'mon on up. Trust me."

Taking Torence's word, Loraine walked inside the empty development reluctantly. Making her way upstairs to join Torence on the next floors, she noticed a lot of renovations were being done, which meant that the building was still used. Walking towards the balcony on the last floor, Loraine felt as though she's meeting another side to this Torence character. Coming to that notion, Loraine began to realize why Torence was so quiet and calm. It gave him the advantage of being unpredictable. Reaching that comprehension, Loraine was now left with expecting the unexpected out of Torence. It was like trying to fill out the blanks to a list of sentences. Yet, ironically, Loraine found that very attractive.

Joining Torence out by the balcony, Loraine stood to his left. Looking back and forth at Torence and everything else below the balcony, Loraine could tell that he's zoned out. With her right hand, she tapped him on his left shoulder. "It wasn't too long ago when I left boot camp. Just know that" she admonished him. Calmly nodding his head while looking at the view outside, he responded saying, "You're good, Raine. You're with me now." Feeling a bit assured by Torence's quiet confidence, Loraine leaned and rested her head against his left shoulder, slowly rubbing her hand across his back. "I was there for too long last year. Ain't no way I'm going back," she said strongly.

"Believe me, you won't."

"Thanks, boo."

"Mmmm hmmm…So…"

"So…"

"Take a look at what I got us."

"Eww, what?"

"A drink…"

"Beer? You got us beer?"

"Yeah…I never tried it, and I figured you –"

"Wait, is that why you burst out the door like that at the corner store?"

"Stuh, yeah…"

"You stole it Torence! Ugh, boy you could've gotten in so much trouble if the store clerk and his people caught you! You know that?!"

"Yeah, but hey, I got away."

"Ugh! Tsk, tsk, tsk, tsk…That there was real stupid what you did."

"Yeah, I know…I only did it because I ain't have enough money to pay for it."

"And you did it for me…and that's cute, boo."

"Mmmm hmmm."

"You know, I thought you were gone after all that."

"Naw, you should know I wouldn't leave you."

"You better never ever."

"I gotchu."

"Really? You got me…"

"Yeah…I gotchu."

"Open up the bottle."

Removing the top off the bottle, Torence and Loraine didn't wait to take any sips off their drink. On the first few sips, they both received a strong buzzing reaction from the bitter taste of the beer. However, after a while, they both got used to the taste. Feeling dizzy and light-headed, they both agreed to sit down on the floor of the balcony. By now, they had practically emptied the bottle. After Loraine finished her last sips, she placed the bottle to her left. Wrapping her arms around Torence's left arm, she then laid her head against his shoulder. "Mmmm," she sighed comfortably while closing her eyes. "Boo, you wanna know something?" she asked Torence. "Hmmm, what's up?" he replied.

"This is actually fun."

"Ha ha…"

"I'm glad I actually let you do what you wanted us to do."

"I'm glad too."

"Boo, you wanna know something else?"

"Yeah, what?"

"I'm-I'm…sorry I said all those things to you that night. You were right to feel the way you did."

"Hmp, yeah, you had a lot to say."

"I know, boo and I was wrong. Dead wrong for talking all that mess. You did right when you walked away from me. I'm sorry."

"You sound like you really mean it."

"Of course, I do…You know I do…Don't you?"

"Hmmm…I'oin know, Raine…"

"What you mean?!"

"Ha ha ha ha okay, lemme stop. I know you're for real."

"Okay…Boo…"

"Yeah?"

"Before everything got all crazy tonight by the store…"

"You mean when I ran off with the drink?"

"Yeah…before all that, I liked how we took the stroll all over."

"Hmp, yeah me too."

"I missed that."

"What, when we'd do that all the time?"

"Yeah…Now you're out with your new friends all the time."

"New friends?"

"Yeah, them girls that be with you…"

"Ooooh, you talking about my clients."

"'My clients', whatever! None of them are as pretty as me."

"Ha ha ha what are you talking about?"

"Don't act like you 'oin know."

"Ha ha ha ha huh?"

"Especially, that girl, I saw you with at the movies…Tequesta…"

"Questa?"

"Questa, Tequesta, whatever her name is!"

"Raine babe, that's one of my best clients. Even Tino –"

"What are y'all?!"

"Like what do you mean?"

"Like what is she?"

"What is she?"

"Yeah, like what is she to you?"

"Raine, Tequesta is –"

"I'oin wanna hear about her!"

"Um, uh okay ha ha ha…"

"Tell me!"

"Um, okay what?"

"Is she prettier than me?"

"Who? Tequesta?"

"Yeah, do you think she's prettier than me?"

"Well, she's never stood me up."

"Oooh and is that why you took her to the movies and not me?!"

"We were actually just meeting up and heading out."

"Right?!"

"Uh…"

"You know what, don't even worry about answering that!"

"Tuh, okay…"

"Ugh!"

"Um…Raine, you…sound…a bit jealous."

"Oh, jealous huh? I sound jealous?"

"Yeah, that's what I just said."

"Eww! I can't stand you."

"Tuh ha ha ha…"

"Rence…"

"What?"

"Look, I don't want you bringing that girl over by mami's house if we're gonna start hanging out again."

"Oh, no?"

"No…You got that?!"

"Hmmm, Raine…"

"What?!"

"You know I can't do that."

"Oh okay, we'll see about that."

"Oh…We'll see about that?"

"Yeah, we're gonna see about that?"

"Hmmm…Okay…"

Several minutes went on without neither of them saying anything to one another. Strangely, the wind isn't blowing as hard as it normally would, which left them hearing one another breathe. Then suddenly, Loraine began to feel some light movement coming from Torence. Looking at him, she noticed that he's got his eyes closed while nodding his head. Curious, she asked him, "What's on your mind?" Replying to her question, Torence opened his eyes saying, "What's on my mind, you ask?"

"Yeah, you're all quiet and plus, you're bopping your head. So, what are you thinking about?"

"Hmmm, I'oin know. Life, I guess."

"Okay and…"

"Hmmm, and some rhymes to go with it."

"Hmmm, rhymes about what?"

"About…what I've gone through…What we go through…you know life."

"I wanna hear it."

"What? My rhymes?"

"No, what's on your mind."

"Hmp, well okay, I guess…"

Day by day, day by night
A bunch of lil' niggas living this kind of life,
We out here where things ain't all that nice
But at the same time,
we always try to make things right.
Till came a nick a time ago,
I made it bout an hour late or so,
To class feeling real glad bout what Ms. Tourez had to show,
I was seeing, hearing, and yearning to learn more
about my peoples and their many methods of lifestyles,
I saw talks about the homies, walks they had at their homes,
Fist fights, foot races and facts I won't get into…

"…ahhh, and I'm a just stop there."

"Hey, boo, that was pretty good!"

"Oh yeah?"

"Yeah!"

"You really think so?"

"Yeah! Baby, I actually like that."

"Tuh, thanks."

"Did you make that up on your own?"

"Yeah, I call it *day by day*."

"Mmmm, nice name for the flow, boo."

"Hmp, I try."

"C'mere. Muah."

With her right hand, Loraine grabbed hold of Torence's jaw and had him face her way. As she leaned in for the kiss, she tightened her grip on his jaw and that's when she began to hear him grunt in a bit of pain. Opening her eyes, she paused to ask him what's wrong. Then as she rubbed his right cheek, she felt swelling and automatically became concerned. "Oh my gosh, Torence, your face is all bruised up!" she said. "I know, ugh," he replied.

"Why didn't you say something?"

"I thought you been noticed."

"Well, it's dark, and you've got on that hoodie, so of course, it'd be hard to tell."

"Tuh, it's not like it matters anyway."

"Yes, it does! Who did this to you, boo!?"

"These boys, Tino and I thumped with this morning."

"Tino huh?! Let me guess: he got you mixed up in one of his bull shits again!?"

"Raine, Raine, calm down, I'm good."

"No, Tino has his own life, and you got yours. If he wanna fuck his up, then good for him. But he can't drag you along with him!"

"Raine, Raine –"

"No, I won't calm down! Mami, needs to hear about this!"

"Oh, Nooooo! Don't do that!"

"Okay, then fine! What happened?"

"J-Roc and a few other boys I never seen before was trying Tino. Tino couldn't take 'em all on his own, so he scooped me up, and that was it."

"He got you mixed up in it."

"I had to Raine...I mean I couldn't leave him hanging."

"And now you've gotta swollen cheekbone."

"I'll be alright."

"I'm sorry, boo. If only I could make things better."

"Well...You still could if you..."

"Hmp, he he...C'mere. Mmmmmmm muah."

Present Day: Rence and Raine

The length of Loraine's complicated but close relationship to Torence was now moving on to a couple of years. Overall, Loraine had known him for practically three years. For Loraine, Torence, was known as a rather laid-back character. To some extent, he at times could be pretty mysterious in his own way. He had a quiet confidence in which Loraine found most intriguing. However, he also had an unpredictable anger that had finally been exposed to Loraine that evening at the park.

Days after lashing out his frustration at his girlfriend and best friend's inability to get along, Torence, on one early afternoon, finally reached out to Loraine. Wanting to hang out, he had her follow him out to his new getaway, which was a relatively remote location. Reaching the area, Loraine took the opportune moment to rest her legs as she sat next to Torence comfortably. They both sat on the grass of a short hill, and before them flowed a smooth murky lake. From afar, they could see a construction that bridged two roads together for heavy traffic. Around them was nothing more than a plain, open field of grass. Now and then, they'd hear the sounds of the soothing breeze blowing against them and their surroundings. *Pretty chill*, Loraine thought as she leaned by Torence's side. "But it's a little too quiet for my taste," said the voice in Loraine's thoughts. "Hey boo, haven't we passed by here a few times," asked Loraine to Torence as she began to recognize the area. "Yeah, we have," answered Torence. "But we never really had a chance to actually sit out here like that," he said.

"My god..."

"What?"

"Nothing...It's just so quiet out here."

"Yeah, I know...It's easier for me to think."

"Think?"

"Uh huh."

"Think…about what boo?"

"Anything… and everything."

"What are you thinking about now?"

"Right now…this may sound funny to you, but I'm thinking about…I'm thinking about a lot of scars."

"Scars?"

"Yep…A lot of 'em."

"Like scars on you? Is that what you mean?"

"Yeah…"

"Tuh ha ha but baby…You barely have any on you. Well, except for the one that used to sit on your right cheek."

"Yeah, I remember how much that one hurt a couple of years back when you squeezed my jaw."

"Hey, hey, hey, hey boo…Now it wasn't me that broke your cheekbone. Remember that!"

"I know Raine, I know."

"It was one of those boys Tino had you all mixed up with that led to you getting that scar on your right side."

"Raine, I know."

"I know you know, but I just wanna remind you."

"Tuh, you 'oin need to do that neither."

"Well boo, that scar faded away a long time ago."

"Babes, I got so many scars, and most of them hurt way more than the one that was on my cheek."

"Bae…just what are you trying to say?"

"You still don't get it?"

"No…Elaborate."

"Elaboray…"

"Elaborate. Like help me out and specify what exactly you're trying to say."

"Oooooh, okay…Well, babe what I'm trying to say is Tye died, Ms. Tourez had it rough trying to hold us together, I've been jumped and thrown in the dump, I still don't know who my parents are…All of those hurt me really bad."

"Ooooh…"

"You see what I mean?"

"Uh huh."

"Those to me are scars. A lot of them…and just like the time I got that scar on my cheek, it hurt. I mean bad…but like how the scar on my cheek faded, some of the –"

"Scars in you faded…"

"Yes, babes exactly! But…When I look in the mirror and see the faded scar on my cheek or the scars on my fists that healed, I still remember the pain. I still remember the pain of getting jumped, chased three blocks, having to live in an orphanage…I still remember…I remember how it felt when I got those scars, Raine."

"So much pain…"

"Yeah…That's what's on my mind right now, babe."

"Wow boo…I would've never known all this was going on inside. You're so quiet."

"I am…But that's just cause there's bigger things going on."

"No, but you're right though…A lot of scars…No one ever made me see it that way…No one but you boo."

"I wanna let people know too, what's on my mind…Kind a like Lee."

"Oh, wait, you mean 'Poetic Lee.'"

"Hmmm…Is that the name everyone's calling her by now?"

"No, it's really more like the name she has everyone calling her by."

"Hmmm...Props."

"Hmp, well, you're probably gonna need a name too boo."

"I'll just run with the name y'all gave me."

"You mean you're adopted name?"

"Yeah…Rence."

"Baby…"

"What?"

"NO."

"What? You don't like it?"

"It's not so much that I don't like it; it's just…okay, yeah I don't like it."

"Why not?"

"Boo, for one, we don't even call you Rence and two, it just sounds lame."

"Well, maybe I'll run with that until people gimme a name."

"'Yeah, well, what if they don't give you a name?"

"Hmmm…Maybe, I could run with my name at the shop."

"The one, the manager calls you?"

"Yeah."

"Doberman? NO."

"Dopamine."

"Well, it sounds like Doberman, and people are gonna ride on you boo."

"Hmmm, I'll think of something."

"Yeah, just keep thinking…"

"Hmp. I will…"

"Hey, boo wanna know something?"

"Hmmm, what?"

"These last few days I ain't seen you, I was thinking about you a lot."

"You were?"

"Mmmm hmmm, I thought about the times people would always look at us when we're together somewhere."

"Oh…So, you noticed it too, huh?"

"Tuh ha ha, yeah, I did, and it made me kind of uncomfortable at first."

"Hah, me too."

"Naw, but I really was conscious about it, though."

"What? Cause you're some 'high school celebrity,' tuh ha ha?"

"Shut up. I'm for real."

"Hmp, I got used to it real quick."

"I hoped you ain't notice."

"Stuh, please, I ain't even care."

"Oh…well, that's good. Anyways, I thought about you."

"I was staying at Tino's new place."

"Wait, Lantino's got his own place now?"

"Mmmm hmmm…Right over by Milleena's place."

"Wow wait till mami hears about this."

"Yeah...Hey, did Ms. Tourez say anything while I was gone?"

"Um, yeah...She was worried and kept asking for you."

"What'd you tell her?"

"Lee and I just said a whole bunch of shit to keep her calm, but she obviously ain't believe us. Even my brother heard she was looking for you."

"Ugh...You think she'll be mad when I come home?"

"Yeah...probably."

"Damn...Look Raine, about that night at the park I –"

"Boy, hush."

"I'm, I'm sor –"

"Shhh...Let's just feel, listen to this breeze... and let all the dust blow out," Loraine reaches over and hugs him.

Chapter 27: Rhyme Spree

Two Hours Ago:

Flowing before a grass on a short hill was a smooth murky lake, and from afar was a construction which bridged two roads together. The area was none more than a plain ol' field of grass and seated comfortably, sat a diamond, yet to have been discovered. While the sun shined and beamed its lens against him, allowing him to glisten, he'd feel, hear the soothing breeze blowing against his entire surroundings. With the black book having reached its last pages, he figured the time had come to mark ink on a new surface (something other than skin). Resting his eyes on the sounding of sounds…that sounded like a continuous rhythmic beat. Nodding his head, the volume in his mind began to pick up. Random words could be heard like flashes of images he couldn't necessarily piece together. And that's when another tone began to emerge…a whole new rhythm, a whole new vibe, a stronger beat began to play and change the mood of the setting, and its listener could feel it.

Later: At Tino's Place
[Chorus: Tyberius]
Like yo, wait a second now, things getting hot,
I mean yo, hold on, this who I think on my spot,
out of line crossing borders got me going out of order,
I'm about to sort a, no, I'm gonna really 'mitta murder!
In the meantime, while the beat plays on continuously, Torence, who happened to be with Lantino, opened up the new dialog, "Yo, that was hot Tino!"

"Yeah, I know! I told you Tye could spit!"

"Was that really him?!"

"Yep, Mr. Top hat himself…You couldn't tell by the voice?"

"Yeah, I could. Just ain't know he was into rhyming."

"Yeah well, he was…"

"How long was he doing that?"

"Hmp, beats me. Hey, how ya like this beat?"

"It sounds hard …"

"Like Tye, huh?"

"Yeah, that's all Tye…"

"Hey well, check out the shit I wrote to this a couple of hours ago before you stopped by."

"Oh shit, for real Tino, you too?"

"Yeah, check out the rhyme…"

"Okay, let's hear it…"

"Hold on, let the chorus playback…"

[Chorus: Tyberius]
Like yo, wait a second now, things getting hot,
I mean yo, hold on, this who I think in my spot,
out of line crossing borders got me going out of order,
I'm about to sort of, no, I'm gonna really 'mitta murder!

[Freestyle: Lantino]
I gotta brag, when ya whoopin' that ass,
I feel the heat that ya have,
for it emerge to be the urge I seem to have,
I'd like to add, with the pen that I have,
I also wrote in my pad, that just like you, I did it all to be a grad!

"Ooooh shit! You wrote that?!"

"Yeah, what do you think?"

"I think that needs to be recorded!"

"Yeah?!"

"Stuh! Yeah Tino! That sounds almost better than what Tye dropped on the beat."

"Tuh, ha ha, get outta here!"

"Naw, real shit. That ought a get recorded."

"Recorded?"

"Yeah."

"Hmp, I don't know about all that."

"Then, what the heck you wrote that for?"

"I don't know; I guess I kept thinking about what you said that one time at your spot."

"At my spot, wait, what'd I say?"

"You know…that one night where you were like 'I'm a write and spit flows and shit.' That time."

"Ooooh, you still remember ha ha…"

"Yeah, I do…Ever since I moved here, flowing's really all I do…At least when I'm here listening to this."

"Hmmm…"

"Yo, why don't you hop on this, Rence."

"You mean like busting a freestyle, real quick?"

"Yeah, c'mon lemme hear you drop some of those rhymes."

"Hmmm, that's the thing I'm a writ –"

"Aww, c'mon! Don't gimme any of that 'Mr. I'm a write and spit flows'!"

"Tuh ha ha ha ha!"

"Naw, just bust one real quick!"

"Stuh, alright but uh, just letting you know…this ain't prewritten."

"So, that's why it's called freestyling."

"Stuh, alright…"

"Here, I'm a play the chorus back."

"Okay."

"You ready?"

"Yeah, yeah…"

"Okay, here it is…"

[Chorus: Tyberius]
Like yo, wait a second now, things getting hot,
I mean yo, hold on, this who I think in my spot,
out of line crossing borders got me going out of order,
I'm about to sort of, no, I'm gonna really 'mitta murder!

[Freestyle: Torence]
Yo, yo, yo, yo when ya come across a fella
like myself who's of another mother,
then ya know I'm going flowing HELL cuz I'm up all in it,
so stupendous when I'm in it, spitting like I'm so tremendous,
no comparing, sitting, dropping, spitting licks a harder than a no
one other…

"Yo keep going!"

"Keep going?"

"Yeah! Keep going! What you doing?!"

"I told ya, flowing ain't really my thing."

"Aww Rence, you supposed to ride to that."

"Shoot, I was about to repeat myself several times."

"Tuh ha ha, yeah, I kind a heard that a little… 'stupendous.'"

"Stupendous, tremendous, ah whatever…"

"Ha ha ha ha nah but it sounded kinda hot though."

"Hmmm, I gotta write it out."

"Naw, naw, it was strong. Just work on your flow some more and…add some punch lines."

"Punch lines?"

"Yeah, throw some of that in there. At least one."

"Wait, first of all, what the heck is a punch line?"

"You don't know what that is?"

"Um no…am I supposed to?"

"Uh yeah, especially if you're gonna write and spit flows."

"Hmmm okay, so what is it?"

"I'd say the easiest way to explain it is thinking of it like this: the last line of a rhyme that brings what you said on point."

"Okay, let me hear you spit a punch line."

"Hmmm okay…uh, yo I ain't need to go to college because I'm a canvas painted with too much knowledge."

"Hmmm… 'I'm a canvas painted with too much knowledge.'"

"Or check out this one…yo I'm so phat, I could die of obesity."

"Tuh ha ha ha ha ha ha ha ha!!"

"Ha ha ha ha ha ha ah, that was weak."

"Ha ha ha ha ha I actually liked that one though."

"Ha ha hey well…"

"So, dropping a punch line is just like how someone would use a metaphor in a story?"

"Hmmm yeah…yeah pretty much that."

"So, I could say 'In this situation her nose was longer than our conversation'."

"Yeah, yeah, there ya go!"

"Hmmm, or better yet, I could say 'the mellowness in his sweet words ain't appeal to her taste.'"

"Hah, well now that ya got punchlines down, why don't you and I ride one time to this beat."

"Oh, uh okay."

"Okay, I'm a shuffle the playlist and…I guess I'll let you go first."

"Hmp, okay."

"Alright, here comes the beat; go head, bust it."

[Freestyle: Torence]
Uh, yo, yo, yo, hey yo, I'm feeling like a chief G.I,
cuz when I spit these rhymes,
 I could go ahead and add a punch line,
It has me knowing that I've reached beyond
and what you've heard thus far,
is truly what meets the eye,
I just take a lil' with a bitta from the temple of my mental,
putta scribble with my pencil on the surface of my paper,
there I go uh, yes, it's written, did I do it, yes, I did it,
did I mention that I'm feeling really pretty so stupendous –?

Lantino cuts him off.
Yo, I've gotta stop ya, I gotta stop ya…I'm a stop ya right there bro,
I gotta stop ya…
"Okay, you've got your right to say you reached this high, like a real big guy, talking all I'm Mista chief G.I,
but let me tell ya Mista chief G.I, when it comes to a rhyme,
the one that matters are the one from the heart
and what I mean by when I say that part,
is the art's sake of the art,
the free flow ya know that gets ya the props,
not to dismiss the scribble with ya pencil on the surface of ya paper
from the temple of ya mental, listen to ya, detrimental,

reciting rhymes, with ya riddles, going hard dropping bars,
but I gotta putta stopping to the lines ya steady talking
but don't get it twisted; the verse sounds pretty straight
but ya are mistaken with what's the true emcee
trait...FREESTYLING!

"Really?"
"Yeah, freestyling is the true emcee trait."
"Naw..."
"Yeah..."
"Naw, and I'm a tell ya why..."
"Okay, let's hear it, tell me why..."

[Freestyle: Torence]
Tuh, yo, yo, what good's a true emcee trait,
when I got what it takes,
reciting lines, spitting hard in ya face,
commemorating from the pen to the pad,
in and out with pizzazz,
you'll be thinking this is better than jazz,
versus the other who might blow the show,
chuckling cause he choked,
got words all stuck in his throat,
rated J for nothing less than a joke,
get outta here, adios, freestyling's just a blizzard of words,
ain't nobody feeling any of that,
all that yackity yack, it's no wonder it's not recorded in
tracks,
it lacks the time goes into a rhyme,
exercising the mind, the rhythm that exists inside of a line,
so, sit over there and shake ya head if you want,
but it's a matter of fact,
the written rhyme is really where it's all at...

"Hmmm...Okay, so that's why, huh?"
"Yeah, freestyling is all just a twist of words with no thought going into it or anything."

"And that's why you say writing is really where it's at?"

"Yeah…I mean; no vocalist could ever take freestyling seriously."

"Hmmm, well okay…Well, let me say this then…"

[Freestyle: Lantino]
Okay, point made about the freestyle bash,
ya split the free from the style,
buck wild and put the T to the trash,
opinionated, getting lost in ya tracks,
dogmatic and all, no pretending it's dead even for sure,
so I'm a stop us from going back here and forth,
sporing bout 'where it's at'
and cutthroat straight deep to the facts,
that any man could grab a pen and a pad,
scribble this and a that,
with metaphors, he's considered real bad
but ask yourself, what's really making him phat,
the raw licks that he spat,
is it the punches that he sprays in his track,?
well may the truth be told to the misinformed,
that the ghostwriter behind the scene hasn't yet been exposed,
with hush money, the proof will never be known,
and the fake will stay gold,
but let's move to what ought to be heard…

"Be heard…Hah, and what's that you suppose?"
"A question…"
"A question, I'm guessing that's for me, I presume."
"Correct…"
"Okay, well I got an answer…So, ask…"

[Freestyle: Lantino]
"What would you do if a nigga put you on blast,
talking shit out the ass,
throwing flags showing hints for a clash,

what would you do if he came after ya shine with his eyes on
a prize,
    saying in full effect that you can't rhyme...
    What would you do? That's an answer I'm a leave up to
you..."

"Hmmm...uh...I'll just make sure I have my rhymes ready."
"Wait, you mean like prewritten?"
"Um...yeah..."
"For every situation, you'll have it all pre-thought out?"
"Uh...something like that."
"Stuh, I know even you don't believe in that shit."
"Look, I'd do something..."
"Oh yeah, like what because as far as we know, you don't think freestyling's an emcee trait. I mean, if I recall, you said freestyling is what 'just a blizzard of words'...So again, my question now is what would you do when someone calls you out on your skills?"
"You really wanna know, huh?"
"Yeah, I'm dying to hear this one."
"Okay, I got one more rhyme for you, Tino."
"Oh, you got one more rhyme for me huh? Well, okay, let's hear it then."
"Alright, turn the volume down a bit. I want you to hear everything."
"Okay good, I'm all ears Rence. It's on you."

[Freestyle: Torence]
Yo, yo, yo, if a nigga came out of the blue,
I'd be like 'What it do' cuz either he or I is gonna be through,
and I know I won't be that guy cuz I'm a pleasant surprise –.

"Stuh...hold on, I messed up that time, lemme run it back..."
"Okay, go right ahead. I'm still listening to hear what you're gonna do."
"Okay, okay, uh...

[Freestyle: Torence]
...Yo, yo, yo, if a nigga came out of the blue,
I'd be like to hell with you,
screw the do and let it do what it do... "Stuh, shit! Naw, that was weak...here lemme start it off different...*

...Yo, yo, yo, my style is so stupendous,
you cannot end this
and that goes for anyone that thinks that they could come out of the blue,
because I'm so tremendous and like Don stupendous...*

"Hold up, how many times did you just say stupendous?"
"Ugh..."
"Seems like someone done ran outta rhymes..."
"Yeah, I'm cold right now."
"Here, lemme finish it off for you:"

[Freestyle: Lantino]
If someone were to come out the blue with his eyes on the prize,
I'd invite 'em to make the best of his time,
I'd look 'em up from head to toe,
take note of his flow
and listen to 'em spit the last of his words
[In unison: Torence and Lantino]
afterwards, I'd go blow for blow,
hit 'em with venomous quotes to let 'em know there's NO antidote!*
[Lantino] *Stumbling, suddenly and collapsed...*
[Torence] *filling the floor up with cracks...*
[Lantino] *that's typically what happens, in fact,*
the thought of thinking he could be the new Mack,
pulling up with that act...
[Torence] *got 'em looking like he fits in a grave...*
[Lantino] *the sound of him grunting under his breath*
[Torence] *is a whisper of death...*
[In unison: Torence and Lantino] *Rest in peace, now ya memory lane!*
[Lantino] *a bitter end of how ya went up in flames...*

[Torence] *to a vapor of shame…*
[Lantino] *vanishing to nothing more than ash…*
[Torence] *So many pieces…*
[Lantino] *I think we'll need us a rag…*
[Torence] *Or better yet, paper bags…*
[In unison: Torence and Lantino] *to clear the streets of a mess full of trash!*

"Whoa, whoa, whoa, whoa…hold on a minute," says Lantino while the last of the instrumentals on his playlist plays on. "So, picking up my punch lines, huh?" he asked with a slight grin on his face.

"Fore-hearable," responding Torence, with a calm tone of voice. "The word I'll use to describe your punches. At least for me."

"You mean you can tell how I'm a drop 'em…"

"Like listening to a beat and waiting for the chorus to come in except the only the difference is, I can hear your punches coming in less than a mile away. Stuh, in like seconds to be exact."

"So, 'a whisper of death'?"

"Yep…heard that coming."

"So, 'blow for blow'?"

"'hit 'em with venomous quotes,' heard that one coming too."

"Stuh, some kind a clairvoyant at my place ha ha ha ha…"

"Naw, ha ha ha ha ha…"

"Tuh, that's what I get for schooling you on punchlines."

"Ha ha ha ha but hey, hey Tino, one thing though…"

"What?"

"Blow for blow…I heard that one before."

"Wait. What?! Tuh, Rence you funny as fuck!"

"I know I heard it from somewhere."

"Yeah, from me. Anyways, getting back to the point; you following me now?"

"About freestyling? Yeah, I get it now."

"It's the trait…the core…"

"The core?"

"Yeah, that's encoded in all emcees."

"Hmmm…"

"Don't you ever forget that, Rence."

"It's just one…One of the traits, but I won't forget, Tino."

"Hey, yo Mista chief G.I, you wanna know something else I don't want you to forget?"

"Hmmm…let's hear it, what?"

"Your flow sounds pretty hot how you went in and spoke your mind about writing."

"Yeah? You thought that was banging?"

"Yeah…Not bad for someone who thinks 'freestyling's just a twist of words'."

"Tuh, ha ha ha ha…Yeah, well I still think that shit you wrote ought to get recorded."

"That? Really? Hmp."

"Yeah…I mean, how long that take you to write?"

"Damn, just those first four bars alone took over an hour, stuh."

"Ding, why'd it take you so long?"

"I don't know; I just feel so restricted when I start writing on paper."

"Restricted?"

"Yeah, restricted…"

"But how?"

"You know what, I don't even know how to explain. I mean, I just feel like once I have that blank white piece of paper, the will to play around with words and all is just gone."

"I think I know what's wrong."

"And what's that?"

"You're missing the vibe."

"That gives me the rhythm and patterns I need, right?"

"Right…I think I know someone that could do something about that."

"Who?"

"Poetic Lee."

"Lee?"

"Yeah, maybe she could go in-depth."

"Wait, but we're talking about a whole different style."

"Yeah, and she writes rhymes on paper all day, meaning she could probably help you figure it out."

"She does floetry, that doesn't count."

"Tuh, alright well, let's see what she says."

"You know what, yeah, let's see what she says."

"I bet you she'd side with me."

"Oh, just like she will side with you about writing, huh?"

"Hey, wait, I ain't say all that."

"No, but you're thinking it though."

"Look Tino; I'm just saying."

"You know what, let's just go."

"Right behind ya."

"Oh, and our debate about writing over freestyling ain't over."

"Stuh, ha ha ha ha…"

"To be continued!"

Part 2: Flow Autopsy

Shining on the edges of the North side's concrete jungle happened to be another, yet to have been discovered, en route to sparkle, she for starters went from vandal to ism to now inscribing descriptions such as the term, 'grad' as part of her new stature, with an entirely new look on the picture, she too like the one mentioned prior had figured that the days of the night writer were probably outnumbered. She thereafter moved, which in turn has led to this page on the chapter, afar from the past, she presently stands, awaiting to 'Poetic Lee' deliver and neutralize the hot topic at hand, a spoken word for word live performer she is, with an icy chill, loosening the iron grip, the chokehold at will…she will, as she prepares to stamp her landmark on stage.

"Recently, there's been a debate over a question," said Milleena, who's standing before a crowd of people. "And this verse I'm about to drop here is strictly for the ones who asked. The question asked… 'What core trait is truly encoded in the rhymer's DNA?'…Well, let's hope this verse you're about to hear answers this question and moreover, put this debate to rest…"

[Poetic Lee]

Meddling, fiddling, do diddling with the written rhythmic style over the likes of the schematic scatting,
premeditated fashion that's supposedly lacking the asset that lands it the melodic pattern...
that necessary passion that's apparent when one's ear hears spitting acid,
though noted when wroted on a blank white 2-dimensional surface the service of its purpose seems to be slacking and now look what's transpiring...
we're left with the mass of the masses asking what's happening with the actions, which then brings me into the address to come replying with my perspective...
     So, check out my flow autopsy...
hear my philosophy's flow autopsy as I spit drop and deliver knee-deep with no regard to any degree of sympathy about me in numerous atrocities, hip hopoly,
ya see in my belief that's only the epitome of what's bound to be when ya peep through psychologically, phonetically coming to the notion of the motion that genetically the written, lit in line of design is aligned to the mind for the time which defines the ties that's assigned between the free flow and written rhymes alike.
So, if I may oblige to set aside a ton of tides, I've come to find that the two of a kind really, factually intertwine like an eye for an eye type of line a rhyme...
so, again, check out my flow autopsy when I tell ya I'm a benevolent, hell of a female a figure that probably ought to be considered an anomaly in today's society is that I'm a crowned queen when I scream my dope theme indeed is that next to the likes of a supreme being ya hear,
for years my pen poured, bled blood, sweat, and tears all in just ink,
     and to make this equivalently to that of a tank,
I'm a unleash, release an arsenal of bars n' all to abate, modify, tone a down, and ultimately choppa style the intensified, inevitably, rectifying some inequities that exist in the hemisphere presently...
     So, to close the prose with a fitting coda,
     if ya didn't get the gist of the twist
     and got lost in the mix,

well then, in some sense, it was meant to leave ya
hang a ling a dangling in the midst.
Poetic Lee…
My Flow autopsy…
Peace.

Cold as Ice
[Ice]
Dear listeners, before when I was living beneath the cracks
on the concrete,
I'd often hear the voices of the misunderstood say
'Eww, she's psycho, bitch belongs in a house full of lokos,
a sis of the struggle, hah, child please!
Bet you, her issues are knee-deep and stay Bugging…'.
With that said, I'd often opt out of saying something.
In fact, nine times out of ten, I'd normally go quiet and say nothing
or better yet, in defense, I'd reply saying, 'Fuck you!
I don't have nothing to say! And there's nothing, and I mean nothing
that you, you or anyone of you could say that'll make me explain.'
You wouldn't understand anyway.
That's why, in my view, you're the misunderstood.
Your presumptions of me are already in place.
Your judging me are already being made
and like that, you've cast me away.
So, shielding you from me, I am.
Try and breakthrough if you can.
Reaching me, tuh, that's a process, but go ahead if you dare
because in the end, I guarantee you won't care…
They…they…they the relatives, doctors, and even the strangers
would say
'Here, take a chill pill, and it'll all be okay.'
Bitch! Fuck you! That's easy for you to say!
Words from the privileged would be something like
get help, make friends, and I swear it'll all come to an end…
Oh yeah, well, stand where I am and see if you could say the same
thing,
for the nerves are struck 24/7,

when the verbal assault comes in,
there's no clear way to manage,
unable to keep the hurt concealed,
an angry character is revealed,
results...bodies, bruised up, laying in hospital beds, that's it.
Yeah, that's how I'd leave 'em...
Now grown, cold, sprouted, and marked with jagged edges,
questions for me from the still very misunderstood are:
'How could you? Are you without shame?
Did you not think of their pain?
What on earth could ever make you do such a thing?...'
In turn, the thoughts of guilt insert my membrane,
but then along comes anger and like that, guilt too becomes
outweighed.
So, flashing back, I can opt-in choosing to say 'To fuck with you!
I'd like to see how you'd handle it!
And I could give a damn if I inflicted any damages!
I could give a flying fuck about you, you, or any of you because even
though I regret it,
ain't a damn thing I can or will do to make things any different.
So, fuck you!
Shit, if they just knew...
Had those bitches only knew...
Before they said what was said...
then they'd know not to have a say...
because this life I know as my own, is trife
and it's as 'cold as ice.'
I am Ice.

Spectate
[Loraine's thoughts on the show so far]
Clap, clap, mmmm hmmm,
yep, I'm a strike my palms to that.
Repeatedly, not in secrecy
because what she did there was 'Poetic Lee,'
and how she delivered it was as cold as 'Ice.'
Yeah, she killed it to the next degree,

redefining the flow autopsy,
so, encore is what I'll say to thee
because this show deserves what one would call
another round of applause.
  Still live with a chill will, I see,
ya came a long way from the program, although, you're still her,
that one girl with the cold stare,
Isis, if I remember right,
this is you, now at your nicest...
Wait, hold on. What it do?
Rence boo, are you still coming through?
Feels like what, I'd say an hour or two.
Tardy again! Where are you?! Eww, I can't stand you!
Ugh! Oh, well, I guess in the meantime while I wait,
I might as well sit down and 'Spectate.'

Aries walks in. Loraine waited and spectated where she was
seated. Despite how good the first couple of performances were, she
wasn't too sure how long she might've stayed for the event. She was
still feeling irritated by Torence's absence. She could feel her blood
beginning to boil as she wandered about where Torence was and
what he was doing. Rolling her eyes back a few times, she started
thinking of what she was going to say and how she was going to say
something, the next time she laid eyes on Torence. That's when she
noticed Milleena back on the stage with a microphone on her hand.
Anticipating another performance from her friend, Loraine sat up
straight to catch every detail. However, Milleena only welcomed
someone else on the stage. This person happened to be a young
white male with long straight brown hair that nearly passed his
shoulders. He had dark brown eyes, slim build, and comparing him
to Torence, Loraine thought they could be the same height.
Watching the microphone being handed to him by Milleena, Loraine
could tell that he wasn't from Chicago. Just looking around, Loraine
figured that practically everyone was thinking the same thing. Using
his bright smile, he seemed to be keeping everyone tuned in to what
he was going to do. Though, there was still some kind of suspense
on what everyone was going to get out of him.

"Y'all give it up one more time for my girl, Lee and your sister of the struggle, Ice!" he said just shortly after introducing himself as an Aries Child. Once the crowd was done clapping, he continued, "This next performance you're about to see here is dedicated to a situation…a situation about not one, nor two, but three newbies…three newbies, who hadn't been on their job for too long but were already showing a lot of promise. So, their employer arranged a meeting to discuss matters about a possible pay raise. Now en route to the setting in which the meeting was going to be held, the three newbies met up along the way. But out of nowhere, they were intercepted by a rival of their employer. In this line of business, the newbies were warned that this person had a reputation of living like a snake in one's garden. He was infamous for being a gamer and twisting up truths. Most of all, his crooked smile was like an omen for the worse that had yet to come. So again, he intercepted them while on their way. Looking at them, he did the crooked smile he's notoriously known for and told them, it's either they get down or lay down. That's the situation. Here's my performance. Hear me and nod ya heads…"

Next came a loud silence that lasted for about a minute or two. Then everyone, including Loraine, heard what sounded like things you'd hear from drum machines or special effects. Except that this time, there were no machine, stereo or turntables. Instead, the sounds were coming from the artist's mouth, lips, gums, throat, tongue, and of course, his microphone. And the sounds he was accurately able to imitate had everyone nodding their heads and moving their shoulders. *Hmmm, he may not be Lee, but this should be enough to keep Mr. M-I-A off my mind*, Loraine thought as she clapped her hands.

Part 3: Tino vs. Roc

After stepping out earlier that afternoon, Torence and Lantino spent the next couple of hours making trips around the city's North/Westside region. In total, both of them had made four different stops between the regions and now were on their way to their fifth stop. However, their fifth stop was still to be determined due to the dispute that was going on between the two of them. "Tuh

Rence, why are we stopping here?" asked an irritated Lantino. "Because Tino, this is Milleena's place, remember," replied Torence. "After all, she does live here," he added as he continued leading the way.

"But Rence, we already stopped here, and she wasn't there. Or did you forget that?"

"Yeah, but that was earlier when we left your place, Tino. Tuwan said she might actually be home around this time now."

"Tuh, I can't believe you're actually listening to Tuwan."

"Tino, how you gonna say that when that's her brother? He of all people should know where she is."

"Man please, I bet you he doesn't even know where he is right now!"

"Tuh ha ha ha ha! What you mean by that?"

"What do you mean, 'what I mean by that'?! Couldn't you tell just by his look?!"

"Ha ha ha ha! He just said he had a little cold."

"Man, damn that! More like a flu! Did you see how he was sneezing all over the place!? Half the time, I didn't even think he was with us, Rence."

"Tuh, he just got a bad cold."

"Well, he's really sick and soon, he's gonna get everyone at his job sick."

"Ha ha ha ha…Anyways, let's keep moving. We're almost there."

"Why don't we just check out Stone Park?"

"Way out there? Please, it's too far out west. We'd have to hop on two buses to reach there, and besides, nobody comes out there anyway."

"Okay well, what about the rec?"

"The rec?!"

"Yeah, let's check out there."

"Haven't you heard?! Out there is like GD central now! Can't none of us come out there right now!"

"Rence, for the last time the GDs got chased out of there weeks ago. We're talking like almost a month ago. That's old news now."

"Stuh, whatever, you won't see me coming out that way. Especially with the street war still going on."

"Rence, I'm telling you were wasting our time! Lee's not home right now."

"Alright, well what makes you so sure?"

"Because we already checked out here and turns out, I was right the first time."

"Oh yeah, just like you were right when you took us out to that one spot near Gurnee Mills, huh."

"I'm telling you, Rence, I know Lee. You won't usually catch her at home around this time of the day."

"Hmmm…then where could she be?"

"Hmmm, I know there's the poetry thing she's been doing lately."

"Yeah, but she only has shows at night."

"Stuh, well, at this point, I don't think we're gonna find her Rence. Plus, there are some rooks I'm a have to meet up within a little bit."

"Yeah…Hey, is it those same rooks you keep telling me about?"

"The three with a lot of promise? Yeah, them."

"How many times did you meet up with them?"

"Tuh, I lost count…But helping them out is the only light I could put on my title as a 'permanent scum.'"

"You must really like them."

"Yeah, I do…Hmp, they kinda remind me of you, Lee and I when we were younger."

"Oh yeah?"

"Yeah…"

"Oh, uh, uh, oooooh shit, I just remember!!"

"What?"

"A show!"

"A show?"

"Yeah! There was this show Raine wanted me to come out to!"

"Wait, in the day?"

"Yeah, yeah, it's on right now!"

"Tuh ha ha, what show?"

"I'oin know, she said it was called 'Flow Autopsy'! Or something, I don't know. All I just know is that I gotta get there!"

"Flow Autopsy…Hmmm, you think maybe that's where Lee might be?"

"Probab-Lee, I mean probably, ahh! I don't know, but look, I gotta go. Peace! Have fun with them rooks."

"Ha ha ha ha! Run Forrest! Hey, but keep your eye out for them Folks."

"Yeah!"

So, rather than making a stop at Milleena's place, the two ultimately parted ways. While Torence was in a rush to join Loraine at the event, Lantino was en route to meet up with his three rookies. In fact, it didn't take Lantino too long to arrive within the setting the meeting was supposed to take place. However, just shortly after his arrival, he noticed that his rookies were nowhere in sight. *Hmmm, something ain't right; they're usually always here before I am,* he thought as he sensed something was off. Listening to his gut instincts, he began to walk a little further than the set destination. Walking about a few yards or two, that's when he automatically noticed one of his rookies running towards his direction. "TINO!" shouted the rookie. "Lil' Red," said Lantino as he looked at his rookie sideways. "TINO!" again, shouting the rookie who was out of breath. "Thank god you're here! C'mon, let's go!" she added.

"Whoa, whoa, slow down Lil' Red! Where's Low key and Eleventh? And why you all sweaty like this? What's going on?"

"We were all on our way here T…"

"But…"

"But we got cut off on our way here…"

"Cut off?! Wait, by who?"

"J-Roc and his boys…"

"You said WHO?"

"J-Roc…"

"J-Roc, huh…"

"Yeah…I know you told us to always stick together, but I had to take off because I knew you'd be here."

"Naw, you did right. You know what, take me to them!"

"Okay…C'mon…"

Infuriated by the news, Lantino was now following his rookie's trail to meet with J-Roc, who, by the way, was not very far away. Though he had walked with a noticeable limp on his left leg, J-Roc was fully recovered from the gunshot wounds suffered by the hands of the Gangster Disciples gang. Five other followers accompanied him. Three of them were Spanish Vice Lords, who believed that he was the top hat according to the VL hierarchy. Before J-Roc and company stood two more of Lantino's rookies, who J-Roc initially was trying to lure into his employment. Instead, he found himself in the middle of a rhyme contest with one of the rookies. Lyrically, the rookie seemed to match well with J-Roc. However, J-Roc clearly had the edge due to his ability to deliver with emphasis. Word after word, J-Roc slowly and surely seemed to be crushing the rhymer within Lantino's rookie. "Eleventh way is what they call you, right?" asked J-Roc while in the middle of rhyming. "Tuh, look chump!" he added. "Ya name's a NO, from head to toe, ya flow and clothes, shit, all that garbage gotsta GO! Matter fact, listen punk…You ain't NO rhymer, ya just a peanut butter, motherfucker, two-time bitch, who fucked with me, ya getcha ass kicked –"

"HEY, YO ROC!!" shouting Lantino as he interrupts J-Roc. "You call that a rhyme? Those lil' corny lines?" he says as he and his other rookie approaches the scene.

"Yeah, that's what I call a rhyme Lil' Tino, ha ha ha," replying J-Roc. "What, you ain't feeling my style?"

"Ya shit is weak, Roc."

"Oh, it's weak, huh?"

"Isn't that just what I said?"

"To fuck with that! Anyways, what are you doing around here? You of all people…Shouldn't you be on your job as a look-out somewhere at someone's meeting, ha ha ha ha ha?!"

"Oh, that's funny huh? Got jokes to go along with your corny rhymes too huh?"

"Ha ha ha ha…Tino, Tino, Tino, after all these years, ya still ain't gotchu a sense of humor."

"And I see ya done replaced Vern with a new rat pack."

418

"He he…Look Tino, on the real, what are you doing here near the Northside?"

"Naw, the real question is, what are you doing fucking around with my rooks, Roc?!"

"Your rooks? Ha ha ha ha…Did you say your rooks, Tino?"

"You have a hearing problem today, or do you always find it this hard to hear? Answer the fucking question!"

"Tuh ha ha ha ha ha! Let me get this straight: you're holding your own meetings now?! Tuh ha ha ha ha ha…But hold, hold, hold on a minute…Since when did you start conducting your own meetings, Tino?!"

"You know since you wanna sit here and waste time clowning around, let me go ahead and make this clear: You stay the fuck away from my recruits, fool! You got yours to sit there and beat up on, and I got mine!"

"Tuh wrong again, Tino…Ya see, I find mine and turn them into real G's as you can see. Only a select few can rock the almighty G-card."

"Yeah well, the bottom line is this: stay the fuck away from mine! Obviously, they ain't want what you had to offer! My rooks ain't dumb enough to stand with you and look like a bunch a cheerleaders."

"You might wanna watch your mouth Tino…Remember, I'm six to your four right now."

"Boy, the hell I look like! You think I give two fucks about you and your five test dummies!"

"Stuh, you should…"

"Tuh, go ahead! Let them find out if I give a fuck! It'll be like roughing up some GDs back in 148th!"

"Stuh, Iyight Tino…You made your point. Besides, I ain't trying to spar with ya like that anyway."

"Fuck you, J-Roc."

"Should've known these were your lil' pep squeaks, Tino. I mean it all makes sense: holding down lil' so-called meetings out here, ha ha ha ha ha…This lil' quiet ass spot that's under construction. 'Lil punk asses probably couldn't hang anyway. Don't know why Tye let them in."

"Stuh, at least they won't have to listen to you spit your weak ass, corny ass lines, ha ha ha ha ha…C'mon y'all, let's get the fuck out of here."

"Wait, just a minute there, Mr. Tino…"

"What now, man?!"

"It's funny how you say my shit is weak?"

"Because it is…What? You don't like the truth? Well, how 'bout some more with my rhythm and poetry?"

"Hah, y'all listen to this nigga talking about rhythm and poetry…So, what ya saying? You rap too?"

"Let's just say, I'll saran rap that ass back to the trash where it belongs."

"You know what, let's do this. I'm tired of your mouth."

"I'm tired of you, period."

"I'm a do you worse than I did your punk ass rook."

"Ight, well, let's hear it…"

"Hmmm…seem like we got a lot of people who came out to spectate like a real show's going down."

"Naw, you're right. We do but quit stalling and put your money where ya mouth is."

"Tuh, stalling huh?"

"Yes…After all, bitches goes first…"

"Okay…but you asked for it, Tino…"

[Freestyle: J-Roc]
Alright, since he wanna tangle,
you wanna shake, rattle and flow,
well then cool, I'm a put 'em in his role,
and let 'em all know like all the rest of my foes who put their best
forth,
nothing but DEATH is all that's known,
so consider yourselves warned my Jehovah witnesses
as I get ready to deliver the business
to one of the biggest bitch made niggas…
Let's start from day one,
when you were just someone else's son,
I remember when you came running to me like one of your punks,

talking bout, you wanted in with your vocal cord sounding lame,
        so I hit up a few of my friends
        and like that, we put several punches in,
        particularly in ya frame, roughing ya up,
        engraving it painstakingly in ya membrane,
        so even if ya had amnesia,
        ya wouldn't forget to remember those hits,
        performing a live Oscar like some ole bitch
        and we marked tracks on ya like a train wreck,
        yeah, that's what it was,
        and that's just the biz of how it's gonna be
each time ya step in thinking you could fuck with me...
        Now here's some case closed facts,
ya only need faith in me, surpass the size of a mustard seed,
        follow my lead and get turned into a real O.G,
        it ain't a shock when ya fucking with the Roc,
        an up line top hat, according to the hierarchy,
        a shining don multiplied and survived by Lords,
        but work with him (Tino) and all ya left with is less,
        nonetheless, the sight, the epitome of disrespect,
don't know what kinda credibility Tye saw in your ability,
        what? Bringing rooks in?
        Boy, please, they look shooked bitch.
        Funny, it took him to die,
        for cuz (Julisa) to see the fool, the jokesta that is,
moreover, look at what happened: she went gay loving a GD,
        a member of Folk Nation?!...
Anyways, I'm a leave that there and state one more thing...
        if it weren't for Tye, you'd never get in
        and that my peoples is a closed case SIN!

Just as J-Roc completes his last line, his followers
immediately start to pat him on the back with cheers of
encouragement. As they're doing that, J-Roc, in the meantime,
chews on his toothpick and stares back at Lantino with a crooked
smile on his face. Staring back with a calm frown, Lantino looks on
silently. And staring at him, his three rookies look on with questions

all over their faces. Glancing away several times, Lil' Red, one of his rookies, then realizes that more than twenty-five other people out of nowhere has shown up to the scene. Some of these people, from what she's able to recognize are affiliates of Rojo. The rest, she's a bit particular about. Anyways, silence has returned to the scene, and her eyes are now drawn back on Lantino. "Tino, it's on you," she whispers to Lantino. Nodding his head, Lantino takes a look around at the crowd saying "Hey, y'all could hear me, right?!"

"YEAH," responding the crowd. Right there, Lantino begins to say his own slur of rhythm and poetry:

[Freestyle: Lantino]
I'd never get in
and that my peoples is a closed case sin'…
Hmmm, so says the serpent which coils on his belly at Rockwell Gardens
and let his words flow as smooth as oil.
And it probably tastes as sweet as honey,
mainly to his 5 test dummies,
man clearly, the tunnel vision in y'all is blurred,
cause y'all thinking, saying this snake
belong among the top of the ranks,
naw that's absurd but like a sound of thunder,
I'm a put all his bull on blast,
starting with some questions asked,
since when was it ever raw to get caught in the midst of bullets,
hands up, guns down, and not shoot back NOT one round?
The fuck you call that? A clown who should've drowned on the pavement he stood on.
You already walk with a limp,
pretty soon you'll be walking with none at all,
just keep fucking with my rooks,
and that ass'll be back in the hospital again,
and we ain't talking lying in bed,
but more like a morgue instead,
or better yet an episode, suited up with rose pedals down below,
after CSI wraps up what's a homicide,

anyways, enough with the art of warring,
it's time light lit on what you've hidden in the dark for too long,
  ya see, while momma was next to your side,
  I managed to connect the dots the whole time,
  and with that said, may real shit get exposed
  as I let the truth be told,
  folks y'all be hold, on the night Tye was murked,
this nigga kneeled and begged for his life that's my word,
not hearing this, well, check this cause I'm a confirm –.

  "Stuh, I begged? The fuck? J-Roc responded as he
interrupted Lantino.
  "Yeah, that's right, begged and I'm a sit here and confirm –"
Lantino replied while trying to get back to where he left off. "Stuh, I
begged," again, said J-Roc, "Man, you know you're full of shit, Tino
–" he disagreed. Cutting him off, Lantino, with a commanding
voice, responded saying, "Hey, hey, hey, quit yapping because I
only picked out ya casket, which means I ain't through killing you
just yet…So quiet when I'm killing you, nigga…"
  Quieting down, J-Roc looks on as he can hear what sounds
like "Ewwws" and "Ahhhhs" coming from the crowd in response to
what Lantino just said. Right there, Lantino continues from where he
left off:
  Now I said on the night Tye was murked,
this nigga kneeled and begged for his life, that's my word.
Not hearing this; well check this cause I'm a confirm…
  Okay, I first said 'Hey, y'all could hear me,'
  then my rooks, Roc and I threw up our signals right,
  so did the shady bunch on his side,
but I couldn't help but notice that one out the 5 threw none at all,
  now that calls for concern,
  I suspect a violations on the horizon in turn,
  cause as I'm flashing my fingers before him,
  he stands there still with silence in return,
hmp…my guess, a pretend from what I've observed,
  moreover, folk in our turf!

Just as Lantino finished he aggressively cuts in the personal space of the follower to J-Roc's left and lurches directly at him. In turn, that same follower on J-Roc's left instinctively jerks back as he clearly wasn't expecting that from Lantino. That's when a silver necklace with the star of David leaked out from underneath the red bandana he had wrapped around his neck. Right there and then, J-Roc's remaining four followers, along with Lantino's rooks make eye contact with the star on the silver necklace. Next, they all turn over to stare back at J-Roc with a look of disbelief. Noticeably walking backward, J-Roc begins to stumble on his words: "Y'all, y'all, y'all, just, just, ch-ch-chill. It ain't like it's a real chain anyway, ha ha…" Dismissing his words, his four remaining followers take another look at the supposed imposter, who's now created a big gap between himself and J-Roc's crew before disappearing into the crowd. Just as they're about to pursue him, Lantino commands them to bring their attention to the one who misled them. "Okay, it's a-it's a… it's a real chain…alright, but the fuck that got to do with me?!" said J-Roc with his arms spread apart. "I mean I ain't know di-di-di-dis whole time," he stuttered.

"You know what, I'm still not done burying you, so quiet," replied Lantino.

"Tino, you need to chill with your rap –"

"Nigga, I said quiet when I'm killing you!"

[Freestyle: Lantino]
Now ya see, a fashion medallion on
with a six-point star as the charm,
it's without question that he cut a side deal with 'em y'all…
A plot to nail Tye in the coffin, which went out of proportion,
landing him on an emergency broadcast station,
ya pig, always talking 'I've been on missions,
also, I got all this on my possession,
I'm the Roc, much hotter than fire',
but in truth, you're just a habitual liar,
ain't no denying, the rooks don't respect ya,
the vets still denounce ya,
and from the looks of it, ya own crew's bout to pound ya…

and its only fitting cause you don't even know which side you're on,

> *it's like you're the vermin that's just rocking our own,*
> *but wait, before I wrap this to put this dirt back in the sand,*
> *I wanna say this to have y'all fully understand,*
> *that Roc's a bitch and here's truly why that is...*
> *Now Roc's rooks listen to me closely:*
> *Ya have Rojo on ya left,*
> *who'll throw you an arsenal of espanol on ya the moment he's upset,*
> *but at least this what you'll get*
> *whenever he catches a fit,*
> *whereas him (Roc), you'll never know his real intent*
> *because you won't know what to expect...*
> *Don't believe me SVLs, well, check with Lil' Red...*

[Final bar: Lil' Red]
Say what you said about me the night they let me in...

"Stuh..." responding J-Roc, who sucks his teeth as he stares back at her uncomfortably in the spotlight.

"C'mon, go ahead, say it," Lantino dared J-Roc. "The same way you did that night she got in."

"Stuh, the SVLs are soft and what," said J-Roc in a low tone of voice.

"Again, and LOUDER, so they could all hear you!" again Lantino dared J-Roc.

"The SVLs are soft," repeated J-Roc, "so what, I said it."

The same followers who patted J-Roc on the back with cheers of encouragement now stood next to Lantino and his rookies. At this point, they each had the look of a time bomb that was about to set off in any second. And being that a majority of the people in the crowd happened to be affiliates of Rojo, they began to hiss, showing their disapproval to what J-Roc said. Being able to sympathize with the fact that the four followers were thoroughly humiliated, Lantino speaks up, telling them that manipulating people is what J-Roc does and who he is. He adds on saying that J-Roc neither knows the meaning nor the spelling of the word loyalty, practically prophesying the dividing of the Almighty Vice Lord Nation. Cutting Lantino off, J-Roc makes one more statement: "Yo, Tino, know this…when the SVLs realize that Rojo is weak, they're all gonna come running to me just like you did ha ha ha ha …"

"Oh, yeah, is that so," replying Lantino. "Well, before you go repeat what you said about the SVLs, Roc."

"Tuh, you know what, fuck you, Lantino," replied J-Roc while flicking his middle finger at Lantino.

"C'mon, repeat what you said about the SVLs, Roc. We're all waiting…"

Wiping the angry smirk off his face, J-Roc, this time stands still in utter silence, being that he now feels overwhelmed with shame. Aware of this the crowd immediately reacts, shouting "OOOOOOH!" all in unison. Shaking his head, J-Roc sucks his teeth and starts walking away. As he does, Lantino watches him and nods his head while his rookies and everyone else applauds him. *Hmp, perhaps Rence is right*, he thought. *I'm a write and spit flows…Maybe there is something to this rapping stuff.*

Part 4: A Closing Performance

In the Shine of the Six
[Benito]
Intro: My mind's all in a haze…taking hits off fumes…but still standing I do (I do)…In the Shine of the Six (in the shine of the six)…
Chorus: In the Shine of the Six…In the shine of the Six…In the shine of the Six
First verse: (One time) A supposed beef is stretching in my speech, between you and I is the one that speak, though, what's present, preexisted in the name of the scenes of the streets that we seize and we claim, anyhow, you're relating to the Pep opened lanes for us, the Folks to throw shades at ya way, but ya roughing up a group of soldiers the Cobras, we're linked to done made ya a danger, from the time ya made moves in this game, I evidently knew from then and on, it was on, the world wasn't big enough for neither one of us, and

there it was apparent that I better make a stand in the shine of the Six...

Chorus: In the shine of the Six...In the shine of the Six...In the shine of the Six...

Second Verse: (Yo) With the Six, I grip my pitchfork strong, abide my Nation's laws, no love for the 5 point star, speak of Nito death will do its part, from the day I was born, One is All till the day that I fall, crossing borders with a GDN, putting dark holes in, on Rice's flesh from limb to limb, you don't get it, we about that struggle, but since ya clapping trouble, then I'm a reach out to your Lord Roc sucka, cut a deal, put a hit in place to see your very end, branch out cuz All ain't well, to hell with that, from each point we rep, to the fullest at that, for my Nation, spect the flag in the shine of the Six...

Chorus: In the shine of the Six...In the shine of the Six...In the shine of the Six...

Third verse: (One more time) Now that thee is out the picture then I figure that I might as well, paint an image of the narrative that all is swell, living large again, baking more than bread, but there's a spar ragging war on my hands, well with that said, I'll take a pause, glance afar, keep my eyes on the cause, feeling cynical, the typical, it is what it is, it happened out of beef, it's fitting cuz it's sweet, according to my creed in the shine of the Six...

Chorus: In the shine of the Six...In the shine of the Six...In the shine of the Six...

Outro: Yeah, ya boy Nito...staying loyal to the Creed...Rest in peace to my fallen brother of the struggle (Rice)...Yeah we here, still standing...In the shine, for the shine...of the Six...We in...One is All and All is One...Folk Nation.

Chapter 28: Birth of Dopamine

Untitled
(Aries Child)
Chorus: Every bit upon a second, minute moving on minute,
from hours going on hours long, tick-tocking but I done did
it, finished (Repeat 1x)
Free verse: Just living on, no limit to the ending till I finish,
what I finished, what I started in the day, going back to back
to the day dating way, way back to a heyday in a year 08,
late nights when I fought rock hard to drop the thoughts that
I'm thinking, writing in a composition with a pencil to the
blank white page to where I'm now chilling, dealing with a
situation, at a point character joint type a shit that I'm
facing, perfect the scene nicely then I repeat with an
imagery, methodically, as you can see read through the
eventful story of a well told tale of a journey, it's about a
bunch a hell a fella fine gal a talent loaded people with no
equals, from the rags to the riches, type edition, kind a
mission, on the go to the goal digging role for the gold
situated bloated wrote it from beginning to what's leading to
the reason of the series with an Aries all up in it, got me
feeling living feeling like I'm feeling floating in the air like I
care when I'm there sky high, uh huh from the minute
ticking, clocking, killing look like a captain take a look
what's happening, dipping n' a dappening harder than a
savage, better than ya average...
Chorus: Every bit upon a second, minute moving on minute,
from hours going on hours long, tick-tocking, but I done did
it, finished...

As the chorus plays on repeatedly, the amateur beat maker, Aries, takes a moment to sit back and critically analyze his work. As he's doing that, he rubs his chin while rocking back and forth on his office chair. Displeased with his work, he shakes his head endlessly, muttering: "Something…or SOMEONE…is missing…The sound is there but…it's still missing that IT factor…Lemme go pick up these blanks now…" Then having a look at his clock on his wrist, he realizes that he's been working for over three and a half hours. "Whoa, 8:30!" he said, "The fuck the time go!? Can only hope that store down the block still open!"

A Few Hours Ago
(Torence)
Day by day,
every night by night,
A bunch a brothers like myself
are living this kinda life
of reality to come and see
what may just come out right,
but society's inequities are really cold as ice,
uplifting anger raises danger
 in the mind of the minor,
I feel inspired by your desires
to show everyone your new fire,
deep down there's something holding way under your breath,
let 'em know what's going on,
express this out of your chest!

"Bravo Mr. Torence," applauding Lantino, who had just join Torence at the park. Thrown a bit off his rhythm and flow, Torence instanteously turns to see who's behind him. "Oh, Tino, it's only you," he sighs in relief. "Tuh, ha ha ha ha what you mean," replied Lantino, "of course, it's only me. Who'd you thought I was?" he laughs.

"I thought-ugh, look, you can't be creeping up on people like that."

"Oh, is that what I was doing ha ha?"

"Look, I'm just saying."

"Tuh, ha ha, big talk coming from the main one who does it all the time!"

"Use to…Use to do it…"

"A lot of times, all the time!"

"Yeah, well not anymore after Loraine got on me about that."

"Anyways, bravo Rence."

"Thanks ha ha…"

"Say, what you got there anyway?"

"Oh, that there, was a lil verse about…you know, the things we go through in life."

"'Let 'em know what's going on, express this out of your chest…' I'm feeling that."

"Raine heard the first one I wrote and told me that I should write more to it."

"Hmmm, I see you're getting good at this writing and spitting flows shit. Maybe, it ought to be you next time at Lee's show."

"Hmmm, maybe…Let's see what she thinks."

"Tuh, that's if we could ever find her."

"Hey, you know what, I heard she was at that last show Raine and I went to."

"You mean the Flow jo, mojo thing?"

"Yeah, Raine told me she performed and all."

"Oh, did you see her?"

"Naw, I had just missed her. She and a whole lot of people."

"But Loraine said she was there?"

"Yeah, and from what she told me Lee really showed out."

"Oh so, it was good then?"

"The show? Yeah! A lot of people came through."

"Hmmm, tell me about the show. Like what happened?"

"Tuh, where do I begin…"

"Well, for one, you could start with what happened the moment you came late."

"Okay…Now mind you, I was late."

"Okay, and…"

"And Loraine was pissed haha."

"Oh shit, she went off on you?"

"Well, yeah, she was on her way to doing just that…But then, out of nowhere this chick that was sitting like literally two seats away from us, just got up and started spitting out of nowhere!"

"For real?"

"Yeah, Tino for real! No joke! And you wanna know the funnier part..."

"What?"

"Bro, it felt as if she was talking about us!"

"Tuh ha ha ha ha!"

"No, for real Tino, even Raine looked at her sideways when she started pointing in my direction!"

"Say what now?"

"Yes, my direction while flowing everything!"

"Wait, so hold on, what was she saying?"

"She said stuff like 'Here's the current situation, fella got his honey irritated' and just kept flowing on and on!"

"What??"

"Yeah, then this one other dude who looked about fifteen or something showed up out the direction she was pointing at, and like her, he was just flowing nonstop!"

"Okay, and what was he saying?"

"I know this is gonna sound crazy, but he was rhyming about how he got caught up hanging out with his friend down the street."

"And you think he was talking about you?"

"I don't know; at the moment, it seemed like the coded words were a message towards Loraine and I!"

"Ha ha ha ha, Rence, did all that really happen that way?"

"Tuh, you could ask Raine, if you don't believe me!"

"Hmmm..."

"I ain't even tell you the rest. That was just the beginning."

"Okay, so what else happened?"

"Okay, so as the chick and the dude step up closer and closer to each other, Raine, me, and everyone else are all tuned in because it looks like they're gonna go back and forth freestyle battling but..."

"But..."

"But then, this white boy shows up near the front of the stage, cuts off the dude and starts flowing too. At that moment, when the spotlight turned to him, everyone and I mean everyone all at once just turned their heads over to him!"

"Oh shit!"

"Yeah, it was…banging!"

"Hmmm…did you say, white boy?"

"Yeah…"

"Hah, that's funny because Low key's white."

"Who's Low key?"

"You know Low key! Remember? He's one of my rooks?!"

"Uh yeah, I guess."

"Anyways, continue…"

"Okay, so um, where was I? Oh, yeah! So, as the white boy's flowing, he's walking up their way, and so are they. When the three of them met in the middle of it all, this guy with a red bandana on his head cuts in and starts blasting punch lines left and right. Soon, everyone's like 'Oooooh' and 'Ewwwww' from one bar to the next!"

"Wish I was there!"

"Yeah, me too, but you know, for some reason, it felt like you were."

"You mean there at the show?"

"Yeah…"

"Like how so?"

"That last guy who showed up kinda reminded me of you because you're always walking around with that same red bandana on your head."

"Hmp, ironic…"

"Yeah, that rap cipher there was my favorite performance. It not only talked to me, but it made Raine, and I squash our little beef."

"Hmp, ironic. Maybe it was a coincidence that homegirl was sitting near y'all."

"Maybe…Raine said she was talking about us, haha."

"Hmp."

"Yeah, I know…And just when I ain't think it could get any better, some other dude out of the blue showed up at the end and started falling on his neck and spinning on the floor! Shit was crazy!"

"Break dancing?"

"What?"

"Break dancing is what you just described to me a moment ago."

"Oh, yeah…that guy had moves…Probably the best I had ever seen."

"From what I've heard, nice is usually the case with most break dancers."

"There were a couple of other performers who came through, but none of them really had me like the last one that went up."

"Hmmm, what was different about the last one?"

"For one, I could tell he's down with Folk Nation from the moment he stepped foot on stage."

"Say what?"

"Yeah, I could tell just by his presence. Let alone his raps."

"He was talking that gangsta shit?!"

"Yeah, he was and a lot of it too. But I wish you would've been there to see this one (especially this one)."

"Hmmm, what makes you say that?"

"You should've heard 'em. Yeah, he's spitting gangsta shit, but…I don't know, he…had a dark, smooth flow about his and somehow, he lured you into his words and made you see things…life in his own perspective."

"So, you're saying you liked it?"

"Yeah…I was feeling it."

"Could I ask you why?"

"I just looked past the bull shit and appreciated the talent being displayed on stage: his rhymes."

"Hmp."

"He even had a catchy line: 'In the shine of the Six'."

"Ding…"

"Yeah, but you should've heard it, though…It was real catchy, 'In the Shine of the Six.' He had some people in the crowd saying it with him or just bopping their heads like Loraine and I."

"'In the shine of the Six,' huh?"

"Yeah, 'In the shine of the Six'…Maybe this is how the Folks and People ought to resolve their issues."

"Through rhyming…that wouldn't be a bad idea. In fact, that'd be better."

"Yeah, you starting to see what I see?"

"Yeah, Rence…"

"Yeah so, I had liked that last one. It was dope, and I wanna do it too."

"You will…Just keep flowing."

"You too…"

"I will…Hey but remember to throw in some punch lines."

"Ha ha, I'll never forget. Anyways, what about you?"

"What about me?"

"Like you been working on your writing?"

"C'mon Rence, you know I don't write."

"Ugh, Tino, I thought we already had this ta_ _ _ "

"Gotcha, ha ha ha…Naw, I have been working on it. Matter of fact, you remember that one shit I wrote?"

"That one you had me listen to, yeah, I remember."

"Well, since that day, I added some more lines to it."

"Oh, snap! Really?! Let me hear it!"

"Alright, lemme see if I memorized most of it:"

[Lantino]
I gotta brag when ya whoopin' that ass,
I feel the heat that ya have,
for it emerge to be the urge I seem to have,
I'd like to add
with the pen that I have,
I also wrote in my pad,
that just like you, I did it all to be a grad,
I'm from the school of hard knocks,
made it through the damn blocks,
now I'm sitting on top
with a grip on my glock,
ain't a way I'm gon' stop,
what I do is on lock,
and if J-Rocka wanna
boy, I'm funna tow' em
from the head on to the floor up
that he stands on!

"Yo, I don't know about you, but I feel like we should write till our hands fall off!"

"Yeah, I do too! You wanna get out of here?!"

"To my spot?"

"Yeah…"

"Okay, c'mon let's go."

Just like that, words were written from left to right and designed into lines of rhymes. Those lines soon formed bars, as those bars turned into verses after verses. Within those verses, profound similes, metaphors, and punchlines were added. And in turn, hooks were improvised to harmonize the rhyme scheme. This rhythm and poetry block was essentially the main highlight for the next couple of hours. The boys had fun writing art to the unheard sound up until the sun began to go down. "Hey, Rence, it's getting hard to see out here," said Lantino.

"Yeah, I know," replied Torence, "What time is it?"

"Like after eight, if I'm right."

"You wanna stop inside where there's some light and maybe write there?"

"Naw, I'm good. I think I'ma clear it; my hands are about to fall off from all this writing. But hey, if you like, you can swing by my place and keep writing. That's if you like."

"Hmmm, okay, but I think I'm a make a quick stop at the store."

"What you getting?"

"Some better pens (I don't like these)."

"Ding, for more writing?"

"Yeah, I'm hooked right now."

"Yeah, I see! You really loving this writing tip, Rence."

"Haha yeah, well, anyway, I'll see ya at the house."

"Yeah…Oh hey, you think you could get me some water?"

"Yeah, I gotchu."

"Preciate ya."

I'm an Emcee
[Aries]

Every bit upon a second,
minute moving on minute,
from hours going on hours long,
tick-tocking but I done did it, finished
Every bit upon a second,
minute moving on minute,
from hours going on hours long,
tick-tocking, but I done did it, finished…

"…Something…or SOMEONE…is missing…The sound is there but…it's still missing that IT factor…Lemme go pick up these blanks now…Whoa, 8:30! The fuck the time go!? Can only hope that store down the block still open!" It was now going on ten minutes since the beat maker rushed through his doorstep, and yet, he still had quite a distance to go before reaching the convenient store. With time winding down, he knew it was only a matter of minutes before the clerk started to shut things down. A trip which started from the front doorstep of his hideaway, through the crowd infested streets of the Northside, now left him feeling a bit antsy and winded. Having finally reached the street in which the convenient store sat on, he wasted no time making his way towards the front entrance. Approaching the front door, he noticed a young man making his way out. He had on a cap that was tilted backward, sand his entire attire was baggy. He appeared younger, though his height and size seemed even to the beat maker. On the one hand, he was carrying a one-liter water bottle, and on the other hand, was a pad along with two pens. Noticing a hasty person in Aries, the young man kindly held the door for him to dash through. Making his way in, Aries toned his pace down, and as he did, his ears captured what sounded like a faultless rhythmic flow. As the words penetrated through one ear and out the other, Aries felt this indescribable sensation of euphoria. A euphoric state which took him surpass the sky's limits or any limit known to his existence; and just coasting away on a scenic route.

Snapping out of his euphoric state, he shook his head, and leaning his back against the front door; he poked his head out to have a look at which path the young man went. Unfortunately, he was nowhere in sight. Uncertain of which way to take, the beat maker asked several people nearby, and in turn, they supposedly pointed him in the right direction. Though, with the young man still nowhere in sight, the beat maker came to the assumption that he was misled. Then with the corner of his eye, he caught a glimpse of the young man across the street entering one of the back alleyways. Making it across the other side, he figured he'd most likely be able to cut him off if he gambled on taking another route. However, he soon came to discover that following the young man was almost like chasing a ghost. Reaching the other side of the path in which the young man took, the beat maker found nothing or no one for that matter. Instead, he saw graffiti marked all over the building walls of the alleyway. Keeping his eyes on the graffiti writing, he began to notice a pattern, which in turn led to him feeling as if he was somehow being guided somewhere. Going with his instincts, he entered the alleyway. Following the graffiti's trail, he then heard what sounded like footsteps. Taking his eyes off the trail, his sight had traveled all over, trying to locate exactly where the sound was coming from. That's when he again spotted the young man, this time casually walking as if he was leaving the back streets. Being that he wasn't too far, the beat maker shouted, "Hey!" as an attempt to get his attention. However, the young man continued with his destination. The beat maker shouted several times while striving to catch up with him. But again, the young man didn't respond nor even take the time to have a look at who was calling him.

To finally close the gap within their distance, the beat maker decided to run as he watched the young man make a right turn into the main road. Just within seconds of turning the corner, the beat maker himself comes to a sudden halt at what's in front of him. Before him sits a crake, and on it is a cap along with a note pad. The same ones in which the young man was holding. *Snaps, he left his cap and pad*, the beat maker thought as he observed the items. "But my question is why?" he asked himself while slowly tilting his head. "Or how? How the heck did he disappear? Matter fact, where'd he g —"

He continued for a short while asking himself several questions till finally, he was interrupted by none other than the young man himself: "You know you shouldn't follow people," said the young man, who unexpectedly showed up out of nowhere. Startled, the beat maker jerked back, knocking the cap and note pad off the crake. "Shit!" he sighed, "You scared me."

"Now normally, Folks get jumped for doing this around here, but…"

"But…"

"You're alone…"

"Wait, but so are you…"

"Hmp, according to whom?"

"What the…"

"Tuh, you're definitely not reading like a Folk."

"Is that why nothings –"

"Happened…to you…Yeah, that's why."

"How'd you know I was following you, though."

"Let's just say; you're in my turf."

"Well, how'd you do that?"

"Do what?"

"The other thing where you showed up…"

"Look, why you're following me?"

"Hehe, oh, yeah, that's right, you would like to know."

"Yes, I wanna know."

"Okay, well, first off, I'm Aries. Matter fact, my real name's Aerion…Aerion Horne. But I run with the name Aries because my birthday falls under the month of the Aries child, which therefore gives me my name, feel me."

"Tuh, okay, but…why'd you follow me?"

"Hold on; I'm getting to it…Now ya see, I'm a beat maker. I make beats for a living."

"Oooooh, I see…Look pal, I ain't buying whatever you're trying to sell."

"Oh no, no, no, no! Wait, I'm not trying to sell you anything!"

"Okay, then what? What do you want from me?"

"Look, what I'm trying to say is, I wanna record you."

"Huh?"

"Like I told you: I'm a beat maker. I make beats. And I've got my own lab down the street –"

"Look guy, sorry I made ya jump, and don't worry about my cap and pad."

"Wait, where ya going?"

"I gotta go."

"So, so you're just gonna leave?"

"Someone's waiting on me."

"Wait, so you don't believe me then?"

"Look, all I'm saying is, I gotta go."

"Listen to me; you need to be heard! I'm for real –"

"Hey, I wouldn't follow me any further if I were you."

"Oh, alright...alright...I gotchu..."

"Stuh..."

"Hey, at least take my business card!"

"A CD? That's your business card?"

"Yeah, take it! It's my sounds! My real sounds that came from my mouth, lips, gums, throat, tongue, and mic...most of it anyway."

"Hmmm..."

"'Cause in this world, our lives are programmed, by society who shovels cards and pass 'em out like a dealer! We are the players of the hemalayers, take charge, play it safe, and set 'em down in your own way'!"

"Tuh, ha ha!"

"You laugh, but what you said back there when you held the door for me at the store...was HOT! ALL THAT SHIT YOU SAID WAS HOT!"

"Hmmm..."

"Look, just listen to my sounds! And I guess we could catch up at the store, maybe."

"Alright, I'm a holla back at ya, Aries."

"When?"

"You'll know...Oh, and by the way, that store won't open again till the day after tomorrow."

"Hah, I done forgot what I needed now, but thanks."

"Yeah."

"Yo...Who are you?"

"I'm Rence…But some people out here know me as Dopamine."

Since the time of their meeting, the days ran through the week as did the weeks through the month, like instrumentals on a playlist. Altogether, this eventually led to a narrative in which Aries, the beat maker, made a quick stop at that same convenient store one evening. This time he wasn't moving in such a haste. Instead, he was the one now casually taking a walk back to his place. On this particular evening, he wasn't taking any different routes towards the back alleys like he'd usually do on some nights. Having concluded that his offer was declined, this Dopamine character was now sitting in back of his mind. Nearing towards his doorsteps, the beat maker stopped for a moment to have a look at the clock on his wrist. And then, that's where he heard the sound of movement out of nowhere. It wasn't loud but rather silent and just clear enough to be heard. Though he heard movement; he couldn't necessarily make out exactly which direction it was coming from. With a peek over his shoulder, he took a glance of the area but found absolutely nothing within the vicinity. Suspecting that he's being watched, he became overwhelmed with paranoia. Not waiting for another second to find out what's to come next, he dug nervously in his pockets for his key. Reaching for his key, that's when he heard someone in a calm tone of voice spoke out and said, "A trailer…I don't see those too often."

"Who's there?" shouting a paranoid beat maker in Aries, who now stood ready to confront the stranger. Again, that same distinct voice was heard this time replying, "It's me…" in a calm tone. To the beat maker, it was like hearing a being trying to lurk from the other side. Shouting once more, the beat maker said, "Me, who?! Where are you?" A loud silence then drew a small gap within their dialogue. But then that distinct voice with the calm tone pierced right through the pitched blackness of the night saying, "I'm right here…Can't you see me?".

"No, I can't! Step into the light!" said the beat maker, who next heard movement once again. Movement, which he could tell sounded like footsteps approaching the lone streetlight that stood across from where he was. Watching the figure slowly creeping out of the darkness and into the light, the beat maker began to breathe with sighs of relief. "Dopamine, it's you…" he said.

"In the flesh," replied Dopamine while crossing the road.

"Dammit, man! Do you always creep up on people like this?!"

"Sorry if I startled you…again."

"Yeah, you did. Say, what took you so long?"

"Let's just say…I got stuck these past few weeks listening to your beats."

"Stuh…"

"Hmp, a nice 'lil spot ya got here…"

"Well, since you feeling my shit, I got some more of where that came from. What do ya say?"

"Yeah?"

"Yeah…C'mon, I'll show you around."

Cutting the light switch on the beat maker paved the way, allowing Dopamine to have a look inside. Taking a look around inside the trailer, Dopamine immediately noticed a couple of leather couches and sofas sitting near the entryway. The beat maker referred to it as the writers' bench area or guest area. Next to it was some small cabinets, a sink, and drawers. With a miniature fridge there as well, Dopamine figured that part of the trailer must've been his dining area. On the walls, he noticed a few photos were hanged up. There were also small tables and counters with cassette tapes, CDs, or even books about music. Grabbing hold of one of the CDs, Dopamine recognized a name scribbled in black sharpie marker. It read 'Lee' which made him come to wonder if this happened to be the same person he knew. Directing Dopamine to the opposite end of the trailer, the beat maker pointed out what he referred to as his office. There, Dopamine noticed a small desk with a laptop and multiple computers. When Dopamine set eyes on the office chair, he realized that it was indeed the beat maker's workspace. "Welcome to what I call 'the laboratory,'" said the beat maker, while spreading his arms apart. Then with his right arm, he pointed to a door. On the door was a small, tinted glass window in which Dopamine took the time to look through. Looking from the glass window, Dopamine saw what immediately made him come to think that the inside must've been a small restroom. However, looking a little further, he noticed foam wedges all over the walls. Not to mention, he also noticed what appeared to be a microphone stand with headphones sitting on it. With that said, he slightly leaned his head away from the glass window, asking if this was some kind of booth. "For recording music, yes," replied the beat maker. "All set up just for you," he added. Staring back with deep curiosity, Dopamine slowly responded saying, "For me?". Nodding his head, the beat maker sticks out his index finger telling Dopamine to "Listen to this," as he clicked on a button from his keyboard. Right there, Dopamine began to nod his head to the instrumental. Joining him, the beat maker began to nod his head as well. "You feeling it?" he asked.

"Yeah, this shit is banging," replied Dopamine.

"Oh yeah, well that's funny."

"What do you mean? This is the best beat I might've ever heard!"

"Stuh, you're only hearing it at its simplest form."

"Well, it sounds done to me!"

"You mean right, haha."

"Yeah, that too."

"But…Tell you what, it's still missing something…"

"Huh? Like what?"

"More like 'who.'"

"Wait…Me?"

"Yeah…This beat's missing a master…"

"A master…A master of what?"

"A master of ceremonies: You…It's missing you, Dopamine. Matter of fact, all these beats are."

"You must really think my shit's fire…"

"Sta! Boy, do I? Look, let's just say from the time I heard you back when you were coming out that store, I already knew…"

"Knew what?"

"That you're an M.C…"

"An emcee…I'm an emcee."

"Yeah…Yo, here take this."

"A mic?"

"Yeah, the cable is already inside. So, you can just hook it up."

"And then what?"

"And then spit fool! Why else you think I brought you in here?!"

"You want me to ride…to this beat?"

"Oh, what, you ain't feeling it? Because if that's what it is, then I'll change it up for you in a heartbeat?!"

"Hey, wait! What are you doing?!"

"I'm adding some changes…"

"Hold on, pause for a second!"

"Alright, okay, so, you're feeling this beat then?"

"Yeah…It's the best beat I ever heard…"

"But what's holding you back?!"

"Stuh…You were really serious when you said you wanted to record me, huh?"

"Dude look, I know I told you this once, and I'm a tell you again: ALL THAT SHIT YOU SAID THAT NIGHT AT THE STORE WAS HOT! And that was just you without a beat! Without a beat…Now your rhymes on my sounds: straight blueprint to money-making! Dope, we're talking more than master of ceremony! We're talking about an all-time dope emcee! The shining of a diamond in the rough…Look Dope, I'm telling you this because I not only hear something, but I feel and see something more and don't ask me how…Cause honestly, I don't know…I just do…"

"Alright, Mister Aries…I'm in."

"So, you're in?!"

"Yeah, yeah…"

"Well, alright then, Dope, destiny awaits you inside that booth, so let's make history!"

"Alright, cool…So you said just hook the cord to the mic, right?"

"Yeah, you'll see it as soon as you walk inside."

"Got it."

"After you hook it up, I want you to tap the mic and say one-two, one-two a couple of times. Got that?"

"Got it," Dopamine said as he heads inside and shuts the door behind him. Shortly, after hooking the microphone to the cable cord, he puts it on the microphone stand. "Microphone check one-two, one-two…".

"Alright, just one more time for me, Dope."

"Microphone check one-two, one-two."

"Alright, hear ya loud and clear!"

"Straight!"

"How's the sound quality on my end?"

"Sounds like you're talking right next to me."

"Ha ha ha ha, you're funny as fuck! But good!"

"You ready to hit the space bar on your keypad? Because I'm ready to ride!"

"Oh, oh, that's the thing I wanted to tell ya about."

"Wait, tell me about what?"

"I already made the additions to the beat."

"What additions?! And why?"

"What you heard a minute ago or so was only the original version…"

"Wait, but I told you it was straight just how it was…"

"Yeah, yeah, yeah but the new sound your about to hear is my mastered version…"

"Naw, naw, just put the other one on!"

"Look, Dope, calm down, and just hear this sound real quick."

"Ugh! You sure about this, Aries?!"

"Look Dope, trust me…I'm a beat maker. This is why I make beats. I gotta ear for the sound just like you got the words for the rhymes. So, trust me…"

"Stuh, I don't know how you get me to listen…but in Aries I trust (I guess)."

"Ha ha ha ha ha…You ready?"

"Yeah, let's do it!"

"Alright, here it comes…"

Pressing the space bar on his keypad, Aries then lifts the volume. Dopamine, in the meantime, is inside the booth with the headphones on. With his hands, he grips and tightly presses each earmuff on the headphones against his ears to ensure that he doesn't miss a sound. With him standing so close to the stand, there's barely any space between his lips and the microphone. Focused, he closes his eyes and licks his lips with anticipation. Silence is heard for the first ten to fifteen seconds. Next comes the sound of heavy rain and thunder in the background. Then he hears the sound of a violin playing in the foreground. And as this sound starts to increase in volume, along comes the rhythmic beating of sticks on a drum, forming the sound of bass. With a minute and a quarter gone by, Dopamine out of nowhere shouts out: "Yo, I'm an emcee!"

[10-minute verse: Dopamine]
It started back in the day,
I'm talking way before I was born,
when my father, David, was walking the Earth,
my mother, Teresa,
another who's worth nothing for the talking
cuz she left me, and I knew I was scared,
as an orphan, a loner walking out of these homes,
different places, situations leading up to Day 1,
I remember, the sweating
that came from the pouring of the running
I was doing when I'd be getting pursued,
by the others,
the wolves of this concrete jungle,
who'd be lurking for the hurting to feed our bods to the
birds,
this a struggle,
a novel 'bout my life as a youngin,
no ray of light was ever-present till the Tourez's home,
though then again, my life was still not bright,
I had to paint my thoughts,
my mind and all, it only served me right,
to aerosol spray, tag shit up,
scribble, scrabble away,
unraveling of what I'm bound to become,
I'm an emcee (emcee)!

[break (beat plays on for less than a minute)]
From birth to early age
to the end of adolescence,
the sole purpose of existence
was to earn me a name,
so then I aimed,
at permanently inking on flesh,
I made an image of my message on the surface of skin,
from right there, the art evolved,
to something more,
even better than whatever before,
moved on to a life of rhyme,
dropping bars and all,
spitting verses through a rhythmic beat,
sit at a park, spit a lick a really venomously,
or rather have a chick like Raine kill a minute with me,
Poetic Lee,
the spoken word's preferred,
first round of applause,
better her than J-Rocka for sure,
a VL sized snake in place,
ya slimy slithering thing,
another Vern, you deserved to be burned,
I'd image Tyke,
need a minute to think,
he's the smallest of us,
but when it's said,
he can throw 'em some twins,
Bear, Train, they're the biggest in size,
front and last of our line,
being led by who other than Tye,
if there's a ridge
there's a Price up the way,
Ro, what up capadre,
Tino, we been through the rough,
spent daze growing up through a maze,
made the nights out okay

which accumulates to me of today,
this who I am,
with rhythm, a lil' poetry,
I've got the elements to say that I'm an emcee,
I'm an emcee (emcee)!!

About the Author

From a security officer in Fort Lauderdale, Florida to a present-day English teacher in South Korea, Manes Marcellon's journey is a riveting tale of perseverance, intrigue, and beauty in an endeavor to keep the arts alive. Throughout his entire life, Marcellon has used the visual arts to not only express himself, but to also serve as his personal doorway, fleeing to a realm apart from our own reality. Regardless of how his art is received, his undying will to create has landed him in numerous exhibits and places around the world. Thus, this has allowed him to meet a wide range of individuals with different skills and personalities. In turn, time has developed a writer within him, and moved him to write about what he's unearthed throughout his experiences.

www.ingramcontent.com/pod-product-compliance
Lightning Source LLC
Chambersburg PA
CBHW072018020726
47501CB00006B/1853